BLUEBEARD'S CASTLE

BLUEBEARD'S CASTLE

A novel
by
Anna Biller

VERSO

London • New York

First published by Verso 2023
© Anna Biller 2023
"Bluebeard" by Sylvia Plath is reproduced with kind
permission of Faber & Faber and HarperCollins

The moral rights of the author have been asserted

1 3 5 7 9 10 8 6 4 2

Verso
UK: 6 Meard Street, London W1F 0EG
US: 388 Atlantic Avenue, Brooklyn, NY 11217
versobooks.com

Verso is the imprint of New Left Books

ISBN-13: 978-1-80429-185-6
ISBN-13: 978-1-80429-186-3 (US EBK)
ISBN-13: 978-1-80429-189-4 (UK EBK)

British Library Cataloguing in Publication Data
A catalogue record for this book is available from the British Library

Library of Congress Cataloging-in-Publication Data

Names: Biller, Anna, author.
Title: Bluebeard's castle : a novel / Anna Biller.
Description: London : Verso, 2023.
Identifiers: LCCN 2023009920 (print) | LCCN 2023009921 (ebook) |
ISBN
   9781804291856 (paperback) | ISBN 9781804291894 (UK EBK) | ISBN
   9781804291863 (US EBK)
Subjects: LCGFT: Gothic fiction. | Novels.
Classification: LCC PS3602.I4366 B58 2023 (print) | LCC PS3602.I4366
   (ebook) | DDC 813/.6—dc23/eng/20230526
LC record available at https://lccn.loc.gov/2023009920
LC ebook record available at https://lccn.loc.gov/2023009921

Typeset in Electra by Hewer Text UK Ltd, Edinburgh
Printed and bound by CPI Group (UK) Ltd, Croydon, CR0 4YY

To Jacques and Claudius, my feline loves

I am sending back the key
that let me into bluebeard's study;
because he would make love to me
I am sending back the key;
in his eye's darkroom I can see
my X-rayed heart, dissected body:
I am sending back the key
that let me into bluebeard's study.

Sylvia Plath, "Bluebeard"

CONTENTS

1.

Fleeing the Castle

Some husbands are pussycats, some are dullards or harmless rogues, and some are Bluebeards. Judith still wasn't sure which type she had married. But she wasn't taking any chances, so she decided to run away.

She hurried through the giant oak front doors and tripped down the wide shallow steps flanked with stone lions, shivering in her thin gown and pulling her cloak more closely about her. And as she set her suitcases down and gazed up at the magnificent castle towering against the night sky, she was seized with an aching sense of loss. She didn't know why she should be sad to leave Manderfield; most of her time here had been fraught with anxiety and fear. But leaving Manderfield was leaving *him*, and she still loved him—an inconvenient fact that would take years of psychoanalysis to sort out. Or so others might scoff, laughing at her neurasthenic and euphoric obsessions. But how was she to blame for loving him? No woman could have resisted him, once he had set his sights on her.

She had wanted so desperately for things to work out. He had whisked her here, to this desolate place which was to have been their fortress, their haven, their fairy-tale castle. It was ironic that she had allowed herself to imagine a happily-ever-after marriage for herself in the first place. She had never believed in love, partly because her parents had loved neither their children nor one another. They were rich, attractive, narcissistic bullies who had destroyed both their marriage and their children's sense of self-worth. Judith, under their influence, had also rejected love, although she had written about it extensively in her books.

At twenty-six, she was the author of seven Gothic novels containing images of windswept moors and crumbling castles full of brooding men and glamorous women, often with poisonous loves and unhappy endings. Her stories helped her to process her lonely childhood, her parents' cruel marriage, her fascination with death, and the legacy of her cold but beautiful mother, after whom she modeled her heroines. And yet despite having delved so deeply into the subject of love in her books, any conscious desire for romance had remained latent in her . . . until she had met *him*.

He had been different — a man simply too good to be true. He had love-bombed her to within an inch of her life, and she had metamorphosed from a plain, unhappy, bookish girl into a beautiful romance heroine, practically overnight.

And then she began to wonder if she had married a Bluebeard.

As the moonlight spilled across her face, which had grown gaunt from self-starvation and suffering, Judith reflected on the grim reality of her situation. She was not normally one to run from difficult situations. She had always fought for what she wanted, and until now, she had been certain that she could fix anything wrong in her marriage through sheer force of will. In fact, winning his undying love in the face of insuperable barriers had become a game to her, a battle she felt sure to win. But now she had no choice: flight was her only option. Because if she remained, her husband was going to kill her.

My husband is going to kill me. She repeated this to herself over and over again, and the tears coursed down her cheeks. No matter how many times she said it, she couldn't believe it. It all seemed like a bad dream, or like something that was happening to a character in one of her novels and not to herself, and yet the evidence was all there.

He had procured a special poison to murder her with, and she had found it hidden in a drawer. Plus, he collected weapons — both guns and knives — so the poison wasn't even necessary. There were few people around Manderfield, and he could easily arrange to be alone with her, so that a gunshot would never be heard. Besides, he was a hunter, so he could always claim that any shot fired had been an accident. He could also facilitate a slip in the bath, or a tumble out of the window, or he could simply choke the life out of her. And then there was the expanse of woods behind the house, where no one would hear her scream.

She didn't know when he would try to kill her, or what method he would use, but she feared her life was in danger each moment she remained at the castle. He could return at any instant and mow her down with his car as she stood there, blinded by his headlights.

3

And yet she hesitated. Was he really going to kill her, or was it all in her head? Even now, she couldn't be sure. Like many young women, she tended to imagine the worst about men, and sometimes she blew her fears out of proportion. But when women worried about men, it wasn't just paranoia — it was a safety mechanism. Being too careful was better than winding up dead. Still, sometimes you could make a mistake and end up demonizing the wrong man.

As she stood before the pain-haunted castle, shivering in the night air, she tried to go back to the beginning and to sort out when and how her life had gone all pear-shaped. She remembered the day they met, and the way he had looked at her, and how it had filled her with a mad ecstasy, which in retrospect had been a nervous breakdown.

But the entire day had been unusual and upsetting. She and her sister Anne had been invited to a week-long celebration for their cousin Victoria's birthday in Cornwall, at a castle hotel on the beach. Judith had been happy for the diversion, for she had just broken up with her boyfriend Tony for the second time, and this last split had been especially painful. No matter how hard she tried, she couldn't fall in love with Tony. Yet somehow he always boomeranged back to her, and she was afraid she might get stuck with him out of simple inertia.

But Tony had followed her there. He wouldn't let her go.

2.

A Good Catholic Girl

Judith stood gaping at Tony as he entered her room. Why had he come? They had said goodbye for the last time. But here he was in her room with its antique furniture, green velvet-flock wallpaper, and gilt moldings, having made the six-hour journey from London to Cornwall. He was obviously expecting something. What did he want? Sex? Validation? Or was he planning to gaslight her into thinking that nothing had changed and they were still together?

Tony was a doctor. Judith's father, Sir Wilfred, pleased with his bedside manner during a minor gallbladder surgery he'd performed on the old gentleman, had invited him to a small dinner party the previous summer at the family's estate in Devon. She had liked Tony right away, and he in turn had quickly fallen in love with her in a puppy-dog sort of way. He had never met a writer before, and he was enormously impressed with her, adoring her wit and imagination, laughing at her jokes, and hanging on her every word.

But although she was charmed by his intelligence, kindness, and good looks—he resembled nothing so much as a model in a 1940s menswear catalogue—she just couldn't muster up the energy to fall in love with him. Their interactions felt safe and dull, and she didn't know how to turn her feelings for him into love. But she was flattered by his attentions, and being with him was better than being alone. So she dutifully dated him, and she tolerated his kisses, and it all meant very little to her. She always hoped that something he said or did would create a spark in her, but everything continued on the same dreary plane.

That is, until her sister Anne let it slip that Sir Wilfred had arranged their meeting as a potential love match. Her family had always considered her unattractive, and she saw her father's gesture as an act of charity for a daughter he considered ugly and unmarriageable. She had found it hard to believe that a handsome, well-adjusted, successful man like Tony could take an interest in her, and she had always assumed that he was merely toying with her affections or making fun of her. And now, with the added paranoia that he might be being paid by her father to make love to her, she unceremoniously dumped him. He eventually won her back by convincing her that his feelings for her were genuine, but a few months later, feeling bored and restless, she dumped him again.

Now Tony was gazing at her with something like adoration mixed with hurt. They stood facing one another, she in her sporty designer skirt and sweater, he in his summer chinos and linen shirt. The sound of guests talking and laughing, and snatches of vintage Latin music, wafted through the window. Finally Judith broke the ice. "Why did you come here, Tony?" She had the type of diction that comes from good British education and breeding—it was one of the things that had made him fall in love with her.

"Can't we try again, Judith?"

The pain in his voice hurt her, but she steeled herself against it. "What's the point? I'm not in love with you." She turned to the brown leatherette-and-wood bar and opened the lid of the plastic marbled ice bucket. Judith never minced words with Tony; she always said exactly what she wanted to say, knowing he'd understand. She held out a glass. "Want a drink?"

"No. You know I never drink during the day."

She felt his sad eyes on her. There was a heavy silence as she plunked ice cubes into the cut crystal glass with the silver tongs. Then he stood behind her and placed his hands firmly on her shoulders. "How can you know what love is when you haven't tried it?" he murmured into her ear.

She knew what Tony meant by love—he meant *sex*. And it was true that she had never tried it. She had experimented with boys at school, and some girls, but she had never yet met anyone with whom she wanted to have sex. Sex, to her, was sacred. She had explored every inch of her body and learned all of its delightful ins and outs, but the person she gave herself to would be the person she wanted to spend her life with.

She emptied a tiny bottle of vodka from the minibar into her glass, and filled the rest with orange juice. She stirred it and took a sip, pretending his hands weren't gripping her shoulders like a vise. "You mean sex. But why would I want to have sex when I'm not in love?"

Suddenly he pivoted her around, planting a firm kiss on her lips. She neither yielded to it nor pushed him away, but simply went limp. She was used to these kisses, and she tried to get into them, but she couldn't; neither did she want to hurt him by repulsing him outright.

When he spoke again, his voice was husky and romantic. "Stop being a good Catholic girl. Or marry me and find out."

She sighed. "So you *did* come here for sex."

He removed his hands from her shoulders as if they'd been burned. "Of course not! How can you say that?"

She stirred her drink. "You're suggesting that I have sex with you to find out if I'm in love with you. But what if we have sex and I still don't love you?"

She was sure her words would cause him to retreat in embarrassment, but he had driven six hours to see her, and he wasn't about to give up so easily. He shifted to a tone of pleading tenderness. "Judith, what do you want? Tell me so I can give it to you."

She laughed. "What do I want? You mean, in one sentence?"

Tony looked mortified. He walked away a few paces to gather his thoughts. "Sorry. That was stupid. I know I can be dense at times. But I love you."

"You *say* that you love me, but I don't *feel* that you love me. When you look at me, I just feel sort of dead. Why don't you ever tell me I'm beautiful?"

This time, Tony was the one who laughed. "Of course you're beautiful," he said with a condescending smile. "But why do you need me to say it?"

Judith frowned. Tony thought he was being modern by

refusing to praise her looks. But his response made her feel like a blob, the way she had when her mother had dressed her doll-like sister as a girl, curling her long, dark, lustrous hair, and Judith as a boy, cropping her fine mousy hair close to her head. No one had ever told her she was beautiful, but the man she married would certainly need to say it—or at least to *think* it. Otherwise, what did he want her for? For her willingness to be his lifelong maid, cook, therapist, baby-mother, and servant? Or as a consolation prize for not being able to capture the interest of the type of woman that men actually dream about?

She couldn't bear to look at him. "Tony, you're a nice person, but I'm afraid you don't understand women."

He knew he had made another gaffe, but he didn't fully grasp what he'd done wrong. "Sorry. I keep putting my foot in it. I may be a bit thick, but my feelings are genuine. I'm sure it's all just some silly misunderstanding. Can't we talk it out?"

Judith felt a crushing disappointment. Part of her had hoped that Tony would say something original or ignite the flame of her desire, but she should have known better; it was the same old Tony, and they were on the same old carousel, going round and round.

"There's nothing left to say."

"All right, Judith. When you need me, just call. I'll always be here for you."

She smiled, grateful that he was making a graceful exit. "Thank you, Tony. Goodbye."

"Goodbye." He took her by the shoulders and planted another unwanted kiss on her lips.

She went limp again, and his face registered a look of hurt and disappointment. Then he turned on his heel and walked away.

She was sorry to see him go. After all, Tony was a good man.

She located the castle chapel and prayed. It was small but atmospheric, with a lofty vaulted ceiling. A large painting of Christ on the cross graced the altar, along with fresh roses and tapers burning in brass holders. She sat on a pew, fingering her beads and making the sign of the cross. She prayed the rosary, and the ritual helped greatly to restore her mind to tranquility.

As she rose to leave, she saw a man standing in the doorway. Due to the lighting, he seemed haloed like the Christ painting on the altar. She stopped and froze, intimidated by the sight of his tall, broad-shouldered frame blocking the exit.

Their eyes met, and suddenly she felt weak and powerless. Not because he was so tall and strong, nor because he was so breathtakingly handsome — although he was certainly all of those things. It was the *way* he was looking at her that took her breath away. He was gazing at her with the look of smoldering passion that men get when they don't care what happens to them — if their wife leaves them or their house burns down or they are killed — as long as their gaze finds its desired object. His glance created an electrical charge in her, making her body feel quiveringly alive.

They stood staring at one another for a few moments, and everything else seemed to melt away. Then she came back to herself and moved towards the door. He stepped aside, and she smiled and walked past him, feeling his eyes burning into her back as she walked away.

The experience was unsettling and frightening, but thrilling. For the first time in her life, she felt like the type of woman that men desire. This man had looked at her as if she were the most exciting woman alive, and it had helped heal her wounded vanity after her deflating encounter with Tony.

She crossed the lobby and wandered over to the pool area, where she ordered a cocktail at the bar to take the edge off her disappointment about Tony. It's all such a charade, she thought, this pretending to be in love just to avoid being alone. I want to love him, but you can't force yourself to fall in love with someone, let alone marry them, just because *they* want you to. Yet Tony seems to think it *is* a good enough reason. Why does he think his feelings alone are strong enough to sustain a marriage? Don't both people have to feel something? Is that what Tony really wants—just to love me in his one-sided way, regardless of how I feel about it? She went over these thoughts in an endless loop in her mind, drowning her sorrows in vodka and schnapps.

The bar was adjacent to the pool, at the end of which was a structure with a turreted stone roof and filigreed wood columns, styled like an Indian palace. A hill with wild grasses and evergreen oaks sloped above, and potted palms gave the area a lush tropical feeling. But the picturesque atmosphere did nothing to lift her mood. She sipped her drink on a tall stool and watched the guests walking to and fro, or reclining on lounge chairs in their designer resort togs. She looked about her, but she didn't recognize anyone she knew.

Suddenly she noticed that two men standing next to her had stopped talking and were staring intently at something. She followed their gaze, and she saw her sister Anne standing at the edge of the pool in a bathing suit. It was freezing on the English coast even in the middle of summer, and no one else was sunbathing or swimming, so she was creating quite a spectacle. She dove into the pool, gliding effortlessly through the water and emerging gracefully at the other end. Then she hoisted herself onto the concrete, pulling off her swim cap and tossing out her long chestnut locks, her figure perfect in her white Burberry bikini.

Anne resembled their mother Ava: tall and slim, with a graceful figure, long, shapely legs, a tiny waist, long, dark, shiny hair, porcelain skin, high cheekbones, striking dark blue eyes, a perfectly sculpted nose, a rosebud mouth, and a movie-star jaw in the mold of Constance Bennett or Gene Tierney. Ava had been a famous model, and then a famous society beauty, and Anne had followed in her footsteps, becoming first a child model, and then a print and runway model.

According to the universe, Anne and Ava were great beauties, and Judith was a nothing. Everywhere she went men and women used to gush, "Your mother is so *beautiful!*" And although she resented the fact that she herself never sent people into raptures with her beauty, she greatly admired her mother for her commitment to herself as a work of art. To Ava, being lovely was the highest pinnacle a woman could achieve. Everyone had wanted to photograph her, to paint her. She had appeared on the covers of a number of fashion magazines and had been a muse for a legion of famous artists and photographers. She had spent a great deal of time crafting her image, and it showed. She loved to quote Marlene Dietrich, who had famously said, "I dress for the image. Not for myself, not for the public, not for fashion, not for men."

Now all of the men around the pool were staring at Anne. Some stared openly, many surreptitiously under their brows or with a side-eye, but they were all acutely aware of her presence through a sort of animal instinct. Her swimsuit-model corporeality put the men into instant competition with one another, and like Penelope's suitors, each imagined himself the one who would knock out his rivals and win her love with his superior strength or wit. For in each man's mind, regardless of his other attachments, this woman belonged exclusively to him.

Anne, aware of being watched, performed her movements with a studied grace. Spotting Judith, she slipped on her mules where they had been tossed under a lounge chair, grabbed her towel, her Dolce & Gabbana cover-up and beach bag, and her pink Versace straw hat, and waltzed over to the bar where Judith was finishing her cocktail. "Why don't you go for a swim, Judith?" she said. "The water's delicious!"

"It's too cold to swim."

"You really should. It's wonderfully bracing."

"And have all the men compare my figure with my sister's? No thanks, Anne."

"Stop dramatizing. You have a lovely figure! Besides, no one is looking at you."

"That's right, Anne," said Judith bitterly. "No one is looking at me."

Anne stared blankly at her as if she had no idea what she

meant. Then she wrapped herself in a towel and rummaged in her bag for sunscreen, applying it liberally to her shoulders. "My skin burns to a crisp in the sun! I'll be a lobster in a minute!"

She smoothed the white cream over her shoulders and arms, glancing around the poolside at the men observing her every move, and assuming a vacant-eyed stare.

Suddenly, Judith got the feeling that she herself was being watched. She turned her head and saw the man from the chapel sitting at the end of the bar, gazing fixedly at her. She blushed, feeling self-conscious. Perhaps she shouldn't have stared at him for so long. At the time she had been powerless to look away, but now she was afraid she had started something she couldn't finish.

Anne was speaking to the bartender now. "Pellegrino with lime, please. And another of whatever my sister is having."

Judith turned away from the man. "I want a sex on the beach."

"What??" cried Anne.

"My cocktail. It's called sex on the beach."

"Oh."

The bartender nodded and pulled out a highball glass, adding ice, orange juice, cranberry juice, peach schnapps, and vodka, and wedging an orange slice onto the rim.

Judith glanced over to see the handsome man smiling at her, amused. She flirted back in spite of herself, and then she turned away as the bartender handed her the drink. She sipped it with a straw, starting to become tight. This was her third cocktail within an hour on an empty stomach, and the bartender had been generous with the vodka.

She put down her drink and sighed. "I broke up with Tony today."

"Again?"

"He's like crabgrass. He keeps coming back. I can't believe he came all the way down here when he wasn't invited."

"And you sent him away? Why are you so mean to Tony? He's so nice."

"I'm not mean to Tony! And he's not that nice. He's just a boring doctor. Anyway, you and John met normally, but Tony was picked for me. Did Dad really think I couldn't find my own man? It's so medieval."

"What are you on about? Tony wasn't picked for you. Anyway, who cares how you met him? He's a good man. You're not likely to do any better."

Judith was enraged. "Why do you think I can't do any better? Why *exactly*, Anne?"

Anne looked away in disgust. "Judith, you're causing a scene!"

Just then, Anne's husband John walked up: dapper, slim, upper-class, good-looking, wearing casual designer clothing. "Hello, darling," he said, pecking his wife on the cheek. "I'm ready for lunch now."

"It's about time. I'm famished! Swimming gives me such an appetite. I think I've gained a pound already on this trip. Do you think I'm getting fat?" Anne turned this way and that, showing herself off. The men at the pool took notice.

John laughed. "No, Sweetie. You're perfect!" He slapped her bottom, and she squealed with delight.

"Ooh, cheeky! Anyway, I *am* getting fat. No dressing on my salad today! Are you joining us, Judith?"

"No thanks."

"All right then, see you at tea." Anne and John turned and made their way towards the restaurant.

Judith looked after her sister, resentment and envy welling up in her heart. But then she suppressed these feelings. Anne couldn't help being beautiful; it wasn't her fault.

She glanced back to the end of the bar, but the handsome man had disappeared. She was disappointed. She would have liked to chat with him, just to pass the time.

She grabbed her drink, her bag, and her sun hat, and she walked along the narrow path that led to the castle garden.

3.

It Was Too Late to Stop Him

Still holding her cocktail, Judith rambled through the castle garden. She passed a crumbling bailey wall covered with moss, large oaks flanked by woodlands and orchards, and bold borders of roses, delphiniums, lavender, peonies, and herbaceous plants. Here and there she came across a nude sculpture of a goddess or a nymph carved from stone, rising from a fountain or languishing under an arbor bursting with wisteria. Her spirits lifted as she absorbed the tranquility of the setting, plucking a rose and inhaling its fragrance, or listening to the sweet calls of the birds.

She reached the end of the garden and came to the top of a cliff, stopping to survey the beauty of the landscape. The turquoise water frothed against the shore, beating against a foot of black rock, and the white sand shimmered before a backdrop of mossy green hills. Seagulls wheeled and cawed. Cornwall was a place of savage beauty, holy and enchanted. It was where Daphne du Maurier had spent most of her life, and where her sublime Gothic novel *Rebecca* was set. To Judith, this gave it an especially enchanted air.

She descended the hill and followed the rough-hewn stone steps to the sand. The beach was empty save for a couple seated on folding chairs, several women making their way back to the castle, and a man walking his dog along the shore. The wind whipped the tall tufts of marram grass and tousled Judith's fine brown hair.

She sat down on her beach towel and gazed at the shimmering water, the glare hurting her eyes.

Suddenly a shadow came over her. She started, and glanced up to see a man standing over her. He was silhouetted against the sky, a masculine cutout with broad shoulders and a narrow waist, his shirtless outline chiseled and well defined.

Judith froze in fear. She had only felt this kind of terror once before: in the woods when she was a child, and a man had flashed at her and chased her all the way home. Then as now, a feeling of dread chilled her bones. For a moment, she thought she was going to be sick.

He circled her until he was lit by the sun, and she saw that it was the handsome man from the chapel. She breathed a sigh of relief. He was wearing only a small pair of briefs despite the freezing wind, and she couldn't help but ogle his beautiful physique.

"Oh! It's you!"

The man smiled charmingly, putting her instantly at ease. "I'm sorry if I frightened you," he said in an upper-class accent, his voice so deep and sexy that it made her blush.

"You just startled me, that's all."

The drinks had given her courage, and she was surprised at her own forwardness as she made eyes at him. "Won't you sit down? I'm Judith."

The man parked himself at the edge of her towel. "Glad to meet you. I'm Gavin Garnet."

"That's an unusual name."

"Yes, it is. Gavin is after Gawain of the Arthurian legends, and Garnet is after the gemstone. I changed it from my family name, Longueville, because . . . well, it's a long story."

He held out his hand and flashed a large garnet ring, which sparkled spectacularly in the sun.

Her eyes widened. "What a lovely ring! I love garnets. Garnet is my birthstone." It was true that she loved garnets. She loved all gemstones, having been enchanted by her mother's fantastic jewelry, but garnets were her favorite because of their blood-red color, and because they were a symbol of Christ's blood sacrifice.

He moved his hand to make the ring sparkle. "My mother loved garnets too. She married my father because he gave her a spectacular garnet ring that had been passed down for generations in his family, along with diamonds, rubies, emeralds, and sapphires as big as the crown jewels. He's *loaded* with cash. Oh, and because of his lineage. He's Baron Hastings. Someday it will be my title."

Judith had known there was something special about this man. That was it . . . he was from the peerage! Now, it all made sense. His obvious breeding reminded her of some of the titled young men she'd met at her parents' parties. But she was amused to think that, because of his stunning good looks, he also reminded her of some of the male models and gigolos there.

"Baron Hastings," she drawled playfully. "That sounds familiar. Weren't you at St. Moritz last season?"

"Yes. I saw you there."

"I've never been to St. Moritz."

"Neither have I."

They both burst out laughing.

"How do you know Victoria?" she said.

"Victoria?" His smile became tight.

"The girl whose birthday party we're here for."

"Oh, Victoria! Of course. Stupid of me. I've always called her Vicky."

"No one calls her Vicky."

"Well, I do. We've known each other since we were children, and I've always called her Vicky. It irritates her like mad, but I love to tease her. Anyway, Victoria sounds too stuffy . . . reminds me of the Queen."

They both stared at the water for a moment. Then he turned to her enthusiastically. "I've been watching you for two days. I wanted so much to meet you, but I was too intimidated to approach you."

"Why?"

"Because you're Judith Moore, the mystery writer. It's not every day one meets a famous author. I'm a big fan."

Judith was startled. It was true that she had written seven books, five of them bestsellers, under the pen name Judith Moore (her family name was de Courtenay), but her readership skewed heavily female, and she had never had a man approach her about her writing, let alone recognize her from her book jacket.

She smiled modestly. "Thanks very much. I'm surprised you know about my books; most of my readership is female."

"Gothic fiction is my *favorite*. You're very young to be such a prolific writer. When did you start writing?"

"When I went to boarding school, at age fourteen."

"You *did* start young! What school did you go to?"

"Malvern St. James, in Worcestershire."

"Isn't that where Barbara Cartland went?"

"Yes. How did you know that?"

"My mother went there. Cartland is their most famous alumna, I believe. And the world's most prolific author. Did you know that she published seven hundred books in her lifetime?"

"Well, I'm not *that* prolific," she said, and they laughed.

"Your novels are wonderful. They're romantic, but they're also chilling . . . they have a dark side."

She basked in the compliment. "I suppose they do. I like to write about my experiences, but also about things that frighten me — like murder. To me, being murdered is the most frightening thing that can happen to anyone."

"I'm interested in murder too." Somehow, it was creepy when he said it — as if he was interested in actually murdering someone, rather than just reading about it.

There was a silence, and then she looked at him and she saw that he was brooding. "Is that why you came down to the beach to see me? Because you're a fan?"

"No." He turned and fixed his gaze on her.

His expression had changed. It was now reminding her of

the way he had looked at her at the chapel. She had liked it then, because she had needed the ego boost after her deflating encounter with Tony, but now she had to face the consequences of her silly flirtation. She had led this man on. And no doubt about it—he was a *man*. Not a boy, not a harmless pussycat like Tony, but a grown man. And she was afraid of what might happen.

The couple on the folding chairs had left, and they were all alone. Judith suddenly felt nervous, wondering what she would do if he made a pass at her.

Now he was speaking again. "I didn't come down to the beach because I'm a fan. I came because I wanted to look at you again."

"Why?"

His eyes ran up and down her body. "I'm a man," he said, in the manliest tone she had ever heard. "Do I have to explain it to you?"

Now things had definitely gone too far, and once again fear crept up and down her spine. She rose and picked up her bag. "No thanks, I'm good." She turned and walked away in the direction of the castle.

"Hey!" he called out, standing and moving towards her. "You're quite the narcissist, aren't you?"

She stopped and turned, genuinely surprised. "Me?"

"Yes. What girl would ask a man why he wants to look at her . . . unless she wants to be told she's pretty?"

Now she was furious. How dare he mock her looks, by suggesting she was so desperate for a compliment? She hadn't asked for his opinion. Being pretty was not her forte, nor did she want it to be. Where she shone was in her mind, and she was disgusted at the way everyone made such a fuss about how women looked.

"I'm not a narcissist," she blurted out. "Anyway, my sister Anne is the pretty one. I'm the clever one."

She couldn't believe she'd said this. She might have blamed it on the three drinks, or on the fact that she'd had nothing to eat all day, or on the way the wind was whipping her hair, and the sea was shimmering like diamonds, and the sand was blinding her eyes. But the real reason she'd said it was that when she was excited, she always said whatever she was thinking. Anne and mother had called it "being dramatic." Fine, she thought. So I said something stupid; now he'll go away and leave me alone.

But her outburst appeared to have the opposite effect. He moved close to her, fixing her with his gaze. "Anne is attractive in an obvious sort of way, but you're the real beauty in the family."

He was standing so close that she could hardly breathe, and she felt overpowered by the scent of his pheromones. "You're crazy," she said. "No one thinks that. Anne is the beauty in the family. Everyone says so."

He smiled, impaling her with his gaze like a lepidopterist pinning a butterfly to a board. "Well, they're wrong. I think you're the most beautiful girl I've ever seen. And I love you."

At these words she became overwhelmed with emotion. All her life, she had lived in the shadow of her beautiful sister. Everyone had always hinted that she was plain, and even after she had blossomed at the age of fourteen, no one had ever told her she was beautiful; but she believed him. For although his confession was implausible, the eyes don't

23

lie, and his longing for her was radiating straight from his eyes to her soul.

She knew that love at first sight was common, and that it happened through the eyes, but she had never experienced anything like this before, and it devastated her. More than anything, it was his urgency that started waves of desire coursing through her body, making her want him with a swooning intensity. When men had expressed interest in her before, it had felt random and impersonal. They hadn't been interested in her as a *specific* woman, but as *any* woman. On dates, they had either been intimidated by her mind and refused to touch her, or else they had pawed her obscenely, without the least interest in who she was as a person. They projected all of their needs onto her, because they thought a woman's job was to take care of a man's needs, including his need for sex. And sex for them was not a spiritual or even an erotic experience, but something banal, a need similar to eating or sleeping.

Tony was different, but with him she didn't feel like a woman. The thing she had been missing in Tony's eyes was what she saw in Gavin's eyes now. She saw in those dark, burning orbs that he wanted her, that he understood her, that he loved her. But she also saw something else — something wild and primitive. His eyes seized hold of her, and suddenly her will was no longer her own. She had never had healthy boundaries. Up until now this hadn't been a problem, for no man had ever been brute enough to force himself upon her. But she had let this man get uncomfortably close, and it was too late to stop him.

She had two options: she could either flee, or she could

surrender. She was strongly attracted to him, but her longing went only so far as wanting to be kissed by him, to be held in his strong arms, to walk along the sand hand in hand as he continued to regale her with all of the ways in which she was prettier than her sister, and most of all, to be plunged into *la folie de l'amour*. The idea of losing her virginity frightened her, and because of this she had an instinct to take to flight. But if she fled, she would never see him again, and she may never again meet anyone else like him.

She wished there could be some third way, but she knew from the way he was looking at her that he would not be satisfied with just a kiss. Sex with him might be the worst experience of her life, or it might be the best, but at least it would be an adventure, and she craved to be shocked out of her life of complacent dullness. She was trembling with fear at the ruthlessness of his masculinity, but because with his eyes he had tapped into the bottomless fount of her unfulfilled longing, she surrendered to his will.

Once she made this decision, she told herself it was what she had wanted all along, and fear and desire combined in a powerful cocktail to convince her that she was madly in love with him. She felt as if she were flying, or falling, or jumping off a precipice to her death. And suddenly, in that moment of intense and unmoored euphoria, she understood what love is. Love, she marveled, is being in the moment, being overwhelmed, being filled with ecstasy, experiencing something deep and profound, being shaken up, being tossed into the fire. It's non-verbal, illogical, inevitable.

For the first time in her life she wanted to be merged with another, to be carried away by voluptuousness, to be inside of the sublime. She looked into his eyes, and his irises were blank projection screens into which she poured all of her longing.

She gazed at him in awe — at his beautiful face, his beautiful physique. Every pore felt alive with his nearness, and the faint touch of his breath on her skin drove her mad. Her desire blossomed and consumed her, and she fantasized about what he would be like as a lover.

He seized her shoulders, flooding her with a sexual ardor that left her almost senseless, and she longed to immolate herself on the altar of his love. She gazed into his hypnotic eyes, in which she saw the ocean reflected. And then something else flashed there, something so cold and terrifying that for a moment she thought he was going to kill her — crush her windpipe with his hands, or hold her head under the crashing surf, or smash her face into the sand until she suffocated.

Her eyes widened with fear and excitement. "I think you're my death," she said.

"Let's die together."

He kissed her. She kissed him back, unable to resist the aching desire that made her crane towards his kiss like a sunflower towards the light. She kissed him with tongue and lips and little ecstatic breaths, and she felt the sandpaper rasp of his chin and smelled his musky male perfume.

And then she collapsed in his arms. She hadn't fainted; rather, she had surrendered her will. She was letting him know, with her collapse, that she was his. No one had ever taken care of her. She had gone practically straight from the womb to bitter self-reliance, knowing she had no one to rely on, no one to save her from danger or death. But now someone would take care of her. Now someone loved her. Her body went limp except for her tenacious fingers, which clung to his neck, and she knew he would take her to her bed, hold her, kiss her, make love to her, make her pain go away.

He hoisted her up in his strong arms, and she opened her eyes and looked at him adoringly. She thought that the image must have possessed a certain eerie romantic charm, like Dracula carrying off his victim.

The gulls shrieked savagely, the waves crashed on the shore, and the pungent odor of the sea mingled with his manly scent as he carried her steadfastly across the sand, up the steps to the ancient castle, through the enchanted garden, and up to the solemn sacrificial altar of her bedchamber, where she would give him her virgin blood.

4.

Trichoplax

Judith lay naked on the baroque bed under the crystal chandelier, atop the rumpled gold satin sheets. Her hair was tousled, and she had an after-sex glow.

She mused about how after guarding her virginity for twenty-six years, she had given it to a man she had known for scarcely two hours, and about how reckless it would sound if she told a girlfriend about it. "You were seduced," the friend would tell her. "You may have even been raped."

But that's not how it had been at all. She was surprised by how quickly he had taken her. There hadn't been much foreplay, and he hadn't asked her how she was feeling, or if she had liked what he was doing. In fact, there hadn't been any real consent at all. She had lain there passively on the bed, and he had done things to her that were strange and pleasurable and sometimes painful. But she hadn't said no—she hadn't pushed him away or offered any sort of resistance—and that had been her form of consent, along with the wanton expression in her eyes.

The first thing she did after he laid her on the green damask bedspread was to have another drink. She was sick from sunstroke and from the sugar in her cocktails, and the alcohol was starting to wear off. She needed a drink to get back into the mood she had been in on the beach, because now she felt alert and nervous and scared. But she had made him carry her here all the way from the sea, and it was too late to back out. So she asked him to get her two miniature bottles of Scotch from the bar, and she quickly drank them down. They calmed her palpitating heart and brought back her hazy sexual heat.

When she had finished drinking, he kissed her mouth, pulled off her shoes, stockings, skirt, and blouse, unhooked her bra, and pulled her knickers roughly down around her ankles. Then he placed his mouth on her sex, licking and sucking with sharp little movements of his tongue, pressing her thighs down with his forearms so she couldn't move. But she couldn't have moved anyway, because she was frozen in fear. This was the first time a man had been down there, and she was filled with shame, averting her head and smashing it into the pillow. But he made her orgasm.

Then he took her knickers the rest of the way off and removed his shorts. She saw him naked, and she was frightened by the sight of his erect manhood, but she couldn't look away. He enclosed her hand around it, and she marveled at its smooth beauty and symmetry, and the way it grew in her hand. He rolled on a condom, and he laid on top of her and licked and pinched her nipples until she moaned. And then, without ceremony, he entered her. She felt a sharp pain and she gasped, biting the pillow so as not to scream. Then he pinned her arms down and began his steady thrusting, and the pain was still there, but it was mingled with pleasure. He finished quickly but didn't withdraw, and he moved slowly inside her until she orgasmed once more.

It was over rather quickly, and she felt sticky, wounded, and spent. And she felt like a woman. Her sensual act with him was memorialized in every cell of her body, and her pudenda, her skin, her temporal lobes, would retain a memory of it forever. He had lain on top of her and broken her hymen and given her pleasure. She lay there afterwards, and her body, bruised and bleeding, still craved him.

She also had a feeling she could only describe as sacred. She loved him the way she loved Christ and the Virgin Mary and St. Catherine, the way she loved living and breathing. She loved him the way she might love an infant birthed from her own body. She loved him, and he belonged to her. Her proprietary feelings were so intense that she felt she would kill any rival who tried to take him from her. Her body, hitherto a site of awkwardness and shame, had become a site of worship. She was loved, not for her intelligence, not for her willingness to serve others, but for herself, as a beautiful, sexual woman. He had given her this gift, and she would be his forever.

And yet she was aware that her feelings made no sense. Why was her heart surging with love for a complete stranger? Was she merely besotted with sex, and not in love at all? Had she really experienced something spiritual and profound, or was her exuberance merely due to a mix of bonding chemicals that would have flooded her brain no matter who had made her orgasm?

She had pretended to faint so that he would carry her in his arms, longing to be swept away, to be completely in his power; but those feelings had dissolved, and she was herself again. And now she wondered if she had confused mere animal instincts for something loftier. Had he hypnotized her into becoming a quivering sexual mass, without thought or reason? She had read in science class about the *Trichoplax*, a tiny cluster of cells lacking stomach, heart, mouth, eyes, and brain, a life form that may have existed 500 million years ago—perhaps the simplest creature to reproduce sexually. Had she become a mere *Trichoplax* under his spell, a simple organism that mates without any will of its own? Had sex taken over her entire being, so that she had no more control over her impulses than a cartilaginous fish? Could such a monstrous thing happen? And if so, could she trust anything she was thinking or feeling now?

She remembered vaguely that he had proposed to her while he had been inside of her. She had said, "Yes, yes, yes!" She had been drunk and delirious, having just consumed two shots of Scotch on an empty stomach. And he had been whispering in her ear, his hot breath and passionate words stimulating her to orgasm as much as his other sensuous efforts.

And then it had been over, and he had run his hand along the bright blood on the sheets, amazed at the sight of it. He hadn't said anything—he had merely taken her in his arms and held her. And then he had rung to have dinner sent up and his clothes brought over from his room, and she had put on a short filmy negligee, something she had picked up at a vintage shop. Dinner had been wheeled in on a small cart with a white tablecloth, and his clothes had been delivered, and he had got dressed. Her Prada tote bag and sun hat had been left on the beach, artifacts of a more innocent time. She was a different person now; she could never go back to that thing she had been, that ignorant girl who had never yet been ravished by a man.

Now he was sitting behind her on the bed framed against the sickly green wallpaper, flushed and romantic, pouring her a glass of champagne.

"No!" she protested. "I haven't had anything to eat all day. If I drink any more, I'll be sick."

"Then have something to eat." He went to the table and daintily selected for her a few small slices of French bread, Brie, Roquefort, Gouda, salami, olives, grapes, and nuts, and he handed the repast to her on a small gilt-edged plate. She devoured the food ravenously. After she'd consumed it, she felt better. She lay back on the bed gazing at him, a feeling of unreality seizing hold of her. Who was she, and what was she doing in this castle bedroom with this strange man? She had a feeling of floating, of not being anchored to anything. She was drifting out to sea.

He raised his glass. "A toast to the bride!"

"You didn't think I was serious about marrying you, did you? I said yes in the heat of passion."

"You little vixen. Why didn't you tell me it was your first time?"

She lowered her eyes. "I don't know."

"You're very responsive," he murmured, looking at her with a pleasantly brutal expression.

His glance sent a shiver down her spine. "I didn't know it would be like that."

"Like what?"

She tried to find the right words. "It was like . . . a religious experience!"

He took her hands and kissed them. "So how does a girl like you remain a virgin?"

"I'm a Catholic. And I was holding out for the right person."

"Am I the right person?"

"Yes," she said darkly.

"So marry me."

She looked at him, disconcerted. The sex had been too soon, and he was asking her to marry him too soon. This was a big red flag. Or was she just being conventional? It wasn't the length of the courtship that mattered — it was the person. But what did she really know about him? Only that he was a baron, from the same social milieu as she. He even knew the people she knew; he had grown up with Victoria, after all. But she had to know more.

"I don't know anything about you," she said.

"I'm a businessman and an aesthete. I was an only child, and I was raised in a fairy-tale castle in East Sussex. I went to Eton, and then to Oxford, where I studied English literature, with an emphasis on Coleridge."

She let out a little squeal. "Ooh, I'm a Coleridge scholar too! And I *also* studied English at Oxford, and I *also* grew up in a castle! Or at least, a country estate. Ours is in Devon. My father still lives there."

"How uncanny!" he exclaimed. "We're like twins!"

"Do your parents still live in the castle?"

His expression grew suddenly grim. "No. My mother died

in a car crash when I was seventeen. Then my father moved away and left me all alone there."

Her mouth dropped open in amazement. "*My* mother died in a car crash when I was *fourteen*."

They stared at one another, stunned at how parallel their lives had been. "How did your mother's accident happen?" she asked.

"I'd rather not discuss it. I lost both my parents that day—first my mother, and then my father, who wanted nothing to do with me after she died. The whole thing was horrible."

"I'm sorry. I know how you feel. My mother's accident was horrible too. She died trying to escape the paparazzi, just like Princess Di. My father had just chased her around the house with a knife, threatening to kill her, so she packed quickly and left. It was right after a photo shoot, and the photographers hid in the bushes and followed her to the house of her Italian lover. They were all speeding along the coast of Devon, when Sergio's Maserati went over the cliffs. My mother was a famous society woman, so it was widely publicized in the tabloids. The details of the love affair came out, and my father nearly went mad."

"I'm sorry. That must have been very difficult for you."

"It was." And then she started to feel sorry for herself, the way she always did when she thought about her mother.

"Tell me about it," he said, with a tenderness in his voice that touched her.

Judith had never told anyone about her relationship with her family—it was too harrowing to discuss—but when he uttered these words in such a gentle and encouraging tone, she felt an aching urge to tell her story. Suddenly she was aware of a great mass festering inside of her, and she had to purge it before it poisoned her.

She took a deep breath and filled her glass with champagne. "All right. You've heard of love children? Well, I was a *hate child*. My mother didn't want me, and she planned to abort me, but she put it off until it was too late. I was premature, so I spent the first few weeks of my life in an incubator. In those days they were deathly afraid of germs, so none of the nurses ever picked me up or held me, and my family only saw me behind glass. Did you know that babies can die from lack of touch? It was a difficult delivery — a C-section — and for years she complained that the scar it left on her stomach ended lingerie and bikini shoots forever. Stop me if I'm boring you."

"No, go on!" he said, gazing at her with an expression of rapt concentration.

She drained her glass, and continued. "Soon after I came home from hospital, my mother abandoned me and left me to a governess. She kept insisting she had been given the wrong infant at the hospital, or that I was of a different race than she was, or that I was a changeling. She couldn't help it — she really felt that way. I think her rejection of me had something to do with the fact that I was an unlovable baby. Also, she hated my father, and she didn't want another child with him. There was a thirty-year age difference between them — it was his second marriage — and she had never really loved him. She only married him because she was pregnant with Anne, and because she was dazzled by his wealth and by Waverly Manor. I'm not saying she married him only for his money—she was quite fond of him at the beginning—but by the time I came around, she hated his guts.

"Anyway, my birth drove her mad. She became nervous and brittle, and instead of sleeping, she would wander around the house every night like a troubled ghost. She couldn't stand the sight of me. Everything I did was wrong. The more I tried to please her, the more it disgusted her. When I said something nice, she accused me of being manipulative and sneaky. When I got good marks, she said I was trying to make Anne look bad. She refused to touch any food I prepared. She hated it when I gave her gifts—you should have seen her frown!—and I never saw them again after she opened them. I think she actually tossed them in the rubbish.

"Anne was two when I was born, and at first she was fascinated with me. But after a while, if she or my father were nice to me in any way, my mother punished them with abandonment. They were both desperate for her love, so they joined her in ridiculing and demeaning me, and I became the scapegoat of the family. Everything that was vile in their minds was projected onto me. I tried to be good, and never to do or say anything that would justify their abuse, but that only made them call me 'goody two-shoes' and 'Pollyanna.' When I stood up for myself, I was told I was 'causing a scene' and 'being dramatic.' And when I hid my feelings, they said I *had* no feelings. They wanted me to be bad so that all of the awful things they said about me would be true, but I never gave them the satisfaction. I was nauseatingly good, and they despised me for it, but it was my only protection against their tyranny."

She walked over to the table, poured herself a glass of

Chianti, and sank down into a velvet dining chair. "I was deeply unhappy. But in spite of how miserable I was, I couldn't hate my mother. I adored her. Everyone did. It was impossible not to love her. She was so clever and funny and beautiful, and she always knew what she wanted. She was like a movie star, and I wanted to grow up to be just like her. I only wish she hadn't died, because I hoped we might mend our relationship someday, and now it's too late."

Telling her story had been like a purgation, and she felt shaken, empty of energy, sucked dry, and desperately sad. And although she tried to contain it, a tear rolled down her cheek.

His eyes shone with sympathy. "I'm sorry. Your family sounds like a bunch of ghouls. And you *couldn't* have been an unlovable baby, because you're the most lovable little girl I've ever met. But you amaze me — you're successful and well adjusted, and you seem happy. It's unlikely that you should have survived such a family, let alone thrived. What was your secret?"

"My secret?" she repeated, in a daze. Usually when she confessed the secret source of her tranquility people laughed at her, but she knew she could trust him. So she looked into the distance, misty-eyed and breathless, and she said, "I discovered religion. Through prayer, I transformed the hate in my heart into love, and I learned to forgive others for the injuries they caused me. The harder I prayed, the better I felt. Often, I prayed until I passed out. Sometimes I wore a crown of thorns and a hairshirt, and I whipped myself with a scourge."

Now he was smiling. "You sound a bit kinky."

"Kinky? I never thought of it that way."

When she had mortified her flesh as a child, it had been a form of penance for her evil thoughts, and a way of preventing more serious acts of self-harm. And yet as her body had developed and matured, she had received unexpected sensual pleasure from her self-flagellations, enhanced by her clandestine reading of her father's erotic literature; so Gavin's irreverent remark secretly thrilled her. She, the nothing, the blob, the goody-two-shoes, being called kinky! Wouldn't her family be shocked to see her now, in a hotel room with a gorgeous, worldly baron, a Coleridge scholar no less, having had deflowering stranger sex with him, and now being called kinky! It was too delicious.

She laughed. "I wonder if I really am kinky?"

"Let's find out." He took her hand and led her to the bed. "Lie down," he commanded. She stretched out obediently on the satin sheets, feeling a burning sensation in her sex that was sharper and more urgent than before.

"First I'm going to tease you till you scream. I'm going to tie your hands so that you can't touch me. And I'll only make love to you once you beg for it."

She watched as he went into her suitcase and found a pair of sheer tights. He cut off the legs with a steak knife, and then he came towards her with a cruel smile, twisting the stockings in his strong hands.

5.

Boundaries Smashed

The sex lasted for hours. Judith experienced sharp pleasure and pain, and the tears streamed down her face, but he went slowly and tried not to hurt her. She drifted in and out of a kind of twilight, and her mind detached from her body so that she was often unaware of what was happening. Half the time she was dreaming, and she had various nightmares.

She dreamed of Gavin as an incubus, looking exactly like the demon in Fuseli's painting. She dreamed of herself as de Sade's Justine, repeatedly tortured and raped, but remaining pious and pure of heart. And she had other nonsensical dreams, mostly of slimy sea creatures that undulated and flapped at the bottom of the ocean, or of ornate gold, ruby, diamond, sapphire, and emerald scepters, crowns, and gigantic necklaces in glass cases at the Tower of London.

She was vaguely traumatized by the things he did to her, but it was exactly what she needed. She had never been held, touched, caressed, and loved, and now he was making up for all of that in one evening; she in turn was letting him into her most intimate spaces. She cried and cried, and her tears were cleansing.

When he finally finished, he held her in his arms and they slept. And this time there were no dreams, but only hideous blackness like the waters of Lethe.

They remained at the castle for three more days, ordering room service, having sex, drinking, and talking. She texted Anne to say that she'd been called to London suddenly by her publisher and to please extend her apologies to Victoria, and then she turned off her phone. They hardly had time to eat or sleep with all of the sex, and she talked about herself until her throat was raw.

By the third day she felt worn down and depleted, her spirit completely sapped by his relentless energy. He took her again and again, and he loved her so tenaciously and thoroughly that she felt completely overwhelmed. Never having experienced love from her family, love was the ultimate aphrodisiac, the only thing that turned her on, and she orgasmed over and over again. She felt isolated and trapped and smothered, but everything he was giving her was something she had always wanted; only, it was too concentrated, a lifetime of missing love and attention crammed into one long weekend.

And he was constantly checking in with her. She would wake up in the morning, bleary-eyed and sleep-deprived, and he would lean over and smile with his maddening scent of man plus sandalwood and say, "How are you this morning?" She couldn't remember a single time that either of her parents had said, "How are you?" They had also never said,

"How are you feeling?" or "How was your day?" Worse, they had never said, "I love you," which he said so often that it almost made up for all the years of never having heard it. The sound of his loving words, and the sight of his handsome face smiling at her, made her feel so loved that she thought her heart would burst.

On the third afternoon, as they were lying spent after a particularly exhausting bout of lovemaking, he said, "So when are we getting married?"

Judith was annoyed. He had mentioned marriage several times each day, insinuating it into the conversation whenever he could, and she was beginning to feel pressured. She had always relied on her intuition for important decisions, but this time, her radar screen had gone black. She loved him, but it was too soon. Anyway, why was he pushing so hard to get married? Was he some sort of gigolo? No—he couldn't be. He was rich, richer than she was. He was from the peerage.

She pulled the sheet over her face. "I don't want to think about that now."

He sat up. It was a violent movement, and his face looked hurt and sad. "Don't you love me?" he asked in a strangulated tone.

"Of course I do."

"Then why don't you say yes?"

"What's the rush? We have plenty of time."

"No, we don't. I have some business to take care of in Paris, and I'm leaving tonight." He rose and dressed, becoming quiet and sinister, like a bomb that was about to explode. Judith watched him, feeling disoriented.

"You didn't tell me. How long will you be gone?"

"I don't know. A very long time. I may not return to London at all."

"Why? What's so urgent in Paris?"

He looked at her as if she were a stranger. "I told you — it's business. I won't bore you with the details." He fastened the buttons on his shirt.

Judith felt a chill of abandonment. All of the trauma of her childhood flooded back to her in waves of nauseous panic. "We'll stay in touch," she said, trying to sound calm. "And I'll come down and see you on the weekends."

"No, Judith." He turned away and braced himself on the dresser, his head hanging down in despair. Soon he began to emit quiet, choking sobs.

She stared at him in alarm. "What is it? What's the matter?"

"It's no use. I don't think we should see each other again."

Molten fear flooded her body. "Why not?"

"I had never been in love until I met you. I had a terrible childhood — worse than yours. Meeting you was the best thing that ever happened to me. If you don't love me now, after all that we've shared, I don't know what's going to convince you. And I . . . I just couldn't take it if we saw each other for a few more weeks or months, and then you got tired of me or found someone else. Oh, I'm so unhappy!" His sobs became violent, the unbearable weeping of a man, and his strong back heaved from the effort.

"No!" she cried. "It doesn't have to be like that. I love you!" She was surprised to hear herself scream this so savagely. It didn't sound like her; but then, nothing she had done in the last three days had been typical. There were so many new emotions and sensations; she was a completely different person than she had been on Friday. Her boundaries had been smashed to pieces, and she had plunged into an unknown, potentially dangerous abyss.

Yet she was deeply moved by his expression of wounded vulnerability, which bonded them together in shared pain. She loved him, and he loved her. What was there to be afraid of, when two people loved each other as much as they did? Why did she always sabotage her chances of happiness? Was it because she didn't feel she deserved anything good in her life? Maybe it was time to stop punishing herself, and to start to believe in love. She was exhausted, her mind was blurry, her head ached, and her nerves were frayed from all of the sex, drinking, conversation, and sleep deprivation, but she had to decide now, or she would lose him forever.

"I've loved you for three days now," she said breathlessly. "I don't know what I'd do if I lost you to another woman — I think I'd kill myself. I don't know why I'm being so cautious. It's stupid of me." Now she was weeping too. "Darling, please marry me. I want to marry you more than anything in the world."

He stopped crying and turned towards her, his face streaked with tears. "Do you mean that, Judith?"

"Of course, darling." He sat next to her on the bed, and they held each other tight.

"Thank you, Judith," he whispered. "Thank you."

She kissed him all over his face. "We're going to be disgustingly happy together."

He sat against the carved headboard, and she crawled over to him and leaned adoringly against his strong chest, while he fondly stroked her hair. "When I become Baroness Hastings, where will we live?" she asked dreamily. "In your castle?"

"The castle's too expensive to heat," he rumbled, in his gentle baritone. "I'll buy you your very own castle."

At this, he removed his blood-red garnet ring with its heavy masculine setting, and slipped it onto her ring finger.

6.

Paris

They went to Paris. Their first day there he left her waiting at the Café de Flore, a charming spot on the Boulevard Saint-Germain, while he attended to his business. She parked herself in a red plastic chair on the street and ordered a *café gourmand*, which consisted of an espresso with a plate of small desserts, including a chocolate mousse, a raspberry cheesecake, a *religieuse*, and a lemon *gâteau*. The waiter brought her order, and she leaned her elbows on the little round rickety table, stirring her coffee with a tiny spoon and watching people go by.

The café was one of the most famous in Paris, having been frequented by the likes of Simone de Beauvoir, Jean-Paul Sartre, Albert Camus, Boris Vian, Georges Bataille, and Guillaume Apollinaire. A large white awning displayed the name of the establishment in green letters, below which were floor-to-ceiling windows encased in glossy black paneled wood, the doors fitted with long brass handles. There were plants and bright flowers on the roof, and the balconies of the apartment building above were fronted with filigreed black iron railings. The tables were crowded close together, and Judith tried to pick up snatches of French conversation from the people at the adjacent table to see how much she could understand.

After she had watched the bustle of the boulevard for a while, she got up and went around the corner, where she stood gazing with inspiration at Saint-Germain-des-Prés, the sublime medieval church across the street, before returning to her seat and consuming most of the dessert (she had a formidable sweet tooth). Then she started jotting down notes for her next novel, thrilled to be part of the legacy of writers who had worked there. She hovered the nib of her fountain pen over her notebook, ideas inspired by her whirlwind romance flooding her mind. She had only managed to write six or seven pages when Gavin returned, all smiles, carrying a bunch of red roses.

Thrusting the roses into her arms, he took her by the hand and whisked her down the street, saying he wanted to take her shopping. They took a taxi to the Champs-Élysées and popped into Fifi Chachnil, where he bought her several exquisite lace-and-satin lingerie sets, four pairs of back-seamed silk stockings, two suspender belts, three corsets in black, white, and nude, two negligees, a slip, and several wiggle dresses. He bestowed on her his mother's antique garnet ring for an engagement ring, with its large emerald-cut stone bordered by perfect diamonds. Afterwards, craving more jewels, they visited a shop where he purchased for her an art deco diamond ring, an Edwardian sapphire ring, and a Victorian ruby ring. They waltzed into various designer shops, where he bought her more dresses, a marvelously tailored skirt suit, high-heeled pumps, makeup, a new handbag, and perfume. He said he wanted to see her hobbling in a tight skirt, high heels clacking on the pavement, waist cinched, like an actress in an old black-and-white French film, and she began to have the same fantasies about herself.

The next day he took her to a salon, and suddenly she became woefully self-conscious about her dishwater brown hair that hung listlessly down, her heavy, shapeless brows, her nondescript eyes, her pale lips, her fresh-scrubbed freckled face, and her chipped, ragged fingernails, but all of that was quickly remedied. She got a facial, a manicure, and a makeover, her eyebrows were slimmed and shaped, and her face was expertly made up to look like a 1950s screen siren. The effect was stunning, and everyone raved about her excellent bone structure. So, she thought triumphantly, I'm my mother's daughter after all!

Gavin stood staring at her after the last touches of powder and lipstick were applied. He formed his thumbs and forefingers into a rectangle, as if looking through the lens of a camera. "I wonder what you'd look like as a blonde?" he said. "A Hitchcock blonde . . ."

Instructions were given, photos were pulled up from his phone, and Judith's hair was cut into a fetching shoulder-length bob, bleached platinum, and toned to a shade of gold reminiscent of Eva Marie Saint's sleek locks in *North by Northwest*. (They had considered the ashier, almost silvery tones of Tippi Hedren's and Kim Novak's hair in *The Birds* and *Vertigo* respectively, but they ultimately found Saint's warmer shade less dated.) When the toner was rinsed out and her hair shampooed, conditioned, blown dry, and misted with hairspray, the stylist stepped back, removed the pink-and-black salon cape with a flourish, and said, "Voilà!"

Gavin had insisted that she wear her new wasp-waisted gray suit, her nude corset, and her 1950s pumps that day, and now she knew why. On instructions from Gavin, the stylist pinned back her hair, studying a reference photo on Gavin's phone. Judith tottered across the room, trying to imitate Judy's walk after she's been transformed into Madeleine in *Vertigo*, and everyone clapped and cheered.

The new Judith walked arm in arm with her handsome beau along the Seine, and everyone stared at them. Men stared at her the way they usually did at Anne, with that lustful darkness in their eyes, and women stared in longing, wishing to be in her place because her man was so handsome. They stared at Gavin too, with all of the same feelings. "They're just jealous, because we're such a beautiful and happy couple," he said, and she knew he was right.

They had left the castle in the middle of the night so as not to be seen by anyone, had hired a car, and had driven all night, arriving in Newhaven early in the morning. There they had enjoyed a traditional English breakfast at a quaint café near the station before embarking on the ferry to France. They had booked a cabin and slept the four hours until their arrival in the quiet coastal town of Dieppe, where they had hurried to the train station and consumed a quick espresso and a sandwich before boarding the train to Paris. Judith had sat gazing out of the window at the scenery going by, miles and miles of rich farmland and grazing cows, peaceful and monotonous, as the train chugged hypnotically along, leading her to a new life.

As her old life slipped away from her, she felt a delirious sense of excitement, but also a profound sadness. She had everything she wanted now, but she'd had to get it all by herself. No one had ever supported her—not in any meaningful way. She felt sad for the sweet child she had been, always trying to help others and be kind to them, yet constantly scorned and derided. She wondered if her family's total abandonment of her had been necessary for her to become a strong and independent person—like James Hillman's concept of the seed that gets exactly what it needs, including privations, to grow into the plant it wants to become—or if it had stunted her somehow. She had long ago rejected romantic love, feeling she would never be able to pull it off. How could she give love, when she had never received it? With Tony, she had sometimes wondered if there was something wrong with her, because she couldn't feel the things for him she wanted to feel.

But now she was a different person, and she hated the person she had been only four days before, who had been so dead to Tony's kisses, so envious of Anne, and so bitter about her own identity as a woman. She had never felt like a "real girl," but that hadn't been by choice. Her mother had forced a boyish identity and clothing upon her as a form of punishment, and as a way of ejecting her from the secret society of girls and women of which both she and Anne were members. The irony was that Anne didn't care especially for feminine accoutrements, and Judith adored them. But she had stopped wearing Anne's hand-me-down party frocks after

51

she had been told once too often that she looked ridiculous in them, "like a drag queen."

Her mother's treatment of her reminded her of the movie *Now, Voyager*, in which Charlotte Vale, played by Bette Davis, has a mother who deliberately tries to keep her dowdy and unattractive so that she'll never become her own self-realized person. But Charlotte sees a therapist and undergoes a stunning transformation, both mentally and physically, and emerges as an ultra-glamorous and sophisticated woman.

Like Charlotte Vale, Judith wanted to reinvent herself as a woman. People thought only men reinvented themselves when they dabbled in feminine glamour, but Judith knew this wasn't true. She had witnessed firsthand the laborious hours her mother had put into crafting her image, and it was anything but natural; it was self-invention, a work of art. Judith didn't find this performance oppressive — stylized feminine entertainers like Mae West and Marlene Dietrich gave her life — nor did she feel that it came from an inauthentic place.

That the glamorous images that populated her mind were always of classic movie stars, and not of stars from her own time, was no coincidence. Although Judith lived physically in the present, she lived mentally in eighteenth- and nineteenth-century novels, in fairy tales, and in classic women's pictures. These artifacts from the past were more real to her than her own life, which had been nothing but an endless source of misery. The Judith who lived in material reality had been self-hating and unhappy, awkward and sad, unattractive and unloved; but the Judith who read books and watched movies could be anything she wanted to be.

As the train rattled along, she daydreamed about the morning she'd been sent away to boarding school after her mother's death, riding in a similar coach from Devon to Worcestershire. She had initially felt that she was being cruelly punished, packed off to a strange place where she knew no one. But once away from her oppressive family, she had blossomed. The outside world found her attractive when her mother and Anne weren't beside her for comparison, and her teachers were impressed with her intelligence and creativity. They encouraged her to write, and the stories flowed out of her, winning her prizes in prestigious literary publications, and making her somewhat of a star at the school. She grew out her hair and learned to style it, and she started to wear dresses and makeup. She remembered her ecstatic pleasure when she had discarded her trousers and replaced them with dresses, and how choosing her own clothing had helped her to come out of her shell, even leading her to become friendly with one or two of the girls.

She had not worn red lipstick at the time, nor purchased items such as stiletto pumps and feather boas, because she hadn't wanted to seem too femme, but the identity politics of her generation exhausted her. Whatever other people might think of her, she knew one thing: she wanted to be a glamorous woman. She wanted it for the pleasure it gave her, she wanted it for the power it gave her over men, and she wanted it as revenge on the people who had wronged her. She would no longer be a sexless blob writing about goddesses; she herself would be a goddess, the heroine of her own romance.

They had arrived in the evening at the Saint-Lazare station and taken a taxi to the Relais Christine, a charming historic hotel on the Rive Gauche. Exhausted, they had showered, ordered a light supper through room service, and gone right to bed. She had texted Anne that she was in Paris, but not that she was with a man. She and Gavin each had to apply for a copy of their birth certificate from England, and they were required to live in France for forty-five days before they could legally be wed.

During that time, they dined at Fouquet's, La Tour d'Argent, L'Ambroisie, and Le Meurice, walked their feet off at the Louvre, the Musée d'Orsay, and the Palace of Versailles, and enjoyed a spectacular can-can show at the Moulin Rouge. They left their hotel room late each day, craving each other's bodies and indulging in all of their most delicious desires before braving the tumultuous streets to soak in the Parisian *joie de vivre*. They saw classic films in French at the Cinémathèque Française, and then tried to speak in broken French afterwards, which made them laugh. In fact, they laughed a lot, despite the seriousness of some of their conversations. She poured out her heart to him, telling him about her childhood, her book ideas, her dreams, her theories about life. They memorized French poetry, and they went to the most medieval places and indulged in the darkest and most *outré* thoughts.

They were drunk on Paris: the modern Paris, but also the Paris of Baudelaire, Proust, Flaubert, Coco Chanel, Louis XIV, Voltaire, Catherine de' Medici, and Eleanor of Aquitaine. They went to see the crown jewels at the Galerie d'Apollon, and he promised he would steal them for her. He bought her flowers every day, and little gifts and fancy chocolates at all the shops, and more clothes, shoes, and lingerie.

He ordered the most expensive dishes at every restaurant, and the rarest wines and spirits. He seemed mad to spend his money, and he begged her to tell him what she wanted, so he could buy her more things. When she protested, he said, "L'amour est une religion, et son culte doit coûter cher."

He started calling her "Princess," because according to him she was a spoiled princess, and "little girl," because he said she was still a sweet, innocent Lolita in bed despite all he'd taught her. This made him want to take her over and over again, and each day they were more besotted with their love. She wondered how a man who was so handsome could also be so intelligent and culturally literate, and then she laughed at herself because she sounded like a sexist man talking about women. But he was just so unreal, like an object that had been created solely for her delectation.

The honeymoon lasted seven glorious weeks, and at the end of it they were married in a civil service at the town hall. He purchased an ivory lace Christian Dior wedding gown for her, and a veil that trailed twenty feet behind, and he had a tuxedo made for himself by the finest Parisian tailor. After the service, they hired a photographer to capture them in their wedding attire running ecstatically out of a church, while she tossed her bouquet to an imaginary bride-to-be.

7.

Manderfield Castle

As soon as they returned to London, Judith got to work on her novel while Gavin hunted for a house for them. He moved into her cozy flat in Hampstead Heath so they would be apart as little as possible, and they continued with their passionate love-making every night, and even during the day. He purchased a house almost immediately, but he kept its location a secret, explaining that he didn't want Judith to see it until it had been repaired and redecorated. All she knew was that it was in the country. He became cross when she tried to find out more, so she had to force herself not to ask any more questions.

After the purchase Gavin was gone much of the time, dealing with carpenters, painters, and decorators. This was a relief to Judith, since she needed to focus on her writing, and Gavin was much too distracting to be rattling around the flat at loose ends, removing her knickers while she was trying to work, or pulling her to the floor for a rough bout of sex. They needed a place where they could spread out, and where Judith could have her own private workspace.

She hadn't introduced Gavin to anyone in the family yet. Anne was dying to meet him, but Judith wanted everyone to see her and Gavin as lord and lady of the manor when they first encountered him, and not as two ordinary people crammed into a bohemian flat in London. Also, part of her was ashamed of her relationship with Gavin. He was her guilty pleasure, and their relentless sexual activity made her feel cheap and vulgar, especially as he often told her that he wanted her to live not in her head, but "in her pussy." She couldn't believe she allowed anyone to say such things to her, or worse, that she secretly liked them. How her own husband, a man of breeding, wealth, and distinction, could make her feel that when they made love she was engaging in an illicit sexual affair, or even a transaction at a brothel, was inexplicable to her; but that was part of his mysterious charm.

Three months later, the house was finished. Gavin had already moved most of their things to the new house, so all they had was one suitcase apiece, which they filled with the few items they had left behind. The thought of having her very own manor was delightful to Judith. She remembered the fancy parties she'd attended as a child at the country houses of barons and earls, where there were swans floating in the ponds, and gardens with mazes cut from boxwood hedges for children to run through. The other children had mostly avoided her because of her cross-dressing, finding her too strange to associate with, but she had greatly enjoyed losing herself in the labyrinthine gardens.

She herself had been raised in a manor house with a dreamy garden, a deer park, and a pond — Waverly Manor, bequeathed to Sir Wilfred's ancestor, Sir William de

Courtenay, by King Edward VI. As a child she had spent countless hours alone in the grounds, reading, dreaming, and making up plays, in which she'd act out all the parts. Sometimes she got lost in the woods behind the house, but no one missed her, and they were never alarmed when she returned late, often well after dark. They didn't seem to care if she fell into the hands or jaws of a predator; indeed, they seemed to *want* her to be eaten by a wolf. Sometimes in her small child's voice she would exclaim, "Mummy, I got lost in the woods!" And her mother would retort, "Don't exaggerate. You didn't get lost." And then Anne would pipe in and add, in her own infantile treble, "Yeah, don't zaggerate!"

But she had always loved the country, and especially the gardens, with their bursts of magenta, purple, pink, yellow, and blue flowers. She thought English gardens were some of the most beautiful and tranquil places in the world, and she knew she would always be happy if she had, as Victor Hugo had put it, "a garden to walk in and immensity to dream in."

Gavin had recently purchased a vintage blue convertible Aston Martin, and one morning they tossed their suitcases into the back of it and made the long drive to the mysterious new house. They took the M4 west, and the M5 south, and they chatted inanely and listened to baroque harpsichord music along the way. When they finally exited the motorway three hours later, she saw that they were in Somerset. A few minutes later Gavin turned off into a country road which wound round and round, surrounded by giant evergreen oaks on either side, and they passed a small village and several farmhouses and orchards.

59

Judith was bursting with happiness. "I'm dying to see the house! I can't believe you've kept it a secret all this time."

"I have many secrets."

"Not for long. Eventually I'll find out everything there is to know about you."

Suddenly she saw a flash of anger darken his face, and then disappear just as quickly. It was a cold, black rage that seemed to emanate from the depths of his soul. She stared at him, frightened. Why would the fact that she wanted to know more about him upset him so much, unless he had something to hide?

Then again, perhaps he was just moody. Her father was moody, and when he went into his rages no one could figure out why. She knew Gavin had been deeply wounded in childhood, but he had never gone into detail. Because they were such soulmates, she imagined that his pain must be similar to her own, and her heart went out to him.

Several miles past the village he took a sharp turn into a long driveway, and they stopped before a pair of massive iron gates set into a stone archway, over which a quaint carved sign read "Manderfield Castle." He pressed the button on a remote, and the gates swung open.

As they moved slowly up the drive, flanked on either side by towering trees, she saw in the distance the crumbling ruin of an old gatehouse, and a gray stone Gothic castle with both round and square castellated towers, its gables dominated by one high central turret. It was bordered with an enormous stretch of overgrown grass bursting with yellow daffodils, and dotted with ancient black oaks. It loomed closer and closer, until at last it towered directly above them.

She shivered as a chill of evil seemed to emanate from its massive walls. Her head pounded violently, and for a moment she thought she was going to be sick.

"What's the matter, Princess?" he asked in alarm.

"Nothing—I just felt a bit nauseated. I'm all right now." Her head still clanging, she gazed up in awe at the fortress. "Oh Gavin, it's splendid! It *is* a castle!"

"Wait till you see the inside!"

"Darling, you shouldn't have! This must have cost a *fortune!*"

They got out of the car, and a young, lanky man moved towards them. "Our bags are on the back seat," said Gavin. "Just bring them up to the master bedroom, that's a good lad."

"Yes, Sir."

Judith walked solemnly towards the castle arm in arm with her new husband, and then up the wide shallow steps. On either side a magnificent couchant lion kept stony vigil, alongside limestone urns overflowing with rhododendrons. She gazed in wonder at the façade, some of it blackened with age, some of it velveted with moss or creeping with ivy, its medieval towers looming above, its windows fitted with leaded panes.

"When was this built?"

"In the eighteenth century. It's a Gothic Revival castle—a folly. Aristocrats built these medieval towers and crumbling castles purely for decorative purposes. It looks more romantic than the real thing, don't you think? I fell in love with it the moment I saw it."

"It looks older than some fourteenth-century castles I've seen!"

"Some of it *is* that old. The original manor house was built in the fourteenth century, and this castle was erected on top of its ruins; only the central tower remains intact. That crumbling wall out there was part of the original house, and the original chapel still stands."

"Oh, Gavin, there's a *chapel*?"

"Of course, Princess. Your very own!"

Now they were on the doorstep, and Gavin slammed the iron knocker on the great oak doors. Moments later they opened, and a lovely young brunette in an English maid's uniform, complete with starched apron and white cap, peeked out from behind them. "Welcome home, Sir!" she said in a working-class accent.

"Hello, Nancy. This is your new mistress, Baroness Hastings."

Nancy curtsied. "Pleased to meet you, Baroness."

Judith was unhappy with the girl's youth and beauty—she couldn't have been more than seventeen, and she was as fresh and pretty as a picture. She nodded curtly. "Hello."

But soon she forgot all about Nancy, as Gavin swept her off her feet and carried her in his arms across the threshold. When he set her down she looked with pleasure at the entrance hall, where an urn filled with flowers on an ornate table formed a centerpiece. He plucked a wild rose from the arrangement and offered it to her, and she sniffed its perfume and gazed at him, more in love than ever.

Yet when he returned her glance, she observed on his countenance an expression that made her recoil in shock. It was haughty and commanding—cruel, even. Her gallant husband had disappeared, and in his place brooded the sadistic lord of a Gothic castle.

He observed her staring, and his expression quickly regained its loving and tender aspect. "Let me show you the house, Princess."

He led her through a pointed arch into the great hall, which featured a carved central staircase, gigantic windows, and magnificent black-and-white marble checkerboard floors. One wall was decorated with swords, spears, and battle axes, and there was a family coat of arms over the fireplace and a suit of armor in the corner. Everywhere were lavish draperies, oil paintings, nude classical statues on pedestals, antique furniture, and costly rugs. The ceiling was lofty, and everything was on a grand scale. But despite the grandeur of the setting, there was a feeling of decay: of walls rotting, wallpaper peeling, ceilings crumbling, rugs eaten by moth larvae, upholstery haphazardly repaired. The whole thing seemed more theatrical than practical, like a mausoleum for antique furniture and gilded objects—as if the décor was itself a folly, a façade, a bit of fakery to evoke grand and melancholy feelings.

"Oh, it's too perfect!" cried Judith.

"Well, it's a solid old place, but it needs a few repairs. The Duke of Belfort was dying to unload it, so I got a good price. Lovely fellow. I was at Eton with his son. Do you see that coat of arms? That's my family's coat of arms. And now it's yours."

They crossed the sweeping hall and entered the drawing room. It had the same air of decadence as the great hall—like a movie set that hadn't been used for decades, but that possessed all the more charm for its fallen pageantry. It featured a large stone fireplace, and the walls were hung with red velvet-flocked wallpaper and wainscoted with dark oak panels. There were long windows adorned with red velvet drapes, heavily carved antique tables and chairs, a sofa and chairs covered in crimson velvet, a sumptuously patterned carpet, paintings in gilded frames, fresh flowers spilling from urns, giant candelabras, and a fully stocked bar. Several of the paintings featured glamorous women in long gowns fleeing from castles, or alluringly menaced by men.

"Oh, Gavin, the *paintings*," cried Judith." They're just like the covers of my novels!"

"I know. I commissioned them from your artist." Then he turned to Nancy, who had followed them into the room. "Go and fetch us some tea."

"Right away, Sir." She turned and left, and Judith watched her wiggle — *deliberately*, she thought — as she flounced away.

"Where did you find *her*?"

"Nancy? She's the gamekeeper's daughter."

"The gamekeeper here?"

"No — at my castle in Sussex. I've known her since she was a little girl. She's turned out quite well, don't you think?"

Gavin noticed her expression and laughed. "Not jealous are you, Princess?" He took her in his arms and kissed her. As always, his touch stopped her thoughts and made her breathless.

Then he stalked around the room, picking up objects, feeling their weight, and setting them down again with a satisfied air. He seemed plunged in an intensely emotional experience as he perused the room in a kind of rapture, looking at everything and shaking his head in amazement. "I've always wanted a house like this . . . a castle all my own."

"What about your family's castle?"

"Oh, that! That's different. That was my family's castle, and this is my *own* castle."

"I know what you mean. I feel exactly the same way." She plopped down on the red velvet sofa. "I hated my family's house, because they lived there. But it's funny when you grow up rich, you know? You can sometimes take all of this beauty and luxury for granted."

At this, Gavin burst out laughing. He laughed and laughed, but she couldn't see what was funny. She didn't recognize him in the person who was mocking her, and she glimpsed again the cruel, diabolical man she had seen when they first entered the castle — that Byronic hero from an eighteenth-century romance. But he was probably just keyed up and overexcited, as she was. Once they had their tea, everything would go back to normal.

Nancy returned and set down the silver tea tray. It included cake, scones, clotted cream, and blackberry jam, all served on the finest bone china. She poured out the tea, and Judith added two lumps of sugar to hers.

Gavin grabbed a slice of Madeira cake. "That was quick! Are you some sort of a witch, Nancy?"

"I was expecting you, Sir, so the water was already at the boil."

"Is there *anything* you can't do, Nancy?"

"Oh, Sir! You're terrible!"

Gavin and Nancy both laughed. Then the housemaid left the room, her large, heavily lashed eyes tossing a backward glance at Gavin; but the Lord of the Manor had eyes only for his bride.

As Judith sipped her hot, refreshing tea, the exhaustion of

the drive, and her fears about her husband, fell away from her. She felt contented and comfortable — she was home.

"You've done a wonderful job with the house."

"I wanted everything to be perfect for my Princess. Now, finish your tea. We have an appointment."

She racked her brain. "An appointment?"

He fixed her with his devastating glance. "You haven't seen the bedroom yet."

They finished their tea, and then they ascended the long, magnificent staircase to the bedroom. It was the most exquisite room she had ever seen; but if truth be told, she mostly saw the ceiling.

8.

Exploring the Castle

For the next several weeks, Judith explored the castle and reveled in the gardens, the woods, the stables, the library, and the chapel. She spent hours traipsing through the crumbling old halls, constantly finding new decrepit rooms with rotting wallpaper and broken-down furniture, musty secret passageways, and superfluous stairways that led nowhere, and she never tired of these adventures.

She had never owned her own horse, but sometimes she had been permitted to ride Anne's. Now she purchased two fine steeds, one black and one white. She named hers Valancourt and Gavin's Montoni, after two characters in the Gothic romance *The Mysteries of Udolpho*. She was surprised that Gavin lacked the training to sit a horse, but he explained that his mother had possessed a phobia of horses due to an accident in her youth, so that part of his education had been neglected. After a few lessons he became quite comfortable riding. His natural dominance, and his quickness at learning commands and cues, put Montoni at ease, and soon he was the undisputed master of the majestic equine. Judith, for her part, became very attached to Valancourt, whom she loved to talk to and groom.

Often she and Gavin would canter together through the woods, he on his black mount and she on her white one. He looked very handsome in his equestrian outfit, and when he was proudly seated on his fiery black steed, he appeared more like an eighteenth-century villain than ever. The sight of him in this aspect gave her a thrill, and sometimes after they rode together they consummated their passion in the woods, or on the grassy bank near the crumbled walls and roofless arches of the ruined gatehouse, and she delighted in his irresistible scent of man mixed with horse sweat and leather.

She found even greater pleasures, if possible, in the old oak-paneled library. Sir Wilfred had gifted her hundreds of Morocco-bound volumes as a wedding present, for the family had purchased enough duplicates throughout the generations to fill her new library from floor to ceiling. She found many wonderful books to occupy her: all of the classics, multiple shelves of psychology, philosophy, and art, and a selection of banned erotica in plain paper covers. One such specimen was Guillaume Apollinaire's *The Debauched Hospodar*, a book that contained some of the most extreme examples of sexual sadism and torture ever published. Little had she known, when she had perused that volume with wide-eyed horror in her early youth, that one day she would be engaging in some of the practices described within its sordid pages with her very own husband. Some of the books were falling apart and some mildewed, the pages foxed and the covers eaten away, for Sir Wilfred had not yielded his best treasures.

But she was pleased to see that her favorite book from childhood was still intact: an enormous and ancient fairy-tale tome, with fantastic color plates. From the time she had first discovered it at age six, she had read the stories over and over again, imagining herself as Cinderella, forced to slave among the ashes by her cruel stepmother and stepsisters until a prince saw her value and rescued her; or as Rapunzel, whose long, golden hair was the ladder that her true love climbed to rescue her from her prison tower. Her favorite fairy tale, however, had been "Bluebeard." This story had held her spellbound, with its bloodthirsty baron, its secret key, and its forbidden chamber full of murdered wives.

While she was exploring the house, she got to know Sarah the cook, James the gardener, Esther who did the scrubbing and mopping but always left before dark, Jonathan the stable boy and dog keeper, and Philip the assistant gardener and errand boy, and she tolerated Nancy as best she could.

Nancy was lazy and insolent, but she could be sweet when Judith took the time to personally instruct her on how to properly iron, dust, hoover, declutter, launder, make beds, or anything else she should have already been trained to do. Judith didn't see the point of having a maid who put so little energy into her work, since this meant she had to do most of it over again herself, but Gavin insisted she would improve with training. The problem was that Nancy's attitude wasn't improving — rather, it was getting worse. And this was because Gavin bent over backwards to be kind to her. Judith suggested that they get rid of her, but Gavin said he owed her father a favor, and that he felt obliged to keep her employed. But the girl was impossibly immature and listless, and Judith suspected that Gavin *wanted* her to do the work, in order to spare Nancy. It was as if Nancy was the princess now, and Judith the housemaid.

Indeed, he greatly enjoyed watching her do housework, rubbing suds on her bottom while she was scrubbing floor tiles, or bending her over at the stove, and she wondered whether her domestic labor reinforced his fantasy of her as a submissive wife. His dominance was one of the things she found most attractive about him, but she was aware that there might be a dark side to it. As of now he only spanked her and ordered her around during sexual role-play, and she made up her mind to set firm boundaries if he ever tried those behaviors outside the bedroom. She had read about Domestic Discipline relationships, where the woman has to ask the man's permission to eat or sleep or go to the bathroom, and she shuddered at the thought of having that kind of arrangement. As for Nancy, she tried not to let his doting on the saucy maid bother her. Nancy was very young, after all, and it was natural for him to want to spoil her.

Once the house was in order, she settled into a routine of reading and writing for several hours a day, taking daily walks in the garden and in the woods, riding Valancourt, and praying at the medieval chapel. This was adjacent to a grave-yard shaded by a giant yew and bordered with crocuses and dahlias. Weeds, grass, and wildflowers grew tall between the tilting headstones, which were worn away with weather and time. The effect was deliciously macabre, like something from an old horror film.

Inside the chapel, stained-glass panels depicting the saints and the Madonna and Child were set into elaborate Gothic windows. Several rows of pews stood on the intricately pieced marble floor, and the sanctuary featured an altar, a pipe organ, richly detailed Gothic carvings, and red velvet benches and hangings. A life-sized wooden statue of the Virgin Mary, once brightly painted but now faded, adorned the altar, along with a gold chalice and paten and dozens of tapers in gold-plated holders. Judith instructed the gardeners to always have the urns filled with flowers from the garden, and each time she prayed she incensed the altar, lit the candles, and knelt on a carved wooden kneeler. Her prayers included songs and hymns, to which she sometimes accompanied herself on the organ.

Beneath the chapel was a vaulted crypt which contained the bodies of the most notable members of the original manor house. Two of the tombs were embellished with marble likenesses of Lord Mordaunt, a baronet who had lived in the sixteenth century, and his wife, Lady Mordaunt, whom he had murdered. The owner previous to Gavin and Judith, the Duke of Belfort, had mysteriously told them, "It is said that her ghost still wanders these halls." The legend gave Judith a thrill, and sometimes she descended to the crypt and gazed upon the effigies of the ill-fated couple. But she never remained there long, as the air was noxious and foul.

She visited the chapel each morning for lauds, and each evening for vespers. While she prayed, her mind often returned to the day she had attended her first church ceremony, at the age of seven. Wandering alone into the village, she had stumbled into the church of St. Mary's in the middle of Sunday Mass. She had been overawed by the beauty and solemnity of the church, and by the priest's orations about the suffering of Christ, with whom she had strongly identified. And she had loved eating Christ's body and drinking his blood, which had seemed magical to her, as if this simple act could transform her into someone entirely new. After that, she made the mile-and-a-half journey to the village every week for Mass.

By the age of eight, she had developed a personal relationship with the Virgin Mary. She had adopted the saint as her real mother—the mother who would always love her. Sometimes Mary appeared to her in visions, and once the little girl had even witnessed her statue in the village church shedding a tear. But Judith's most cherished memory dated to the time after her mother's death, when Mary had appeared and wrapped her arms around her in a divine embrace. Afterwards, Judith's wrists had bled in holy stigmata. The wounds had been excruciatingly painful, and she had lost a great deal of blood and gone through many bandages, but they had healed spontaneously after seven days. This episode had nearly committed Judith to an institution, but she soon realized that babbling about holy stigmata wasn't helping her case. So she lied and said she'd accidentally cut herself on some brambles and had been scratching the wounds open in her sleep, and they left her alone after that.

She didn't know anyone else who was religious, let alone Catholic, and she had received a steady stream of ridicule throughout her life for her religious practices. Everyone she knew thought of Catholicism as something from the Dark

Ages, but that was why she liked it. And while she abhorred the Church's views on women and homosexuality, she loved its theatrical aesthetics and its gaudy gilded grandeur; above all, Catholicism was deliciously *Gothic*. She might have become a Catholic for the architecture alone, especially after having visited some of the most magnificent cathedrals in France. She loved the religion for its poetry, its pageantry, its fetishistic artifacts and rituals, its martyrs, its sacred and sublime energy, and its iconography of the Virgin Mary. She was amazed that for hundreds of years, men who had consistently disparaged women as evil had bowed in reverence before images of the Holy Virgin, just as the pagans had worshipped their goddesses.

For Judith loved goddesses, from Aphrodite to the Virgin Mary to Joan Crawford and Ingrid Bergman. Her worship of these idols was about loving women, including herself; and she desperately needed to love herself, and to populate her world with images of admirable women to emulate. So she watched movies featuring glamorous actresses, and she prayed to Mary, and she read novels featuring bold, self-possessed heroines, and she dolled herself up like a 1950s screen siren, and in these rituals she created an all-encompassing world of feminine fabulousness for herself.

As she explored the castle and grounds, she felt as if she had slipped into a dream, but she hadn't questioned the change. She had always lived so much in her fantasy life that the transition had been seamless for her. Why *shouldn't* she live in a castle, with a handsome baron, and horses and stables and staff and all the rest of it? She was so in love that she would have been happy living in a hovel as long as it was with him, but that the beauty of her surroundings should match the beauty of her love for him seemed to her as natural as breathing.

Two weeks after they arrived at the castle, she invited Anne to tea. It was now early autumn, but the weather was positively balmy. Judith purchased a romantic ensemble for the occasion: a pink cotton frock with a pattern of small flowers and a deep ruffle at the hem, and a pair of high-heeled sandals to match. Anne wore a similar frock in blue, her hair in a fetching updo with little curls coming down.

As soon as she arrived, the couple gave her a tour of the castle. Anne was impressed, although it was a bit Gothic for her tastes. But she loved the master bedroom and the garden, with its stately hedges flanked by rare blooming shrubs, its rows of planted beds, wildflowers, and herbaceous plants, its enchanting lake, its shady paths and hidden grottoes, its fountains, its apple and pear orchards, and its views to the blue-tinted forest beyond.

The tour ended in the little walled garden adjacent to the kitchen. Gavin went to fetch something from the house, and the ladies sat down. Presently Nancy wheeled out the tea, along with cakes, scones, clotted cream and jam, fresh raspberries, and little triangle sandwiches, all served on Royal Albert china.

Soon, a large Persian cat bounded up and jumped on the table, and Judith kissed its wet nose. "Oh, Romeo!" she cried. "You're too scrumptious!" The feline gazed at her adoringly and purred.

She had adopted Romeo shortly after moving into the castle,

and he had promptly become the love of her life, supersed-ing even Gavin in her affections. He was exceptionally sweet, good-natured, and handsome, with long, thick white fur and bewitching blue eyes—he could have been a Fancy Feast model, she thought—and he followed her wherever she went. It had always been her greatest fantasy to become intimate with a cat, but she'd never had the opportunity until now. She reflected that in a dizzyingly short time, she had acquired the perfect home, the perfect man, the perfect horse, and the perfect cat. Her life couldn't have been more perfect.

She sighed. "Isn't it a dream, Anne? I've never been so happy."

"Yes. It does seem like a dream. The house is lovely. And that husband of yours is so handsome! He's like something from one of your novels."

"Yes, he is, isn't he?" Judith beamed with pride as she dolloped cream on a scone, followed by a smear of black currant jam. "Sometimes I almost feel as if I've invented him!"

Anne sized Judith up. "You look very feminine. Have you hired a stylist?"

"No—I've just started dressing as I please."

"Really? I never thought of you as the feminine type."

Judith was piqued by this comment, but her sister ignored her aggrieved expression and rambled on. "Anyway, we were all very shocked when we found out you had eloped. It was very impulsive."

"I didn't make the decision lightly. I knew he was the One right away. Sometimes it happens like that."

Anne poured herself another cup of tea. "I was very surprised that I recognized him. You don't forget a man like that. I noticed him around the pool area at Victoria's birthday party. Is that where you met him, or did you know him before?"

Judith realized it would sound tawdry to tell the truth. "Only casually," she lied. And then she couldn't resist blurting out, "Do you know what he said? He said I was the most beautiful girl he'd ever seen!"

Anne looked at her doubtfully. "Are you sure he's not a gigolo?"

Judith went into a rage. "How can you say that? Is it because you think I'm incapable of attracting a man like that, without my money? If he's a gigolo, then how was he able to buy this castle? Or pay for our honeymoon in Paris? Explain *that*, Anne!"

Anne looked away, embarrassed by Judith's outburst.

Just then, Gavin waltzed up with two boxes: a small one and a large one. The women lit up when they saw him, looking devastatingly handsome in a stylish blue suit, but Romeo hissed and bristled. Gavin handed the smaller box to Anne and bent down to kiss her. "This is for the pretty lady," he said.

Judith was horrified that Gavin had called Anne "the pretty lady," as if there was only one pretty lady present. She pouted childishly. "Where's *my* kiss?"

He laughed and kissed her, handing her the larger box. "Open it, Princess."

She did so. The gorgeously wrapped package contained a Jean Harlow–style white satin bias-cut dress, a vintage double-stranded pearl necklace, and a pair of art deco silver sandals. She held the dress up to her. "Oh, Gavin, it's lovely!" she cried. "It makes me feel just like a goddess!"

"As you are, Princess." Then he turned to Anne, his eyes shining as he took in her fresh, dewy beauty. "Now, open yours!"

Anne tore the paper off the little package and removed from it an exquisite antique garnet necklace. She went into raptures as she admired it, smiling winsomely at her benefactor, but then she caught Judith's appalled expression and put it back in the box.

"I can't accept this," she said, flushing a becoming shade of pink. "It's inappropriate."

"Nonsense." Gavin seized the necklace and fastened it around Anne's delicate white neck. At first Judith was jealous, but then she thought, I'm not going to be one of those wives who falls apart every time my husband looks at another woman. That's the surest way to kill love.

And she willed her jealousy to die.

9

The Princess Room

Judith's bedroom possessed ceilings carved with gilt-edged squares, tall leaded windows with blue velvet curtains and window seats, a thick pale-blue carpet, an enormous Italian marble fireplace, and a canopied bed made of richly carved black oak, hung with pink and purple sheers and heavy blue velvet draperies. The walls were fitted with blue damask and oak wainscoting, and the furniture included a Louis XVI dressing table, a Chippendale loveseat, and two matching armchairs upholstered in blue velvet. A shrine to her mother was displayed on the dresser, including a photo of Ava in a blue evening gown, a candle that burned night and day, a pair of her white kid gloves, a bottle of Chanel N°5, and a strand of her blue crystal beads.

Roses, lilies, and dahlias bloomed on every table, emitting a sweet, intoxicating fragrance, and paintings of nightgowned women fleeing from castles ornamented the walls. It was the one room in the house that had been completely redone, with fresh carpets, curtains, and paper. It was reminiscent of a boudoir in a classic Hollywood film—the type where, no matter the era, the luxurious feminine décor sets off the leading lady and her wardrobe in the best light. It was so extravagant that when she gazed at herself in her vanity mirror, or glided around the room in a negligee, she felt like a classic movie actress in a period film, or a heroine from a historical novel. And indeed, if anyone had seen her, they would have thought the same thing. There was little or nothing in her life now that one might call "modern," and more than ever, she felt she had become the heroine of her own Gothic romance.

Although they both slept in the master bedroom, Gavin had dubbed it "The Princess Room," because he said it was fit for a princess. He also called it "The Blue Room," because everything in it was blue. He had his own dressing room which he rarely used, except to nap in occasionally during the day.

It was late afternoon, near dusk. Judith, in a silk robe and lingerie with satin mules, sat at her dressing table, and Romeo dozed in an armchair nearby. She was hosting a cocktail party that evening—a sort of wedding party and housewarming combined. No one except Anne had met Gavin yet, and she was excited to show him off. All of those relatives who had found her so plain and bookish would now see her as the beautiful and glamorous wife of a rich, handsome baron.

But something was bothering her. They were spending a worrying amount of money, what with the mortgage payments, the household expenses, and the unpaid invoices from decorators and contractors, and Gavin hadn't settled a single bill. She had little understanding of his business, because whenever she asked him about it, he said it was too boring to discuss. Whatever it was, he seemed never to be doing it, as he occupied his time entirely with the leisure activities of a gentleman. She had assumed that once they were settled in he would go back to work. But he only wanted to hunt, ride Montoni, polish and maintain his weapons, work out and pump iron, shop for clothes, lock himself in his study, and make love. She was loath to confront him about money, but she made up her mind that she would bring it up during their next conversation.

She looked at her reflection and sighed. Life with him was wonderful — idyllic, really — but some things about it disturbed her. She had grown accustomed to the new, lordly air he'd affected since he first entered the castle, and now she rather liked it; but her knowledge of who he was as a person hadn't deepened since their honeymoon. She had expected that they would share everything about their lives, but she was the only one doing the sharing. She had blurted out her entire life story to him in Cornwall and Paris, and the relief of finally talking to someone had been so great that she hadn't noticed that she was the only one doing the talking. Once she had purged her soul to him she had craved for him to do the same, but he had remained curiously opaque.

Sometimes being with him was like looking in the mirror, because of the way he echoed all of her tastes and values without adding his own. Sometimes she felt he didn't exist at all, but was merely an illusion created by her desire — a composite of all of her favorite romantic heroes rolled into one. He was all style and charm and wit, with hints of an authentic self that would flash in his eyes for an instant, and then disappear. And a wall went up in his eyes when she asked him certain questions, like a drawbridge rising up over the moat of a stone castle, barricading it beyond reach.

His mysterious nature had given her the idea for her next novel, inspired by the fairy tale "Bluebeard." She had been working out the themes for some time, and now, feeling a sudden burst of inspiration, she decided to begin. So she took out her notebook and prepared to start writing, first going over her notes:

Bluebeard personifies the dark side of masculinity, and his bloody chamber is where men stuff all of their violent and antisocial thoughts. Men such as Bluebeard are the backbone of romance literature, in which sexy male brutes are routinely tamed and brought to heel through the love of a virtuous woman. The heroine conquers her lion, puts it on a leash, domesticates it, and turns it into a pussycat.

But Bluebeard is a man who refuses to be turned into a pussycat. He is an exhibitionist, teasing his wives to peer into his monstrous interior, but forbidding them to use the key. He knows they will disobey him, because wives want to know their husbands out of love, or fear, or self-preservation. Disobeying such a man might be rolling her eyes at something he says, or yawning when he's speaking, or asserting her will, or serving dinner late, or failing to keep the children quiet, or denying him sex, or contradicting him; or, worst of all, trying to escape his control. Thus the forbidden chamber, where Bluebeard stores his dead wives, represents raw male power—the side of men that women can't tame.

And yet not all mysterious men are Bluebeards, she thought. Many are just wounded, or reclusive, or inarticulate, or insecure, or socialized not to reveal their feelings. For instance, Gavin is the wounded type. I knew it the moment I saw him weep so pitifully in that hotel room in Cornwall. That was when I knew for certain that I could tame my lion. But as of now, he's far from tame!

As she opened her notebook to a blank page, she thought, this book will not be about my mother, but about me. This time, for once, *I'm* the beautiful heroine. And my name is . . . She went through a list of typical romance names in her head: Isabella, Sarah, Catherine, Emily, Jane, Eleanor, Abigail . . . Abigail! And Gavin is Barrett . . . no, *Beaumont*.

She picked up her pen and wrote, in her graceful longhand: *Bluebeard's Castle, by Judith Moore*. She paused, and then continued:

Abigail was attractive, but she was never confident about her looks. Raised in the shadow of a cold, beautiful mother and a distant father, and unable to compete with her famously ravishing sister, she became bitter and misanthropic, and she developed an innate distrust of men and a severe dread of marriage. But all of that changed when she met the handsome, dashing Beaumont. As soon as he swooped into the village and asked for her hand, giving her a garnet ring and whisking her away to his castle, she knew the first moments of passion in her young life. No one had ever been interested in her for herself, as the vibrant, fascinating woman she knew herself to be. In the mirror Beaumont held up to her, she was beautiful, alluring, amusing, and bewitching. He was her shadow side, and without him she was unable to express all of the things inside her that made her feel alive. Abigail knew one thing for certain: she would rather die than go back to being a pale, sexless shadow of her glamorous sister.

Suddenly, the sound of distant gunshots shattered the air. She laid down her pen and looked anxiously towards the window. Although hunting was popular among her class, Judith hated it. It seemed so cruel to kill animals for sport. And even when they consumed the animals they slaughtered, it still upset her; she didn't want to hear her animal friends from books labeled as venison, or to find their body parts served with French sauces on her plate. She was glad at least that they had a cook who knew what to do with the carcasses Gavin dragged into the kitchen, dripping blood all over the floor. Sarah refused to dissect the deer, though. She left it up to Gavin to behead and dismember them, which he did with great relish, brandishing his sharp knives with precision.

Judith's family cook had owned an old volume titled *The Complete Game Cookbook*. Within it were recipes that began with instructions like "gut a young deer, and saw off its head," or "hang a hare to bleed for seven days," or "soak a drained woodchuck in milk overnight." As a child, she'd had a morbid fascination with this book. The instructions on how to flay and dissect animals, or how to use the organs and blood and brains, were like horror stories to her, and the full-color plates made her stomach turn. In her family home, she never saw the game until it appeared at the dinner table in various braises, roasts, and stews — or worse, in fried sweet-breads, kidney pie, grilled heart, pickled tongue, and blood soup — for she always fled the kitchen when she heard the men coming home from the hunt. But here at Manderfield, sometimes she saw the animals being dragged through the back door, and Sarah rushing in and scrubbing the blood off the tiles.

She was yanked out of her reverie by the sound of dogs barking. She rose, went to the window, and looked out. Below, Gavin was sauntering through the back garden bordering the woods, past the ancient crumbling wall, the giant hedges, the banks of flowers, and the Roman fountain, and across the intensely green lawn. He was carrying a shotgun and a brace of dead rabbits, his two beagles barking joyously beside him. He looked up at her with his devilish smile, blew her a kiss, and disappeared beneath the eaves of the house.

Judith sighed and moved back to her dressing table. She hated his hunting, but she couldn't ask him to stop; in any case, it would have been futile. If she knew anything about men, it was that a man does what he likes. She felt sorry for his dogs, though. They were *his* dogs, not theirs, and Gavin insisted that they live in the kennel, as the comforts of the house would spoil them. She was forbidden even to speak to them, lest she corrupt them with her soft and womanly ways.

She spritzed on some French perfume — Joy by Jean Patou, once advertised as "the costliest perfume in the world" — lined her lips, and smeared them with the vintage red of a lipstick. Then she shaped her brows with an eyebrow pencil and glued on a pair of long, thick eyelashes, the greatest weapon in a glamour girl's arsenal. Nowadays when she made up her face, she gave it the works—foundation, blush, lipstick, eyeliner, eyeshadow, mascara, eyelashes, powder—and it was only armed with this mask that she felt ready to tackle life.

Soon she heard the front door slam, and Gavin's heavy boots stomped up the stairs. He entered and plopped his bloody rabbits down on a table. She shuddered. "Do you have to bring them in *here*?"

"Sorry. I'm in a bit of a hurry. The guests are arriving in an hour."

She spoke to him in the mirror. "Is it that late? You'd better dress, then."

He flung off his hunting coat and crossed to the bathroom. Soon, she heard the shower running.

"Gav?" she called out.

"Hmmm?"

"I got a call from the bank today. We're behind on our mortgage payments."

"What, Princess?" he yelled from the bathroom.

"Never mind. I'll tell you later."

She heard him step into the shower and close the door. A few minutes later he emerged from the bathroom in a robe, drying his hair. "What were you saying?"

"The bills. We're behind on our mortgage payments."

"Oh, that. Well, I'm a little short just now. Can you take care of them?"

She frowned, confused. "What do you mean, you're a little short?"

He came behind her and smiled at her in the mirror. "Well it's a bit awkward, but I seem to have run out of money."

She gaped at him, trying to figure out if he was joking. "Run out of money?"

He grabbed his clothes from the closet. "Yes. I spent everything I had on the honeymoon and on the house, and now there's nothing left."

"You mean you don't have any savings? What about your assets? Can't you sell your family castle?"

"No," he said, pulling on his trousers. "It's in such disrepair that if I sold it now, I'd get practically nothing for it. Besides, I don't want to sell it."

"What about your father?"

"He's never helped me, and he never will."

"Is he coming tonight? Maybe we can speak to him."

"Of course he's not coming. I told you, we're not on speaking terms."

Judith stared at him helplessly. "But you must get dividends from your business?"

"I'm afraid not. The stock went bad last year. I'm sorry, Princess, I know I should have told you all of this before, but it's so bloody tedious to talk about money."

For the first time, his smile failed to charm her. She looked around in despair at the giant castle bedroom, the luxurious furnishings. "Gavin, what were you thinking? Did you really expect me to pay for all of *this*?"

"Why not? Do you think the man should always pay?"

"It's not that . . . it's just that I *can't*. How much money do you think I have?"

He looked genuinely shocked, and then he laughed. "It doesn't matter. We'll get by. I have plenty of business deals in the works. I'm just going through a rough spot. I can build up a fortune very quickly; I've done it before. We'll have millions before you know it."

Her mind raced to find a solution. "All right. I'll use my savings to pay our debts, and we'll borrow from Father until we can get back on our feet. But we'll need to sell Manderfield."

"Sell Manderfield? Never!" She was surprised at his vehemence; there was a desperation in his voice that she'd never heard before.

"But, darling," she protested. "Do you realize how high the monthly payments are? How much did you put down as a deposit?"

"Five percent. As soon as I told the bank manager I was your husband, he would have trusted me for any amount." He fastened his diamond cufflinks, a wedding present from Judith.

She sighed. He was such an irresponsible child, but it was difficult to be angry with him. "I'll have to insist," she said firmly. "The situation is completely impossible."

He came behind her and nuzzled her neck. "I bought the castle for *you*. And I'll work and slave to make sure you never have to leave it. I always want to see you like this: a jewel in a velvet box."

She laughed. "You don't want the castle for *me*. *You're* the one who has an unhealthy obsession with it."

He ran his eyes up and down her body. "There's only one thing I have an unhealthy obsession with — and that's you." She blushed as he devoured her with his eyes. "My naughty little girl. Is that new lingerie?"

"Yes. I sent away for it from that shop in Paris. Like it?" She slipped off her robe, posing in her vintage-styled underwear.

"Darling, you're a sex goddess!"

She went to the full-length mirror and surveyed her figure; it *did* look rather good. "Do you think so?"

He squeezed her from behind, wrapping his strong arms around her waist. "You'd better get dressed before I rape you."

She was instantly turned on. He could always do that to her; it was like turning on a tap. He carried her to the bed and tossed her onto the blue velvet coverlet, kissing her face and neck.

"Don't! My makeup!"

"To hell with your makeup," he growled. He was like a wild beast, kissing and biting her all down her body. She gasped and moaned, furiously undoing his shirt studs. They rolled around on the bed, madly in love, going at it like horny teenagers.

10.

The Cocktail Party

A smattering of guests mingled in the hall, faintly bored as at most parties, while servers passed around little trays of wine, champagne, spirits, and hors d'oeuvres.

Gavin had showered again after their wild bout of lovemaking, whereas Judith had been loath to wash his manly scent off her body. So she touched up her makeup and came down first, flushed and blooming with sex. She was wearing the white satin outfit Gavin had given her, plus elbow gloves and a short white ostrich cape.

She felt the eyes of the men on her as she descended, and she basked in the attention, walking slowly for maximum effect. And then she saw Tony standing at the base of the stairs, gazing up at her with an eager, shining face. She hadn't seen him since her elopement, and she was nervous about what would happen when he and Gavin met. She imagined them having a duel, Tony shouting, "You stole my woman!" and inviting Gavin outside to draw pistols. But no, Tony wasn't like that; he would never do anything to hurt her. Above all, her happiness was more important to him than his own.

His eyes were aglow with admiration and love. "Hello, Judith. Congratulations on your marriage."

The expression on his face moved her — he was fighting back tears — but she tried not to notice. She leaned on the banister, feeling like a vamp. "Thank you, Tony. How have you been?"

"All right. Nothing very interesting to report. It's been a long time, hasn't it? The last time I saw you was at that castle in Cornwall." His voice quavered, and Judith reflected that the day she had shattered Tony's heart had been the most important day of her life; but not because of him.

A server stopped before them with a tray of champagne in little flutes, and they each took one. They clinked glasses and drank. "By the way," he said, "where is that mysterious new husband of yours? I'd like to meet him."

"He'll be down in a moment."

His sad eyes scrutinized her. "Judith, are you happy?"

"Isn't it obvious?"

"Yes, you look fantastic. Beautiful and radiant." This was the first time he had ever told her she was beautiful. It made an impression, but it was too late. Her vanity had been carved into an exquisite sculpture from years of abuse, and he had been one of the sculptors.

"All of this was so sudden," he continued. "Are you sure you made the right choice?"

"Yes, I'm sure."

He winced a little. "Then I wish you the best."

Suddenly the room went quiet. Judith looked up and saw Gavin descending the stairs in a beautifully tailored blue suit. His charisma and good looks stunned everyone; it was as if sunshine had entered the room. Everyone stared at him, and there were audible gasps of delight. One woman blurted out, "What a handsome man!"

Judith was thrilled by the reaction. Gavin was her man, and all of these people knew it. She grabbed his arm as he reached the bottom of the steps. "Gavin, this is my friend Tony. Tony, my husband, Gavin." The two men took an instant dislike to one another. Tony was offended by Gavin's good looks and charisma, and Gavin glared at Tony so viciously that the doctor actually took a step back.

"Tony, will you excuse us?" said Judith. "I want to introduce Gavin to Father."

"Of course."

Judith led Gavin into the drawing room, where guests mingled in their smart expensive outfits, holding cocktails and chatting against the red velvet wallpaper, under the enormous crystal chandelier. All of the women turned their heads and stared at Gavin as he passed, and all of the men stared at Judith, who was commanding quite a bit of attention in her sleek satin gown.

Judith spotted her father and strode towards him, with Gavin on her arm. "Dad!" she called out. Sir Wilfred, a lovely, impeccably dressed older gentleman with white hair, very English and upper crust, turned and glanced at her. At first he registered confusion, and then delight.

"Judith, I didn't recognize you! You look so . . . pretty."

Judith was shattered by the backhanded compliment. "Dad, this is my husband, Gavin. Gavin, my father, Sir Wilfred."

Sir Wilfred shook Gavin's hand. "Gavin! Glad to meet you. Judith's been keeping you from us."

"Judith thought an elopement would be more romantic."

"Very sly of her. She's a sneaky girl, Gavin. Can't be trusted. A real bitch! Of course, I'm only joking." Sir Wilfred chuckled, pleased with himself. He'd had a few drinks already, and in his opinion he was being witty — the life of the party.

Judith, who had turned scarlet with shame, felt a warm hand in hers and a loving squeeze. "I support Judith in every way," said Gavin, smiling into her eyes. Judith was eternally grateful; she had never been more in love with him than at this moment. Finally, she had someone on her side: someone who would stand up for her against her family, and against the world.

Sir Wilfred slapped his son-in-law on the back. "Gavin, my boy, Judith tells me you're from the peerage."

"His father is the Baron of Sussex," bragged Judith.

The old man nearly choked on his drink. "You must be joking. There hasn't been a baronetcy in Sussex for over three hundred years!"

"Judith is a bit mixed up. My father is Baron *Hastings*, not the Baron of Sussex."

Sir Wilfred racked his brain. "Baron Hastings? Are you sure?"

"Gavin grew up in a *castle*," said Judith.

Gavin smiled blandly. "Will you excuse me, Sir Wilfred? I have to see a man about a horse." He turned and walked away.

Sir Wilfred stared after Gavin, puzzled. "Baron Hastings? Extraordinary!" he muttered to himself. Then he disappeared into the crowd, leaving Judith standing alone.

As Judith watched her father wander away, abandoning her for more stimulating company, she hated him. This man, whose drunken rages had terrorized the household for so many years, now seemed a pathetic old fool, unable to be the least bit kind or attentive when it mattered most. Both of his children had been accidents, as he was fond of pointing out, and he often lamented that they had sucked away all of his time, although he had spent remarkably little time child-rearing. He treated girls and women as either pretty baubles or ugly invisibles, and he assumed they didn't have a thought in their heads, no matter the evidence to the contrary.

Judith shared so much with her father — their tastes in books and music and art — but he had never taken her seriously as a person or as a writer, and he dismissed her ideas as a load of feminine claptrap. His vicious nicknames that lampooned her childhood plainness, and his casual sexist remarks, cut her to the core; he had even tried to impress her husband by calling her a bitch. His own failed marriage had blinded him to the possibility of harmonious matrimony, and he assumed all men liked to bond over deriding their wives. But Gavin hadn't played; Gavin loved her. Only weak men hated women. Her father had only truly loved her mother after she was dead; maybe because dead women couldn't speak. They were marvelous dolls to be admired from a distance, like Millais's painting of Ophelia's drowned corpse floating down the river at the Tate Britain. And that's the way Judith's father liked his women: beautiful and mute.

Her reverie was broken by a bright voice, as Anne and John pressed through the crowd to greet her. "Hello, Judith," said Anne. "I've been looking everywhere for you."

Anne looked ravishing as always, in a long black gown with a full taffeta skirt and a square neckline, very Grace Kelly. But she wasn't used to Judith appearing so attractive, and she looked askance at her sister's revealing bias-cut dress. "That dress is rather clingy, don't you think?"

Judith smiled vampily. "The men seem to like it." Anne gaped at her sister, startled by her new aplomb.

John was more enthusiastic about the change. "I say, Judith, you look spiffing. Can I get you another drink?"

"Yes, thank you John."

John meandered away to find a server, followed by Anne. Just then, a tall, striking brunette in a long red sequined gown sauntered up to Judith. "Ms. Moore? I'm Selene, your neighbor. I live just down the road. I'm a huge fan of your books. I loved *The Honeymoon Murders*! Will you sign it for me?" She thrust a book and a pen into Judith's hands.

"Of course."

As she was handing the signed book back to Selene, she caught a glimpse of Gavin across the room, surrounded by a group of women who were hanging on him and laughing at his every word. Selene followed her glance. "He's such a *marvelous*-looking man! I just about fell over the first time I saw him."

"That's my husband."

"Oh, I know, dear! But how *ever* did you land him?"

"With a fishing pole and a net."

Selene eyed her doubtfully. But then she was distracted by Nancy, who had materialized before them with a tray of champagne. They each took a glass, and Judith downed hers quickly.

Selene watched as Nancy sashayed away in her little uniform, which on her looked like a sexy Halloween maid costume. "That girl is simply *darling*! Did you hire her for the evening?"

"No. She's our full-time maid."

"Really! Don't you feel uncomfortable, having such a young and pretty housemaid? I know *I* would, with a husband like yours."

"No. My husband doesn't look at other women."

"Well, you never know. I'd sack her just in case."

"I can't at the moment. I only have two housemaids, and I don't have time to find a replacement."

"This house is much too large for just *two*," observed Selene, scanning the room.

"I can manage. I like to do some of the housework myself."

Selene laughed. "How quaint! You know it's funny, but your husband's *exactly* the same way. Doesn't care about appearances at all. If he did, he never would have married that tarty blonde. You know the type—all fur coat and no knickers."

Judith tried to conceal her shock. "I beg your pardon?"

Selene continued, with thinly concealed delight. "Well," she said, "when your husband was working with the decorators, I stopped by to bring over a cake and say hello. And just as I was leaving, a gorgeous blonde named Constance came by the house all dolled up, saying she was his ex-wife and asking for money. He begged her to go away, and after she left, he told everyone she was crazy."

Judith's stomach dropped. "I know all about that. Gavin and I have no secrets between us. But that woman *was* crazy. Gavin's never been married before."

97

"I'm just telling you what I saw. Lovely to have met you. Cheers!" And she sailed away.

Judith ground the heel of her palm into the sofa, reeling from an attack of vertigo. She suddenly recalled the horrible look on Gavin's face when she'd said she wanted to find out all about him. Is that what he was concealing — an ex-wife? What else was he hiding? She had romanticized his mysteriousness as a side effect of his masculinity, but now she began to wonder if he was hiding a dark past. Why had she, normally cautious to a fault, married a man she knew absolutely nothing about? There must be some misunderstanding; Selene must have got her facts wrong. She was just a vicious gossip, the type to repeat anything she heard whether it was true or not. Gavin would explain it to her later.

She wished she could speak to him, but he was still surrounded by a gaggle of adoring women. He's certainly comfortable around them, she thought. It wouldn't surprise me if he was a womanizer. Could he have actually been married before, and kept it from me? Is he capable of such duplicity?

John returned with Judith's cocktail. By some miracle, he had brought her a whisky highball. She drank it down eagerly, and the sweet, harsh liquid warmed her and gave her strength.

John made a priggishly disapproving face at the way she polished off her drink. "So I hear you're working on another novel," he said. "What's this one about?"

"It's about a sociopath who kills a series of wives . . . until he's stopped by his last wife."

"I can't understand how you ladies end up with sociopaths. Are women really that stupid?"

Judith's blood boiled. "No, John, women are *not* that stupid. Sociopaths are very good at love-bombing and gaslighting their victims. They're so good at it that they rarely fail. Anyone can fall for a sociopath. *Anyone*. Even you, John."

"Well, I suppose so. But you would think that an intelligent woman could see . . ."

"It's got *nothing* to do with intelligence!" she shouted, the alcohol loosening her inhibitions. "You wouldn't believe how many letters I get from women who say they thought they were too intelligent to end up with an abuser . . . until it happens to them. And once they're in it, it's hard to get out, and hard to explain to people why it's hard."

"All right then, explain it to me. Why *is* it hard to get out?"

The drinks had taken effect, and her eyes burned bright. "Well, sociopaths can fake emotions, so they pretend to be everything the woman has ever dreamed of. Later, when the mask comes off, she feels like a fool for having fallen for him, so she turns a blind eye to his bad side, and she tries to stick things through."

"I see — in for a penny, in for a pound — sort of a confirmation bias."

"Exactly. Plus — and this is really important — often, she's really and truly in love with him. Love is madness, and no one can really understand it except the person who suffers from it. So she becomes desperate to save her relationship, and the more she tries, the more hooked she gets. It can get pretty grim."

"That sounds fairly straightforward. So why is it hard to explain?"

She uttered a wicked little laugh. "Because of people like you, who call victims stupid!"

John crimsoned with embarrassment. "Sorry—I see what you mean. So this sociopath in your book . . . how does he get away with the murders?"

"He makes them look like accidents." She perched herself on the arm of the sofa, grabbing a drink from a passing tray.

"That doesn't sound so easy."

"Well, it is. It's incredibly easy to kill someone and get away with it."

Several people had gathered around to eavesdrop. Soon they had all stopped talking, and were listening to Judith with rapt attention.

"You mean, like the perfect murder?" asked Selene eagerly.

Judith, quite drunk, was enjoying being the center of attention. "Yes. The key is to make it look like an accident, so you don't have to do away with a body."

Anne was shocked. "That's horrible, Judith! How can you say such things?"

"Well, think about it. If you found someone dead in the bath, how could you prove it was murder and not an accident?"

Gavin had a fascinated gleam in his eye. "You could perform an autopsy."

"You can't always tell from an autopsy. For instance, a man could bludgeon his wife on the head, and it might look as if she'd fallen and struck it on the edge of the bath. Besides, they usually don't order autopsies for household accidents."

Murmurs went around the room. "That can't be true!" cried Sir Wilfred.

"They must order autopsies!" exclaimed Selene. Soon they all started speaking at once.

"But they usually don't," resumed Judith, and they all quieted down to listen. "Not unless something looks terribly wrong. For instance, I once read about a man who claimed that his wife had just drowned in the bath. But when the police came by, the wife and the bath were both dry. *That's* when they order an autopsy."

People started murmuring again amongst themselves. Then Tony interjected, "Judith is right. It's shocking, the number of corpses we see at the hospital that are assumed to be accident victims, when they have absolutely no idea how the person died. There's usually no investigation at all."

"Says the white knight," said Gavin with a sneer. He glowered under his brows at Tony, and his expression was so hostile that Tony bristled. They stood glaring at one another for a few moments, and Judith thought, oh dear, we're going to have that duel after all. But then Tony looked away, and the showdown was over.

The room became very still as the guests let their imaginations run wild about the love triangle on display. But then Judith continued effervescently, "It's really shocking what people get away with. I read a story about a woman whose boyfriend called 999 because supposedly she slipped and hit her head in the bath. She was covered with bruises when they put her in the ambulance, and she died three days later. It wasn't until the family hired a private investigator that the police finally entered the house. When they did, they found blood *everywhere* — all over her clothing and the floors and the walls. Her boyfriend hadn't even bothered to clean up all that blood. If he had, he might have easily got away with it."

Everyone looked shocked. Then Gavin stood and paced the room. "You can't believe everything you read."

"It was in the *Spectator*."

"All right. But that story is probably an outlier."

"I'm afraid not. When you read true crime, you come across *dozens* of stories like that."

They all began murmuring again. Judith, in her intoxicated state, was rather enjoying disturbing her guests.

"What about poison?" suggested Sir Wilfred. "They would jolly well catch *that* in a coroner's report!"

"They only test for poisons they suspect are there. If it's an unusual poison, chances are it will never be detected."

Anne looked horrified. "Then people must get away with murder all the time!"

Judith suppressed a gleeful smile. "The fact is . . . they do!"

The guests exchanged shocked glances, and then Gavin started laughing. He laughed so hard that everyone else laughed too. They laughed and laughed, and Judith laughed hardest of all.

11.

What Is Going On?

The guests finally left, and Judith sat at her dressing table in her pink chiffon negligee, brushing out her hair. She had swallowed nothing all evening but a canapé, a spinach-and-cheese triangle, and three Swedish meatballs, and she felt sick. But the alcohol was beginning to wear off, and what she wanted most of all was another drink. A drink, to give her the courage to face Gavin, to ask him about his ex-wife, and possibly to cause the whole house of cards that was their marriage to start toppling down. Would he lie? Would he be angry? Would he have a plausible explanation? If so, would she believe him?

Gavin, in striped pajamas and a silk dressing gown, came behind her carrying a glass of cognac. It was their nightly ritual: he would pour her a snifter of Rémy Martin from the drawing room bar and bring it up the stairs to her on a silver tray while she was removing her makeup.

He set the glass down, trying not to disturb Romeo, who was stretched out on the dressing table; but the cat hissed and cuffed him, drawing blood on his cheek. His eyes blazed with anger, and he raised his hand to strike; but then he saw Judith's expression and he changed his mind. "Here is your cognac, little girl," he said, dabbing his face with a tissue.

Judith expertly warmed the cognac in her hands, drinking it down in one gulp. Then she lifted off her eyelashes one by one and carefully removed her eye makeup with cold cream and cotton wool. Gavin sat on the bed, and they watched each other in the mirror as she finished her bedtime ritual.

Suddenly she began to lose courage, and she wondered if she should wait until morning to broach the subject of Constance. Maybe she would never bring it up; maybe it was better not to know. Many marriages were destroyed because of too much transparency. But she had to know, eventually. And if she didn't ask him now, she might never have the courage later. So she took a deep breath and she said, "Gav . . . you know that woman Selene?"

"Selene? She lives down the road, doesn't she?"

"Yes. She told me some interesting things tonight."

"What did she say?"

Judith tried to find the right words; she didn't want to sound as though she was nagging. "She said . . . she said that you were married before, and that your ex-wife — Constance — came here asking for money."

Gavin laughed. "Oh, Constance! She wasn't my wife. I'm sorry, I probably shouldn't laugh. It's actually kind of sad."

Judith was surprised by his nonchalance; this wasn't the behavior of someone who'd been caught in a lie. "Who is she, Gav?"

He wrinkled his brow, embarrassed. "She used to rent a room in my house. She was living on the streets — I don't have to tell you what type of work she did — and I offered her the room in exchange for some housekeeping. But then she fell in love with me. She was furious when I kicked her out for plying her filthy trade in my home, and she started stalking me and spreading lies, saying she was my wife and a load of other bollocks. I finally dodged her, but she tracked me down. I warned her never to show her face here again, or I'd put the police on her tail. Ha — that scared her off! She's a complete nutjob, poor thing. It's all rather unpleasant."

His manner was so sincere that she was certain he was telling the truth; she was a fairly good judge of these things. She felt silly to have believed Selene's vicious gossip; but then, she had known all along that there must be some reasonable explanation. She laughed into the mirror. "She sounds dreadful! But Selene says she's very attractive."

"Attractive? Not to me; but you know I detest trollops of that sort."

She tried to rise, but Romeo, jealous of her attention, meowed and hooked his claw into her dressing gown. She freed herself from the cat's tenacious grasp and joined Gavin on the bed, enormously relieved.

She leaned back against him, and his arms enfolded her. "Love me?" she whispered.

"Madly."

She lost herself in the comfort of his embrace.

Judith borrowed a considerable sum from her father and paid their debts. She now felt guilty for having hated him. She had to admit that he had been rather nice lately, first with the gift of books for her library, and now with the generous loan. She sometimes had to remind herself that Sir Wilfred had been a good father when he had enrolled her in a proper school where her talents could be cultivated. If her mother had had her way, she would have been sent away to live with distant relatives, disowned, and disinherited. It was only due to her father's intervention that she had been allowed to remain in the house at all. Her mother had suppressed her personality, ridiculed her dreams, willed her to fail, and kept her in a state of suspended terror.

And yet she loved her mother fiercely. Judith was one of those rare people who was able to see the good in everyone no matter how they treated her, and she was dazzled by her mother's beauty, wit, and sparkle. Her mother was her ideal—the woman she had always longed to be. She had carved out her own path and become successful in a competitive field, despite a husband who had tried to stifle her ambitions, and children who had threatened to suck up all of her time and energy. And Judith admired her witty, wisecracking personality, which reminded her of the fast-talking sassy dames in the classic women's pictures she loved.

Also, there was something indefinable—some quality of inner goodness she saw shining through her mother's sarcastic personality, turned bitter by living in a misogynistic world with a brutal husband. Ava had been a great person, if not a great mother, and she had taught Judith by example all of the things a woman could do and be.

But Judith had paid a steep price for loving a person who had committed on her, in August Strindberg's words, a "soul murder," placing her in lifelong emotional thrall to her tormentor.

Gavin was starting a new business. He had been driving up to London on the weekdays to find investment partners, and also to visit his club, where he worked out on the machines and swam in the Olympic-sized swimming pool — he always kept his body in perfect shape.

Judith missed him terribly when he was away. She had to banish her jealousy at setting her handsome husband loose in a large city without her supervision, but she believed in his ability to make a fortune quickly, and she was glad of his efforts. For now, she had him on a fixed allowance, but he was always asking her for more money as new expenses cropped up. She couldn't very well say no to him; she knew it was humiliating for a man to ask his wife for cash. But she'd had to dip into her savings and retirement accounts and to sell some of her stocks, and she was afraid to let her capital dip any lower.

Sometimes when Gavin was in London or out hunting, she had Tony over for tea. Without the sexual and romantic pressure she was more relaxed around him, and she found that they shared a lot of the same values. It was a deeper friendship than she'd enjoyed with any of her girlfriends at university, who had all abruptly dropped out of her life after she had published her first story in the *New Yorker*. Tony would never cut her off like that, with no explanation; he was a true friend. Unlike her husband, he hid nothing from her, and the process of getting to know another person intimately was deeply pleasurable for her. But after the first visit she omitted mentioning Tony to her husband, whose glowering glances and sulky withdrawals taught her to conceal his visits, however harmless they might have been.

So life at Manderfield continued harmoniously . . . until one fateful morning. The couple always breakfasted in the dining room, with its lofty ceilings, giant crystal chandelier, immense fireplace, and oak-paneled walls, next to a bank of mullioned windows that overlooked the lawn and let in a gray English light. Large silver candelabras decorated the table, and the sideboard featured an impressive display of fine china.

As usual, they were in their dressing gowns and slippers. The table was long, so they sat together at one end of it, with Romeo on a booster seat in the chair next to his mistress. Judith was having poached eggs with crème fraîche and spinach, Gavin was having a gourmet English breakfast with sirloin steak, black pudding, grilled vegetables, fried eggs, and fried bread, and Romeo was having a poached egg yolk. Everything was laid out nicely on the white damask tablecloth. They were eating late, as they had slept in, and then indulged in a particularly wild bout of lovemaking. Sarah had cooked their breakfast and then run to the market for the day's shopping, so Nancy was waiting on them at table.

Gavin leaned over and kissed her. Her senses were still alive from their bedroom antics, and his touch sent a shock of electricity throughout her body. Then he whispered into her ear, "Princess, can I have ten thousand quid?"

"Why?" she murmured. "What do you need it for?"

He pulled away abruptly, his chair screaking on the floor. "Do I have to account for every penny I spend? As if you didn't know, hunting is very expensive. And the horses need re-shoeing. And I need some new clothes. It all adds up. I hate to ask you, but it can't be helped."

Judith sighed. "All right. But I'm not made of money, you know."

Gavin turned away from her, brooding, and they ate in silence for a while. Judith took a sip of her coffee, and found it cold. This typical example of Nancy's slipshod service annoyed her. "Can you warm my coffee please, Nancy?" She pushed her cup to the edge of the table.

Nancy rolled her eyes, heaved a big sigh, and picked up the silver coffee pot. Gavin winked at her. "Nancy, don't let your mistress work you too hard."

Nancy giggled. "I won't, Sir," she said, looking back at him flirtatiously as she disappeared into the kitchen.

Judith was beyond irritated. Why was Gavin telling Nancy not to work too hard? How could she work any *less* hard? And how difficult was it to warm a pot of coffee? She had never known a more listless or sullen child, and yet Gavin doted on her. She tried to think of it as a paternal sort of doting, but deep down she knew it wasn't. Nancy was the type of girl one might describe as a vamp. It wasn't just her looks, it was every-thing about her — her voice, her laugh, her walk, the way she lowered her chin and raised her eyes demurely, or glanced over her shoulder and fluttered her eyelashes — moves Judith thought had been retired with Louise Brooks.

Indeed, she resembled Brooks not a little, with her dark hair, her porcelain skin, her perfectly symmetrical features, her large, heavily fringed eyes, and her lithe, delicate frame. And she was always hiking her skirt up to her crotch and adjusting her stockings and suspenders. All of this was certainly deliberate: a way to fascinate Gavin, and possibly to depose Judith as Lady of the Manor. But Judith had firmly decided not to be jealous of her husband unless she had something to be jealous about, and it seemed clear that he saw Nancy as nothing more than a pretty doll to look at.

Still, his indulgence towards the girl was directly responsible for her lazy, spoiled attitude. Sometimes she found Nancy sprawled on the drawing room sofa, taking a nap during working hours. And when Judith would shake her and order her to get up, she would rise very slowly, staring at her mistress with a look of sullen hatred. This morning, the situation was rankling her more than usual, so she decided to say something.

"The way you speak to Nancy . . . it's as if you're *asking* her to disrespect me. And now she despises me."

"Despises you?" Gavin wiped his mouth with his napkin. "That's a bit far-fetched, don't you think?"

"No. I've seen the way she looks at me. I don't think you should get so familiar with the staff."

"Not get familiar with the staff?" He roared with laughter. "I never knew you were such a snob!"

Judith was shocked by his cruelty; his laughter was like a knife stabbing her heart.

"I'm not a snob. I didn't mean that we're superior to her, it's just . . . she has no respect. And it's because you spoil her."

"Why shouldn't I spoil her? She's had a hard life. She deserves some kindness."

"Yes, but she's here to work. Do you really want me to do the housework myself, just so Nancy can lie around and paint her nails?"

"Of course not. You're overreacting."

Nancy returned from the kitchen with the silver pot and poured Judith's coffee. Judith took a sip and involuntarily made a face.

"This coffee is stale. Can you please make a fresh pot?"

"Make it yourself."

Gavin chuckled, amused at Nancy's snark, and then the two of them started laughing uproariously together. Judith couldn't believe what she was hearing, and neither could Romeo, who jumped off the chair and fled the room. The sound of their cackling was grotesque, obscene. Her own husband was laughing at her — with *that little tramp*.

Judith stood up, flushed with anger. "Whose side are you on, anyway?"

"Yours. I'm on your side." But he still had that awful grin on his face.

"No. You're *not* on my side. You're laughing at me . . . with *her*. I don't know what I've done to deserve this treatment." Then she did the worst thing she could have done. She sat down and cried . . . in front of *that girl*.

There was a silence as Gavin took in the situation, and then he sighed heavily. "I'm sorry. I didn't mean to hurt you, Princess. I was just having a bit of fun." He turned to Nancy. "Nancy, you're a good girl. But it's not working out."

"Sir?"

"I'm giving you your notice, Nancy."

"But Sir, I was only — "

"It can't be helped, Nancy. You'll get two weeks advance pay. Now, go and pack your things."

"As you wish, Sir."

Judith felt a surge of relief. This girl had been a thorn in her side ever since they had arrived at Manderfield. Now Gavin had sacked her, and she would go. He had been a lout, but he had supported her in the end, as he always did; and now everything would go back to normal.

But Nancy wasn't leaving the room. She was staring at Gavin with a kind of dark fury in her eyes. She really is an entitled brat, thought Judith. She has no ability to reflect on her bad attitude or learn from her mistakes.

But it was more than that. She was accusing Gavin of something with her eyes, and Gavin was studiously avoiding looking at her. Judith watched as he innocently cut into a piece of black pudding, and she thought, *What is going on between Gavin and Nancy?*

12

Bluebeard's Study

Nancy left Manderfield the next day, and Judith started interviewing housekeepers. None of them were to her liking, so she found herself in the position of making beds, hoovering, dusting, and keeping ahead of clutter. She didn't mind the work, now that it was no longer a question of picking up Nancy's slack. In fact, she found it quite relaxing, and she especially enjoyed dusting and polishing objects and making them shine.

One day, she received a call from *Vanity Fair* requesting an interview. She had been bombarded with requests ever since Anne had leaked on her Instagram that her sister was a famous author living in a Gothic castle, a fact that had greatly captured the imagination of the press.

A fortnight later, three stylish young women from the magazine visited the castle: a journalist, a makeup artist, and a photographer. The former asked Judith why she wrote Gothic romances, and she answered, "Romance is written by women, *for* women. My books pose the questions: Is it a crime to be a woman — to be feminine? Is it a crime to desire the wrong man — or to desire sex *at all?*" The photographer snapped pictures of Judith in the castle and on the grounds, including several of her fleeing the castle in a frock provided by the magazine, her hair styled long and glamorous. But they especially wanted a portrait of her with her new husband. Everyone had heard how devilishly handsome he was, and the editor had specifically requested a photo of the two of them for the cover.

Gavin had been out hunting all morning. When the ladies told Judith they wanted to take his picture, she said she was sure he'd be happy to comply. So they all sat down for tea in the little walled garden and awaited his return. When Judith heard him charging in the back door with his dogs, she ran to greet him in her diaphanous Oscar de la Renta gown. "Darling, the *Vanity Fair* people are here. I'd like you to meet them!"

She dragged him by the sleeve through the kitchen and out to the tea table. "This is Julia who's writing the piece, and this is Louise the photographer, and this is the makeup artist, Emma. Don't you *love* what she did with my hair? I must wear hairpieces more often! Anyway, they want to take a photo of us together for the cover. Ladies, this is my husband Gavin."

The women brightened when they saw Gavin, who was looking virile and handsome after the hunt, but his face darkened into a scowl. "No one told me about this," he growled.

"Oh! We thought your wife told you," said Louise.

"She didn't tell me you wanted to take my picture."

"That's probably my fault," said Julia apologetically. "But would you mind terribly posing for just one photo?"

"Yes, I would mind," he fumed, and he stormed away.

Judith knew it was no good speaking to him when he was in this mood. "I'm so sorry. He gets a bit irritable when he's been out all morning . . . blood sugar problems, you know. He'll feel better after he's had a bite to eat."

"Do you think we should get the photo after he's had his lunch?" asked Louise hopefully.

"No. I'm afraid he'll be no good for the rest of the day. Do you have enough photos otherwise?"

"Yes, we do. I'm very pleased with the way they turned out. You're positively glowing in them."

"Because she's in love," teased Emma, and everyone laughed.

"You know what," suggested Julia, "Maybe we can make something of your husband's attitude in the article. We can say you have a brooding, dangerous husband, like the ones in your novels. Do you think he would mind?"

"I don't know, and I don't care. It serves him right for being such a pill!" And they all laughed again.

The day after the *Vanity Fair* interview Judith went on a cleaning spree, and she set aside some clothing to donate to the Halloween bazaar. But just before the ladies from St. Andrew's Church arrived to collect it she removed Gavin's clothes from the bag, fearing his wrath lest he should miss them, although they were old and shabby and he never wore them. She couldn't bear to return them to the closet in the condition they were in, so she decided to store them in the tower until she could get him to go through them.

She had been up and down the spiral stairs of the medieval tower numerous times, but she had never visited the room at the top; she had always intended to poke around in there, and she felt now was as good a time as any.

She climbed the stairs to the second floor, and from there she wound her way up the steep flight of worn steps, with Romeo close at her heels. As she reached the top, she came to a heavy oak door.

But just as she was about to turn the knob, she jumped back as she heard noises issuing from within. It sounded like heavy chains were being dragged across the floor, and as if something or someone was insistently pounding on the wall. Romeo arched his back and flattened his ears against his head, his nerves and fur on end, emitting a low growl.

She pressed her ear to the door, and to her amazement, she heard the sound of quiet sobs. She stood listening in rapt concentration, her heart pounding wildly, and Romeo stood at her feet, equally rapt.

She was mystified as to the origin of these noises. Could an animal be making them — a mouse, perhaps? Was what sounded like sobbing only the wind in the trees? But then she thought, what if there's a *person* in there, weeping and dragging her chains along the floor, and pounding on the wall as a cry for help? What if it's *Constance*?

She knew such an idea was absurd. And yet she wasn't surprised that her mind had gone to Constance, because she had thought about Constance nearly every day since the cocktail party. This was because, in retrospect, Gavin's story about Constance hadn't sounded quite right. Perhaps his ridiculous story was an elaborate construction to conceal the truth. And although he certainly hadn't locked his embarrassing first wife up in a tower like the infamous Rochester, there had to be *something* in there, and Judith didn't want to go away without seeing what it was. So she braced herself and opened the door, which creaked uneasily on its hinges.

The room was cold and black as pitch. Her fingers scrabbled for a light switch, but when she flipped it, nothing happened. Then she heard a screeching sound, and something came flying straight at her head. She screamed and ducked, and a horrid furry bat, its fangs dripping, went flapping past her and down the spiral staircase. Romeo chased after it, nearly knocking her down.

It took her a good ten minutes to calm down and catch her breath. No sounds now came from the chamber — all was still. But she had a sick and sad feeling that she couldn't describe. She felt like someone was shaking her or choking her, and it was so awful that she burst into tears. After a few moments, it passed.

Recovering herself and drying her tears, she lit a silver candelabra on the hall table and carried it into the little room. Cobwebs accosted her from every direction, draping themselves over heaps of furniture, bric-a-brac, tools, Victorian steamer trunks, and other miscellaneous objects. Stacks of ancient books were rotting away and covered with droppings, and the foul stench of urine permeated the room. She let out a stifled scream as she perceived the beady eyes of a large black rat staring at her from atop a pile of books.

Her scream sent it scuttling into a corner, where it dived into a small hole in the floorboards.

Uttering a sigh of relief, she set down her candle and opened one of the trunks. Inside, she found a number of splendid antique theatrical costumes in silks and velvets with the most exquisite trims, some of them studded with costume jewelry.

She held up a gold Renaissance-style dress, and her eyes sparkled with pleasure as she admired it. And she discovered other old-fashioned garments and accessories: gowns, shoes, gloves, hats. But everything reeked of mothballs, and the dust was making her sneeze. So she shoved Gavin's clothes into the trunk, tucked a few of the costumes under her arm, and moved towards the door. Then the light from her candles spilled onto a painting leaning against the wall.

It was an oil portrait of a woman in a heavy frame, but it was so filthy that she couldn't make out the sitter's face or costume. Intrigued, she picked it up and carried it downstairs with the other items, planning to have everything professionally cleaned the next time she was in town.

She entered the kitchen, where she shuddered to see the ghastly bat wheeling around overhead squeaking, and Romeo observing it with fascination, his tail switching. She set down her burden and shooed the screaming thing out of the door with a broom, much to the cat's chagrin.

Heaving a deep sigh, she scrubbed her hands and arms thoroughly, put the copper kettle on to boil, and sat down to have a cup of tea and a jam tart. Romeo spent some time sniffing the old, musty costumes, and then he jumped onto the kitchen table, washed his face and whiskers, and fell asleep.

While she sipped her tea and watched Romeo's side rise and fall with each little feline breath, she was amazed to think that she had just characterized her life as a scene from a Gothic novel — specifically *Jane Eyre*, with its horror of the mad wife in the attic. But the forbidding castle, and Gavin's mysterious and brooding air, made such comparisons inevitable. Indeed, her husband was the perfect amalgamation of the secretive Rochester, the passionate Heathcliff, and the intimidating Max de Winter.

Comparing him to these characters comforted her. For if she were to believe the novels they inhabit, these brooding men who seem to be hiding terrible secrets are actually madly in love with you, and all they need is your kindness and support to reward you with their undying love.

She rose from the table. Feeling better after her spot of tea, she was seized with a renewed zeal to clean and declutter the castle, and she set her sights on Gavin's study. He had never allowed anyone in there, and she was sure it was filthy. He might be angry at first that I went in without his permission, she reasoned, but when he sees it all tidied up, he's bound to be pleased. So she traversed the dark, narrow gallery that separated the central area of the castle from the east wing.

After stealing down the lurid green hall carpet and passing a number of unfurnished rooms, some of them littered with broken furniture and assorted rubbish, she found it. She inserted each key on her massive ring into the lock until one of them turned with ease, and the door swung back with a groan.

She strode into the room and pulled open the green velvet curtains, releasing a cloud of dust. The afternoon light flooded through the long windows, revealing a once charming room in great disarray. The chairs and sofa were upholstered in bottle-green leather, the tables were of polished mahogany, and stag and boar heads—gruesome trophies from Gavin's hunting forays—were mounted on the wall. The bookcases were stuffed with books and crammed with various outré objects and tasteless ornaments. A display case featured an assortment of antique guns and knives, and the coffee table was littered with weapons, dirty rags, and gun oil, along with piles of books, newspapers, and magazines, half-eaten scones, empty water bottles, and rancid cups of tea, one of which hosted a large eye of mold.

Overall the room was cluttered and filthy, with dirty socks lying everywhere, along with crumpled dressing gowns, empty tubes of personal lubricant, tennis shoes, gym clothes, and dumbbells. Books, magazines, and DVDs were stacked on tables and strewn all over the floor. The books were mostly horror novels and esoteric and erotic literature, and the DVDs and magazines were all fetish porn, along with a few scattered issues of bodybuilding magazines. She wondered why he hid his porn collection from her; she wouldn't have minded him sharing it with her.

She gingerly picked up the items, placing them neatly in piles or back on the shelves, or tossing them into the rubbish bin. After she had tackled the worst part of the clutter, she strode over to Gavin's desk and ran her finger along the thick dust coating it, clucking her tongue at the filth. Then, as she swept her feather duster energetically across the surface, lifting objects to get them out of the way, her arm jostled a small wooden jewelry box. On impulse, she opened it. Among the cufflinks, rings, lapel pins, and shirt studs, she found a little golden key.

She held it up to the light, and the sun created blinding glints as it glanced off it. She didn't know why—perhaps it was its bright gold color, or its dainty size—but the key seemed magical to her. She inserted it into the lock of his desk, and to her delight, it turned with a click. She rifled through the drawer, disappointed to find only the usual clutter: pens and refill cartridges, stationery, business cards, rubber bands, paper clips, receipts, cologne samples, nude playing cards, plastic monster toys, takeaway menus. Then she noticed a little leatherbound volume peeping out from under a pile of papers. Pulling it out, she observed that it was a photo book. She opened it eagerly and proceeded to examine it.

The first photo was of Gavin several years younger, standing with a group of actors in a dressing room. They wore satin period outfits trimmed with lace, and long curly wigs. It looked like a French play—perhaps a farce by Molière. Gavin was the only one not in costume. He looked very handsome, with that devilish grin of his.

The subsequent pages revealed a number of selfies, mostly of him posing before National Trust castles. There were no pictures of his parents or his castle; she had often asked to see such mementos, and he had told her they were all in storage.

But then she saw something that made her frown. It was a faded photo of Gavin with a woman on a boat. She was stunning, with long blonde hair, wide blue eyes, and high cheekbones, and he had his arms around her. Flipping through the pages, she discovered several more photos of this woman.

In some, she and Gavin were hugging or kissing. In one, she was laughing and touching her collarbone, and her hand sported a large garnet ring.

Judith picked up an antique magnifying glass and held it over the photo. The emerald-cut stone was the same as on her own ring, as was the gold setting, and the number and size of the accent diamonds. And then she noticed a slight flaw in the stone. She held up her hand and compared her own ring with the one in the photo, and she cried out as she realized that the inclusions on the two rings were identical. Her engagement ring had been his mother's, intended for his future bride. But this woman had worn it before her!

She flipped over the photo. On the back were the words, "Constance, my queen."

Trembling with shock, she slipped the photo into her pocket, locked the book in the drawer, and fled the chamber. Then she staggered back through the long gallery and dragged herself up the stairs to her room.

She collapsed onto her bed, feeling sick and feverish, and trying to remember everything she knew about Gavin. When she had searched his name on her phone in Paris, she had discovered a few photos and mentions of Peter Longueville, Baron Hastings, but none of his son. And when she had asked him why he had no internet presence he had only laughed and said that any peer worth his salt wasn't about to have his information blasted all over the internet. She had written to Baron Hastings about his son and received no answer, and then she remembered that he and his father were not on speaking terms, and she felt guilty for prying.

She knew she could have conducted a deeper search into

his past, but the thought of doing so chilled her; after all, marriages were built on trust. But now that trust had been severed, for he had lied to her about Constance. Judith was only his princess . . . but Constance was his queen!

As she languished in the deepening shadows, she thought, Selene is right—she's gorgeous. She's classically beautiful, with a perfect figure and bewitching eyes; just the type to create a lifelong obsession in a man. How could I hope to compete with a woman like that? Is he still in love with her? Am I living in her shadow?

She wished she could speak to Constance and find out the truth about her relationship with Gavin. For a moment, she had the crazy idea to drive over to Selene's house; perhaps she would know Constance's last name. But if Selene knew she was inquiring into Gavin's past, it was sure to get back to him. And she couldn't bear the thought of Gavin knowing she had spied on him; a thing like that could ruin a perfectly good marriage.

She felt dizzy and weak. She wanted to get up and drink some water, but she didn't have the strength. And as she lay there feeling sick and sorry for herself, she realized she knew very little about navigating a marriage. When did you confront your spouse, and when did you keep silent? How many crises would disappear on their own if you *did* keep silent? Her only model for a marriage had been her parents, and neither of *them* had kept silent. Their lives together had been nothing but mistrust, suspicions, rage, and violence. When her drunken father had insulted her mother, it had been an enormous welling up of hate, as if she was responsible for all of the wrongs every woman had inflicted on every man from the beginning of time. It had been biblical, medieval, grotesque. And her mother had been no shrinking violet: she had retaliated in kind, turning the knife and stabbing him with her cruel words and glances. Sometimes, when she triumphed over him in an argument, or mocked and ridiculed him, or threatened to leave him, he hit her — although no one in the family ever acknowledged it. But the children knew. They heard her screams and cries. Then, late at night, she would wander up and down the halls in a cloud of white nylon chiffon, and they would hear her quiet sobbing; and the next day she wore heavy pancake makeup to cover the bruises.

Judith wondered whether her parents could have been happy if either of them had ever apologized or backed down. They both wanted the same thing — to be loved by the other — but neither of them would say, "I'm sorry, darling, I didn't mean it. I love you." And while she sided with her mother over her father, feeling there was never any excuse for physical violence, she wished her mother had used more strategic compliance, rather than continually fanning the flames of his rage.

The last thing Judith wanted was to duplicate the loveless marriage of her parents, so she determined to solve the problem of Constance in the least confrontational way possible. There would be no digging into Gavin's past, no accusations, no cross-examinations. She would simply show him the photo, and ask him to explain it to her.

13.

Who the Fuck Are You?

That night, Gavin returned later than usual after spending the day in London. She had never seen him in a blacker mood, but each attempt to find out what was wrong was met with merely a grunt or a glare. She knew better than to vex him when he was in such a foul temper, so she decided to wait until the next day before broaching the subject of Constance. Instead they sat at either end of the long dining table before the fire and consumed a light supper of carrot soup, roasted wild rabbit, asparagus hollandaise, baby lettuces from the garden, and Châteauneuf-du-Pape, and afterwards she went upstairs and drew him a bath. He said not a word to her throughout supper, and the steaming tub, filled with mood-enhancing juniper oil, left him as bad-tempered as before. In fact, he was so agitated that he paced for hours up and down the hall before finally retiring to sleep in his dressing room.

The next day, Gavin remained at the castle instead of going up to London. They had been invited to a Halloween party at Selene's house, but neither of them had put together a costume, nor were they in the mood to socialize; so they decided to stay in and watch horror movies instead. Judith picked *Peeping Tom* and *City of the Dead*, both of which had scared the living daylights out of her as child.

They breakfasted as usual. Gavin hunted all day, and Judith read, took some notes, and carved a jack-o'-lantern, which she stuck on the terrace. Then she put on a brown houndstooth skirt suit and a stylish black cape, and she went down to tea while Gavin showered and changed.

He met her in the garden and took her arm, and they strolled over the dewy grass, past the boxwood hedges, and into the woods, where they wandered through ancient oaks with intensely orange autumn leaves, and fairylike silver birches with mottled trunks and witchy branches. It was the time of day that photographers call the magic hour, and the light was preternaturally beautiful. The birds had gone to sleep, save for a lone raven cawing on a bough, and the only other sounds they heard were the chapel bell ringing four o'clock, and their feet crunching on desiccated leaves. They walked in this way for a time, their arms sweetly linked, each enjoying the other's wordless presence.

Although she was loath to spoil the tranquility, she was dying to ask him about Constance. Planning to insinuate it casually into the conversation as soon as the moment was right, she asked, "How's business? Have you found any investors?"

"Things are going quite well. It helps to have connections, let me tell you. My family name goes a long way in getting these meetings."

"I'm so glad. I miss you when you're in London. I'm absolutely chuffed about your business, but I had got rather used to having you around. Now I hardly ever see you."

He sighed wistfully. "Like normal couples, who have day jobs. Not like the glamorous baron and baroness that we are. But we're happier than normal couples."

"We're disgustingly happy. But you're still so mysterious to me — I know hardly anything about you. What were you like as a child?"

He fell silent. Then, after a pause, "I was very lonely as a child. I never had any friends."

"Neither did I. I was tutored at home, so I never got the chance. But then I made some friends at school. Did you go to boarding school?"

"Yes, I told you, at Eton," he said, a hint of annoyance creeping into his voice.

"Did you make any friends there?"

"Why are you so obsessed with whether I had friends or not?" he snapped. "What are you driving at?"

She flinched from his tone. "Nothing. It doesn't matter."

"Well, it seems to matter to *you*. So I'll tell you: I *tried* to have friends. I tried very hard. But it never worked out. I just couldn't get along with people."

"Why not?"

He stopped and turned towards her with a furious scowl. "Because people are bloody miserable. Have you ever had a look around you? Most people are so rotten, I wouldn't spit on them if they were on fire!"

He had never spoken to her like this before, and it shook

her. He had a bitter, angry look on his face, as if remembering unspeakable things. She scrutinized him, wondering where all of this fury was coming from.

He noticed her staring, and suddenly his expression became light and charming again; the drawbridge had closed, and the darkness was once again hidden away within the depths of the castle walls.

"But you're different," he said. "I always dreamed of having a playmate. And now I do."

"You mean I'm your first playmate?" she said teasingly. "Surely you must have had girlfriends before me, a man with your looks and charm?"

"Well, yes, I've dated a bit. But you're the first girl who's really meant anything to me."

"Really? What about *her*?"

Judith whipped the photo of Constance from her pocket and handed it to him. "Who is Constance to you, Gav? And why is she wearing my ring?"

Gavin snatched the photo away. His face darkened with rage, the veins on his neck stood out like those of a restive horse, and his eyes glowed red like the eyes of a demon.

"Where did you get this?" he snarled.

She shrank back in fear. "It . . . it was in your study."

"What were you doing in my study?"

"I was cleaning. And I . . . I happened to come across your photo book."

"*Happened* to come across? How did you *happen* to come across it?"

She tried to smile to deflect his anger, but all she could manage was a grimace. "It was in your desk drawer."

"Was the drawer lying open?"

"No. It was locked."

"So you didn't just *happen* to come across it, did you?"

"No. I went into the drawer."

"How did you do *that?*" he cried, his eyes glowering under his brows.

"I . . . unlocked it with the key."

"And why was it locked in a drawer with a key?"

Her face sagged into a sad theater mask. "Because . . . it was private?"

"Yes, Judith. Because it was *private*," he said, with a fearful frown. "Privacy is a basic human right. Don't you agree?"

"Yes."

"Do you also agree that people can't live decently together when they don't respect each other's privacy?"

"Yes."

"So! You expect to continue living as my *wife*, when you have no respect for my basic rights as a human being?"

"No," she whimpered. "I don't expect that."

"Then, what *do* you expect?"

Judith was so frightened that she could barely speak. "I don't know," she pleaded, beginning to cry. "Nothing. Please forgive me."

"Forgive you?" he roared. "You have violated a basic law of human decency, and you dare ask for forgiveness! Why can't I have just one tiny corner in the world where you're not spying on me, trying to look inside of my soul? Who the fuck are you to judge me? *Who the fuck are you?*"

Gavin's voice had risen to a shriek. His wrath was so great that words could no longer express it, so he raised his hand to strike. Then, hovering it there for a terrifying instant, he changed his mind and enclosed both of his hands around her neck, shaking her like a doll. She tried to pry his fingers off, but he was so strong that she couldn't budge them a single inch. She tried to scream, but it was no use; she couldn't scream, much less breathe. And yet she felt no pain. She had no physical sensations at all, other than the feeling of being shaken. If anyone had seen them, they would have been certain they were witnessing an attempted murder, and yet she didn't feel that he was actually strangling her; it was as if they were performing a scene in a grotesque play.

His rageful face hovered over her, and his eyes were blank and rolled up into his head, as if no human inhabited the brain behind them. She was chilled and numb, and beads of sweat stood out on her brow. She became more and more terrified, and then her body went limp, and she sagged unconscious onto the hedge.

When she came to, he was cradling her in his arms and gazing at her sadly, and her terror knew no bounds. "No!" she moaned, her pupils dilated with fright. "No!" She struggled to free herself from his grasp, holding her arms out stiffly and pushing him away from her. "Let me go! Please, let me go!"

"Judith!" he cried. "My poor Judith! What have I done to you?" And then he saw her loathing of him, and her fright, and her heart that was broken and would never be whole again. "Judith!" he cried again, sobbing like a child.

The light began to fail, and the rays of the setting sun threw a golden gleam on the vermillion-leaved oaks. As they sat there in the gathering darkness, like two lost and frightened children, the progress of twilight spread its tints over the landscape, and obscurity began to overtake the dying glimmer. The sun sank lower in the sky, until finally it expired in a bloody collapse behind the hills. He had released her from his grasp, but she hadn't moved. She was frozen in shock, and he was frozen in grief, and they sat there in silence as dusk turned into night.

The pale moon rose, and the nightingales began to sing. Judith slowly came out of her severest shock, but she knew she would never fully recover — that this terror would forever be part of her nervous system. Where was the Judith of half an hour ago? She no longer existed. She would have done anything to bring that Judith back. Nothing in her life had prepared her for this moment, when the man she had loved and trusted more than anyone in the world had put his hands on her neck and tried to . . .

But what *had* he tried to do? She was breathing freely, and her throat wasn't sore, and there was no pain where his hands had been. Had her husband tried to kill her, or only to scare her? Did shaking someone by the neck count as domestic abuse? And even if it *wasn't* domestic abuse, surely it was *emotional* abuse? It was also possible that he *had* tried to kill her; she knew that adrenaline can delay pain for hours after a shock. But surely, she would *know* if she had been strangled?

Now he was talking. He was still crying, but she no longer cared. Crocodile tears, she thought. He spoke slowly, and his handsome, chiseled face was streaked with tears. "My father used to beat me unconscious," he said. "He would hit me with anything at hand — a frying pan, a belt — he was a brute. The other children laughed at me because I stuttered. Do

131

you know why I stuttered? Because if I said the wrong thing, my head would get smashed in."

Judith listened to his words with a troubled heart. So that was it—he was a battered child. She finally understood his moodiness, his rages, his reluctance to speak about himself. She knew what it was like to be abused and neglected and to want to lash out at the world. This is the real Gavin, she thought, the Gavin who has been hiding all this time—and it's taken a crisis of this magnitude to bring him out.

He resumed, "My mum was no better than my dad. She would be right there in the room when he hit me, and she never lifted a finger to help me. Later, she would deny it had happened, or she would say she didn't remember. It wasn't her fault—she was scared to death of him. She knew if she stood up to him, he would kill her. I asked her why she didn't leave him, and do you know what she said? She said she loved him." His mouth hardened into a thin line. "Sometimes when my father was beating me, I would hold on to something—the leg of a chair, a stuffed animal—and I'd pretend I was choking him. I'd squeeze and squeeze until I blacked out.

"Just now I felt that same type of rage . . . like there was a beast inside me. It was when you showed me that photo. I'm sorry I lied to you about Constance. We *did* date for a few months, but I hated her. I was obsessed with her body—it was a sickness—but she was cruel and evil. I keep her photos in my desk to remind me of what I once was: a slave to an insane woman. She used to steal my mother's ring and show it to people, telling them she was my wife. She would taunt me, belittle me, threaten me. She said she would go to the police and press domestic abuse charges if I didn't marry

132

her. I knew she was capable of harming herself and blaming it on me. And I knew they'd believe her. Finally she found her next victim, another poor idiot who was smitten by her beauty, and I got away. I thought I'd got over her, but when I saw her picture . . . something in me snapped. Hate can do terrible things to a person, but that's no excuse for what I did to you."

He turned and fixed his eyes on her, and they were full of the sweetness and love she had seen in them that first day. And he vowed, "But I promise by everything that's holy that I'll never hurt you again. You are more precious to me than myself, and I'd rather die than harm a hair of your head. I know it's probably too late — the damage has been done. But if you could find it in your heart to forgive me . . ."

And just like that, she loved him again. He was finally giving her the gift of opening up to her, and it was ugly, but it was honest. He had never loved Constance . . . he had hated her! She, Judith, was his one true love, and always would be!

She looked into his eyes, and she saw no raised drawbridge, no heavy stone walls to protect him from her prying stare. Maybe now they could speak openly, and their love would grow day by day. It wouldn't be the same love as before — that fresh, new love of youth, full of endless possibilities; it would be a mature love, a love that becomes stronger the more adversity it faces, a love where dark secrets are destroyed by exposure to the sunlight.

"I forgive you," she breathed, and he sighed with gratitude. He held her in his strong arms and he wept, and she wept too. The incident had brought them closer together, creating a bond of shared trauma. But all she wanted was to reverse the clock, to go back to a reality in which her husband had never put his hands on her neck. Maybe she *could* go back. Maybe she could remain innocent, untouched by the cruel fingers of shock and trauma. Maybe she could sleep, and her dreams would be black and still.

"Shhh," he said, trying to take away her pain, to banish the nightmares to the shadows. "Let's forget it ever happened."

Forget, she thought. I must forget. *If I could only forget.*

14.

Why Can't a Man Be More like a Cat?

For the next fortnight, Judith devoted herself to finding a new housekeeper. She finally hired Jane, a sensible and solid woman in her forties who managed the household with a clockwork efficiency. With Nancy gone there was no longer any drama in the house, and Gavin was on his best behavior; but something had changed between them.

She had hoped that they might kiss and make up after the unspeakable incident in the woods, but instead they had walked back to the castle in rueful silence and stiffly said goodnight, and he had slept in his dressing room. She had tossed and turned until dawn, crying and feeling her neck with her fingertips and staring terrorized into the night.

The following day he went up to London, and she didn't see him until supper. They ate in silence in the cavernous dining room, for neither of them was in the mood to talk. She wished she might have lifted the lugubrious atmosphere with light banter, but she couldn't think of anything to say.

After dinner she retired to her bedroom and put on a pretty nightgown, waiting for him to come to bed. He did come in, but only to get into his pajamas, brush his teeth, and say goodnight, bending down to give her a tepid peck on the cheek before he left.

She was disappointed, for she had hoped that they might lie together side by side and heal the pain between them, but she understood why he didn't want to sleep in the bed. She trembled when he came near, and her heart rate increased, and she alternated between chills and sweating, butterflies and nausea. Her body remembered his violence, although her mind had tried to forget it. Whenever he bent down to kiss her, or took her hand, or reached across her at table, she froze in terror. And then she saw the sadness creep over his face and the feelings of loss overtake him. The more she tried to relax, the stiffer she became, and the smile she performed to convince him she was happy was a tight, puppet-like grimace.

The weeks went by, and he settled into a routine of sleeping in his dressing room. Eventually she relaxed as the terror of that night grew more and more distant, and she began to crave his touch. But he was no longer interested in intimacy. For he had withdrawn into himself, much farther than before, and she couldn't reach him. Her only consolations were Valancourt and Romeo. She poured out her troubles to the horse daily while brushing its mane, and she bonded with the cat as if they shared one spirit. The expression on Romeo's sweet face, and the touch of his velvet paw on her hand, told her that he understood her, and that he would always be there for her. Why can't a man be more like a cat?

she thought. Cats are so loyal and uncomplicated. If you're nice to them, they reward you with headbutts and purrs. And if you're still, they eventually come to you.

Judith had spent weeks being still, and she had waited and waited for her husband to come to her, but he never had. He thinks I hate him, she thought, and it's traumatized him. He will see that I love him, and he will come back to me. She tried to be as sweet and loving as possible, to take down the barriers he had erected against her. But nothing she did could bring him back. He doesn't love me anymore, she mourned, and she became filled with a gut-wrenching terror. For she had grown to depend on his love, and she was firmly convinced that without it she would vaporize, and nothing would be left of her at all.

Sometimes, in the middle of the night, she would hear him in the hallway, walking up and down, up and down, his feet creaking on the floorboards. And the wind would sigh and moan and rattle the windows, and she would lie awake and listen to all of the unsettling sounds of the night, feeling terribly lonely.

As the weeks went by, she became so estranged from her husband that she started to forget what he was like and to substitute a phantom for him. This phantom was a perfect specimen of manhood: strong, kind, affectionate, funny, warm, gentle, brave, and sexy. But she had to admit that he had always been a phantom — a fake man she had invented in her mind. At first she had created him to fill in missing details, as we all do when we first meet someone, little by little replacing our projections with reality; but he had remained so opaque that his true self had never fully materialized. She was disturbed to think that the man she loved and craved was not Gavin at all, but his fantasy double. He was her Frankenstein monster, her Adonis with the chiseled jawline who never spoke enough to make her grow tired of him, who mirrored all of her tastes and interests, and who seemed to know everything she wanted without being told. But how had he come to exist in the first place? How had he sprung up in his amorphous perfection, as a blank projection screen for her most secret desires?

All she knew was that she preferred the phantom to her real husband — not only because of his shocking violence, but because she didn't want a husband who was too real. Her heart had gone out to him when he had opened up to her about his problems, but his confessions had also made him seem weak and ordinary, like other men. She knew it was selfish, but she didn't *want* a man with problems. She wanted a problem-free man, a fantasy lover from a romance novel.

One night as she lay drifting off to sleep, listening to his footsteps in the hall, she began to fantasize about the day they had first met. She had fallen in love with her phantom, and he had kissed her, and she had collapsed in his arms, and he had carried her to her room, and she had let him take her. She jolted awake at the phrase *she had let him take her*. Surely, *to take* meant *to rape* — in Latin *rapere*, to take, seize, snatch, steal, abduct, obtain by robbery.

She had often used the phrase *he took her* in her books to describe an unequal sexual situation — in other words, a rape. Her readers liked this phrase, because many of them had rape fantasies — or at least, fantasies about being *willingly overpowered*. And now, she was using the phrase *he took me* to describe her own deflowering. Was this because, like many of her readers, she secretly romanticized being over-powered as a way of eschewing responsibility for her sexual desires? Or was it because she felt she had *actually been raped*?

This question had thrust itself into her consciousness again and again, because she still wasn't sure if she had lost her virginity to him because she had wanted to, or to make the best of a bad situation. She had been dimly aware that if she tried to leave, he might catch her and overpower her. He was much stronger and faster than she was, and if he had been bent on having her, she knew she couldn't have got away.

Not that she had been totally innocent; she distinctly remembered having wanted him to *take her* as he had carried her across the sand, while people had gaped and stared. She was less clear about what she had wanted once they had entered her room, but by then she had no choice: they were going to have sex whether she liked it or not.

Judith languished in her bed, feeling confused and fever-ish, as the floorboards creaked outside in the hall. Why was it so important for her to know what had happened? Was it some absurd prudery on her part, that she should deny having wanted sex, despite having swooned in his arms to orchestrate it? Yet even before he had stripped off her cloth-ing she remembered thinking, *I made my bed, and now I have to lie in it*. And he must have seen that she was drunk. A decent man would not have had sex with a girl who was too intoxicated to offer consent. Viewed in that light, didn't his conduct imply . . . a lack of *empathy*, at least? She recalled her meeting with Tony earlier that day, when he had asked her to have sex, and she had turned him down. If Tony had ignored her refusals and had gone ahead and *taken* her, *would she be married to Tony now?* The thought made her ill. Was that how she made her decisions—based on which man was willing to transgress her boundaries, and the boundaries of society, and even the boundaries of *the law*?

She couldn't solve it, because the answer lay with him: if he had loved her when he had taken her, it was not rape. If he hadn't loved her, then it *was* rape, because she wouldn't have surrendered to him unless he had loved her. But of course he had loved her—he had put a ring on her finger and entwined her life forever with his. And although it had been a quick, brutal consummation, she had felt an almost religious rapture afterwards, and she had retained that feeling all these months. It had been like living in a fever dream, and she hadn't wanted to come out of it. For the first time, she'd had the feeling of being a whole self, merged with another who could fulfill all of her deepest needs.

But now she was in danger of being rudely awakened from that dream, so she clung to her phantom lover and discarded anything that was inconvenient about him. The less she saw him the more unreal he became, and the stronger his phantom grew. They still chatted at breakfast and at dinner, and their interactions were pleasant enough; but the wall between them was growing deeper and wider by the day. And as the man himself grew more distant, her sexual fantasies about him became wilder and more intense, taking forms that were almost Sadean in their voluptuousness. Sometimes late at night she would imagine that he was there in her bed, making love to her as he used to. And when she came back to herself and realized she was alone, she would sob herself to sleep.

She remained in this state of suspended reality for several months, and she scarcely noticed anything around her. Christmas and the New Year came and went, and she performed her social duties like a sleepwalker. She maintained a pleasant exterior, so that no one knew there was anything wrong — but Tony knew. He came over once for tea and asked if she was happy, and she became angry and defensive at his questions. After that, afraid that her fragile existence might crumble under the scrutiny of a concerned friend, she stopped inviting him to the house.

During this period, she had frequent nightmares. Initially, they were just fragments — half-remembered images from Paris, past conversations that were now thrown into a sinister light, scenes of him at his parents' castle, cracking a whip and laughing maniacally. She largely saw these nightmares as non sequiturs, with no connection to her life. But deep down she knew they were working to dismantle her carefully crafted denial, which she'd cast over herself like a magical mist to protect herself from truths that were too painful to bear.

15.

Living in a Gothic Novel

One stormy night, thunder rumbled, lightning flashed, wind howled, and torrents of icy rain beat against the windows. As Judith twisted and turned in her sleep, wearing a romantic white ruffled nightgown with long sleeves gathered at the wrists, she dreamed she was walking with Gavin along the drawbridge of a medieval castle.

He looked handsome and sinister in lordly attire, and when he fixed his gaze upon her, his smile was chilling. She tried to turn back, but he seized her wrist and roughly pulled her along. "Where are we going?" she said, shivering with dread.

"To my castle, Judith." And he laughed a deep, frightening laugh.

The moon was shining bright, and the reflections of the torches shimmered yellow on the moat. She gazed up at the forbidding fortress, its black walls frowning down upon her. "No," she cried. "I don't want to go in there!" She tried to release herself from his iron grasp, but he merely laughed and kept dragging her along.

The drawbridge seemed endless, and when she peered at his profile she was terrified at the sight of his evil and commanding expression, and at his hair blowing wildly in the wind.

Finally they reached the great castle doors. He slung her over his shoulder and carried her across the threshold, and the doors clanged shut behind them. Then he set her on her feet and took her hand, and they glided weightlessly down a corridor flanked with flaming torches.

Soon they stopped before a massive door studded with iron nails, and he flourished a giant ring of keys, dangling them before her with self-satisfied pride. "When I became lord and master of this castle, they gave me the keys," he said. "In the old days they had heavy doors, thick walls. They really knew how to keep people in or out. And they knew how to lock people up till they rotted away. Do you know how many human bones were piled up in those fetid towers? That's what castles and dungeons were all about. Raw power. That's when might was right. Those were the days!"

He laughed awfully and turned the key in the lock, and the door swung open with a sickening groan. Then he shoved Judith into the chamber and followed after her, locking and bolting the door behind him.

Judith stared at the room in terror and amazement. The stone walls, dripping with blood, seemed alive and weeping with pain. A fire blazed in a gigantic stone hearth, large enough to roast a bear. Daggers, rifles, and shotguns were strapped to the walls and piled on tables, and various medieval torture devices were displayed throughout the room: the rack, the iron maiden, the pillory, the chair. A large, rough-hewn table, encrusted with gory remains, dripped with the blood of the animals that had been carelessly tossed there: a deer, a wild boar, piles of rabbits, heaps of pheasants and partridges. A foul smell permeated the chamber.

Judith shuddered as she took in the horrors of the room. "These are my weapons, and those are my instruments of torture," he boasted. "Are you frightened, Judith?" A thunderous laugh followed that shook the walls, and she shrank back in terror.

"Get under the table and fetch my dagger," he commanded. She crawled under the slab of slaughtered animals to retrieve the hunting dagger that had fallen below, narrowly avoiding the blood that was plunking in great drops to the floor. She handed the blade to him gingerly, and he took it and made an incision into a rabbit. Blood spurted out, and he drained it into a chalice and guzzled it down, licking his chops while it dripped down his chin.

When he had surfeited himself with the beverage of his choice, he said, "I love the smell and the taste of blood. But you have to be careful. If you have too much blood all you can think about is getting more blood, and that's not healthy." He smiled vilely at her, his eyes glowing red like a demon.

As she turned away in disgust, she spotted his keys glinting on the table. She snatched them up and ran to the door, sliding the bolt and turning the key with trembling fingers. She ran out with the demon at her heels, turning and pushing him so that he fell to the ground.

He cursed her as she flew down the corridor, into the great hall, out of the enormous doors, over the drawbridge, and onto the grassy moors, where the moon was bright and clear.

She glanced over her shoulder to see if he was coming after her, and then she saw him: a tiny figure at first, then larger and larger, a menacing caped figure from a nightmare . . .

She awoke screaming in her bed. Lightning flashed and thunder rumbled as she sat up gasping, her heart jumping out of her chest. At first she stared wildly around the room, fearing that the monster was coming after her, but gradually she realized it had only been a dream. And then she recollected the events of her nightmare, and she felt sick as she remembered her husband's real-life violence, his dominance, his obsession with weapons and killing, and his fearful rage. She took a few deep breaths, and eventually her heart slowed and regained its natural rhythm.

She turned on the lamp, but the power was out. She sighed and donned her robe and slippers. There was enough moonlight to see her way to the table, where she lit a match and ignited the long white candles of a silver candelabra.

Romeo stared at her from an armchair, his bright blue eyes gleaming in the moonlight. "Oh, Romeo," she cried. "Thank God you're here!" The cat blinked at her, a magical love blink, and then he jumped on the table and pressed himself to her side. The feeling of his warmth against her, and the vibration of his hypnotic purr, sent healing waves throughout her body.

Once the candles were lit, she smiled bemusedly to herself at the picturesque figure she cut: she was a woman alone at night, in a castle, in a long white nightgown, wielding a candelabra, worried and afraid of her mysterious husband — it was a scenario right out of one of her novels.

She glanced up just in time to see lightning flashing on a painting of a woman in a nightgown fleeing from a castle. That's me, she thought. Did I dream myself into this existence, or have the Moirae, those fickle goddesses of fate, already determined my destiny?

But even as she allowed herself to revel in this romantic fantasy, she knew that being a heroine from a Gothic novel wasn't all glamorous nightgowns and moonlit castles — for there was always the element of danger posed by the brooding man of the castle, which her dream had so horrifically illustrated.

She heard the heavy tread of her husband's footsteps creaking up and down the hall, and suddenly she felt foolish for being afraid of him. She saw him every day; they chatted cordially at meals, and nothing seemed to be wrong. It was true that he should be coming in, kissing her goodnight, lying down next to her, and going to sleep. He shouldn't be up all night, walking about like a restless ghost. The pacing indicated a troubled mind — it belied his Stepford husband demeanor.

But it was irrational to be afraid of his footsteps. What was she afraid of? His insomnia? She laughed at herself. Maybe writing crime novels had got to her. She saw murderous motives in everything; her nerves were so jangled that even a frown could indicate a homicidal impulse.

Her laughter dissipated the remaining vestiges of her fear, and suddenly she felt guilty for having demonized him. She saw now that she had been neglecting him, pushing him away, objectifying him both sexually and as a violent male, and she was seized with remorse at how unfair she'd been. It was absurd to think he didn't love her; if she was a nervous wreck, it was her own fault. A drink, she thought, that's what I need. But when she went to the decanter, there were only a few drops left. So she snatched up her candelabra, opened the door, and peered into the darkness.

The corridor was as silent as death.

Girding her loins, she crept into the dim passageway and made her way carefully down the magnificent staircase, her candles casting fantastic shadows on the walls, her white robe sweeping behind her.

She gained the drawing room bar and poured out a generous amount of cognac from a cut crystal decanter. As she drank it down, it calmed her nerves and filled her with a pleasant glow. In the soft moonlight the castle now appeared tranquil and innocent of horrors, and the remaining traces of her nightmare began to float away.

She glided to the mantlepiece and held up her candelabra to the painting she'd found in the tower. It was a portrait of Lady Mordaunt—the very lady who was rumored to haunt the castle. She was a delicate sixteenth-century beauty wearing an exquisite gold dress, with raven-black hair, mysterious dark blue eyes that seemed to follow you around the room, and an enigmatic and bewitching smile. Something about the lady reminded her of her mother. Perhaps it was nothing more than the unusual combination of dark hair and blue eyes, or the imperious gaze shared by all women who know they are unmatched in beauty, or—dare she think it—the tragic aura of women who are fated to die at the hands of jealous lovers. Of course, her father hadn't *actually* killed her mother—Sergio had been driving the car, and the paparazzi had caused him to drive recklessly—but if her father hadn't chased her mother around the house with a knife, she would still be alive today: beautiful, cruel, and alive.

While she was deep in her reverie, a gust of wind forced the window open and blew out her candles. The window clanged open and shut in the wind, and she went to fasten it, shivering as a cold blast of rain struck her face.

Somewhat shaken, she returned to the bar and poured herself another drink. Then, hearing the creak of soft footsteps, she looked up to see something padding towards her in the darkness, its shadow looming gigantic on the wall. She dropped her glass, her eyes dilating in terror as the shadow covered her. She screamed, nearly falling senseless with fright as strong hands seized her by the shoulders, gripping her like the claws of a monster.

But it was only Gavin. His handsome face registered concern, and his dark eyes, bordered by long, beautiful eyelashes, were moist with hurt. "Princess! Don't be afraid—it's only me. I came down to check the fuse box; all the lights are out."

16.

A Terrible Tragedy

Over the next few weeks Judith spent most of her time alone, and her relations with her husband remained polite, but nothing more. Their encounter in the drawing room, during which she had screamed bloody murder at his shadow, had caused him to retreat even further into himself, and she knew it would take some time for him to trust her again. She was willing to wait years if necessary to win back his love, for she refused to let her marriage disintegrate into one of hate, grudging tolerance, or indifference, like that of her parents and so many other married couples. And she would *not* get a divorce. Her passionate love for her husband, and her belief that he was the only man in the world for her, precluded this option.

One thing that had distracted her mind of late had been her pursuit of information about Lady Mordaunt, the painting having aroused in her a burning curiosity about the lady and the circumstances surrounding her death. An exhaustive search through the stacks of the British Library had yielded a paragraph or two about her husband as a baronet in the service of Queen Elizabeth I, but there was nothing about the murder of his wife, and the only mentions she found of the lady herself were blurbs on a number of tourist websites that repeated the legend of her ghost wandering the halls of the castle.

One day she was sitting in the drawing room before a cheerful fire, writing in her notebook while enjoying a pot of tea. Romeo was stretched out beside her on the sofa, looking particularly fetching. She scratched his thickly furred white belly and asked, "So, Fluffy McWetnose, what's it like to be an English country cat?"

"Miaow," replied the cat. Sometimes these days she was so enamored with Romeo that she thought she might just kick her husband out and live an idyllic existence together with her adoring feline.

Just then Jane, the new housekeeper, entered and began to dust the mantlepiece. Judith watched her lazily for a while, avoiding working out a problem in her novel. She was grateful that Jane wore her uniform below the knee, unlike that horrible tart Nancy who was always bending over and flashing her knickers at anyone who would look. Jane was proper and efficient, but she kept her distance like the rest of the staff, and this increased Judith's loneliness; she would have liked to have Jane as a friend. She watched as the housekeeper glanced curiously at the painting of Lady Mordaunt.

"Jane," she said. "Do you know who that lady is?"

"Yes, Ma'am. It's Lady Mordaunt, who used to live in the old castle."

"Do you know how she died?"

"Yes, Ma'am." She crept towards Judith until she was standing quite close, and then she uttered in a low voice, "Her husband gave her poison. He was jealous, and he suspected her of having a love affair. But they say she was faithful to him, and that she never even looked at another man."

Judith shuddered as she imagined Lady Mordaunt living in the same castle and sleeping in the same bedroom as she, and dying violently from a draught of poison administered by the man she loved. "Do you know what her husband was like?"

"Well, Ma'am," returned the housekeeper with relish, "all I know is the rumors I heard in the village. They say he was a knight, and that he was drunk on his power. He was cruel, and he would thrash a man for looking at him the wrong way. Not only that, but some of the village girls that came to work at the castle disappeared, and no one ever saw them again."

Judith felt a pit at the bottom of her stomach. Was there no end to male violence? And why did evidence of it pursue her wherever she went? It was true that she had folders stuffed with newspaper clippings of women killed by men in the UK, but the stories kept coming at her whether she sought them or not: true crime shows about serial killers, notices in local papers about women dismembered in various ways, woods littered with female skeletons, random girls disappearing from castles. "How horrible!" she said. "What do the people in the village think happened to them?"

"He murdered them, as sure as I'm standing here," declared Jane, with an air of satisfaction.

"That stands to reason. Jane . . . have you heard the rumors about Lady Mordaunt wandering the halls of the castle?"

"Yes, Ma'am. Everyone in the village knows the castle is haunted."

"Do you believe the castle is haunted, Jane?"

"No, Ma'am. I don't believe in ghosts. But a few people told me not to work here because of the ghost. Most of the local people believe it, one way or another. And Esther is afraid of the ghost, which is why she won't stay here after dark."

"Has Esther seen the ghost?"

"She says she's heard it crying, and clanking its chains — they say the poor lady's husband used to punish her by locking her in the tower and chaining her to the wall — but I believe it's just her imagination. Likely what she's heard is the wind sighing and moaning, and rattling the iron gates."

Judith shivered, despite the heat from the fire. "Thank you, Jane, you've been very helpful."

After the housekeeper exited, Judith felt an unnatural chill, and she clasped Romeo in her arms for comfort. She had blotted out those awful sounds in the tower completely from her memory, but now they came back to her with a horrible clarity. What had been in that room? The bat may have been knocking against the wall, but what unearthly creature had been dragging its chains — or crying like a woman?

She nearly melted with fear as she recalled that awful presence. Ghost stories were never scary to her, but a real ghost . . . she couldn't describe the feeling. It was like being shaken to death . . . like being in a tomb. Once again, she burst into tears. Something was shaking her violently, trying to hurt her … Romeo was howling, he felt it too … but no—it couldn't be. It was merely that her nerves were on edge, and she was upsetting the cat. There was no such thing as ghosts. The simple explanation was that she had read so many Gothic novels featuring wives locked in towers that she had conjured up the whole thing in her imagination. Still, the image of Lady Mordaunt chained in the tower made her blood run cold. She wasn't superstitious, but the acuteness of her senses caused her to feel the castle's dark history like a crushing weight on her soul.

Judith decided that most of her problems stemmed from being too isolated. So after weeks of not asking anyone to the house, she invited Anne over for tea. Relations between herself and her husband were beginning to thaw—he had even started chastely kissing her goodnight, encouraged by her loving constancy—and she was finally coming out of her gloom. But she craved company outside of her husband's intangible presence.

The day Anne came to tea, Romeo went missing. Judith set the entire household to searching for him, but to no avail. At first she feared he may have got out. But he had never escaped before, and the servants were careful about the doors. He's probably just exploring some new part of the castle, she thought; he'll come back when he's ready. She was certain that wherever he had wandered to, he would soon return, rubbing against her leg as if nothing had happened. And then she would scold him in the gentlest manner, pressing his wet nose against her cheek, listening to his adventures, and giving him treats as punishment for his waywardness.

Anne arrived at about two o'clock. It was the first day of spring; it had been raining, but now the sun burst forth in all its glory, and the earth was freshly scented. As it was too early for tea, the sisters decided to work in the garden. Judith lent Anne some gardening clothes, and they crouched on the ground in their fetching cotton trousers, button shirts, straw hats, and gloves, cutting back roses and hydrangeas, pulling out weeds and dead growth, and snipping begonias, daphnes, and camellias, which they placed in large flat baskets.

After they had been working for a while, Anne said, "How's everything going, Judith?"

"Fine. I've been having trouble sleeping, though. Lots of nightmares."

"Nightmares? What about?"

"Nothing important."

Judith was hesitant to confide in her sister. But she needed to talk to someone, so she decided to take the risk. "Gavin never sleeps in the bed anymore," she ventured. "I wonder if he still loves me."

"Of course he still loves you. Don't be silly."

Judith sighed at this typical dismissal of her concerns. "I'm *not* being silly. Things have changed between us. I don't want to repeat Mum and Dad's marriage, and have everything fall apart because of a lack of communication. I don't mind getting in the trenches — I know marriage isn't a walk in the park — but he has a frightful temper. Or, at least, he lost his temper once, and it scared me. Could it be that I'm afraid of men? No one prepares you for what it's like to live with a man, so how are you supposed to know what's normal? I remember Dad used to get angry like that.

Is that what all husbands are like? Why didn't anyone warn me?"

Anne sniffed a rose. "Don't be so dramatic. Every husband is different, like every wife. And you're never going to find a man who's perfect. I think Gavin is very nice. Honestly, you're lucky to have him."

"I do feel lucky. It's just, I don't know if something is wrong, or if I'm overreacting. I realize that you can't expect people to be on their best behavior all the time, especially when you live with them, but it's hard to know when someone crosses a line. Does John ever lose his temper?"

"Of course. Everyone has their moods."

The women continued pulling weeds. Then Judith continued, "It's not just that. He keeps photos of a woman he used to date locked in his desk. I suppose I can't begrudge him for having a life before he met me, but he's been so strange and secretive — and he lied to me about her."

Anne was admiring the camellias. "That's weird. Why would he lie?"

"I don't know. But he went into a rage when I showed him her photo. And then he . . . he put his hands on my neck."

"He what?" said Anne, gathering camellias into a bouquet.

Judith could no longer hold back, and the words flooded out of her. "I'm not sure if it was domestic abuse, or if I'm just . . . he went into a sort of trance, and he put his hands on my neck. He didn't realize what he was doing, and when he came to, he was sorry and he cried." Her eyes filled with tears. "I've tried to forget it ever happened, but I can't. And now I'm afraid of him. As far as I remember, he wasn't applying any pressure, and I didn't feel any pain. But it scared me so much that I passed out. What I want to know is, could I have actually passed out due to lack of oxygen? His anger was so scary—he was like a demon. He said it was the woman's picture that set him off, but I think it was when he realized I'd gone into his desk. He hates it when I pry."

There was a brief silence as Anne continued her gardening. "Then don't pry!"

Judith looked over at her sister, who was tranquilly absorbed in snipping camellias from a bush, and she felt enormously deflated. Her heart was pounding at having confessed her shameful secret to someone, and her sister hadn't even been listening. "You haven't heard a word I've said!" she cried.

Anne turned to her sister with a bright smile. "Yes, I have. You said that Gavin hates it when you pry." She glanced with pleasure at the pink camellias. "These flowers are so pretty! Your garden is lovely, Judith. I do miss living in the country. Look at that shade of yellow!" And she leaned over to cut the stalk of a tulip-like yellow flower.

Judith shoved her hand away. "Don't touch that! It's aconite. It's highly poisonous. I've repeatedly told the gardener to take it out."

"Yes, you don't want your cat eating it. By the way, where *is* Romeo? Usually he's all over you when you're gardening."

"I haven't seen him all day. I've looked all over for him, but he seems to have disappeared. I've got the whole household looking for him."

"Maybe he got lost chasing a squirrel or something. Your garden *is* rather large. I could get lost in it myself."

"I'll be very cross if he's in the garden—everyone knows not to let him out unsupervised. But it's odd that he didn't come when he heard me calling. He's like a dog that way; he always comes when I call."

"Naughty boy! You'll have to scold him when he returns."

Judith frowned, seized with a new worry. "If he was in the garden, he'd be here with us. Unless he's caught under the house or something." She rose and walked back to the castle, followed by Anne.

"Sometimes the workmen open these little windows," she explained, "and an animal can get in, and get trapped inside." She knelt down and unlatched a small mullioned window at the base of the thick stone wall, leading to the basement. "Romeo! Romeo! Are you in there? Romeo!" Her voice echoed in the cavernous space, and she listened for the sound of a meow.

Anne searched for more openings. "Maybe he's hiding from us."

"He might be sleeping under a bush. Sometimes he does that. But he usually still comes when I call." The two women perambulated the castle, looking under every bush and tree, and opening every little window. "Romeo!" they called out. "Lover! Here, kitty, kitty!"

After they had navigated the perimeter of the castle, Anne moved beyond the holly hedges and started checking under the various shrubs bordering the vegetable garden. Suddenly she stopped short and cried out, "Judith! Oh, Judith!"

Judith walked over. "What is it?"

"Don't look!" implored Anne, trying to shield her sister's eyes.

But it was too late. Judith was standing next to Anne, and she saw what Anne saw.

Romeo was lying under a holly bush, his neck strangled in

a snare. She crouched down and touched him, and his body was stiff and cold.

Judith smothered a cry and sagged to the ground, clutching her face in her hands. Anne put her arms around her and held her as she wept. "Who do you think let him out?" she said. "Why was the snare even there? Who put it there?"

Judith shook her head, too grieved to speak.

And then, in the distance, the clap of gunshots ripped through the air. The women turned their heads in terror at the sound.

17.

Grief

Anne helped Judith into the castle and up to her room, where she collapsed on the bed and began shivering violently. Jane covered her with a blanket and called Doctor Graham, a local physician from the village. He was an older gentleman with white hair, who wore a black wool suit with an argyle tie and carried a little black doctor bag.

When he arrived, Judith was moaning softly, unresponsive to everything around her. The doctor examined her heart, lungs, eyes, and throat, and checked her reflexes and motor responses. Then he smiled soothingly at Anne. "There's nothing to worry about. Your sister is suffering from nervous shock. She needs complete rest and quiet. Give her broth, water, aspirin, and solid food if she asks for it. And apply cold compresses to her head. She'll be all right in a week or two."

Just then, Gavin swept gaily into the room holding a brace of dead rabbits, his shotgun slung over his shoulder. But when he saw Judith lying there catatonically, her lips white with shock, and the drawn, worried faces of the doctor and the two women, his cheerful expression vanished. He flung his kill on the table and rushed over to the sickbed, his hands stained with rabbit blood.

Judith snapped into consciousness. At first he recoiled from her horror-glazed eyes, which fixed themselves upon him with a furious judging stare, but then he regained his composure and turned to the doctor. "What's the matter with her?"

Anne glared at him accusingly. "Her cat was strangled in a snare."

Gavin's face collapsed into an expression of remorse. "I *did* put a few snares in the garden to trap foxes. But I never thought the cat would . . . Oh, darling, please forgive me!" He rushed over to the bed and clasped Judith's hands, weeping.

She pushed him away violently. "No!" she screamed, in such a loud voice that they all drew back. "Go away! Make him go away!"

"Princess! Please forgive me!"

"Go away!" She covered her face with her hands, emitting a deep, anguished moan.

The doctor, Anne, and Jane stood there awkwardly, watching Judith recoiling in horror from her husband, and Gavin crying in the most maudlin and unseemly manner. Finally the doctor pulled him away. "You had better go. Your presence seems to upset her."

Gavin nodded, his face contorted into a mask of grief. "I only want what's best for her." Then he turned mournfully to Judith. "I'm sorry, Princess. I'm a brute. I'll make it up to you somehow." And he left the room.

For a minute or two, no one spoke. Then the doctor turned to Anne. "Can you stay on and take care of her?"

Anne shook her head. "Sorry, I need to get back to London."

"I'll take care of her," volunteered Jane. "I have some experience with nursing."

"And you are . . ."

"Jane, the housekeeper."

"That's good of you, Jane. I'll ring tomorrow and see how she's getting on."

The doctor left, and Anne sat by her sister's bedside. She tried to make conversation, but Judith only stared bleakly off into space. After an hour or two, she also left.

After that Jane cared for her mistress, giving her water, broth, and aspirin, speaking to her soothingly, and applying cold compresses to relieve the heat and pain in her head. Judith drifted in and out of consciousness, seeing only vague shapes and hearing only fragments of sound and speech. The only thing she distinctly remembered was the sight of Gavin crying in such an exaggerated manner that it had shocked her to the core. It had seemed so fake, and she even thought she had seen him gloating; although, in retrospect, she was sure she had imagined it. No one could be that cruel—it wasn't possible.

When she awoke the next day, she was seized with a panic that Romeo's body would not be properly cared for, and she gave Jane detailed instructions as to his burial. After the housekeeper promised to follow her directives to the letter, she sank back into a torpor, exhausted with the effort. But then she rallied again, and she ordered Jane to set up a shrine to Romeo at her bedside with candles burning, and a photo of him in a gilded frame. This was erected, and Judith kept vigil there night and day, praying while clutching some claws and whiskers and pieces of fur she had collected, and wetting the relics with her tears.

A week later, she began responding to Jane's questions: was Madam feeling okay, was she hungry, did she want more wood on the fire, did she need her pillows plumped. No one had ever cared for her the way Jane was doing now. She knew Jane didn't really love her — she was simply performing her duties, and when Judith was well again, she would return to her brusque, impersonal ways — but realizing what she had missed out on by not having a mother's love made her feel sad and broken, and she became murderously jealous of all the loved children in the world.

Gavin had been barred from the room. The doctor had forbidden him to enter unless Judith should request him, and she never had.

She convalesced for a fortnight. She had become ghastly pale in the course of her illness, and she looked like a wraith. She had survived, but to what end? Romeo was dead, and there was nothing to live for. She kept thinking she saw him out of the corner of her eye, or heard his meow, or smelled his fragrant fur. And when she realized he was really gone she felt a stabbing pain in her heart, and no amount of sobbing and wailing could take away the pain. She became obsessed with the little bits of fur she had saved, and she crawled along the floor and searched for more under the bed or stuck in the heating vents. She touched the clumps of fur, whiskers, and claws, and she wished she were a witch who could bring him back to life with just these precious fragments.

Once she felt well enough to think clearly, she turned the tragedy over again and again in her mind. Gavin killed my cat, she thought, and I'll never forgive him. He must have known that if he set snares in the garden, Romeo might fall into one. But why would he do a thing like that? Can he be that evil? No one would deliberately kill a beloved pet. Except that people do. I read a story once about a man who shot his wife's cat while she was away, and then he tried to replace it with a different cat, thinking she wouldn't notice. He thought he could fob off a strange cat on her, because he was a psychopath. But it's ridiculous to compare Gavin to a nutcase like that. Gavin's not a psychopath. It was obviously an accident—a mistake. But if he's innocent, then why am I blaming him?

She had always had a hard time trusting people, and sometimes she thought they were scheming against her in intricate ways. People were savages. How could you know what evil they were plotting? But she had to trust someone. She couldn't just shut herself away forever and never speak to anyone; she should at least be able to trust her husband. But her husband was the person she was most afraid of. Her husband was a killer. He had killed her cat.

She went round and round in this way, exhausting herself. She was sinking into a bottomless abyss, being dragged into the mire. The mire of her own madness, or of being married to a killer? She didn't know. She felt like she was living in a horror film, where the protagonist is being gaslighted and loses her grip on reality.

Gavin wasn't evil. Or was he? She remembered the frisson of evil she'd felt when his shadow had covered her on the beach, and her terror when he had shaken her by the neck. That had nearly scared her to death, and now she was afraid to ask him anything. Because what if she said the wrong thing, and he put his hands on her neck again? And what if next time, *he squeezed harder?*

This thought plunged her into an unspeakable terror. The wind began moaning like a sad ghost, and the windows rattled like lugubrious chains, and the rain pattered down like knives stabbing her heart. She cried herself to sleep, and she slept through the night.

The next evening she felt well enough to rise. She tossed a cloak over her nightgown, grabbed a torch, and descended the stairs.

When she exited the castle, her view was obscured by a thick blanket of fog. But with the aid of her torch, she made her way carefully past the fortress, across the rose garden, and through the iron gates to the churchyard, searching for Romeo's grave. After shining her light on each one, her beam fell on a wooden cross on which was painted the single word *ROMEO*. This was just a placeholder; the headstone would not be ready for some weeks. And then she would have a funeral. But who would come? She flung herself on the grave and wept many tears. Poor, sweet Romeo. Her feline love.

Then she rose and stood looking at the headstones littered eerily throughout the moonlit yard, and at the crosses with their arms outstretched like congregants gathered to hear a sermon. Suddenly she felt she was not alone, but connected to the souls of those who had died here hundreds of years before. And as she felt the energy of the dead surging around her, she became aware of being merely a tiny particle in an endless cycle of life and death, her troubles insignificant in relation to the whole. Her grief somewhat dissipated, she continued through the churchyard and into the chapel.

As she entered, she faded up the sconces and chandeliers, crossed to the sanctuary altar, and lit the tapers. Once the altar was blazing with light, she sang a hymn and read from the Bible. Then she incensed the altar, and she sat at the organ and played the Magnificat and the Gloria. The organ's sepulchral chords filled the church, and to this she added the sound of her clear soprano voice. Finally she said the closing prayer and uttered the last blessing and invocation.

Normally this ritual made her feel centered and serene, but now she felt as troubled as before. She glanced madly around the church, trying to soak up its sacred atmosphere, but her efforts were in vain. And as she turned her eyes to the vaulted ceiling and the awe-inspiring stained-glass windows, she thought, I'm going insane. I want to die.

She knelt before the statue of the Virgin Mary, her tears flowing. "Mother Mary, please help me," she whispered. "Should I flee from the castle, or should I stay and try to make things right?"

As Mary looked down piously at her, Judith remembered that divorce is a mortal sin. She bowed her head before the Holy Virgin, feeling a great weight on top of her heart.

What she couldn't admit to herself was that remaining with her husband had nothing to do with her vows. She was chained to him by invisible bonds of love and desire, and because he had taken her virginity, and because they shared so much in common, and because she was his princess, and because she couldn't bear to give up on him now, when she had been so sure of him. Her instincts told her to flee, and yet she knew she could never leave him.

At this shocking revelation, she cried, "No matter what he does, *I still love him!*" For the second time in several months, she felt her heart break. She sobbed herself blind, and she fell senseless to the cold stone floor.

She awoke just before dawn, frozen to the core. She rubbed her limbs to get the circulation flowing and managed to rise. Then she snuffed out the few candles which were yet burning and made her way back to the castle. The fog had lifted, and dawn was breaking in the pink-streaked sky. She entered the castle, climbed the grand staircase, and taped a note to her door, forbidding anyone except Jane to enter. Then she locked herself in her room and returned to her bed, sinking into a deep depression.

When Jane came in with the breakfast tray, she was alarmed at her lady's state of health. She had formerly been improving, but now her face was tinged with a deathly pallor, except for her eyes, which were red and swollen from crying. Judith told the housekeeper not to worry, but she knew she was sinking fast. She had lost all appetite for food, and she felt she might die of inanition. Indeed, she welcomed death; anything would have been better than the state of suspended terror she'd been plunged into by loving and fearing her demon in equal measure.

Jane continued to wait on her, and she deteriorated a little more each day. Eventually she grew so weak and disoriented that she began to believe she was really dying. I'm a dead maiden, she fantasized deliriously—a necrophile's delight! In her crazed state she became half in love with easeful death, and she secretly hoped she might just dissolve and fade away, like Sylvia Plath when she crawled under her mother's house to die.

On the sixth morning she heard the customary knock on the door, which meant that Jane was arriving with her breakfast. "Come in, Jane," she said, coughing. But when the door opened, the demon himself darkened the doorway, gripping the tray in his strong hands. "Get out!" she shrieked. "Get *out!*" But he merely smiled and strode over to the bed, setting the tray before her. She rang the bell furiously, and Jane came.

"Jane," she screamed. "Get him out of here!" But Gavin whispered something in Jane's ear and she nodded, smiled knowingly, and slipped out of the room. "Jane! Jane!" she cried, hysterically ringing the bell.

"She's not coming back," said the monster. "So you may as well eat your breakfast."

Judith turned her head away and refused to look at him. But he stayed and chatted with her—or at least he talked, and she listened—and his manner was so sweet and charming that she soon relaxed. Her appetite returned, and she drank some coffee and ate part of a scone. After she had eaten he took away the tray, promising to look in on her later.

He did so, and she found that she didn't mind. In fact, she was glad of his company. Day after day he continued to dote on her, and gradually his gentle attentions relieved her confused mind and banished her fears. After a while she felt terrible for having doubted him, and they started to laugh and have fun together again. But they never touched or kissed, and she wondered if they would ever be lovers again. To ameliorate the situation, she began parading around the bedroom in short transparent baby-doll nightgowns with matching knickers; but he never seemed to take any notice.

One night, they were lying side by side on the blue velvet bedspread, drinking claret from giant goblets and watching *Cleopatra* on the television, which was ensconced within an antique faux-Elizabethan cabinet decorated with nude figures, lion's heads, and fluted columns, fitted with a pair of blue velvet curtains to hide the modern abomination from sight when it wasn't being watched. Only, he wasn't paying attention to the film. He had propped himself on one elbow in his underwear like a *Playgirl* centerfold, and he was staring at her with big, sweet, adoring eyes. "Have I ever told you how pretty you are?" he purred.

"Like a million times. But I never get tired of hearing it."

"I still can't believe I got so lucky. The shape of your mouth, for instance, is perfect."

She knew her mouth was one of her best features, and she glowed at the compliment. "Not as perfect as Liz Taylor's mouth," she said, indicating the screen, on which Taylor as Cleopatra was seducing all of Egypt and Rome.

"Nonsense. You're much prettier than Elizabeth Taylor."

She laughed, delighted. "Now you're just flattering me."

"No, I'm not. Her face isn't that interesting to me. She may be Cleopatra, but you're Helen of Troy. Your pretty little mouth could launch a thousand ships, but all I want to do is kiss it. May I?"

170

She nodded and closed her eyes, and he kissed her. Then he slid his hand under her diaphanous baby-doll nightgown, and he touched her in a way that inflamed her senses. She moaned, and he kissed her mouth again, and he raised her nightgown and kissed every part of her body that his lips could reach, while she lay limp and quivering under his touch. That night, they made love.

He was careful with his lovemaking now, keeping the sex vanilla to avoid triggering her, but she didn't care either way. Now that he was amorous with her again, her imagination was awake to the suggestion of every passion. After that, he slept in the bed every night, and they made love two or three times a day. She reveled in the sight and smell and touch of him, and she orgasmed again and again.

Sometimes she orgasmed just from his glance, which made her feel so desirable that she became wildly aroused by her own body, and now she knew why women are afraid of the male gaze. The unwanted male gaze is bad enough, but what about the gaze you *respond* to? That gaze can ruin your whole life. It can make you do things you don't want to do — things you never thought you were capable of. It can make you follow a man, whether he's the right man for you or not. She knew Gavin was the right man for her, but she shuddered to think that even if he was the wrong man, his gaze would have made her follow him to the ends of the earth.

So everything went back to normal, and Judith was contented once more with her handsome beau; but deep down, she was still troubled. She had never had "the talk" with her husband, never confided her fears and anxieties to him. So although things seemed harmonious, and they had resumed their relationship as lovers, there was still a barrier between them. Sometimes she dreamed of him as a demon or an incubus, and she would awake in a cold sweat, unable to get back to sleep.

Often, on windy nights, she heard the distant sound of a woman weeping. She would lie awake listening in terror, wondering whether it was a ghost, a fanciful interpretation of the sounds of the wind, or a hallucination, produced by the effect of the legend of Lady Mordaunt on her imagination. Sometimes she thought it was the sound of her own tears in her mind, weeping pitifully for the lonely girl she had been, and the lonely woman she had become.

Due to these disturbances to her rest and peace of mind she developed insomnia, which exhausted her so thoroughly that she could scarcely keep her eyes open. Her writing suffered, and she was usually too tired to leave the house, often spending the entire day in bed. Sometimes she forgot to eat or bathe or dress, and she even stopped riding Valancourt. Gavin still spent a great deal of time in London, and while he was away, the bottle was her best friend; for it was only when she was drunk that she could truly forget.

18.

I'm Afraid of My Husband

Spring melted into summer, and life at Manderfield settled back into a pleasant routine. But underneath, Judith was plagued with depression and anxiety.

One morning, she was rudely awakened by the sound of whistling. She had finally dozed off after hours of sleeplessness, and she groaned and pulled the covers over her head. But it was too late; she was awake. She opened her eyes and saw Gavin across the room, whistling a cheerful tune as he rummaged through his closet. A shaft of sunlight pierced her bleary eyes and she winced, the glare splitting her head.

Gavin emerged with his coat and walked over to kiss her, perching on the edge of the bed. She inhaled his sandalwood scent, and she felt the touch of his smooth, hard cheek and his soft lips against hers. "What, little girl, still in bed? You've overslept yourself. I've already had my breakfast."

Judith took in the sight of his twinkling eyes and his clean, manly beauty. She herself was deathly pale with dark circles under her eyes, the result of too many sleepless nights and too much alcohol. "I didn't know it was so late," she said.

"Do you know what today is?"

"Thursday?"

"It's our anniversary."

"That's right. Happy anniversary, darling." But for some reason it meant little to her.

"Always forgetting things! And you need to start taking better care of yourself . . . you look a bit seedy. You're drinking too much. Only a year of marriage, and you're turning into a frump."

Judith sighed and slipped on a robe. "I know I'm a mess. I'll be all right if I can just get some sleep."

"I'm leaving now. Follow me downstairs." He picked up his briefcase and strode into the corridor and down the stairs, with Judith tagging behind. "I'm worried about you. Why don't I send for Doctor Graham?"

"There's nothing wrong with me."

"Yes, there is. You're depressed."

"I guess I am. But Doctor Graham isn't a psychiatrist."

"True, but he's very knowledgeable. He's studied the mind, nutrition — everything. Maybe he could get you to change your diet, or run some tests. He could even refer you to a mental specialist. I'll give him a ring now and ask him to make a house call."

"All right."

"And why don't you get yourself a new outfit for this evening? Selene is throwing a party, and you know she likes people to dress. Take the day off and do some shopping. Buy whatever you like."

"Of *course* I'll buy whatever I like. It's my money!"

"Don't be a witch, darling."

"Sorry. I *do* need some new things. I'll go to Harrod's."

"Good girl. Anyway, I'm off."

They had reached the door, and he stood on the threshold and embraced her. She lost herself in his kiss, craving the feeling of his strong arms around her, and then he was gone. She watched him drive away with a bemused smile on her face. Her husband had just called her a frump, a drunk, and mentally unstable; she really needed to get her act together.

She ascended the stairs to the bedroom, and showered and washed her hair. Then she donned a pink Chanel dress, clasped an immense pendant around her neck, and applied her makeup. While she was dressing, Gavin texted her that Doctor Graham would be there at noon, so she went down to the dining room and rang for Sarah to get her breakfast. A funereal light filtered into the room as she sat alone and waited. She glanced at the empty chair next to her, and her heart ached for Romeo. Then Sarah came in with bacon, eggs, toast, and coffee. She ate the bacon and eggs, but she had a lump in her throat, so she couldn't get the toast down.

Then, as she thought about her life, the lump in her throat grew larger, and the tears came. She had tried to fix her marriage, but she had failed. She had been afraid to call her husband out for his toxic behaviors, and she had allowed him to remain elusive and uncommunicative. The result was that she was still afraid of him, and he was still a stranger to her. Not only that, but her endless idealizing and demonizing of him over the months had worn her down and left her a shell of her former self.

At twelve o'clock sharp the doorbell rang, and Jane announced Doctor Graham. Judith escorted him into the drawing room. He inquired after her health, having been alarmed by her state of mind after her cat had died, but she assured him she was much better now.

They sat on the sofa, and he asked her about her lifestyle. She lied about her drinking, telling him she was only having one or two drinks per day, and exaggerating the amount of exercise she was getting—precious little lately, for she had taken to her bed instead of going on long walks and riding Valancourt as she used to. She also hid the fact that she was skipping meals and eating lots of cakes and sweets; the last thing she wanted was a lecture on how to eat, which she knew the doctor was dying to give her. She told him about a new symptom she had—chronic pain—and she admitted that her sleep was spotty, and that many nights she got no more than two or three hours. This she chalked up to worry and anxiety, and to her constant nightmares.

After the interview he checked her heart with a stethoscope, tested her reflexes, felt her lungs, looked in her eyes, ears, and nose with little instruments, and made her stick out her tongue—"You're a bit anemic," he said—and now he was holding her wrist and timing her heartbeats.

He looked at her gravely. "All of your vital signs are normal. What concerns me is the nightmares and the lack of sleep. My guess is that you can't sleep because you're afraid of something. We call that hypervigilance. Have you experienced any trauma lately?"

"None that I can think of." But then she added, "Except . . . I'm afraid of my husband."

"Why is that?"

She wasn't sure if she should tell him anything or not; it might get back to Gavin. But he had such a sympathetic look on his face that she trusted him. "It's his anger. He has a violent temper." She hadn't breathed a word about this to anyone except Anne, and Anne hadn't been listening, so the disclosure terrified her.

"You say he has a violent temper. What do you mean by that?"

"Nothing. I don't mean anything. It's just that he raises his voice sometimes, and he . . . well, it's nothing out of the ordinary, I'm sure."

"Men are different than women," said the doctor condescendingly. "Anger for a man is like tears for a woman. We have to let it out sometimes."

"Oh, I know. I don't believe people should censor their emotions. And anger can be healthy — righteous anger, especially. But it's just . . . no, there's no problem. He's actually very sweet. He lost his temper with me once, and it scared me, that's all. And now sometimes I . . . I dream of him as a demon. But the thing is, he's not like a demon at all. At least, it was only that one time."

"No one is a demon or an angel," explained the doctor, with an easy confidence in his own paternalistic wisdom. "We're all a mix. When we're angry, we often see people as demons. That's perfectly natural. Does he know how you feel?"

Judith shook her head.

"Then you need to speak to him."

"I can't."

"You can't sustain a marriage without communication," said the doctor sternly.

"I know. But I tried talking to him once, and he —" her hand involuntary flew up to her throat. "He didn't respond well."

Doctor Graham smiled. "Well, maybe he just needs some space."

Judith was startled. "Some space?" she repeated incredulously. As if she didn't give him enough space! If he had any more space, he would be living on the moon!

"Yes," said the good doctor. "Men are funny that way; if you give us space, we always seem to sort things out for ourselves. As for the diagnosis, you appear to have post-traumatic stress disorder."

"PTSD?" said Judith, feeling stupid right after she said it.

"Yes." He whipped out a pen and a pad of paper and wrote out a prescription. "I'm prescribing something to help you sleep, something for anxiety, and something for chronic pain. You can fill these today."

Judith took the piece of paper. "Thank you."

19.

The Vampire

Judith filled her prescription at a quaint chemist's shop in the village. As she exited the shop the wind pierced her bones, and she pulled her coat more tightly around her. She was about return to her car and make the long drive to London, but then she spotted the magnificent old cathedral across the street, and something compelled her to go in. She walked towards it briskly, gazing with wonder and inspiration at the façade, her pumps clacking on the pavement.

As she entered the building, admiring its stained-glass windows and marvelous vaulted ceiling, she passed a group of people leaving Mass, and then a priest in full regalia, who nodded kindly to her. She considered going into a confession box and spilling her guts, but after her experience with the doctor that morning she decided she'd had enough of sharing her secrets with men for one day. She had confessed often in her life, but just now she didn't want to say anything that might make her feel guiltier than she already did about her drinking problems and her failing marriage. Confessing so much over the years had caused her to blame herself when people were cruel to her, and she resented this. Usually when people are cruel to you it's *their* fault, and you shouldn't have to apologize to God for being upset about it.

Being inside a church always made her feel good, and her anxious brow relaxed as she absorbed the peaceful and uplifting atmosphere. A few people were milling around admiring the architecture, and several worshippers were praying. She brushed past a group of tourists and sidled down one of the pews, groping in her handbag for her rosary. She touched the first bead and murmured to herself: "In nomine Patris, et Filii, et Spiritus Sancti. Amen."

She opened her lips to continue, when suddenly she was distracted by a young woman in an advanced state of pregnancy waddling down the aisle. She wore a short black maternity dress with a white dickie collar, her black patent leather Mary Janes clopping along the floor. As she came closer, their eyes locked.

The woman was Nancy.

Nancy paused, and then averted her eyes and hurried to the back of the church.

Judith sat confused, her heart pounding wildly. The girl looked miserable, and suddenly Judith felt guilty about the way she had been fired. She had nothing to fear from Nancy now, so she decided to ask how she was getting along.

She rose and strode to the back of the church, where Nancy was lighting tapers and placing them in black iron holders. She gazed at her pretty little face, grown solemn with the weight of pending motherhood. "Hello, Nancy," she said. "How have you been getting on?"

"All right, I guess. I got another position. I've taken some time off for the morning sickness though."

Judith thought she looked heartbreakingly young. "Congratulations on the baby. I didn't know you had a young man."

"I don't."

"I'm sorry."

"Me too. It ain't been easy."

The priest walked by in his gold-trimmed robes, smiling and nodding, and the women stopped talking until he had gone. Then Judith said, "Let me know if there's anything I can do to help."

Nancy's tone became bitter. "Don't bother yourself. Anyway, your husband's already helping a bit."

Judith was seized with confusion. "My—husband? Why is my husband helping you?"

Nancy looked at her contemptuously. "Don't you know?"

"Know?" repeated Judith, a wave of panic sweeping over her.

"Because he's the father."

Judith stared at Nancy in speechless horror, hoping it was some sort of joke. But then, as she looked at the girl's hurt and angry face, she realized it must be true.

She rushed from the church and hurtled across the street, her eyes blinded by tears. A horn blared, and a car screeched to a halt. She jumped back. "Hey, look out!" a man's voice cried out.

She looked up in a daze. "Sorry."

"You ought to be more careful!"

Pedestrians stopped and stared. "Are you all right?" a woman asked.

"I think so."

"Here, let me help you." The woman took her arm and guided her across the street. "Do you need a ride somewhere?"

"No, my car is just there."

"I don't think you're in a condition to drive."

"No, I'm fine . . . really. Thanks for your help." And she got into her car and drove away. The woman was right; it wasn't safe for her to drive. But somehow, she made it home.

She drove back to Manderfield in a state of shock, her head splitting with migraine. She was angry with Gavin, and sorry for herself, and she felt like a fool. He has never loved me, she said to herself. The whole thing has been a lie, from the very beginning. That poor girl. I'll send her some money.

She pulled up to the castle and got out of the car, her headache so intense that she thought she would faint. Then she staggered up the drive and let herself in, dragging herself up the stairs one by one until she finally reached her bedroom.

Once inside, she tore open the bag from the chemist and gulped down a handful of pills with water. She undressed, slipped on a yellow nylon tricot nightgown, and lay on the bed, staring at the ceiling. She lay awake for a while, feeling nothing save the blinding pain of her headache. Then, miraculously, the pain subsided and she became drowsy. Sleep, she thought as she drifted off. Sweet, beautiful sleep.

She was awakened by a dulcet-toned voice insinuating itself into to her consciousness. "Wake up, Princess. It's time to get dressed for the party." She opened her eyes and recoiled in horror. Her husband was hovering over her in his blue velvet smoking jacket, with his charming Dracula smile. "What's the matter?" he said.

"Go away. Leave me alone!"

The day was dying, and the sunset bathed the room in a bloody light. He turned on the lamp, which flooded his face with a hard incandescence.

"What's the matter?" he repeated.

She sat up shakily, woozy from the pills. "I ran into Nancy today. She's pregnant with your child."

"Is that what she told you?"

"Yes. Don't try to deny it. Now I know why you fired her. It's all clear to me now!"

He walked away and poured a glass of water, the lamp casting diamond glints onto his hair. She stared at his handsome profile, and she hated herself for loving her vampire, with his commanding air, his glowing eyes, his pale face, and his slicked-back dark hair. But he didn't love *her*; he had discovered other charms.

Finally he turned to look at her. "I'm sorry about Nancy," he sighed. "It was all a stupid mistake. But I only did it to ease the pain."

"The pain?"

"Yes. The pain of Tony and you. It's obvious you're in love with him."

"But I'm *not* in love with him. Tony and I are just friends!"

"Then why did you lie to me about his visits?"

Judith fell silent, woozy and confused from the drugs. Then she said, "Because I knew you didn't like him."

"An emotional affair is just as bad; you can't blame me for finding someone too. But maybe it's for the best. I don't like you seeing Tony, but I'm not going to forbid it. And perhaps you wouldn't mind if I saw a friend now and then as well."

Judith felt plunged into a nightmare. Was he really suggesting an open marriage? And why was he trying to shove her into Tony's arms? "I don't want to have affairs with men," she said, trembling with indignation. "And I don't want to share you with other women. If that's the way you want it, it's over."

He crumpled onto the bed. "How can you be so cruel?" he cried in an anguished tone. "I'm your husband, the only person in this world who loves you! But maybe you're right to go. I've made a mess of things. And that slut Nancy, she . . . oh, I don't want to talk about her. She doesn't matter. But I suppose something like this was bound to happen, sooner or later. I'm just a savage — a beast. I've been so isolated in my life that I've never learned certain skills — like how to be monogamous. It seems I just wasn't ready for marriage."

She gaped at him, stunned. She knew she should be furious with him, but his words were so outrageous that she was more astonished than angry. He *was* a savage, but he couldn't help it; he had just never had a good woman to civilize him. She, on the other hand, had spent her entire life trying to placate cruel and brutal people, so she was in the perfect position to help him. Women must be constantly throwing themselves at him, with his good looks and charm, but none of them had made him *want* to be monogamous. Besides, he hadn't married them; he had married *her*. She was enough woman for any man, and she would prove it to him.

She smothered her anger and spoke calmly, like a therapist speaking to a patient. "You were the one who begged me to marry you. Why did you do that, if you knew you couldn't be faithful?"

"Because I thought I could change."

"And *can* you change?"

There was a long pause. And then he said, "Yes . . . I think I can. I have two selves: the good self that loves you, and the shadow self, that's full of darkness. But with your love, anything is possible. You can make me whole again." He gazed at her, and she saw the same love light shining in his eyes that she had seen that first day at the beach. He'd had an affair, but he had come back to her, loving and repentant. She had kept her man, and that was all that mattered.

She lay back, exulting in her victory. She was surging with pride at her deftness in handling her wayward husband. She felt loved and cherished once more, and warmth and happiness flooded her body. "All right. But I'm a one-man woman. If I take you back, you have to promise to be faithful."

"I promise." He took her in his arms and kissed her. She closed her eyes during the kiss, which was long and intensely pleasurable. But she was so knackered from her weeks of sleeplessness, from the emotions of the day, and from the pills she'd ingested, that she dozed off.

Soon she felt a light tapping on her shoulder. "Princess . . ."

She opened her eyes and saw her husband standing before her with a paddle, a pair of handcuffs, rope, chains, and a blindfold, all of it new with tags.

"Happy anniversary, little girl. I got you some new toys."

"Thank you," she said faintly.

"Show me your arse. You're going to get a spanking."

She looked up at him, feeling exhausted and ill. But she didn't want to refuse him so soon after their reconciliation, so she dutifully turned over and presented her backside to him. Delighted, he roughly pulled down her knickers and struck her bottom with the paddle. Why was he spanking her? They had just endured a horrible trial, the worst of their married life, and she was still traumatized. Normally she liked being spanked, but now it just seemed like a punishment. She felt like one of the dolls she used to drag around by the hair and sadistically pull apart.

At first his pleasure in witnessing her submission was evident, but soon he noticed her lackluster expression and he stopped. "Princess, what's the matter?"

"Nothing. I'm just not in the mood."

His face darkened, and he yanked away the paddle and threw it violently across the room. "All right, Little Missy. I've done everything you said. I even agreed to be monogamous. But if we're issuing ultimatums, then I need to demand some things of you as well."

She lay back exhausted on the bed, pulling up her knickers. She was so tired; she just wanted to sleep. "What would you like me to do?"

"For one thing, you need to be more expressive in the bedroom. I'm bored to death with your vanilla lovemaking. All you do is lie there."

She sat up, stunned. "But you *ordered* me to lie still! I'm not even allowed to —"

"True, but you don't put your heart into it. You're just going through the motions. I want to see genuine fear in your eyes."

186

"I'm sorry. I'm just so tired. Maybe tomorrow . . ."

"It's not just tonight. You used to be a good sport, but you don't want to do *anything* anymore. All you want is vanilla sex. I can't even spank you, let alone flog you! If I could just draw blood *once* on those lovely buttocks of yours . . ."

Normally she reveled in light flogging and other humiliations, which brought her to a greater pitch of ecstasy than milder amusements, but in her present state of exhausted illness something snapped in her, and she felt disgusted by the suggestion. "Why would you *want* to draw blood? Are you some kind of a *sadist*?"

"You really need to stop your kink-shaming. It's offensive."

"My — *kink-shaming*?"

He got up and paced again. "Yes. You're turning out to be a sex-negative prude. I've always slept with any girl I wanted, and marriage has really put a damper on that. So you can at least cater to my sexual tastes, if nothing else!"

She looked at him incredulously. She felt like a meal he had ordered in a fine restaurant, that he was sending back because the chef had not prepared to his liking. "Your — *sexual tastes*? I'm not just a girl you picked up on the street. I'm your *wife*. And you're treating me like a *whore*!"

"What's wrong with being a whore?" he parried, with mocking amusement.

Her heart welled up with rage. "How dare you call me a whore, you — you *Dracula*! You stole my innocence, and you groomed me to be your sex slave. I was a *virgin* when I met you. I was completely innocent. And then you told me that you *loved* me, and you *hypnotized* me, and you — you *raped* me!"

His eyes burned with a proud exultation. "You can't sell that tale to *me*. Remember, I was *there*. Little Miss Virgin made me carry her all the way back to the castle. And then she stretched herself out on the bed like a naughty Lolita, and she stared at me with bedroom eyes that said, *take me*."

"No, I didn't! I was drunk, and you—"

"You wanted an *adventure*. That's the phrase you use in your books, isn't it? In other words, you wanted me to *ravish* you."

She had never felt so confused and disoriented in her life. She *had* wanted an adventure, but not in the way he said. She had wanted him to kiss her, but she wouldn't have had sex with him if he hadn't cornered her, and if she hadn't been drunk. He must have known that, and yet he had deliberately . . .

She flung herself on the bed, the tears streaming from her eyes. "I *loved* you. And you took advantage of my innocence!"

"That's *your* story. It's a story that preserves your virtue intact, which is very convenient for you. Tell yourself anything you like, if it makes you feel better. But the fact is, you're not the innocent little girl you pretend to be. You were *begging* to be seduced. You've never loved me. All I am to you is a man who flatters you and pleases you in bed. If our marriage is a failure, *you're* to blame. You live in a fantasy world. You don't even care who I am as a person. You just want to fit me into a mold of the perfect lover, like one of your book heroes. I'm nothing but an object to you. If you want to know the truth, I *did* love you. But your heartlessness has killed that love!"

Judith's mind became tormented with a creeping panic.

She *had* objectified him. She *had* tried to mold him into the perfect lover, in deliberate ignorance of his actual personality. Had she read too many romance novels, which reduced men to their rippling muscles, their piercing dark eyes, their eroticized sense of menace, and their ability to pleasure a woman where and when she wanted? Her heart filled with anguish at the thought that she may have killed his love with her foolish romantic fantasies. "That's not true!" she screamed, her mascara pooling her tears into black rivulets. "I *love* you!"

At this, he erupted into crazed laughter. "Love! What is love to you anyway? A man who whispers sweet nothings in your ear, who plucks flowers for you, who tells you you're beautiful night and day? You don't love me — you're in love with *yourself*. You fell into my arms the moment I said you were more beautiful than your sister, even though you knew it wasn't true!" He laughed again, and his laughter was like knives piercing her heart.

She had believed him when he had told her she was beautiful, and it had *made* her beautiful, because of the boost it had given her confidence. But at these words, all of that confidence drained from her in an instant, as if a vampire had sucked out every last drop of her blood. And now that he had taken everything from her, including her self-esteem, she hated him with a burning passion. "You *monster!*" she shrieked. "Get out of this house. *Get out!*"

She threw a flower vase at his head, and he ducked to avoid it.

"Yes, I'll go," he said, his lip curling with contempt. "It's not worth it, being shackled to you!" He stalked to the door and stormed out. His steps thundered down the stairs, and the front door slammed with a sickening finality.

The room swirled around in a blur, and she fell to the floor. She felt as if she had turned into a liquid and was being sucked into a vortex, like Marion Crane's blood in *Psycho*. She spiraled round and round, trying to hold on to the sides, but to no avail. She heard loud sucking noises as she slipped down the drain, and she screamed, "No!"

And then everything went black.

20.

Regrets

Judith stirred her tea with a spoon, round and round. How many lumps of sugar had she put in? A frightful amount. It would be undrinkable. But she wasn't paying attention to the tea. She was gazing out of the window at the expansive lawn and the stately oaks, remembering when she and Gavin had first driven to Manderfield the previous autumn, and their joy and hope at starting a new life together. He had carried her across the threshold and shown her the castle, and they had gone up to the bedroom, and he had made passionate love to her.

And then she recalled their idyllic honeymoon in Paris, where they had shared all of the same tastes and interests, and they had laughed so much and seen so much art, and he had bought her dozens of presents and styled her like a screen siren. She couldn't believe all of that had happened only a year before; she felt she had aged a hundred years since then. Since he had gone, she had felt empty and incomplete, like a person who is missing a limb.

A few hours after he had left her, she had awoken at dawn and found herself lying on the floor. She had been heartbroken, and she had lain there and cried until Jane had discovered her and put her to bed. She had told the housekeeper that Gavin was gone for good, and that she wanted to die. Jane had not wanted to take any chances, so she had rung both Anne and Doctor Graham. The doctor had rushed right over, and Judith had lied to get rid of him, denying any suicidal thoughts. After he had lectured her extensively on her role in a happy marriage, and she had agreed with everything he said, he declared her out of danger and went away, much to her relief.

Anne had come by a few hours later with a suitcase and had remained by her side at all times, fearing she might take her life if left alone. Judith had fallen mute, responding to Anne's questions with only nods and shakes of the head. She had checked her phone every hour to see if he had texted her, and when he hadn't, the tears had flooded out in torrents. She hadn't wanted to speak to the monster, but she had wanted him to be contrite, and she had hoped that he would beg her to take him back so that she could kick him to the curb.

But after she had spent countless hours in anguish over his depravity and cruelty, she began to rationalize his position. She went over and over their last conversation, and his words echoed through her mind and haunted her. Once again, she became tormented by several inconvenient facts about herself. I *did* objectify him, she thought. I *am* in love with myself. I *did* want an adventure. Are my lofty sentiments about love hiding a purely sensuous drive? She had wondered about this right after they had first had sex, so his words had rung true for her.

It wasn't the first time she had been called out for being sex-negative, either. A girlfriend had accused her of this when she had questioned if she really liked being choked and slapped by her boyfriend during sex. That friend had never spoken to her again, and now she knew better than to say anything about other people's sex lives. And she started to imagine that her offense at being called a whore was problematic too; the last thing she wanted was to be whorephobic and to slut-shame other women.

What's wrong with being a whore, anyway? she thought. Why am I, a sexually experienced married woman, holding on to this absurd notion of myself as pure and virginal? Is it some sort of fetishistic self-fantasy — do I imagine myself as innocent as one of Dracula's virgin brides? I'm like a relic from the Victorian era. Women have reclaimed the word whore. There's no shame in being sexually active, in wanting sex, and even in financially profiting by it. I don't mind my husband pushing my boundaries in the bedroom — in fact, it gives me a thrill — and now that I know he wants me to be wilder in the bedroom, I'll surprise him with how far I can go. He was upset that I'm so stiff in bed, and I can't blame him. A man has his needs, after all, and I'm sure my lack of enthusiasm has made him feel unloved. That was bad enough, but then I had to go and objectify him! I know that hurt him terribly. That's why he insulted me; but I'm sure he didn't mean it. He was lashing out in pain. I'm certain that if I love him properly, we can be happy again. I never thought of him as a person who needs love, but of course everyone needs love, including men. I made him into my man toy, without considering his feelings at all. No wonder he had that affair! But now I'll love him so thoroughly that he'll have no further urge to stray. He said that he's never learned how to be monogamous; well, I'll teach him! He's still a wild animal, but he won't be wild for long. I *will* tame my lion!

She smiled as she fantasized about taming her wild beast by giving him everything he wanted in the bedroom, and thus enslaving him. She wanted desperately to apologize to him for losing her temper, to tell him she understood why he was upset, and to promise to be a more adventurous and attentive lover. But he hadn't contacted her, and she had sufficient pride to refrain from contacting him, although it took every ounce of her willpower not to do so. She wanted to text him and say, "Sorry about the other night. Love you. Talk soon," but she knew it was a bad idea. Besides, he might not respond, and she wouldn't have been able to tolerate that. More than anything she wished he would call her, so she could apologize and tell him she forgave him, and hear the love and gratitude in his voice, and his profuse apologies for having insulted her, and his declarations of love, in his noble, sweet, courageous, chivalrous, protective, sexy, manly tone.

Thus, she dreamed of a glorious reunion, but the more time that passed without contact from him, the more her feelings for him deteriorated. She once more characterized every word he had uttered that night as monstrous and cruel, and when she remembered how he had told her that her sister was more beautiful than her, she felt only a white-hot hatred for him, and she fantasized about stabbing him to death.

Now she was starting to come out of her severest depression, but she still saw no compelling reason to live. Her sense of self had been utterly shattered by his abandonment of her. That was how she characterized it to herself—as abandonment—even though *she* had kicked *him* out. Because if he loved her, he would have called her by now. If he loved her, he would have taken her in his arms and refused to leave, shedding tears of remorse at how he had hurt her with his lurid affair and his insults to her vanity. But there were no calls, and no tears; in fact, there was nothing. A void had opened up where he had been, and nothing could fill it. And where her heart had been, there was only a ragged hole.

As she stirred her tea, round and round, she became aware that someone was speaking to her.

"Judith? What are you thinking about?"

Startled out of her reverie, she saw Anne gazing at her with an expression of concern. "Nothing."

"Feeling better?"

She continued to listlessly stir her tea. "No."

"I've never seen anyone cry so much. You must have cried three buckets of tears this week."

"Sorry."

"No need to apologize. I'm sure you needed it. Anyway, I'm glad you're coming out of it. I was so worried. But you'll be all right now."

"I will?" returned Judith with an air of gloom.

"Yes, you will. But you shouldn't be alone in this big house. I'll stay with you until your divorce comes through."

"You don't have to do that."

"I want to. It will be like taking a holiday. You *are* getting a divorce, aren't you?"

"Of course."

Anne was surprised at Judith's mournful expression. "You're not still in love with him, are you?"

"No. I hate him. He can rot in hell."

"Well, I say good riddance to bad rubbish. I don't know what happened between you two, but any man who can make a woman cry like that is no good."

"You have no idea," said Judith, with daggers in her eyes. "He truly is a monster."

Anne laughed. "The Monster of Manderfield! That's the perfect name for him, don't you think? Anyway, that's that. You don't have to think about him anymore. But we're going to have to pull you out of this funk somehow. You should go out, meet new people."

"I don't want to meet anyone."

"You will."

They chatted a bit more in this vein, and eventually Judith's spirits started to lift. She had never felt she had a real family, and now Anne was pulling through for her when it really mattered. They never spoke about anything serious — their family dynamic had been so traumatic that it could never be discussed between them — but they bonded over superficial subjects, and their light chatter relieved Judith's mind from its byzantine tortures.

That weekend John visited, and the three of them took tea in the garden. Anne surveyed the charming landscape. "Do you remember when we were kids, and we would go to those masked balls at Lord Clifford's house? Your garden reminds me of his. I do miss those days."

Judith recalled bitterly how Anne had got to be a pretty lady in a gown at those parties, whereas she'd had to dress as a dandy gentleman in velvet knee-breeches. She heaved a deep sigh. "I always thought Manderfield would be a great place for one of those balls, but now it's too late."

"Why?" asked John. "It's no longer a liability to be a divorced lady—in fact, it makes you rather mysterious. And no one's seen the castle, apart from a few of our closest friends."

"That's right," said Anne. "If you agree to have it, John and I will make all the arrangements—we'll make the guest list, and hire the staff, and manage the catering."

"Well . . . money is a bit tight now," said Judith.

"Why? Has Baron Hastings been holding out on you?"

"Worse. He's broke."

"Broke!" screamed Anne and John unison. "How can he be broke?" cried Anne. "He's a *baron!*"

"Well, he made some bad investments or something. He promised he would be flush again soon, but I have no idea what's going on with his new business."

"Don't you guys ever talk?"

"Not much."

"Then what did you *do* together all that time you were married?"

If you only knew, thought Judith. "Well, he was away a lot," she said vaguely.

"No wonder the marriage fell apart! If you don't talk about things, how do you settle disagreements? John and I talk about *everything.*"

Judith felt a twinge of jealousy over Anne's stable marriage, and suddenly she felt she would like to have the ball after all. What did money matter? They would sell the castle once they were divorced, and this would be her last chance to use it for something truly memorable. She smiled impishly. "I think I *will* have that ball. As long as you'll arrange everything. We can do a Renaissance theme. It will go perfectly with the house."

John clapped his hands together in glee. "Splendid! I know a theater company where we can hire the costumes."

"What about the entertainment?" asked Anne. "I remember you used to love fairy tales. How about engaging some actors to perform a fairy tale? What was that one you liked so much — Blackbeard?"

"Bluebeard."

Judith started to feel truly happy for the first time in months. She was free of her nemesis, and mistress of her own manor, and she was starting a new life. This ball would be just like the fancy-dress party in *Rebecca*, except that hopefully it wouldn't turn out so horribly! But there was no chance of that. There would be no forbidding husband like Max de Winter to judge her costume; in fact, there would be no man to answer to at all. She was finally free, and she could do exactly as she pleased.

21.

The Masked Ball

For the next several weeks, the castle was in a flurry of excitement as John and Anne made guest lists, sent out invitations, hired musicians and caterers, and worked with a theater company to outfit the guests in authentic fashion. Judith wrote a libretto for a short opera dramatizing the Bluebeard story, and she sent it to a friend, Vladimir, to compose the score. Once it was finished, Vladimir booked singers and musicians, and Judith hired a scenic painter to make some simple theatrical backdrops. Anne, in her turn, hired model friends to serve food and drinks.

Judith had the gold dress she'd found in the tower cleaned and pressed. Once the odors were gone and the wrinkles steamed out, she realized it was a replica of the gown worn by Lady Mordaunt in the portrait above the mantlepiece. It was an Italian Renaissance confection fit for a princess, in gold tissue silk glittering with little glass beads, metallic gold trim, and rhinestones, to dazzling effect. It had a low, tight bodice that pushed up the breasts, full sleeves tied at the upper arms, elbows, and wrists, and a pleated skirt, the top layer split in front to reveal a second skirt underneath. Judith was extremely excited to wear it, and she stored it in a box with tissue paper and lavender to keep it fresh.

Finally, the day of the ball arrived. The castle had been decorated with potted palms, and banks of fresh flowers had been brought in from the garden and the greenhouse. Costumed musicians played period instruments on a little stage that had been erected in the great hall, and the sounds of the lute, recorder, drum, shawm, and dulcian soared out, clear and pure. The catering was magnificent, designed to replicate a medieval feast, and long wooden tables had been set up with a display of gorgeous breads, cheeses, fruits, chicken, pheasant, beef, wild boar, fish, lamb, salads, roasted vegetables, puddings, pies, and cakes. The sight of the guests in their period finery sweeping into the castle and across the marble checkerboard floors was quite a spectacle, and Judith reflected with a thrill that the inhabitants of the original castle must have been similarly attired.

John and Anne were habited exquisitely as Cesare and Lucrezia Borgia. Judith looked charming in her gold dress, which she wore over a chemise, petticoat, and farthingale, and accessorized with a sparkling rhinestone necklace, a papier-mâché half-mask on a stick, a long dark wig with a little golden crown, and dainty gold brocade shoes. When she looked in the mirror, she felt a delicious thrill as she compared herself to the portrait of Lady Mordaunt, who had swept across the halls of the old castle in balls many times more lavish than this. But she experienced a pang of grief as she wished her mother could see her now, and she fantasized that Ava would finally be proud of her and tell her she was the prettiest girl at the ball.

She left it up to Anne and John to greet the entering guests as she wandered around, drinking in the spectacle. Beautiful young models masquerading as wood nymphs, wearing transparent green dresses and garlanded with flower wreaths, served the guests, along with sexy young fauns with furred legs, faux split hooves, and bare chests. They glided around with trays of goblets filled with spiced wine, and Judith grabbed several in succession and gulped them down. The guests continued to trickle in wearing their magnificent costumes, and Judith spotted some interesting animal and bird heads amid the usual variety of carnival masks.

As the hall began to fill, a string ensemble joined the other instruments, and the music took on the form of a waltz. Some of the guests began to twirl round and round the great hall, the women holding their full skirts in one hand, the men sweeping dramatically around with their mysterious masked faces and swirling capes. Judith wished she had someone to dance with, and the thought that she was now single made her feel achingly alone.

She moved through the crowd as the hall filled up, smiling and saying hello to the guests. None of her family friends recognized her, having known her only as the peculiar girl who had cross-dressed as a boy. But she noticed that many of the men were staring at her lustfully, the way they had in Paris. She was surprised at first at the half-lidded stares, but then she remembered that she was now an incredibly alluring woman, made even more so by her exquisite costume and the mystery it gave her.

She fastened her eyes on some of the attractive young men, and she smiled. She might have any man she wanted. She could even have a different man every night — perhaps several men at once! She remembered a girlfriend at Oxford who had practiced serial dating, and how she had described her situation as "raining men." That wouldn't be so bad, she thought. Let it rain men!

But other than the flattering attention from the men, being part of this crowd was not as pleasurable as she'd thought it would be, for it dredged up painful memories of her parents' parties, and of the falseness and snobbery of the guests there. This group looked down on people below their social class, and their attitude disgusted Judith. The more of these toffs she saw filing in, the more determined she was to get good and drunk.

She wandered around, squeezing through the crowd to pick up another glass of spiced wine from a nymph's tray, when a strange man bumped into her. He had a long, craggy face heavily made up with theatrical greasepaint, and a shocking blue beard. He was standing next to a young woman with large, luminous eyes and a waist-length wig, also heavily made up. They both wore elaborate blue robes. The man showed his teeth in a ghastly smile. "I beg your pardon."

Judith was ecstatic. "You must be the singers! I'm so glad you could come!"

An event photographer asked her to pose with Bluebeard, and he snapped a Polaroid of them together. It zipped out and began to take on a ghostly image. The singers moved on, while Judith watched the image of herself standing next to Bluebeard materialize in shocking color.

She surveyed the room to see if there was anyone she knew. Soon she spotted Victoria, looking stunning in a wine-colored velvet gown. She made her way over to her, all smiles.

"Victoria! Thank you so much for coming!"

Victoria looked strangely at her. "Hello, Judith. Nice party."

"The last time I saw you was at your birthday party. Did you know I ended up marrying your childhood friend?"

"I heard you got married, but I don't know the man."

"Yes, you do. My husband is Gavin Garnet, the future Baron Hastings."

"I remember you caused quite the scandal at my birthday. People saw a very handsome man carrying you up to your room, but no one seemed to know him. And I don't know any Gavin Garnet."

"But he said he's known you since you were children, and that he used to call you Vicky. Maybe you know him as Gavin Longueville?"

"No, I don't. I don't know any Gavins, or any Longuevilles either. He must have been pulling your leg." And then someone grabbed her by the hand, and she laughed in delight and began whirling around in the waltz.

Judith stared after her, stunned. Victoria must have had her own reasons for pretending not to know Gavin, for she certainly wasn't a liar. And then she wondered if her husband had a bad reputation amongst Victoria's crowd. Had he seduced Victoria perhaps, or one of her friends?

Her reverie was broken by a voice calling out, "Princess!" The word sent a chill down her spine. She looked up to see Tony standing there, looking obscenely handsome in a short toga which showed off his broad shoulders and slim waist to perfection, with a laurel wreath around his head, sandals that were tied with leather strings around his strong calves, and a prop lyre. Until this moment, she had never noticed what a beautiful body he had. "Tony!" she cried. "Thank God you're here! Anne didn't tell me you were coming."

"I wanted it to be a surprise," he said in his rich baritone.

"Have a drink with me, Tony?" She grabbed two glasses of spiced wine from a passing tray and handed one to Tony; she was beginning to feel pleasantly tight.

His eyes lingered on her. "You're looking very pretty."

"So are you. Who are you supposed to be?"

"Orpheus. They said Renaissance or mythical, and mythical was cheaper."

"Kiss me, Orpheus!" She grabbed him and pressed her lips to his, feeing for his tongue. It was a long, sensuous kiss; perhaps the best kiss she'd ever had.

Tony was pleasantly surprised. "You've never kissed me like *that* before."

"You were never Orpheus before. Now you can rescue me from the underworld."

He looked at her with great sympathy in his eyes. "Have things been that bad?"

"You have no idea! I've been in the clutches of a vampire."

Suddenly she had the uncanny feeling that she was being watched, and she scanned the room. But all she saw was a blur of masked faces whirling around in the waltz, and other masked people socializing and drinking.

"Are you looking for someone?" asked Tony.

"No . . . I think someone just walked over my grave." She took his arm, and they walked through the hall and out to the garden, where they were enchanted by the sight of a *tableau vivant* of three naked men sitting on a pedestal, white from head to toe, appearing like statues until they moved and struck a different pose. Nearby, two dancers costumed as caterpillars performed a *pas de deux* in front of the Roman fountain, which was spouting jets of water colored with a thousand tints. The woman entwined her thigh-length black hair around the man, enveloping him in it as they circled one another in a slow erotic dance. Then she sprouted wings and became a butterfly, and he held her aloft, displaying his proud queen as she fluttered in his arms.

Judith and Tony were riveted to the sex-sodden spectacle. Then he said, "I'm sorry your marriage didn't work out—I truly am. I know how much it meant to you."

"Now you can say 'I told you so.' And you'd be right. I don't know what I was thinking, but love isn't always rational."

"I know. For instance, I'm not very rational. Because I'm still in love with you, and I shouldn't be."

"Why shouldn't you be? I'm a soon-to-be-divorced lady, and we're on an equal footing now. I was a child before, and now I'm a woman."

"I've noticed."

"I mean it," she said drunkenly. "I'm a real woman now. I could show you some things, Tony . . . you'd be *shocked*."

"I'll take you up on that sometime."

They were standing very close, and Judith felt a warm glow of desire radiating from him. Now that she was no longer a virgin he was properly amorous with her, and she found his new energy incredibly erotic.

"How about after the party?" she whispered.

"It's a date." They looked into each other's eyes.

At that moment she wanted Tony so desperately that she almost suggested going up to the bedroom with him on the spot. But it wasn't just his eroticism that transfixed her; he was gazing at her with an expression she had never seen before. Gavin's glance at the beach had pulverized her senses, but this was different. That had felt like being seized to be sacrificed on a pagan altar, and this felt like she and Tony were seizing one another with their eyes, playfully and with abandon, in a pleasurable *pas de deux*. Was this, then, what love was? Not a sacrifice to an all-powerful god . . . but rather, a dance?

She led Tony back to the hall, smiling at him with coquettish glances, and they began whirling around together in the waltz, becoming dizzy in each other's arms as the walls flashed by.

"I love you," he said, looking into her eyes, and Judith nearly swooned with desire.

"Oh, Tony, I . . ."

But then the music stopped, and the wood nymphs went around tinkling little silver bells. "Gather near, everyone!" they cried. "The performance is about to begin!"

The crowd pressed towards the stage. It was now illuminated with a spotlight, and a simple set had been added, consisting of a pastoral backdrop and a fountain. John as Cesare Borgia stepped onto the stage, striking his glass with a spoon.

"We have a special surprise for you," he announced. "Judith has written the libretto for a short opera, with music by Vladimir Semenov—who, sadly, couldn't be here tonight. And now, without further ado, I present the world premiere of . . . *Bluebeard's Castle!*" John stepped down, and everyone clapped as Bluebeard and his wife mounted the stairs to the stage.

Tony turned to Judith admiringly. "So you wrote this?"

"Shhh!" she hissed. "It's starting!"

The lights dimmed, and a spotlight came up on the stage. The musicians began to play a sad pastoral tune with undertones of menace, and the scene opened on two sisters in peasant attire dancing and playing around a fountain. Bluebeard wooed the young girls in an aria, using his castle and his great wealth as a lure. The older one was frightened of his blue beard, but the younger was charmed and sang about how she would be honored to marry him.

The next scene opened against the frightful exterior of Bluebeard's castle. His new bride sang plaintively about how she was frightened of the dark and foreboding fortress. Bluebeard sang that there was nothing to fear, and their exchange turned into a soaring duet.

The lights faded down, and came up again on Bluebeard and his wife standing in the gloomy castle interior. Bluebeard handed his wife the keys to the castle, singing that he forbade her to open the chamber that the smallest key fit, on pain of death. Then he departed on a long journey.

Once Bluebeard was gone, his wife explored the castle. She opened several doors, and she sang in turn of his riches, his jewels, his weapons, his ladies' costumes, and his room full of tears. Then, curiosity overcoming fear, she unlocked the door to the forbidden chamber.

As she did so, the lighting on the scrim changed, and several dead women were revealed hanging behind it, their throats slit, blood running down their chemises. Several audience members gasped, and a child began to cry. Bluebeard's wife dropped the key into a pool of blood. She tried to wash it off, but to no avail.

Bluebeard returned early from his journey, and she was forced to render the keys to him. When he saw the blood on the key, he knew she had disobeyed him and entered the forbidden chamber. The music became violent and discordant as he sang, his voice deep and full of rage, about how she must die and join the other ladies she had seen there. His wife's fear turned to fury, and she sang:

> I loved you and I trusted you, and yet
> You only wished to stifle me of breath
> Murdering the members of my sex,
> And drenching all the world in blood and death.
> You're drunk with power, and to you a wife
> Is one to strangle, stab, and rob of life.

Then Bluebeard, gloating triumphantly, sang:

> To murder and to silence worthless girls
> Is all I live for in this bloody keep.
> And now this knife will slice your pretty throat,
> Consigning you unto eternal sleep.
> You'll join my other brides within that room,
> And soon you will be sealed within your tomb.

Bluebeard's wife addressed the audience and sang, her eyes blazing with a fearful rage:

> Let all who look upon this awful scene
> Shun this man, who's rotten to the core.
> The blood of women ever stains his hands
> And he will have no peace forevermore.
> Now other women will avenge my death,
> And Bluebeard will exhale his final breath.

She held her last note for a long time. And as the music trailed off, she turned and disappeared into the chamber which was her tomb. The door closed behind her, and Bluebeard stood on the stage frozen in melancholy thought. His spotlight faded, and he became dimmer and dimmer, until finally he was ensconced in total blackness. The dulcian droned out its last brutal note, and there was a heavy silence. Then the lights faded up, everyone applauded, and the singers took their bows.

Judith turned excitedly to Tony. "Wasn't that *fabulous*?"

"Yes, it was, rather. I'm impressed."

"This is the first time I've heard it performed. Vladimir is a *genius*."

"I agree. And your lyrics are marvelous. Rather dark, but I like that."

"Tony, darling," she drawled, "I'm absolutely *dying* of thirst, and I don't see any of those nymphettes around. Would you be a dear and get me a drink?"

"Certainly. I'll be right back." He turned and disappeared into the crowd.

Just then, a tall, good-looking young man in a *commedia dell'arte* harlequin outfit approached Judith, handing her a glass of mead. His form-fitting costume of red and white diamonds was enhanced by a red cape, and a sequined mask covered his eyes.

"Here's a fresh one for you, Sweetie."

Judith took the mead from him and drank it down. "Do I know you?"

The harlequin removed his mask. "My name is Montgomery," he said, his voice that of a flamboyant gay man. "I used to model with your sister, and I'm an old friend of your husband's. I run into him from time to time at my athletic club. One day I overheard him talking to the concierge, and I realized he was married to you. I recognized your name, because my ex-boyfriend used to read your books, and I saw your feature in *Vanity Fair*." He took a gander around the room. "I haven't seen your gorgeous husband all night. Is he here?"

"No. We're not together anymore. I've kicked him out. I don't care *what* happens to him. He can live in his old leaky castle and freeze to death for all I care!"

The harlequin threw his head back and laughed. "That's hilarious!"

"What's hilarious?"

"I've known your husband for *years*. Believe me, I know all about his castle fantasies."

"What do you mean, *fantasies*? You *do* know he's next in line to be Baron Hastings, don't you?"

The clown looked at her askance. "I'm sorry . . . I thought you were joking. I mean, so you really don't know? You married him thinking he had a title and a castle?"

"Of course. Because he does."

"I hate to be the one to break this to you, but he doesn't have a title, and there isn't any castle. He comes from the working class."

Judith suppressed a laugh. "The *working class*? I hardly think so. You must be mistaking Gavin for someone else."

"His name wasn't Gavin when I knew him. His real name is Sam Jones."

"*Sam Jones?* Now I'm *sure* you have the wrong person."

"I'm afraid not. Sammy was the caretaker at the Royal Haymarket, where I used to perform. After the show, after he'd swept and cleaned up, he would join us at the pub for a few pints. He used to have us in stitches with his stories."

"I believe you're making a mistake," she said, with less conviction than before. Suddenly she remembered that photo of Gavin with actors in a dressing room, and the way he had stood out because he wasn't in costume.

"You don't have to take my word for it. But anyone who was there at the time would tell you the same thing. Anyway, we liked him; he was entertaining. He was always telling everyone he was a baron and putting on airs."

Judith's mind tried to process this, but her attempts only produced a cognitive dissonance.

Orpheus returned with her wine, and Judith downed it in one draught. Then she said facetiously, "This clown here has been telling me about Gavin's past. Apparently, he isn't a baron at all. He comes from the working class!" She laughed uproariously, and Tony looked at her, worried.

"I'm not surprised he didn't tell you," said Montgomery. "Sammy *hated* to work. Always thought he was too good for it. He was so ashamed of being poor. If you ask me, I think he married his last wife for her money."

Judith struggled to focus. "His last wife?"

"Yes, Constance. She was an heiress. Didn't you know?"

Judith frowned, her mirth quickly fading. "Oh yes, Constance. She wasn't his wife. She just told people that."

"You're quite mistaken. I was at their wedding in Italy."

The harlequin continued to speak, but Judith's head was filled with clanging, so she didn't hear him. And then the wine, the noise, the pressing crowd, and her own anguished mind proved too much for her, and she fainted in Tony's arms.

Tony lifted her gently and moved towards the staircase. The music stopped and the room became hushed, as the guests gaped in mute amazement at the spectacle of Judith unconscious in Tony's arms. Then Anne rushed up to him at the base of the stairs.

"Is everything all right?"

"She's just had a little too much to drink. I'm putting her to bed."

22

Bad Men, and the Women Who Love Them

In a bizarre déjà vu that echoed Gavin's epic journey across the sand holding a limp and intoxicated Judith in his arms, Tony carried the gold-clad princess up the magnificent staircase and into her chamber, where he laid her on her canopied bed.

When she came to a few minutes later, all she wanted was to erase the horrible new reality that had shattered her soul. She instructed Tony to lock the door, and she undid her bodice and lifted up her skirts and gazed at him, pulling him down to the bed. In her tribute to authentic Renaissance fashion she wasn't wearing any knickers, and the awareness of how sexy she looked in her semi-nude disarray made her wild with desire.

"Make love to me, Orpheus," she moaned.

"No. You're drunk."

She pouted, pulling him down to her and kissing his mouth. "Don't you love me?"

He savored the sweet kiss, in which their tongues deliciously mingled, and then he pulled away. "Of course I love you. But you can't consent when you're drunk."

"Yes, I can. I'm fully in possession of my faculties."

She placed her hand on his hardening manhood, easily accessible under his toga—something she never would have dared try with Gavin, who forbade her to touch him without his consent. "Please, Tony. Make love to me." She kissed him again and pulled his mouth down to her breast. He teased her nipple with his tongue, and she squealed with pleasure, pressing her half-naked body to his. Then she moved his head down and let him taste of her nectar. After that he could no longer control his desire, and he stopped protesting.

She found him to be a tender, thoughtful lover, less dominant than Gavin but more sensitive, and her passion knew no bounds. After they had been locked together in kisses and caresses for half an hour, he removed her exquisite costume in all its layers, and then his own scanty clothing, and he went slowly with her. Despite her drunken state, she found his lovemaking to be incredibly arousing. She didn't feel like a body detached from a soul, the way she did with Gavin. With Tony as her lover her entire being was involved in the act, and she blossomed under his touch like a rose.

But something bothered her about Tony's lovemaking. At first she couldn't put her finger on it. Then she realized what it was: it was Tony's touch, and not Gavin's touch.

And so, as he continued to touch her in all the ways that drove her mad, she began to dissociate, imagining she was making love with Gavin instead of Tony. Gavin loves me, she said to herself. Gavin is making love to me now, and he is touching me in this way because he loves me. He has always loved me, and he loves me now more than ever. I will always be his. And when she opened her eyes and gazed into Tony's face, she saw Gavin's face. And she felt the softness of Gavin's lips, and Gavin's body merged with hers, and she reached the heights of ecstasy over and over again. She fell asleep sweetly in Tony's arms, imagining them to be Gavin's arms.

Judith awoke just before dawn with a splitting head, and the first thing she did was to rapturously recollect the delicious lovemaking of the night before. But when she saw that it was Tony lying next to her instead of Gavin, at first she felt confused, and then disappointed, and then guilty. Tony had surprised her with his passion, and she had experienced intense pleasure with him, but the thought that she had cheated on her husband gave her a sick, empty feeling. And then her conversation with Montgomery flooded back to her, and she was shocked anew as she remembered that she was married to a fraud, a swindler, a con man, a gigolo.

She gazed once more at Tony's handsome face, and then she crept silently out of bed and into her luxurious bathroom, where she quietly showered the party, the alcohol, and the sex off her, donned her robe and slippers, and left the room. She descended the stairs, and below in the hall she observed the carnage of the night before: ribbons, feathers, melted wax, dead flowers, discarded carnival masks, confetti, half-empty glasses and bottles, cigarette butts, vape pens, plates of partially devoured food, and other assorted debris. Mice banqueted on the remains. She picked up a Polaroid from a random pile, and she found herself staring at a photo of herself with Bluebeard, which was so lurid and theatrical that she laughed.

She shuffled into the kitchen and made herself a pot of coffee, which she took to the library with her.

The dawn was just beginning to break, casting a sepulchral light through the sheer white curtains in the wainscoted room, with its shelves of old, comforting books. As she lit the silver sconces with their frosted glass globes and sank onto the crimson velvet sofa, sipping her coffee and absorbing the tranquility of the atmosphere, her mind became tortured with thoughts about Gavin, and the web of lies he had spun. He obviously hadn't attended Eton or Oxford. His father wasn't a baron, his mother hadn't attended Malvern or died in a car crash, his family had no coat of arms, and he had never lived in a castle, in Hastings or anywhere else.

And then she wondered: *is* there a castle in Hastings? Why did I never look it up before? Seized with a burning curiosity, she set down her cup and began searching in the numerous shelves for something. Finally she found it: a large, hardbound, coffee-table volume titled *Castles of England*.

She pulled it out and lugged it over to the sofa, flipping through it eagerly until she found the entry for Hastings Castle. To her horror, the large, clear color plate depicted an ancient ruin overlooking the English Channel. Nothing remained except for fragments of a few crumbling foundation walls, and part of a burnt and blasted tower. Skimming the accompanying text, she found that it had become a ruin as early as 1287, when large parts of its façade had fallen into the sea.

Judith sighed and closed the book. So this is Gavin's castle, she thought. It's a perfect metaphor for our marriage: something that seemed strong and magnificent, but is really just a crumbled ruin.

She sank into a deep dejection as she considered the reality of the person she had married. Not only was he a fake, but he was worse than she ever could have imagined. He had likely made up a list of rich, single women to target, and had crashed Victoria's birthday party solely in order to meet her. He had probably been stalking her for months: shadowing her at cafés and restaurants, listening in on her conversations with her sister, reading her novels and interviews, studying her lonely and unsatisfying life. He had clearly targeted her for her money and had never found her beautiful or interesting at all. She should have known something was wrong when she saw him staring at her instead of Anne at the pool, because no man ever noticed her when Anne was around. There were so many red flags: the way he had called Victoria Vicky; the way he had made that gaffe about St. Moritz; the way he had pretended to be a fan of her books; the way he had refused to allow her to meet his father or see his castle; the way he had manipulated her into marrying him; the way he had no internet presence or history; the way he refused to talk about himself; the way he had turned out to be shy of cash.

Then she reflected on her own insane actions, trying to assess them honestly in the cold light of day. I allowed myself to be seduced by a stranger, she lamented. I allowed him to take my virginity, and to push my sexual boundaries in ways that made me uncomfortable. I allowed him to love-bomb me into a slave-like compliance. I continued to believe that he was fabulously rich and titled, even after he put a five percent deposit on a castle and left me with the tab. I excused his abhorrent and bizarre behaviors: putting his hands on my neck, setting traps in the garden, his sexual sadism, his affair. And I bought his ludicrous lies about Constance. I've fallen victim to a highly skilled serial seducer. And what's worse, I'm still in love with him.

Why me? she thought with anguish. Did my desolate childhood, bereft of love, fashion me to be the ideal mate of this monster? Was I exquisitely and perfectly crafted through misery, neglect, and cruelty to endure, nay, even *welcome*, such a hellish union? Were my boundaries eroded and my heart broken at such a tender age that I was destined to fall into the arms of such a vicious predator?

Her tears flowed, and her heart was filled with so much pain that she thought she would die. She was familiar with this deep, stabbing anguish, which she had experienced all throughout her life. She had cried herself to sleep countless times as a child, promising to be better the next day in order to finally win her mother's love. That love had never come, but she had never stopped striving for it. And now she was doing the same thing with her husband: making excuses for his cruelty, sweeping his lies under the rug, forgiving his every transgression, all to extract any crumbs of love that might be gained for her good behavior. She had thought she was being rebellious and independent when she had decided to marry Gavin, but now she realized that she had merely fallen neatly into the plans of a sociopath.

She dragged herself to the mantlepiece and stared at his photo in a silver frame, looking bewitchingly handsome in his riding clothes, and she smashed it to the floor in a rage. She couldn't believe she had actually married a sociopath. Why hadn't she seen the patterns? She rose and fetched a well-worn book from a shelf in the psychology section, titled *Bad Men, and the Women Who Love Them*. She flipped to a bookmarked page and read:

Abusers pick women who have weaknesses they can prey on and love-bomb them into oblivion. Then they start to display small amounts of rage and violence, often triggered by being caught in lies about other love affairs, and the ratios eventually reverse so that there are fewer loving moments and more abusive moments. The woman craves the love that is starting to disappear, and she forgives the abuse because the man convinces her that he's the one who is hurting. So she takes him back, and she pours all her energies into healing him. That is, until he blows up or has another affair, and the process starts all over again. Each time they fight and make up the man seizes more control, until finally she has no boundaries left at all, not even in her mind. It's at this point that the woman becomes either so fragmented or so brainwashed that she agrees to live her life as an emotional and sometimes a physical prisoner of this man, or something snaps in her and she leaves. When a woman in this situation tries to exit, the man often goes berserk, because he has long ago stopped thinking of her as an autonomous human being (if he ever did). So he sets out to stop her at all costs, often by violently killing her.

Judith closed the book, shocked that this familiar passage described her own husband to a tee, and horrified that, although she was now consciously aware of his evil, she was still irresistibly drawn to him. She had an overwhelming passion for him that was insensible to thought or reason. She was attracted to his dark side, which mirrored her own, and to his troubled masculinity. No one could ever love her the way he could, and if she lost him, her life would be forever dull and empty. When he loved her, she loved herself, and her life was glorious and whole.

As she reflected on these feelings in herself, she felt a black despair. Why can't I love a man like Tony, she thought, who is decent and kind? Tony is good and Gavin is bad, and yet it's Gavin I love, and Gavin I fantasized about last night, even after I discovered his diabolical web of lies. No matter how hard I try, I can't switch my love from one man to the other. If only love were rational, and I could bestow it on the man who deserves it! But that's one of the mysteries of life: you can't help who you love, any more than you can help who you hate.

The thought that she would forever love Gavin, even if it killed her, plunged her into a paralysis of terror. She would always love her mother, and she would always love Gavin. Once a therapist had told her that she couldn't begin to heal until she stopped idolizing her mother, but she could never do that. Because then she would have to acknowledge that her mother had never loved her, and that would surely kill her.

Tears came to her eyes as she recalled how her mother had accused her of being sneaky, manipulative, deceitful, artful, and wicked; how she had wished her dead; how she had glared at her with a despotic eye of ice; how she had disparaged her face, figure, and personality; how she had been openly bored and disgusted in her company; how she had become enraged if anyone was ever kind to her; how she had once told her to her face that she hated her. Afterwards she had taken it back, saying, "No, I don't hate you. I can't hate you—you're my child. But I hate your *ways*." That had made it so much worse. And then she started to remember other specific instances of her mother's mistreatment of her—scenes of such unimaginable cruelty that they cannot be recorded here.

23.

No Man Is Perfect

After Judith had spent some time absorbed in the blackest grief, she emerged from her hellish trip down memory lane to find herself chilled to the bone. She rose and tossed some paper and kindling into the fireplace, warming her hands in the blaze. As the fire took away her chill, her terror began to dissipate, and her relationship with her husband appeared to her in a rosier light. Gavin was nothing like her mother. He had always been sweet, kind, and attentive. He had encouraged her to write, to think, to dream. He had made her feel beautiful and wanted. He had only lost his temper twice, and he had always been faithful, except for that one affair . . . but she had still kicked him out. *She* was the heartless one, not him.

She was aware that her thought processes, no matter where they started, consistently made him lovable again in her eyes as through a sort of diabolical witchcraft; but she finally resigned herself to the fact that she had no power over the process. Whatever logic she used to get there, the result was always the same: she was his wife, and she loved him, and she could never leave him.

She stared into the flames, resigning herself to her fate. She now knew that she had fallen victim to a sociopath, and yet she didn't care. No man is perfect; all men have their flaws, and you have to accept the bad with the good. Some men expect you to mother them, or make you into their maid. Others ignore you, or lecture you, or misunderstand everything you say, or are fussy about trivial things. A bad man can kill you with a knife, but a good man can kill you by boring you to death! Her worst nightmare was to be married to a stodgy fool who understands nothing about a woman's soul, and who promises a tedious, dreary life, like Madame Bovary's husband. Nice guys imprison you within the patriarchal strictures of duty and wifeliness, whereas bad men whisk you away from all expectations of proper behavior into a life of sublime and mindless pleasure.

She knew she wasn't alone in her attraction to a bad man. Years of writing dark romances and receiving confessional letters had taught her that many women crave a strong, masculine man to sweep them off their feet, and that these men can be dangerous. But she felt she could handle any difficult situation that arose, and she believed in the power of her love to transform her beast into a prince. Surely, if Jane Eyre could tame her domineering, dissimulating, gaslighting Rochester, she could tame her counterfeit baron! She no longer had any illusions about him; she knew he was, like Lord Byron, "mad, bad, and dangerous to know." Now, her task was to figure out if he was worth keeping.

She continued to pace the room. The sun was higher now, but it was filtered through a heavy bank of clouds, and the grayness of the day reflected her mood. And as she paced, she exonerated the man she loved from every crime and blamed herself for every problem in their marriage. Soon she felt guilty for having objectified him, and she began to paint him as the poor, disenfranchised plaything of a rich, heartless woman. She had emasculated him with her wealth, and oppressed him with her class. As for the rape, that was just her paranoid interpretation of his undying passion for her, and her prudish schoolgirl attempt to absolve herself of responsibility for her carnal desires.

Then, as she sat down and poured herself another cup of coffee, she began to tackle his lies about his background. Gavin had *always* told people he was a baron, so he hadn't been specifically bilking *her* with that fiction. That he had lied about his financial status was pretty bad, but he had been generous to the point of extravagance in Paris, bankrupting himself to surround her with pleasure and romance. He may have initially targeted her for her money, but her woman's intuition told her that their desire had been mutual, and that by the time she had agreed to marry him, he had been deeply in love with her.

By the time she had performed all of these tricks in her mind, he seemed like the perfect man again. She knew she was spinning the facts, but she was like a drowning woman, clinging to any piece of floating wreckage to justify her love for her diabolical Adonis. She was consumed with an intense desire to turn back the clock to the way things had been in Paris, and to win him over with her virtuous and all-consuming love, the way her book heroines always did. But it gave her a start to realize that she had once again slipped into thinking of herself as a heroine in a novel. Had her mind been addled by romance to the extent that she was willing to wreck her life over an absurd and wildly unrealistic hope? Or was she like Captain Ahab, determined to capture her quarry and force it to her will, even if it meant expiring in the process?

As she finished her second cup of coffee, she realized that as long as she was single and unattached, she wasn't safe. She didn't trust herself to stay away from Gavin, especially while he was still her husband. She would have to remain locked in the house until her divorce was final and never be left alone, lest she be tempted to go to him. She felt like Lucy in *Dracula* who, although guarded night and day, finds a way to break both the bonds of her bedroom walls and of human decency to keep a tryst with her demonic and unnatural lover.

Exhausted by her tortured thoughts, she sank down onto the sofa, gazing vaguely into the distance in an attitude of melancholy. Suddenly the sun burst through the clouds, and the library, latterly shrouded in gloom, became infused with a soft glow. She strode to the long windows and flung open the curtains, letting in a flood of light. The wholesome sunshine, and the sight of the luxurious verdure and the stunning blues and magentas of the castle gardens, broke the spell of her morbid obsessions, and she laughed. The cobwebs in her mind began to dissipate, and she suddenly saw her husband as no more than a pathetic and ludicrous gigolo. His dark narcissism no longer seemed interesting to her and had no further command over her spirits. She would no longer wreck herself against the rocks and destroy her mind, body, and soul to win his love; he simply wasn't worth it.

But then, just as she was about to turn from the window, she detected a figure walking through the trees in the faraway mists at the edge of the forest. Her heart leapt with joy as she recognized Gavin's gait and posture, and she ran barefoot out of the castle and across the wet grass, panting heavily with the effort. But by the time she reached the woods, the figure had disappeared.

Perspiring, frustrated, and filled with dejection, she turned back towards the house. She encountered the gardener as she was crossing the lawn, his ancient face wearing an expression of eager anticipation as he made his way over to the boxwood hedges holding a pair of large shears. She ran up to him breathlessly. "James, have you seen the baron around these parts today?"

His eyes wandered hungrily up and down her body, and she pulled her dressing gown more closely about her. He shook his head. "I ain't seen the maister since 'e left."

"Were you walking in the woods just now?"

"No, Ma'am. I coom from the cottage."

"Thank you, James."

As she made her way back to the house, she thought, all I saw was a man. He was so far away that it could have been any man, but my mind went instantly to Gavin. Why was I so delighted when I thought was him? And why did I run to him and yearn for him to take me in his arms? I had just disavowed him as a pathetic gigolo in my mind, but the sight of a man I perceived to be him was enough to instantly throw me back into the raptures of love. I *am* the vampire Lucy, and I *can't* be trusted to stay away from Dracula. Fine — then I'll just have to make sure I'm never alone. All I have to do is survive this nightmare until the divorce, and I'll be free of the monster forever.

Fortified by this decision, she made her way into the hall and ascended the stairs to her bedroom. She stepped over her gold dress, brocaded shoes, long black wig, and petticoats, and Tony's toga, gold rope belt, sandals, and lyre, and sat at the edge of the bed.

Tony had just awoken. He raised himself seductively on his elbow. "Oh, there you are! I was starting to think I had dreamed you."

She lay down beside him and put her arms around him. "Do you still love me?"

"I'll always love you."

"You're sweet, Tony."

He raised an eyebrow. "Just sweet? I thought I'd done a bit better than that."

"Yes, you were marvelous."

She rolled onto her back and held his strong, beautiful hand in hers. "What are we going to do, Tony?"

"You mean about us?"

"Yes."

"You know how I feel. I would marry you in an instant if you'd have me, the moment you got your divorce."

"I'd like that."

"Are you sure you're not still in love with Gavin?"

"No. I *hate* Gavin. He lied to me. He never was even a baron." Her tears trickled down her cheek and onto the pillow.

"He's the worst. I'm not surprised he told you all those lies. He's the devil, through and through."

"I know. He told me Constance was a prostitute, when she's really an heiress! That's what he thinks of women: that we're all worthless whores. Not that it's bad to be a whore, but *he* thinks it's bad. You should hear the tone in his voice when he says it! Honestly, he scares me. I never told you this, but he put his hands on my neck once."

Tony looked startled, then angry. "You shouldn't tell me things like that. Because if I ever see him again, I'll — "

"No — I just want to forget about it. But I know *you'd* never do anything like that. That's why I feel safe with you." She snuggled up to him.

He smiled gently. "That's not the declaration of love I was hoping for. But I guess it's a start."

"You're very nice, Tony."

"Nice and safe. But not very exciting." The hurt in his voice was apparent.

Suddenly Judith looked at Tony and she actually saw him: Tony, the man, with his own pride and vanity, his own tastes and desires, his own wisdom and expertise, his own gentle masculinity and sense of humor. He had always been so kind that she had failed to really see him. He had focused so ardently on her, and erased himself so skillfully, that he had effectively disappeared. Suddenly she felt a flood of love for this utterly decent man, and a twinge of guilt at her own selfishness.

"I didn't mean it that way. Oh, Tony, I've been so unfair to you! I should have married you instead of Gavin. I don't know why I didn't."

"Maybe you're afraid of happiness."

"Could that be it?"

"Or maybe I'm just too well adjusted for you. I'm not a project, something you can fix."

"How did you get to be so wise?" she asked, gazing into his beautiful, long-lashed eyes.

"By observing you. You're not that difficult to read."

"Is that an insult?"

"No, darling. It's what makes you fascinating. You're so expressive and alive. I admire your spirit."

"Maybe you admire me too much. I'm not used to being loved and admired. I thought Gavin loved me, but he didn't."

"Don't worry. You'll get used to being loved. I guarantee it."

Judith fell silent, contemplating his words. She should have been touched by them, but she was afraid of them. She couldn't afford to lay herself bare to the scrutiny of Tony's love. He was a "normal" person, and she had never been able to please normal people, who inevitably grew disenchanted or disgusted with her. She was too obsessive — too dark for Tony. She was pathological, excessive, manic, morose, perverse, needy. How long before he saw these traits and ceased to love her?

Tony was nuzzling his feet against hers. Suddenly he stopped, staring down. "What's that on your feet — mud?"

"Yes. I was . . . I went for a walk this morning."

He smiled. "Barefoot? You really are a wild thing."

Judith wondered if Tony would still marry her if he knew she had just run like a madwoman after Gavin's phantom, hoping to be taken in his arms. He would probably forgive her, as he always did, and the thought made her sad. Tony was too good for her; she didn't deserve him.

They lay there like that for a while, quietly holding hands, and then he untied the sash of her dressing gown and admired her beautiful body. He kissed her breasts and stomach and thighs until she craved him desperately, and they made love again. And this time when she looked at Tony, she saw and experienced him as himself, and she was not disappointed. But at the same time, she felt ashamed of her adulterous behavior.

Afterwards, as she and Tony lay quietly in each other's arms, she saw the curtains rustle, and she was seized with the irrational terror that she was being watched by a pair of demonic, glowing red eyes.

24.

The Curse

A cleaning crew came in and got the castle back in shape, and Tony drove back to London, promising to return on his next day off. Judith spent her days working on her novel, reading, walking, and riding Valancourt, and Anne spent her days walking and riding with Judith (she *adored* Montoni), binging television shows, shooting selfies in the castle and grounds and on the horse, watching videos, posting on social media, texting friends, chatting with John, doing vigorous dance exercise, and knitting.

During these weeks, Judith really came to appreciate Anne. Their small talk was banal, and the time they spent together unremarkable, but she was deeply grateful that her sister had taken time off from her busy life to be with her. Anne was not particularly empathetic or loving, and she could be shockingly shallow at times, but she was still family, and Judith knew that her weaknesses weren't entirely her fault. All throughout their childhood Judith had been insanely jealous of Anne's relationship with their mother, but now she could see that Anne had paid a steep price for playing the role of golden child to a narcissist. Anne had not been allowed to function as a person in her own right, but only as an extension of her mother, who had expected to have the same control over Anne that normal people expect to have over their own arm or leg. For even as she became a facsimile of her mother, and her greatest admirer, she remained a mechanical robot limb, an inferior copy. And her mother was her harshest critic: "Anne, that top makes your breasts look droopy!" or, "Anne, you're getting freckles! Stay out of the sun!" When her mother gazed into Narcissus's mirror and saw Anne reflected, she demanded to see an image as perfect as her own. Because of this, Anne had never fully developed her own identity; her identity was whatever her mother wished it to be. And what was that? Merely a girl. A lovely girl. A lovely, obedient, charming girl.

So Anne could be vapid, but her vapidity was a highly polished object, crafted to please. Sometimes Judith caught glimpses of a more complex personality beneath Anne's blank exterior. But she seemed contented with the life she had chosen, and her beauty, and the attention it elicited, gave her great pleasure. In a way Anne was similar to her sister, constructing her life around the desire to be loved in the way that was easiest for her, just as Judith had done. Only Anne's currency was her beauty, and Judith's was her brain, as adults had constantly pointed out to them in their childhood, irreparably shaping both of their destinies. They had cut each little girl in half, telling her she could be either body or mind, but not both, and each child had been permanently imprinted with her perceived inadequacy.

Whether Anne's shallowness was natural or something forced on her by duress, Judith felt that she personally benefited from her sister's insistence on keeping conversations light, superficial, and amusing. With Anne, she could be *girly*, and it's difficult to express how much that meant to her. Their badinage took her mind off more serious things, and she came to see it as a relaxing form of self-care, like going to the spa. Because she had never been allowed to be a girl when she was growing up, sharing girl time with Anne was profoundly pleasurable, and she finally felt part of the much-coveted girls' club she had always yearned to belong to.

Several days after the ball, Anne and Judith were taking afternoon tea in the little walled garden, in pastel frocks and wide-brimmed hats. Suddenly, Anne turned to Judith. "Why didn't you tell me your house was haunted?"

Judith looked at her sister with interest, hoping she'd find out more about the haunted castle than she already knew. "Who told you that?" she asked, spooning gobs of strawberry jam on her Victoria sponge cake.

"Loads of people were talking about it at the party," returned Anne, grabbing a cucumber and watercress sandwich from a gilded Limoges plate. "Didn't you hear them talking?"

"No, I didn't really speak to anyone except Tony. What were they saying?"

Anne sipped her tea. "Well, *apparently*, the lady you have hanging over your fireplace was murdered right here in this very castle by her husband. And ever since, she's been wandering the halls, and rattling her chains, and crying. Have you heard her?"

Judith put down her fork. "Well, I've heard some eerie sounds around the castle at night, but I'm sure it's just an effect of the wind. Anyway, that legend is on all the tourist websites. I thought you might have heard something new."

"Well," continued Anne with relish, wiping her pretty mouth with a napkin, "Valentina said that according to the local people, the castle is *cursed*."

"Cursed?" For some reason, the word caused a chill to pass through her bones. She felt as though someone had been whispering it in her ear for months. But where had she heard it — in her sleep? From the weeping ghost dragging its chains in the hall? She tried to appear calm, but her voice sounded stiff and unnatural. "Cursed? How so?"

"Because of all the tragedies. A lot of young brides have died here. And according to the legend, they see the ghost of Lady Mordaunt just before they die!"

Judith had once fetishized the idea of living in a haunted castle, but such fancies no longer felt romantic; they just felt creepy. And she felt sick at the thought that she herself might have become a dead bride that night in the woods, if her husband had actually squeezed her neck instead of just pretending to. "All old houses have tragedies," she said. "And women died young in those days — in childbirth, and from various fevers and diseases."

"But don't you think it's queer that so many brides died here?" persisted Anne. "In 1972, a bride hung herself from the bell tower just after she saw the ghost. And the Duke of Belfort's wife died here in an accident just five years ago. Supposedly she fell out of the window. But what if she saw the ghost and jumped . . . or what if *he* saw the ghost and *pushed* her?"

Judith laughed, and her voice sounded hollow and shrill. "That's utter bollocks! I've met the duke, and he'd never do anything like that. And if she jumped, she must have been depressed or mentally ill."

"So you don't believe in the curse?"

Judith picked apart her cake with her fingers. "No. Every old house has ghost legends, but there's never anything really convincing." And then the harrowing reality of her life with her husband welled up within her, and she blurted out, "But Gavin *did* start behaving like a medieval tyrant as soon as we got here!" She uttered a dry little laugh, as if it had been a joke.

Anne's jaw dropped. "Ooh, that's wicked! Do you think he's possessed by the spirit of the murderous baron?"

"He might be," said Judith facetiously. "And I'm probably possessed by poor Lady Mordaunt, because I'm definitely a woman in peril!"

Anne put down her teacup abruptly, and it clattered loudly in the saucer. "So does that mean you believe in the curse?"

Judith grew thoughtful. She had never believed in ghosts or curses, but there was definitely something off about the house, and she felt sure it had changed them in sinister ways. "No," she said slowly. "I'm not superstitious. But I think houses have auras . . . and that Gavin and I have been affected by the energy of the castle's bloody past."

Anne shuddered. "That sounds kind of dark," she said.

A week later, Judith's father secured a solicitor to handle her divorce, a Miss Mary Crumpet, and Judith drove up to

Soho to meet her. She had never met anyone with the name Crumpet before, but Mary Crumpet had formerly been a burlesque queen, so the name may have been chosen for its saucy connotations. But as she sat at Berners Tavern around the corner eating mac and cheese and downing two martinis, she thought, if it's a burlesque name, then why *Mary*? Can it be possible that her name is actually *Crumpet*?

Arriving at the solicitor's office after her luncheon, pleasantly sloshed, Judith met Miss Crumpet, an attractive redhead with an hourglass figure, glamorously coiffed and attired. After they had exchanged pleasantries, the two ladies sat on either side of the solicitor's desk in front of a bay window overlooking a row of quaint shops and restaurants. Judith discussed her finances, expressing concern that she might owe Gavin spousal maintenance.

The solicitor looked surprised. "Anything preventing him from working? A disability?"

"No. It's just that he doesn't like to work."

"Oh, dear! He's that type, is he? No, Luv, you won't owe him anything. Do you share any bank accounts or credit cards?"

"Not anymore. He can't be trusted with money. I had him on a fixed allowance, but he was always asking for more. I don't know how he's living now. I thought about sending him some cash, but the bloodsucker is probably already leeching off another woman."

Miss Crumpet threw back her head and laughed for two minutes straight. Judith laughed too, releasing a flood of pent-up anxiety. "What a clown!" shrieked the solicitor. "So he's a male gold digger, is he?"

"I suppose so," answered Judith, trying to recover from her fit of laughter and wiping her tears with a handkerchief. "But he *did* have some money before we were married. He made the deposit on the castle, and he paid for our honeymoon, and he bought me some jewelry—real diamonds and rubies—and a ton of designer clothing."

"He bought you diamonds and rubies, and a *castle*, Luv? If he doesn't have any income, how do you think he got the money?"

Judith furrowed her brow. "I don't know. At first I thought he'd inherited it, or earned it as a businessman, or in the stock market. But now I know that was all lies."

Suddenly it dawned on her where the money had come from. She remembered Montgomery's words: *If you ask me, I think he married his last wife for her money. She was an heiress.* She said, "You know what, I believe he got the money from his ex-wife."

After they went over a few more details, the session ended with Miss Crumpet assuring Judith that she was in a good position to keep all of her own assets.

Judith drove home in high spirits. She had made the first step towards getting rid of her rotten, worthless husband, and it was a great feeling.

But as soon as she turned into the driveway and saw the Gothic castle looming before her, her exhilaration disappeared, and her spirits sank at the thought that her beautiful life with her fraudulent baron was over forever. How could she live here, in her fairy-tale castle, with Tony? He wasn't a "castle" person at all. Besides, he had a busy practice in London; he would never agree to move down here and become a country doctor. She had lived her dream, and it had been beautiful while it lasted, but it was over.

As she trudged lugubriously up the drive, past the stone lions, and up the wide steps to the castle doors, she felt incredibly depressed. For although she was aware that he was a worthless gigolo, she still couldn't shake her obsession with her mad, bad, dangerous baron.

She entered the drawing room and rang for tea, and Jane brought the tray. She absently spread jam on a scone, having intended to put the cream before the jam. "Bloody hell!" she cried, flinging it across the room. She hadn't felt so cross for a long time, and she rose and paced to and fro. As she stormed around the room, her glance kept returning to the bewitching portrait of Lady Mordaunt, whose eyes were admonishing her. Men are no good, they seemed to say. He's not worth it. Get rid of him!

As she watched the lady's haunting orbs following her eerily around the room, she felt more and more agitated. Who was this lady to tell her what to do? What did *she* know about Judith's life, and her Great Love?

Suddenly she felt terribly alone, and she missed her husband with an aching urgency. The thought that she would never again feel his touch was intolerable, and she wished he would sweep into the room, take her in his arms, and ravish her.

But as soon as she allowed this fantasy to take hold of her, she felt a strong self-disgust, knowing that her love for such an evil man was unwholesome and unclean. My husband is gone, and I'm safe now, she thought. So why do I long for his return? Is the curse working on my mind to speed my destruction? Has fate situated me in this blood-soaked castle to repeat, with my own life, the tragic destiny of the unfortunate Lady Mordaunt?

Just as she was sinking beneath the weight of these fancies, her phone rang. It was Anne, ringing her from the garden. "Would you like to take a walk, Judith? It's lovely out."

Judith was greatly relieved by the distraction. "I need to change. See you in a bit."

A few minutes later, the sisters were rambling by the pond, wearing ruffled dresses and high-heeled sandals, and carrying embroidered white parasols to protect them from the sun. Swans glided across the water, creating an atmosphere of fairylike enchantment, and there were clear views to the forest, and to the expanse of blue hills beyond. What fun to be a pretty girl, in a pretty dress, carrying a parasol on a sunny afternoon, thought Judith. It makes me feel innocent again. I haven't felt pure in ages, but now I'm determined to reclaim my lost innocence!

And yet she wondered if she would ever be clean again, after having received the vampire's kiss.

Then Anne broke into her reverie to ask her how it had gone with Miss Crumpet.

"She was brilliant. Seeing Gavin through her eyes made me see what a complete clown he is. A male gold digger! I can't think of anything more despicable."

Anne stopped and stared at her. "So it's not just you he's sponging off?"

"No. I think he embezzled money from his ex-wife, who's an heiress."

"Maybe he's still in *love* with her," said Anne, pursing her lips knowingly. "Maybe he's gone *back* to her."

Judith gaped at her sister in shock. "Do you think so?"

The model shrugged. "Why not? Especially if she's an heiress."

"I never thought of that." A pang of jealousy stabbed Judith's heart as she imagined Gavin kissing another woman, making love to her, flattering her, deceiving her. Yes, even that. How dare he dupe another woman!

They strolled a bit more, picking their way through the tall grass. Judith glanced over at Anne in her summer dress, and she couldn't believe how pretty she was: sun-kissed freckles, pouting lips, long, thick hair, winsome waist, dreamy blue eyes . . . the type old men creep over, and teen girls tear out of magazines and pin up on the wall. Then she thought of something. "Anne, do you remember Montgomery? He said he used to model with you."

Anne's face lit up. "Oh, yes, Montgomery! He came to the party with some of the models. He's *such* a sweetheart."

"Do you have his number?"

"No, but I can get it. Why?"

"Well, he knows Gavin's ex-wife, and I'd like to speak to her."

"I think Holly has it. I'll give her a ring."

When they returned to the castle, Anne texted Holly and got Montgomery's number, and she handed it to Judith on a pretty lavender-scented scrap of paper.

25.

You Can't Speak to Constance

Judith flounced up the stairs to her bedroom. Finding her frilly frock stiff and confining, she flung it on the bed and donned a blue chiffon peignoir set and matching slippers. Then she fixed herself a whisky highball and put on the Rachmaninoff piano concerto from *Brief Encounter*.

Sipping her cocktail as the music ebbed and swelled, she stood at the window and gazed at the darkening woods, which the setting sun streaked with blood. Suddenly, the abjectness of her situation seized her: she was a woman living alone in a castle, with only a handful of taciturn domestics, who secretly envied and despised her, for human company. What would become of her once Anne left? Would she slowly go mad? Her future with Tony suddenly seemed unreal to her. She would die here, alone and unloved; she would never leave the castle.

Oppressed by a dreary solitude, she fetched her phone and called Montgomery.

"Hello, this is Judith — Gavin's wife," she said. "We met at a ball the other night."

"Judith! I'm so glad you called. I wanted to apologize for all of those things I said the other night."

She clung to a wild hope. "You mean they weren't true?"

"No, they *were* true. But it wasn't nice to throw it all at you at once like that."

"That's all right," she sighed, with crushing disappointment. "But I wanted to ask you: do you have Constance's number? Because I'd like to speak to her."

"I'm sorry, but that's impossible."

"Oh! Well, I'm not going to harass her. It's just . . . I think Gavin may owe her some money, and I want to see if I can help."

"You can't speak to Constance," he said in a strange, muffled tone.

"Why not?"

There was a silence, so long and drawn out that Judith's mind began to fragment into a web of tortured fears. And then he said, "Because Constance is dead."

"*Dead?*" cried Judith, collapsing onto a Chippendale armchair. "How did she die?"

"It was an accident. She slipped and cracked her skull in the bath. Such a tragedy."

She gasped. "In the bath? Are they sure it was an accident?"

"Yes. Tragic, isn't it? She was so young."

"I see." She was too upset to continue, so she said, "Thanks for your help," and she hung up.

Her head splitting, she sank into the cushions of her armchair as night succeeded day, her hands clutching the armrests, waiting for her heart to stop pounding.

Constance was dead. She had fallen in the bath. People slipped and fell all the time; there was nothing sinister about that. At least, not normally. But nothing about her husband and his relations with women was normal.

After sitting paralyzed with doubt and fear for what seemed like an eternity, she plucked up courage and rang Montgomery again. "Sorry to bother you," she said. "But do you happen to know Constance's last name?"

"Yes, it's Somers, with an *o*. I remembered it because Sammy — Gavin, I mean — said they needed to be married in the summer, because her name was Somers." He laughed in spite of himself.

Judith winced at the bad pun. "Thanks very much."

She stood up and switched on the lamps. Then she took a deep breath and typed into her phone, "Constance Somers obituary." A news story came up right away. It was just a little notice in the *Sunday Times*, and it read:

SOMERS HEIRESS, 28,
DIES IN FREAK BATH ACCIDENT

Constance Somers, 28, heiress to the Somers fortune, was at her home in Fitzroy Square when the tragic accident occurred. She failed to show up for a dinner date with her fiancé Michael Wilding on Friday night, 30 October, and he had been unable to reach her since Friday afternoon. On Sunday he called 999, and the police went to her home to investigate.

When officers entered her townhouse with Wilding on Sunday afternoon, they found Somers lying dead in the cast iron bath. An investigation determined that she had slipped and cracked her skull, and that she subsequently died by drowning.

Ms. Somers was a fashion illustrator, and she is survived by her parents, James and Diana Somers, and by her brother, Percy Somers.

Judith, already startled at the discovery of Constance's death, became alarmed almost beyond belief. She went to the window and leaned on the sill, drinking in the night air and trying to think.

Constance had died on the 30th of October, the day before Halloween. Gavin had returned from London that night in the blackest of moods, so she had refrained from mentioning Constance's photo. And the next day, when she showed it to him, he went half mad with rage. He'd said he had lost his temper because he was upset by Constance's picture. But what if he was upset because *he had just murdered her?*

She turned back into the room, her head screaming, her heart pounding, her insides revolting. Her husband was a murderer who had killed at least one wife, and if he got the chance, he would kill her too. He was *literally Bluebeard!*

Trembling with emotion, she rang the police. But as soon as she heard a voice at the other end, she hung up. What proof did she have that Gavin had killed her? Her manner of death had been ascertained. What evidence would she need to have the case reopened? Maybe I should contact her parents, she thought. But what would I say . . . I think my husband murdered your daughter, because the day she died, he was in a beastly mood? Besides, it would only dredge up painful memories of her death. And what if I get them to do an autopsy, and I'm wrong?

She swallowed some pills and paced the room, turning over in her mind any potential motives he may have had for killing Constance. Money? Hate? To escape prosecution? To shut her up? But then she laughed at herself for these conjectures. He may have been a liar, a fraud, and a gigolo, but he wasn't a *psychopath*. And only a psychopath could have murdered his ex-wife and then returned home a few hours later with nothing more than a cross mood to show for it. The idea was patently ridiculous! But even as she stood there laughing at her absurdity, she was still badly shaken, and not fully convinced.

Deeply agitated, she went to the bar to fix another drink. As she plunked ice cubes into the glass, she thought, all right, so maybe he *didn't* kill Constance, but he's still *capable* of murder. And as the whisky glugged over the ice, she thought, most people could never kill, but *he* could. I saw it in his face in that cruel look he gave me when we were driving up to the castle, and when we had that terrible row, and when he tried to strangle me . . .

She gasped, and the glass slipped from her hand and fell to the carpet, splashing its contents over her nightgown. Up until now, she had successfully banished the word *strangle* from her mind, telling herself that he had only put his hands on her neck, or shaken her; but now the ugly truth of that night burst like a battering ram into her consciousness.

And then she saw his demonic red face, and his eyes glowing with a murderous rage as he tried to choke the life out of her, and she collapsed to the floor in a heap.

As she lay convulsing on the carpet, she had a latent memory of pain. The pain of his hands crushing her windpipe. The pain of feeling she was going to die.

The pain of being murdered.

She staggered to her feet, careened over to the bed, and flung herself upon it. She wept until there were no more tears, heaving and moaning, her throat sore, her eyes swollen, her temples on fire, every muscle and joint aching. She had never wanted to die so much as at this moment, when she had to face the fact that her husband had thought of her as a disposable object, to be done away with simply because she had dared to ask a question. How can I have continued to love him all this time, she lamented, when he values me so little that he tried to murder me? Why did I imagine I could fix a man like that? Because I believe in my own power to tame the untamable? What sort of hubris is that? Or is it some insanity that comes from reading too many Gothic novels? He's not a romantic hero. He's a monster—the Monster of Manderfield!

After she had wept her guts out, she stared at the ceiling, her eyes blazing defiantly in her white, wratihlike face, and she thought, but I'm *not* insane—I forgave him because I loved him. And I loved him because he's handsome and charming and sweet. I suppose he *is* a romantic hero in his way; but he's the shadow side. He's not the Heathcliff who loved Cathy—he's the Heathcliff who hated and abused his wife Isabella. He's not the Max de Winter who loved his new bride, but the Max de Winter who murdered his first wife, Rebecca. He's not the Rochester who loved Jane—he's the Rochester who locked his mad wife Bertha up in the attic.

Where is the wife's side of the story in these novels? We only have the husband's side. The husband who wishes to discard an inconvenient wife. *Me.* I'm that wife.

She was too distraught to go down to supper, so Jane brought the tray to her room, shocked at her dreadful appearance. Judith was repelled by the sight and smell of the loin of venison with Bordelaise sauce, the truffled potatoes *au gratin*, the glazed Vichy carrots, and the *petits pois aux lardons*, and she refused to touch it. But Jane urged her to take something, so she pushed the food around with her fork. And then she said, "I have dined. You may take the tray," and her tone was so final that the housekeeper obeyed her and left her to herself.

Her mind was a blank, and all she could focus on was the distant sound of the dogs baying at the moon. Were they lonely for their master, as she had been before she realized that he had tried to murder her? She lay there staring at nothing, in a torpor of abjection. And then the deluge came once more, and she wailed in her agony and loneliness, wetting the sheets with her tears. Finally she fell into an agitated slumber, and she had a nightmare.

26.

It Was Just an Addiction

She was standing in a white nightgown with Gavin in the hall of a medieval castle, before a roaring fire. He turned and frowned at her, looking handsome in a blue doublet and hose with a sweeping cape, his eyes monstrous and cruel. "Yes, Judith, I did strangle you," he said. "This time I spared your life, but the next time you stick your nose into my affairs, I'll kill you."

He dangled a large set of keys before her. "I am going on a long journey. Here are the keys to the castle. Go anywhere you like, except the chamber at the end of the hall that this key fits. That door must remain locked. If you're tempted to open it, just remember what happened when you went through my photo book."

Then he glared at her under his dark brows, dropped the keys into her hands, and stalked away into the night. Soon the door slammed, and she was alone.

She stared into the flames, trembling with indignation. "His precious photo book! His stupid locked room! Men and their horrors! He can't scare *me*. Bloody hell! I'm going in."

She picked up a silver candelabra and moved swiftly down the gallery to the forbidden chamber. As she turned the little key in the lock, the door swung back into a cavernous blackness. She crept around the room, her candles creating stars of light as they glanced off thousands of sparkling jewels and gold and silver coins in countless bowls and chests.

Then her tapers illuminated five female mannequins piled on the floor, their limbs twisted together. They wore jewel-colored gowns and synthetic wigs, and there was blood on their plastic throats and over the fronts of their gowns, dripping down and pooling on the floor.

She heard a squeaking sound, and she looked up to see a mannequin in a long blonde wig gliding towards her on wheels, its arms outstretched. It wore a tattered white gown crimsoned all over with blood, its full sleeves hanging in shreds, its fiberglass face sporting blue glitter eyeshadow and long, thick lashes. A garnet ring gleamed on its finger. As it slid forward, dozens of candles and sconces lit themselves, and the room dazzled with light. Then it transformed into the living Constance.

The other mannequins likewise came alive. They stretched their arms, yawned, and opened their eyes as if waking from sleep. Then they rose eerily and distributed themselves around the room posing on little pedestals, their pretty mascara-fringed eyes alert and watchful.

"You're Constance, aren't you?" asked Judith, marveling at the ghoul's lovely face, with its sharp cheekbones, perfect lips, wide blue eyes, and painted-on mannequin makeup.

When Constance spoke, her voice was ghostlike and dreadful. "Yes. Our husband murdered me and put me in the bath. He murdered us all. You're next."

"Why did he kill you?"

"Because we discovered his secret. Do you know what a man's secret is? It's that he wants us dead, but he also wants our love."

The dead brides stepped hypnotically off their pedestals and glided forward. They opened a gilded chest and removed from it a silver gown, some silver slippers, and a diamond necklace and crown, all of it smeared and stained with blood.

Then they slid nightmarishly towards Judith, pulling the bloody dress over her head, slipping the bloody slippers onto her feet, fastening the diamond necklace around her neck, and placing the glittering crown on her head.

As the weight of the jewels crushed her down, her eyes opened wide with shock, and she became dead like the others. The brides smiled and laughed, and their teeth were black and rotten.

"Now you are dead," said Constance. "Do you know our husband's name? It is Bluebeard."

Judith awoke in a cold sweat, just before dawn. Her heart was still pounding, and her dream gave her an oddly terrified feeling. For days she was haunted by images of the beautiful dead Constance, and the ghastly dead brides.

She tried to think what her dream reminded her of, and she realized it was the Italian thriller *Blood and Black Lace*, which she had watched recently with Anne. The fashion models in the film who are murdered one by one, and dragged by their pretty long hair across the grounds of Italian castles, resembled the dead brides in her dream. Anne had adored the film, but Judith hadn't cared for it. She loved beautiful actresses, but she preferred to watch them alive and speaking interesting dialogue, rather than mute and dead. She always thought about characters you weren't supposed to think about: the girls and women who are murdered in slasher films rather than the final girl, the mad wife Bertha who throws herself from the roof rather than the victorious Jane Eyre.

Over the next few months, Judith and Tony grew closer. They hadn't made love since the morning after the party, since Judith wanted to wait until the divorce was final. But they chastely kissed, and watched movies, and took meals and tea together, and went on long walks, and rode the horses, whenever Tony could get away from the hospital. She made him watch awful B movies like *Berserk!* and *The Legend of Lylah Clare*, and he was a very good sport about it, laughing and groaning in all the right places. His easy laugh, the gentleness of his disposition, the consistency of his moods, and his relaxed attentiveness, all had a tonic effect on her rattled nerves. Being with him was *natural*. With Tony, she didn't have to be anything in particular, and she never felt any pressure to perform; whereas with Gavin, everything had been a performance, including — or especially — sex.

Sometimes during sex he had taken out his phone and filmed her, issuing orders like a director on a set. She had often fantasized about becoming an actress, and she was chagrined to think that her only roles thus far had been her pornographic performances for his camera. She hadn't minded being filmed; it had made her feel beautiful and desirable, and there had been something deliciously dirty about it. He even played the footage back to her sometimes and critiqued her performance, telling her to remember where the light was, and to project her voice "beyond the footlights." Even outside the bedroom they were like two actors performing roles, as the line between reality and fantasy was often blurred. But although she was always able to remove the greasepaint after the show, with him there was no face behind the mask. He seemed to have no center from which his character sprang, and this made him appear insubstantial and hollow. He was a fake, just like the castle—a thing constructed purely for effect.

Tony, on the other hand, was a real person, with real character, and his love for her was also real. He loved her no matter what she said or did or how she looked; in fact, he seemed to prefer it when she didn't take any special pains with her appearance. Often she didn't bother with makeup at all anymore, and she went out with her face raw and clean. She even wore plain, mismatched underthings, knowing no one would ever see them. With Tony she felt like a human being, rather than a sex worker catering to the fantasies of a punter, and it was glorious.

One day they were out riding together, and the horses had slowed to a gentle walk through the dappled woods. She felt especially contented, and she said, "You know, Tony, I'm finally starting to feel like myself again."

"I've noticed. You seem much happier lately. It's wonderful to see."

"You know what I was just thinking . . . I was thinking

that if I hadn't met Gavin that day in Cornwall, you and I probably would have got married."

He raised an eyebrow. "Why do you say that?"

"Because I think that eventually we would have got back together and worked things out. I didn't think we had any chemistry, but when you approached me that day to find out, I was too shy to have sex with you."

"You weren't too shy to have sex with *him*," he grunted, more than a little annoyed.

"Yes. But that's because he didn't give me a choice. When he seized me and looked at me I sort of broke down, and I didn't feel my will was my own anymore. It was either flight or surrender, and I surrendered."

Tony was silent for a moment as he processed his feelings. "Now I hate him even more," he said, his mouth hardening. "You're telling me that he raped you."

The finality of his statement crushed her. "I suppose so. I've been trying to tell myself that I was bewitched, or seduced. The whole thing has been so humiliating." And a tear rolled down her cheek.

"There's nothing to be ashamed of. It wasn't your fault."

"I know. Things have been really difficult. I lost myself for a while, but now I'm back."

"Welcome back," he said, and his gentle, masculine smile was like a flame warming her heart.

They continued riding through the woods, listening to the rhythmic thud of the horses' hooves. "Now that I'm no longer under Gavin's spell, I wonder what I saw in him," she said. "But I think it was just an addiction."

"Yes. You have the same symptoms as an alcoholic or a drug addict: an ecstatic high, followed by a harrowing crash, comedown, or rebound, and an intense desire to repeat the process over again."

"That sounds accurate. But I think the poison of him is slowly starting to exit my veins."

"Good girl."

They fell silent again. She was glad she could speak to Tony so freely, and yet she was sorry she had told him. He didn't need to hear about her addiction to Gavin. Why did she torture him with such information? She was unaware of any intentional cruelty on her part, but she made a mental note to be more tactful in the future. Tony seemed like a man who could take anything, and yet every man has his breaking point.

The thing she hadn't told him, and never would, was that she was a typical addict, in that detoxification from the addictive substance required complete abstinence. As long as she didn't see Gavin or hear his voice, the cure would go as planned. Seeing him would be like giving a sip of wine to an alcoholic, and the cycle would start all over again.

27.

The Sex Ghost

Judith was surprised when Miss Crumpet informed her that Gavin wasn't planning to contest any of the terms of the divorce. He had behaved like a perfect gentleman throughout the proceedings — the ex–burlesque queen had found him exceptionally charming and attractive — and his graciousness made Judith wonder if she'd committed an injustice by characterizing him as a heartless gigolo. The entire affair had been handled by their solicitors, so she'd had no contact with him since their separation, and she was glad to be rid of him.

Yet her mind, which should have felt exhilarated at its freedom from its shackles, remained shrouded in gloom. She wrote pages and pages each day — mostly, tortured monologues from the depths of her heroine's soul — but the hero had disappeared, and without him, there was no story. So she laid aside *Bluebeard's Castle* and started a new novel, *Murder on the Moors*. Her insomnia became nearly intolerable during this period, and she lost nearly all interest in food, eating only the bare minimum to sustain her; except for puddings and sweets, which she devoured ravenously.

A week before Judith's divorce was to become final, Anne announced that she had received a modeling offer she couldn't refuse. It was one of those surrealist "Fantasy and Fashion" spreads in *Vogue* magazine, and it was to be photographed and styled by friends of hers. Judith urged her to return to London with her blessing, but Tony was extremely worried about leaving Judith alone in the castle.

The morning of Anne's departure, the two girls walked to Anne's car, each carrying several pieces of luggage, with Tony trailing behind, carrying several more.

The sisters hugged. "Thanks for everything, Anne! I'm going to miss you."

"Me too. I'm sorry I have to leave. But I think you can manage on your own now."

"Yes, I'm sure I can."

"Anyway, I'll give you a ring tomorrow and check up on you."

"All right. But really, I'll be fine."

Anne climbed into her black Bentley Continental. "Don't do anything I wouldn't do!" she said, laughing.

The couple watched as she zoomed away. Then Tony turned to his fiancée with a frown. "I've got to get to the hospital. Are you sure you'll be all right?"

"Of course."

"I could cancel my patients for the day."

"That's ridiculous. They need you."

"Then come with me to London and stay at my flat."

"I have too many things to take care of. I'll come live with you as soon as the divorce is final."

"We should have hired you a companion. I don't like the idea of leaving you here alone."

"I'm not alone. The domestics are here."

He smiled wanly. "All right. Take care of yourself, sweetheart."

They kissed, and Tony got into his car and drove away. Judith looked after him sadly, feeling a slow panic creep over her. I should have gone to London with Tony, she thought. Something terrible is going to happen. She stood there, paralyzed with fear. And then she gazed around at the majesty of her surroundings, and she realized she was being ridiculous. Here she was, chatelaine of her own castle, with her own staff about. What could happen? Her husband had not contacted her in over three months. He didn't want her, and she didn't want him. She had nothing to fear; she was free. She breathed the crisp air in long draughts, feeling mistress of herself again, and she strode into the castle.

She made her way up to her bedroom and collapsed on the window seat. She had a hangover, and she'd had nothing to eat that morning, and little the day before, so she thought she was going to faint. But then she recovered, and she gazed disconsolately out of the window at the garden. She reminisced about the many times she had watched Gavin striding across it, beagles in tow, the animals he had just slaughtered slung over his shoulder. She missed him achingly, and she could no longer bear the sight of the resplendent landscape below, which now seemed bereft of all beauty and charm.

She turned away from the window and reclined on her bed. Again, she had that queer feeling of loneliness that had plagued her just minutes before. She hadn't been without Anne or Tony since Gavin had departed, and their absence left her dangerously vulnerable to self-delusion and uncontrollable, demonic desires. Now that Tony was gone, she no longer recognized the girl who had been so fearful and confused about Gavin's seduction of her. So what if he had forced her into sex? All that meant was that he had been unable to control his desires, so overwhelmed had he been by her charms. She wouldn't have had him spare her for the world! Not every girl could inspire a man to that kind of passion, but she was the most beautiful girl he had ever seen — she was his naughty Lolita! What man could have resisted her?

She panted with lust and ran her hands along her body as she remembered how he had deflowered her. She longed to feel his hands on her, tearing off her clothes, caressing her flesh, and sweeping her into a world of forbidden pleasure. She had been bitten by the vampire, and no reason or logic, not even fear of death, could keep her away from him.

An uncertain amount of time passed as she became lost in the wildest sexual fantasies, until eventually, exhausted from lack of sleep and nutrition, she dozed off.

Suddenly, she was jolted from slumber by the distant sound of dogs barking. She sat up in bed, listening. The din became louder and louder, and soon she perceived that it was coming from the garden.

Rushing to the window, she saw two beagles barking joyously, their tails wagging behind them, and Gavin alongside them, grinning at her with that devilish smile of his. She called out, "Gavin!" but he didn't respond, and he and the dogs disappeared from sight as they passed beneath the eaves of the house.

"I knew he'd come!" she cried. Smoldering with desire, she removed her clothes and slipped into her prettiest lingerie. Then she sat at her dressing table, spritzed on perfume, and put on her makeup, quivering with anticipation.

Soon she heard his heavy tread on the stair, and she glanced expectantly towards the door. He entered, movie-star handsome, and plopped his shotgun and rabbits on the table. He looked at her without a word, admiring her body as she slipped out of her robe and posed for him in her Paris lingerie.

He came towards her and seized her by the shoulders, kissing and caressing her roughly and pulling her down to the bed. She moaned and writhed as his strong hands gripped her, and he covered her with kisses in a fury of passion. And then he entered her, and the intensity of her passion, and her weakened state, proved too much for her, and she blacked out.

When she came to, he was gone. She gazed at the spot on the bed where he had been, missing him with an ache in her heart. Looking up woozily, she saw no trace of him. The only signs that he'd been there were the sticky emission on her thighs, and the lingering scent of sex and sandalwood soap.

She rose, dressed, consumed a Miss Crumpet with butter and jam, and searched for him all over the house, and then in the garden and the woods, but she found no trace either of him or his car. Then she returned gloomily to her bedroom and lay down, exhausted. She rang Jane and asked her if she'd seen Gavin; she had not. So Sarah was fetched, and James, and Esther, and Jonathan, and Philip. But no one had seen a car pull up, nor Gavin himself since he had departed months before.

She dismissed the staff, feeling depressed and disoriented. Gavin had come back, and he had made passionate love to her. He was hers once more. But *where was he?*

She lay in bed as afternoon turned into evening, and evening into night. She had nothing for supper but a chocolate croissant, and she finished the decanter of whisky. Finally she drifted off, but her sleep was troubled by dark desires, and she tossed and turned, whispering Gavin's name. She awoke in agitation, listening to the wind sighing and moaning, the thunder clapping, the rain beating down on the windowpanes, and the rusty iron gate clanking in the wind. She stared lustfully into the night, thinking about her lover.

A few moments later she heard soft footsteps, and he entered quietly and stood gazing at her from the edge of the bed. Her eyes glittered as she took in the sight of him. He said nothing, but only ravished her with his eyes.

Then he climbed in next to her, and she inhaled his maddening scent. He touched and kissed her with the greatest passion, and she felt his wondrous lips against hers, filling her with sublime ecstasy. They made love, and it was both painful and pleasurable, as he took her to dark and dangerous places with his ruthless manliness. She was addicted to his body, and she was his wife; she couldn't believe she had ever let another man touch her. She was his alone, and she always would be. Afterwards, she wrapped her arms around him. "Darling! Where did you go? You left me all alone. Don't leave me again!" And she wept tears of sorrow and joy and dozed off in his arms.

When she opened her eyes, he was gone. "Gavin, my love!" she shrieked. "Where are you? Please come back!" The tears trickled down her face, and she felt more alone than ever. She knew she hadn't dreamed him; his intoxicating scent still lingered, and every inch of her body was alive with the sensual memory of him. But where did he keep disappearing to? And why was he so strange, never speaking to her, but only materializing in her bed in order to ravish her?

Just as she was about to get up and search for him, she saw him again. He was across the room, gliding silently along with his arms outstretched stiffly, and then disappearing into the hall. She screamed. It wasn't Gavin . . . it was a ghost! He had never been there at all. Each time he had visited her and made love to her, it had only been his phantom!

Now she *knew* the castle was haunted. Over the past few months, she had come to believe that the dark energy of the house had worked upon their imaginations to transform her husband into a Byronic villain, and herself into a woman in peril. But she had never believed that it was *literally haunted*. She had always told herself that the sobbing sounds were an effect of the wind, or an echo of the sobbing in her own heart. And although from childhood she had seen and heard things that other people hadn't, she had always been able to explain them away either as spiritual visitations, or as outward manifestations of her inner distress.

But this time, she had actually been visited by a *ghost*, and had *sex* with it! She was amazed that she had fantasized about her husband so intensely that she had conjured up his ghost out of the ether, and she began to feel uneasy about sleeping alone in the castle, without Anne or Tony to protect her.

Then she sat bolt upright in bed as a terrifying thought seized her: if Gavin was a *ghost*, did that mean he was *dead*?

In a panic, she turned on the bedside lamp and rang Miss Crumpet. "Mary, it's Judith. Sorry to bother you at this hour, but can you please call Gavin and make sure he's okay?"

"Why, Luv? What's happened?"

"Nothing. I just have a feeling something may have happened to him."

"Bloody hell! Can't you call him yourself?"

"No, I can't. Would you please do this one favor for me?"

Miss Crumpet heaved a sigh. "All right — I'll ring you back."

The next ten minutes were sheer torture, and Judith drank two shots of Drambuie to stop the shakes. Finally, the phone rang. "He just texted, Luv. He's as right as rain."

After she hung up, she felt incredibly foolish. But even more, she felt depressed. Gavin was alive and well, but he wasn't there with her. She had banished him from her life, and he was never coming back. And this thought had been so unbearable to her that she had hallucinated him making love to her in her own bed. Worse, her hallucinations had been so palpable that she had been unable to distinguish them from reality. Was she losing her mind?

Her religious visions hadn't frightened her, and she told herself she shouldn't be frightened of this vision either. In addition to her visitations from Mary, she had sometimes seen St. Catherine of Siena, her spiritual twin, floating above her bed. They had a great deal in common: they had both adopted the Virgin Mary as their mother, they both had holy visions, they had both mortified their flesh and starved themselves to get closer to God, and they were both writers and intellectuals. Only, Judith had married a flesh-and-blood husband, and Catherine had married Christ, bathing herself in his blood and sanctifying their holy union not with a wedding band, but with his circumcised foreskin worn in a ring on her finger. Being in Catherine's presence always made her feel calm and centered, the way Mary's presence made her feel.

But her religious visions felt cleansing, and her erotic visions felt psychotic; not only because they were so carnal, but because they were indistinguishable from reality. She had even gone so far as to imagine his semen trickling onto her thighs, and she still felt the stickiness there. She was truly frightened at this new deterioration of her mental state, which had already been at the breaking point. Tears of shame stung her cheeks, and she felt crazy, unhinged, hysterical, unlovable, and worthless. She was sinking into mental debility, and the realization that she no longer had control over her thoughts, feelings, actions, and senses filled her with unspeakable dread. She was truly going mad.

She knew there were razor blades in the bathroom, and she considered fetching one and opening her wrists. It would be so easy: five or six more cognacs, and she would feel no pain. Seven or eight, and she would drift off to sleep and never wake up again. She didn't want to wake up; she wanted to die.

The thought of dying was very attractive to her. She had always known she was not wanted, even when she had lain alone those first few weeks in the hospital incubator; and because of this painful awareness she had remained partly in the spirit world, closer to death than to life. It was to this liminal state that she attributed her religious visions. Her despair throughout her childhood had been so intense that she had often longed to die, and she was still amazed that she had survived that unhappy time. Two things had saved her: prayer in her early years, and writing in her adolescence. Her ability to sublimate her despair through prose had effectively prevented her from suicide these last thirteen years, but now nothing was adequate to distract her mind from its gloomy and disordered madness.

She taped a note to her bedroom door, forbidding anyone to enter for any reason. Then she locked the door, stretched herself out on the bed, and lay there until the sun was high in the sky, planning to fetch the razor blades and end her life in a bloodbath, but too weak to rise. I wonder where they'll bury me, she thought. Certainly not in the churchyard; suicides can't be buried on consecrated ground. Maybe they'll bury me next to my mother? No, they would never do that. She couldn't stand being around me in life, so why would she want me around her in death? I wonder if there are any dead people that might like me? I'd love to meet Noël Coward . . . and Marlene Dietrich . . .

Then her lids grew heavy, and she fell asleep.

She awoke several hours later, parched and hungry. She threw on a long floral print dress in autumn colors and descended to the kitchen, where she consumed a cold leftover quiche and a salad that Sarah had saved for her, and she drank some coffee and a glass of water. Feeling better, she decided to take a walk. So she gathered herself up and trailed through the drawing room and out of the back door, where a light rain drizzled, and the day was as cold and gray as a tomb.

28.

He Only Shook Me

When she stepped outside she felt a chill, but she was too tired to fetch a coat. She paused as she considered taking the dogs with her — she could really use the company — but although Gavin was gone, she felt uneasy about disobeying his prohibitions. So she turned away from the kennel and crossed the lawn past the flowerbeds, the fountain, and the massive hedges. Then she slipped through the iron gate and wandered into the woods.

As soon as she entered, her mood lifted. She stood silently in the white mist, watching the quiet life of the forest unfold. She marveled at the individual existences of all the plants, insects, and animals, the whole of nature working together in a sublime and unified plan.

As she continued walking, she glimpsed through the trees a vivid green meadow abundant with wildflowers, where she spotted a fox and a stag, each of whom stopped and looked her in the eye. She passed through a pine forest and breathed deeply of the air, savoring its fragrance.

Then the sun burst through the clouds and slanted through the trees, and a red peacock butterfly fluttered on a nearby branch. Overwhelmed by the beauty of nature, she slowly came back to life, like a vampire who has just received an infusion of fresh blood. Everything is going to be all right, she thought. I'm alone, and I'm not even thinking about him. *I'm free.*

And then, she saw it: a shadowy figure emerging from the trees. A man. He was tall and broad, and he was lumbering straight at her with a slow and steady determination, like something out of a nightmare. Feeling a frisson of evil, she shrank back and screamed.

It was Gavin.

He continued walking towards her with an inscrutable smile, and then he stopped several paces from her. "Hello, little girl."

He looked as handsome as he had when he had appeared to her the night before as an incubus. Her senses thrilled to see him, but at the same time she was deathly afraid—mostly of herself and of what she might do. "What are you doing here?" she demanded.

"Judith, I need to speak to you."

She turned away. No, she thought. I can't look at him. He's Satan, and he's going to draw me back into his clutches. "Go away or I'll call the police."

"Please listen to me, Judith."

"Why should I?"

"There's no earthly reason why you should. But please give me a chance to explain. And then I'll go away and never bother you again."

There was a long pause, and then she replied, "All right. I'm listening."

"First, I want to say that I'm sorry about the things I said that night. I only slept with Nancy because I was mad with jealousy about Tony and you, and I wanted to hurt you."

"There was nothing between Tony and me. You're just using that to excuse your own disgusting affair."

"Nothing between Tony and you? You're marrying him, aren't you?"

She blushed. "Yes. But I wasn't in love with him before."

"Then why did you fall into his arms at the first opportunity? Don't look at me like that — I know you slept with him at the ball."

"How did you know that?"

"Because I was there."

She trembled with rage. "You were there? How *dare* you!"

"I wanted to look at you again. But just as I was about to unmask myself and speak to you, I saw you kiss Tony. Later, we all saw him carry you up the stairs. It reminded me of when I carried you up to your room at that castle in Cornwall, and I almost died with jealousy. But I knew by then that I'd lost you forever, and I only hoped he'd take good care of you."

Judith's cheeks burned with shame. So he *had* been a witness to her adultery! He had probably also been hiding in the room while they had made love; she had felt his eyes on her. "Well, now we're even," she said. "We've both had our affairs; only, mine is for life. I'm in love with Tony, and I'm going to marry him. So let's behave like adults and part ways amicably."

"Not yet. I have a few more things to say to you."

All her feelings of hurt and betrayal now flooded to the surface. "What is there to say?" she cried, fighting back tears. "You married me for my money; it's as simple as that."

"I don't deny that. I knew who you were, and I crashed Victoria's party to meet you."

She sniffled, and he handed her a handkerchief. She took it unthinkingly. "You pretended to be interested in my books, and in Coleridge."

"But I *am* interested in your books, and in Coleridge! I love Gothic fiction, and your writing is some of the best out there. I admit that my main motivation for wanting to meet you was because I knew you had money, and I wanted to get in with your social class. But then something happened that I hadn't counted on."

There was a tenderness in his voice that she'd never heard before. And then he murmured, "What I hadn't counted on was falling in love with you."

She laughed bitterly. "Do you really expect me to believe that?"

"I know it sounds unlikely, but it's true. At first, I only wanted your money. But when our eyes met in the chapel, it was like magic. I know you felt it too. I wanted you so much that I thought I'd die if I couldn't have you. I admit it was only desire at first. How could it have been otherwise? You were a stranger. But by the third day in that hotel room, I was madly in love with you, and the more I've got to know you, the harder I've fallen. I didn't realize how much I needed you until you were gone."

"All lies!" she said. Did he really think she would be taken in by his glib seducer's patter?

"The eyes don't lie," he said. And he looked at her the way he had looked at her at the beach.

Judith turned away from him. No! she told herself. Don't fall for it! He's trying to trick you into taking him back!

He shivered. "It's a bit chilly. Should we walk?"

She glanced at him, and he was smiling gently; she could detect no threat or guile on his face. She nodded, and they began to walk together through the sun-dappled, faun-stepped woods. After they had been strolling for a few minutes, she broke the silence. "I met your friend Montgomery. He told me the truth about you. Why did you tell me you were a baron's son?"

"I'd been posing as Longueville's son for years. I'd done it for so long that I almost started to believe it myself. I wanted to tell you the truth so many times, but I was afraid of losing you. Of course, now I regret it."

"Who are your parents?"

"I never knew my parents; I was a foundling. I could be Prince Andrew's son, for all I know. I used to fantasize that I might be some secret abandoned child of the peerage, and I wanted so much to live in one of those National Trust properties they took us to at school — all of those castles and palaces. I couldn't believe people still lived like that. It gave me a taste for luxury, and I've had it ever since. My own life was much grimmer. I grew up in a succession of children's homes, each more horrible than the last."

"Then that story about your father beating you wasn't true?"

He stopped and leaned heavily against a tree, struggling with his emotions. "He wasn't my real father. He and the lady I called my mum adopted me from the children's home when I was four. But when I was nine, I smashed him over the head with a chair. He wasn't seriously hurt, the bastard. The next day two social workers took me away and put me back into the system. I was never adopted after that; no one wanted to take the risk."

His face was hard with misery. He'd had a terrible life, and she became painfully aware of her wealth and class privilege. Her own struggles with her family seemed petty by comparison. Of course, even wealthy children died of neglect. It happened to the children of movie stars, and to children that grew up in castles, and to princesses locked in towers. It could happen to anyone. But obviously, it was worse for the poor, and especially for orphans and the homeless. Her family had hated her, but at least she'd *had* a family, and a lovely house to grow up in, and nice food to eat, and wonderful books on the shelves. Suddenly she had a fierce longing to protect him — to be his buffer against the world.

He saw her expression and he said, "I believe you are really sorry for me."

She was unable to answer him, because her emotion threatened to choke her. She looked straight ahead, feeling shy in the presence of this hard luck, working-class man — a dizzying shift from the baron she thought she knew — and for several minutes they stood listening to the songs of the starlings and the wrens, and the rushing of a distant stream. Then they resumed walking. "Why did you pick Hastings Castle?" she asked.

"I liked the romanticism if it — the fact that it was like a Byronic ruin. I'm surprised you didn't look it up sooner; it would have been an easy thing to check. I almost hoped you would, so I could tell you the truth about myself."

She felt incredibly foolish. Why hadn't she checked up on him? Had she been afraid of what she might find? Or had she really not cared who he was or where he came from, as long as he satisfied her sexual and romantic desires?

Now they were entering the garden. He stopped and turned to her. "Should we finish talking in the house?"

A voice inside her was screaming, No! Don't let him into the house! He's trying to trap you! But this was ridiculous; he was harmless, as long as she kept her wits about her. So she let him take her arm, and they strolled together through the garden and towards the house, enveloped by wafts of delicious perfume from the autumnal blooms. She hadn't felt this contented since the last time she'd walked arm in arm with him in this way. A feeling of elation flooded her body, and she knew that she always wanted to be with this beautiful man, hanging on his strong arm. This was her rightful place in the world.

They entered the house, and he popped into the kitchen and asked Sarah to bring them a decanter of wine and some individual meat pies and salad. Sarah gaped at him as if she had seen a ghost.

Then they ascended the stairs to the bedroom, and she sat on the blue velvet loveseat while he lit some kindling in the grate. Soon the flames were dancing brightly, and she felt cozy and contented. He lifted her feet onto an ottoman, tucked a shawl over her shoulders, and seated himself in an armchair nearby, his handsome face lit by the yellow glow of the fire. Presently she asked, "Did you marry Constance for her money?"

"No. I thought I was in love with her. But she turned out to be mentally ill. It wasn't a happy marriage."

"How did you get all that money? Did you steal it?"

"No. She lent it to me. I promised I'd pay her the whole thing back with interest, and I would have eventually, but then she had that horrible accident."

Judith scrutinized him, but she saw no signs of guilt or duplicity on his face.

"I think it's a remarkable coincidence that she died that way," she said in a sinister tone.

He looked up, startled. "What, in the bath? Why is that a coincidence?"

"Because I told you how easy it is to kill someone in the bath and get away with it."

"You did?" He looked genuinely surprised. "I don't remember."

She studied his face. "It was at the cocktail party."

"Oh, yes! That's right. You were blotto, and you were shocking the guests with your murder stories. And they certainly were shocked. I remember their faces!" He laughed.

"Yes, I suppose I *was* trying to be shocking. But I never thought I was giving an *actual murderer* a blueprint for how to create *the perfect crime!*"

"The perfect crime? What are you talking about?"

His face registered only a blank amazement. She knew sociopaths could fake emotions, but no one could be *this* good. "Never mind," she sighed.

The verdict was in; he obviously hadn't murdered Constance.

Sarah brought the supper and laid it out nicely on the table. Judith declined to eat the meat pies because of a Charles Dickens story she'd read as a child called "Captain Murderer," about a man who kills a series of brides and uses them as filling for meat pies; but she picked at the salad, and she found the wine enormously rejuvenating.

While she sipped her Bordeaux, she continued to interrogate him like a member of the Spanish Inquisition, and he answered every question calmly and reasonably. When she grilled him about his polyamorous tendencies, he said, "I didn't mean it about wanting to be polyamorous, Princess. Or if I did, I don't feel that way anymore. I don't want anyone but you. I swear, if you take me back, I'll never be unfaithful again." She was amazed at how easy it was to speak to him. There were no walls going up, no anger, no defensiveness, no violence, no games, no manipulation; just sincere and honest disclosure.

At one point she asked him, "Did you try to kill me that night?" And then she gasped, nearly fainting with terror that the question might excite his rage.

He was taken aback. "When?"

"When . . . when you tried to strangle me."

His mouth dropped open in amazement. "I don't remember doing that."

"It was in the woods. When I showed you that photo of Constance, and you . . . you lost your temper."

"Oh! You mean, when I *shook* you?"

He looked so comically hurt and sad that she laughed. "Yes," she said, laughing helplessly, "when you *shook* me." Her laughter was infectious, and he laughed too.

His minimizing of his violent act was so effective that the trauma of it vanished like magic. Poof! He had said there was no strangling, so there was no strangling. A great weight was lifted from her as she realized she had been making a mountain out of a molehill. They had even *laughed* about it!

She began to wonder if she had misunderstood him all along, and if she was not herself to blame for the disintegration of their marriage. She had demonized him as a man who was suspiciously brooding and silent, and thus hiding dark secrets. But if he brooded sometimes, what of it? Was not a man allowed to brood? Was he to police his face every waking moment, erasing every expression save those which signaled his undying love for her?

She had been afraid of men ever since she was a little girl, and she wondered if she had been unconsciously punishing her husband due to her fear of men as a category. But she had to admit that he was also someone who genuinely inspired fear. She was terrified that some minor transgression might cause him to wreak his vengeance on her the way he had the night he had shaken her, but it seemed to her that he had changed. Had her love transformed her lion into a pussycat, the way she had always hoped it could? She gazed at him, and for the first time in months, she loved him without fear or ambivalence.

He gazed back at her, his eyes full of affection. "I know we got off to a bad start, Princess, but I'm sure we could mend things if we started over again."

In spite of how she yearned to tell him she was his forever, she still hesitated. "I don't know. You've lied so much."

"I'm sorry. I'm not very good at love, but you can be my teacher. I'll do anything you say. In any case, let's drop this charade." He smiled into her eyes. "I'll tell you one thing: you *are* more beautiful than your sister. And I'll tell you another thing: I'm the only man for you, and you know it. No one will ever love you the way I do. You're mine, and you'll always be mine."

At these words, she became nearly insensible with love for her beautiful, sweet, sexy man. "All right," she said. "But if I take you back, you have to promise to be monogamous, and to let me take charge of every decision regarding the marriage and the household. In return, I promise to be more adventurous in the bedroom. If you ever so much as glance at another woman, or shout at me, or shake me, or put your hands on me in a non-consensual way, or order me around outside the bedroom, you're out. Those are my terms; take them or leave them."

"I accept your terms. And I promise to love you forevermore. But that shouldn't be difficult; I already love you more than I love myself." With this, he looked at her in that devastating way of his. And then he seized her and kissed her, and she collapsed in his arms.

He carried her to the bed and laid her down. "So you've finally come back to me."

He held her, and they wept. "I saw you as a *monster*," she sobbed. "I must have been *insane!*"

"Shhh. It doesn't matter now. All that matters is that we're together, and we're in love." And then he began to make love to her, and she let him take charge, and her world was whole again.

At one point she murmured, "Darling, get the horse whip."

"Are you sure?"

"Yes, get it!"

So he did, and she lay on her stomach, naked except for her suspender belt and stockings, and he struck her with the whip, at first lightly, and then harder and harder, until she spent in an ecstasy of passion. Afterwards he licked the blood off her buttocks and pressed his lips to the bleeding sores, kissing whatever presented itself to his lust. Her tears flowed with the pain, but she would have done anything he asked at that moment, so desirous was she of pleasing her handsome lover.

When they had sated their passion to the point of exhaustion, they lay in each other's arms until well past sunset. The room grew dark, except for the moonlight silvering their faces as they clung to one another in the enchanted bedroom, which their love made magic.

But then Judith's phone rang. Gavin glanced at it. "It's Tony," he said with a frown, turning on the lamp.

"I'm not going to answer it."

"You have to. If you don't pick up, he'll think something's wrong, and he'll drive over here. Answer it."

Judith reluctantly picked up the phone. "Tony? How was work? I'm fine. No, I haven't been lonely. I've had too much work to do."

Gavin began nibbling her ear, and she pushed him away, giggling. "Oh, nothing, I'm just laughing because I'm so happy to hear your voice. Tonight? Oh no, you really shouldn't make the drive. Anyway, I'm *exhausted* . . . I think I'll make an early night of it. I was practically asleep when you called. No, don't apologize! But I should go to bed soon, or I'll be up all night. You know how I am. You too. Talk to you tomorrow."

Judith hung up, feeling guilty.

"When are you going to tell him?"

"Soon."

"Tomorrow, or I'll be very cross with you."

"All right. Tomorrow."

"Promise."

"I promise."

29

This Is My Castle

The next day, Judith called Tony and told him she had reconciled with Gavin. He tried to talk her out of it, reminding her of the anguish Gavin had caused her, and his adultery, and his violence, and his lies. Then he became desperate, telling her how much he loved her, and reminding her how happy they had been together. But Tony had already dropped out of the picture. She now saw him only as a threat to her happiness with Gavin. He heard the coldness in her voice, and he knew they were finished. "Good luck, Judith," he said. "I won't wish you happiness, because I know you'll never find it with him." And he hung up.

Judith felt terrible, but what was she to do? She loved Tony, but not the way she loved Gavin, and she had been forced to make a choice. She decided to put the whole thing out of her mind, and to focus on being a good wife to her husband. She exulted in the fact that by sticking things through, she had come out victorious at the other end. She was a real woman, with real dimensions, capable of giving and receiving love as her parents never could. She was a queen, and she never let Gavin forget it.

In fact, she had become quite imperious and demanding. She now had *attitude*, and she was surprised to discover how well her new diva persona suited her. She no longer feared him, since she'd made it clear that the moment he slipped up, he was getting the boot. She now dominated him — except in the bedroom, where he was the undisputed master — and she enjoyed every moment of her rule. Gavin seemed to enjoy it too. He relaxed into being her boy toy, her flatterer, her manservant, her masseur, her sounding board, her Lothario, and anything else she wanted him to be, and he was an exceptionally good sport about it. The key was keeping things *light*. As long as she kept things light, and stopped herself from complaining or arguing about anything, or demanding anything except in a gay and amusing manner, they got along splendidly.

She was so excited about her new insights into male psychology that she was tempted to start a marriage counseling practice, where she would advise beleaguered wives, "Just keep things light!" She now realized that she'd misunderstood men all along. They didn't want to be treated like intimate partners, but like someone you'd just met at a cocktail party. Nor did they desire a doormat; what they wanted was a *queen*. Judith's queen persona included a strong hand to bring her husband into line, firmly but lightly, like those dog whisperers you hear about; only, she was a *man whisperer*.

They celebrated their reunion with chilled champagne of a very good vintage, the finest Belgian chocolates, and a delicious light supper, and he gave her several boxes of exquisite Paris lingerie, just as he had on their honeymoon. Having recently dyed her hair a flaming red to match her new personality, she was also aflame with desire, and she lay on her princess bed in her delicate new things, including a silk chiffon negligee with ostrich trim. He entered naked and thrust into her arms a mass of juicy red roses he had snipped from the garden, growling in his best Jean Marais impersonation, "Belle . . . vous volez mes roses. Et il se trouve que ce simple vol mérite la mort!" The sex was thrilling, and she had an out-of-body experience as he took her to both the depths of debauchery and the heights of ecstasy.

A week later she purchased a new kitten, a Persian with blue eyes that was the spitting image of Romeo, and she named it Lovelace, after the seducer in *Clarissa*. When she picked it up, a tiny fluffball with a bold, unafraid glance, she thought no woman in the world could be happier than she.

The months passed by, and she remained blissfully happy. But they were in serious debt, and her father had refused to lend them another penny. He had already invested large sums in Gavin's businesses, but they had failed one by one, and Sir Wilfred had regretfully informed the couple that he could do no more. As Judith well knew, it was wildly expensive to maintain these old castles and estates, for it was illegal to hire anyone to repair them other than certified restorers. And Waverly Manor had begun to spring leaks in the roof, an inconvenience which was tying up all of Sir Wilfred's cash at the moment.

The house expenses were also high at Manderfield, and Judith's cash flow was insufficient to meet their needs. She had already sold all of her stocks and run through her savings, and her book royalties were not large enough to support their life in the castle. So she began to push harder for Gavin to contribute to the household expenses.

He had recently become interested in a plot of land in Bournemouth, and he only needed fifty thousand pounds to buy it. But he had no development money, nor any business partners, and he was unlikely to acquire any. Although he was charming and well-liked by friends and acquaintances, his temper was so frightening that at the first dispute, any potential partners would flee from him. None of the banks would lend to him, and he had worn out all of his personal contacts.

Judith had a sneaking suspicion that he sabotaged all of his business opportunities on purpose because he didn't *want* to be in business. He was more allergic to work than anyone she'd ever met, including some of the toffs she had grown up with. Gavin's idea of the good life was spending every waking moment taking his pleasure. And for him, business was the antithesis of pleasure, so he avoided it like the plague. In fact, she was beginning to think that he never conducted business at all when he went up to London, for he often came home glowing from a workout at the gym, or loaded with packages from his incessant shopping sprees—activities that would have left him precious little time for meetings, especially when combined with the long commute. She was worried about their debts, but she was loath to create any friction between them. So she avoided raising the subject, until one day when the situation had become so insupportable that she was forced to speak.

She was sitting in the garden taking tea in a white summer

frock. Gavin was nearby, shooting at a target. Lovelace, now a full-grown cat, was lapping up a saucer of cream on the table, and she was rubbing his ears and kissing him all over. "Oh, Lovelace, you're too scrumptious!" she cried.

A shot ripped through the air, and she instinctively put her arms around the cat to protect it. She knew it was ludicrous to think that Gavin would hurt Lovelace, let alone shoot him point blank, but her protective instincts remained. After all, he was a cat in peril!

She watched as Gavin fired more shots into the target, hitting the bullseye every time. Then he stalked over to the table and grabbed a ham and Brie sandwich, eating it voraciously while standing. "Princess," he said with his mouth full, "can you lend me five thousand quid? I have a few debts to take care of."

She sighed, still shielding the cat. "I suppose so."

"I hate to take money from you, but it's only temporary. Soon we'll be swimming in cash."

"I'll believe it when I see it. None of your schemes have panned out so far."

"That's because I haven't had the capital. All I need is a loan from your father."

"Another loan from father? That's out of the question. If you don't make some money soon, we'll have to sell the castle."

"Sell the castle? Never! This is *my* castle. I've worked and slaved for it, and there's no way I'm going to lose it. Just wait. I'll get the money somehow."

His claim to have worked and slaved for the castle mystified her, and he had a wild, desperate look on his face.

She smiled indulgently. "All right. I knew you'd be against

it. So I've arranged a meeting with the National Trust. They're coming by next week to assess the property."

At this, he became so furious that he almost started jumping up and down. "The *National Trust*? Do you know what those vultures will do? They'll pay our debts, and turn our home into a museum, and rope off the furniture, and have tourists in and out all day, and set up a nasty tearoom that serves stale tea bags in paper cups, and force us to live in a tiny corner of our house! Are you *mad*?"

"Never mind. Let's just drop it."

She gazed at his handsome, brooding face, which looked demonic in the late afternoon light. She reminded herself that he had the perfect right to brood, and she refused to read any meaning into his forbidding glance.

Judith finished *Murder on the Moors* and sent it off to her agent and her editor. She felt satisfied to have another completed novel under her belt, and she returned with interest to *Bluebeard's Castle*. She had stopped at the point where Abigail had been poised to flee from Beaumont's castle, and now she continued with Abigail deciding to remain, unwilling to do violence to herself by tearing herself away from the man she loved. Seated at her vanity table in a long glamorous house dress and a silk velvet dressing gown, Judith opened her notebook and wrote, "She knew now that she could never leave him. He was her mirror soul, her twin flame. They completed one another."

She laid down her pen and gazed in the mirror, imagining her face merging with Gavin's. "Gavin is me . . . I am he," she said. Then she started musing to herself about how much she loved him. He had confessed to having a good self and a bad self, and she was the same way. All her life she had repressed the dark part of her nature, and it was only with him that she could express it. Otherwise, she was only half a person, and she would have done anything rather than revert to the good, proper girl she had been when she had first met him. She was drunk on his love, and she didn't care what happened to her, as long as she got her daily fix. "He may be a demon," she said to her reflection, "but he's *my* demon."

She laughed, her love for him flooding her with fond feelings and reminiscences. He's such a child, she thought. He has so many toys—his knives, his guns, his traps—and he must constantly play with them. I really wish he wouldn't hunt, but you have to let men do what they want. Otherwise, you can't live with them at all. You have to be very sweet—that's the only way to control them. Then they're eating out of your hand. For instance, Gavin doesn't realize I know what he's up to, asking Father to go hunting today. I've *told* him he won't get any more money out of him, but he *will* try to cajole him until he relents . . . and who knows, maybe he'll succeed. He's a very naughty boy, asking Father to go hunting, with his bad heart!

She laughed again, thinking about Gavin's naughtiness, which she found quite endearing. In fact, she was sure she couldn't love him if he hadn't been a rascal and a rogue. What would be the fun of loving a man who always played by the rules? She began to apply makeup, wielding her lipstick, eyeliner, and mascara wand like a pro, and afterwards surveying her face with the proud vanity of a screen siren. I'm really quite lovely, she thought. I've grown more beautiful from suffering; it's given me a certain distinction.

After she finished her makeup, she misted perfume over her bosom in a circular motion. Then she paced the room, feeling on edge. To steady her nerves she had two gin and tonics, and then she stretched out on her bed and closed her eyes. Soon she drifted off to sleep, and she had a dream.

She was lost in the forest. She was trying to get back home, but the fog was so thick that she could scarcely see an inch in front of her. She turned blindly this way and that, her arms outstretched, bloodying herself on branches and pine needles. Then she heard a fox bark, and she hid behind a bush. The fog cleared, and she saw a demon with a fox's head in dandy ruffles and velvet knee breeches dragging a woman who seemed to have fainted along the ground.

As they got near, Judith saw that the woman was her mother. A diamond ring glittered on her finger. The fox-demon tried and tried to pull off the ring, but it was tightly fixed; so finally, cursing and swearing, he drew his sword and cut off her hand. The hand jumped into the air and landed at Judith's feet. The demon looked around for it, but he didn't think to look behind the bush, so he resumed dragging her mother away.

Just as she was about to seize the hand and take it to the authorities, Gavin and Sir Wilfred appeared in their hunting clothes. They had their guns and their dogs with them, and they were excited and in good humor for the hunt. The dogs raced over to a bush, sniffing excitedly. Soon a hare lolloped out into the open and stood there stupidly, its ears erect and quivering. Gavin shot it, and it let out a terrible squeal, limped a few steps, and lay still.

Judith screamed and cried, but no sound came out. Then

she noticed that the Monster of Manderfield had turned his shotgun away from the poor dead creature and was pointing it at Sir Wilfred. He stalked towards the old man with an odious smile, training the gun on his heart with the steely determination of a trained assassin.

All of the blood drained from Sir Wilfred's face. His breath came in labored gasps, and he stumbled backwards, clutching at his heart. He cried out, "Help! Help me!" and he fell to the ground with a thud, convulsed, and lay still.

The assassin stood over the body and kicked it maliciously in the head. Then the dogs started barking wildly, and she woke up.

30.

The Statistics Don't Lie

Judith awoke to the sound of a dog barking. She gulped down some water to shake herself awake, but then she realized that what she heard wasn't part of her dream, but the live barking of a dog outside the castle. Then the doorbell chimed, and chimed again. Suddenly she remembered that Jane had taken her car to the village for repairs, and that she would have to get the door herself.

She raced down the stairs and pushed open the front door. A policeman stood on the step, and another stood close behind. Two police cars were parked in the drive.

Judith watched in confusion as Gavin scooted out of one of the cars with his beagles. A third policeman emerged from the other car, trying to restrain Sir Wilfred's Jack Russell terrier. The dog was barking and lunging at Gavin like mad, its jaws snapping. The officer led it down the path, and the barking grew fainter.

"What is it?" asked Judith in a daze, blinking in the sunlight.

"Ms. Moore?" said one of the policemen.

She strained to hear above the barking. "Yes?"

"I'm afraid we have some bad news."

"Bad news?"

"It's your father, Madam. He's dead."

"*Dead?*" A wave of vertigo struck her, and she sank against a stone lion for support.

"I'm afraid so. He had a heart attack while he was hunting with your husband."

Judith slowly turned her head and looked at Gavin, who was smiling at her from the bottom of the steps with vacant, soulless eyes. She uttered a cry and covered her face with her hands. "Oh, my God."

"Are you okay, Madam?" asked the second policeman.

"Let me handle this," said the demon, rushing up to her. The policemen moved away to give them privacy.

The monster seized her with his claws. "Princess! I'm so sorry. He just . . . fell over." He began to cry in an exaggerated manner, just as he had the day Romeo had died.

Judith wrenched herself from his talons and ran over to the policemen. "Don't you realize this was murder?" she whispered savagely.

The officers exchanged pitying glances. "Don't take it that way, Madam," said one of them. "I know it's hard now, but you'll get used to it. We all have to go someday. Would you like to come to the hospital and see him?"

Judith shook her head no.

Satan strode over to Judith and seized her hands. "I'll go, darling. You've had a great shock. You need a rest."

"Yes," said the officer. "You'll need to come down to the station and make a statement."

"I'd be happy to." Then, turning to Judith, "I may be gone a few hours, Princess. Try to rest." He tried to kiss her on the mouth, but she turned her face away, and his lips landed on her cheek.

It was the first time she had ever hated his kiss.

Beelzebub got into one of the police cars. The policemen handed the leashes to Judith, and she watched as they drove away. The terrier had calmed down now, and she stroked its silky head and ears. Then Jonathan, the dog keeper, came up and took the leashes. "We have a new dog," she said catatonically. "Her name is Ava. Be kind to her." She watched as Jonathan led the dogs in the direction of the kennel, and then she disappeared into the house.

Somehow she made it up the stairs and into her bedroom. She dragged a suitcase from her closet, flinging clothes into it while the hot tears stung her face. As soon as she was able to speak she rang Tony at the hospital, her eyes swollen from crying.

"Judith? I'm with a patient. Can you make it quick?"

"Hello, Tony? Thank God you're there! Something awful has happened. Make any excuse, but please get here right away!"

A ponderous silence. And then, "I'll be there as soon as I can."

She hung up, breathing a sigh of relief. Tony would cancel his patients for the rest of the day. He wouldn't keep her waiting.

She fixed herself a Scotch on the rocks and collapsed onto the window seat, waves of shock coursing through her body.

Gavin had killed her father. He had asked him hunting on purpose to kill him, just as in her dream. Should she file a police report, accusing him of murder?

As she looked out onto the garden, she thought about how awful it would be to endure a lengthy trial, and how much worse to send Gavin to prison. He couldn't help being evil; it was in his genes. And punishing him would do no good — it would only create a dangerous enemy for life. No — she didn't want to see him caged like an animal. She only wanted him out of her life.

She packed a second suitcase and plucked from her closet a 1950s burgundy skirt suit and matching pumps, a pair of black silk stockings, and her new Burberry trench coat. Then she dressed, washed her face, put on makeup and perfume, admired herself in the full-length mirror — I'm *terribly* sexy, she thought — and grabbed her suitcases, lugging them down the stairs to the drawing room.

She placed the suitcases next to the sofa and fixed herself a whisky highball, waiting for Tony. She didn't know what she would have done without Tony. She had spoken to him now and then since their breakup, and he had been civil, but nothing more. Something had changed in Tony. He was still in love with her, but he held her at arm's length, and he was often cross with her. In some ways, she preferred this new Tony. She found his gruffness sexy, and she was always more comfortable around people who were mean to her. Now he would come and whisk her away to safety.

She spent some time reading an excellent novel by Elisabeth Sanxay Holding called *Lady Killer*, about a woman trying to solve a murder aboard a cruise ship, but she couldn't concentrate on it. Then Lovelace plopped down next to her on the sofa and washed his paws, getting his rough tongue between each pink toe. After that he vigorously cleaned his chest and his stomach, and she stroked his belly for an inordinate amount of time, enjoying the sight of his back legs pointing ridiculously into the air. Then he heaved a deep sigh and fell asleep. Soon he started twitching and crying out in sharp, short chirps. What was he dreaming about? Birds, probably, or mice. She watched him fondly for a while, and eventually he stopped twitching and fell into a deep and dreamless slumber.

She wondered if he knew she was leaving, for cats always know when you're sick, or distressed, or going on a trip. She would take him with her to Tony's. Tony lived in a small, cramped flat in Pimlico, but they would be comfortable there. Lovelace was used to his garden, though; he would be very cross to give it up. She liked her garden too. It would be a shame to leave it.

Suddenly she felt desperately alone, and she grew restless. So she fixed herself another highball, and she began to fall into that comfortable haze of drunkenness that had sustained her so well throughout her married life. She felt so good that she put on a 1950s crime jazz record and danced around the room, pretending she was captivating a room full of men.

Soon the doorbell rang, and Jane's footsteps clacked along the entrance hall as she opened the door. A moment later, the housekeeper was standing in the drawing room. "It's Mr. Tony, Madam."

"Show him in."

Tony entered, and the first thing he did was to march over to the stereo and turn it off. He looked at her with disgust, the blaring music, the empty whisky glasses, and the wild look in her eye suggesting to him that her call may have been frivolous. But he gave her the benefit of the doubt, as he always did. "Judith—I came as soon as I could."

She rushed up to him and flung her arms around his neck. "Tony, thank God you're here! Something terrible has happened!"

Tony's expression changed to alarmed concern. "What is it?"

"Father is dead! Gavin killed him!" She burst into tears, dampening the shoulder of his coat. She had never cried on his shoulder before, and the feeling of his strong arms around her was bliss.

But now he was pushing her away and looking gravely into her face. "Tell me exactly what happened," he said, leading her to the sofa and sitting her down.

As soon as she could speak, she said, "Some police officers came to the house and told me my father died of a heart attack. But I know Gavin killed him—I had a dream about it!"

Tony looked at her skeptically. "I'm very sorry about your father. But why do you think Gavin killed him? Because of your dream?"

She tried to focus through her drunken haze. "No. I told him we needed money, or we'd have to sell the castle. Today he invited Father hunting, knowing he had a weak heart, and that any sudden excitement could be fatal. He must have done something on purpose to frighten him!"

He furrowed his brow. "So you think he *scared* him to death? That's a bit far-fetched."

"No. In my *dream* he scared him to death. But there are other ways to stop the heart. Just a few sips of poisoned coffee could do it. I use that in one of my books — strychnine in coffee — and he's read all of my books. In fact, I'm *sure* that's how he did it. He wouldn't risk trying to scare him to death and failing." She nestled up to him, leaning against his strong chest. "It's all my fault. I should have known something like this would happen. But I refused to let myself believe he could be that evil!"

She glanced up to see his response, and the look on his face infuriated her. She rose and faced him defiantly. "If you don't believe me, then at least you might believe Sir Wilfred's *dog*. She was going berserk, trying to *kill* Gavin. She must have witnessed the whole thing!"

There was a long pause, as Tony let everything sink in. Finally he said, "I believe you." He rose and paced the room. "I knew that guy was no good. Are you going to tell the police?"

"No. I don't want an investigation — I just want him out of my life. I'm through with Gavin. That's what I wanted to tell you!"

She rushed over to Tony and wrapped her arms around him. But he merely stood there, brooding. "Did you hear me, Tony?" she said manically. "I've left Gavin. We can finally be together! We have to hurry — he'll be back soon. Kiss me!" And she planted a drunken kiss on his lips.

He detached her arms from his neck. When she observed the hard, stony expression on his face, she began to panic. "Tony, what's wrong?"

"I'm sorry, Judith. It won't work."

Waves of adrenalin coursed through her body, and she felt as if her life was ending. "What do you mean?" she cried.

"I'm not going to live with you when you're still in love with him."

"But I'm *not* in love with him. I *hate* him!"

"You said that before."

"I mean it this time!"

His expression turned to disgust. "Do you? I know I'm not a mysterious baron from a romance novel, but I think I deserve some consideration. Don't speak to him for six months, and get a divorce, and then we can discuss it."

She stared at him in shock, realizing she could never do that.

"You see? You can't. You're addicted. Like all addicts, you need to hit rock bottom before you'll change. I hope that once you do, it won't be too late."

"What do you mean, too late?"

His face became grim. "Often when a woman comes to hospital with bruises on her neck, the next time we see her she's on a stretcher, headed straight for the morgue."

"How dare you say that? Gavin would never hurt me. Gavin loves me!"

"You told me he tried to strangle you once. The statistics don't lie. Over forty percent of women who are murdered by their husbands were strangled by them within the year. The chances of murder go up exponentially if he has a gun, and Gavin *collects* guns. And he's already killed your father. What do you think he'd do if he found out you *knew* he'd killed him? Do you think he'd let you live? And what if he decides to murder you out of simple rage, or in an argument, or for your money? Do you think anything could stop him, once he'd set his mind to it?"

Tony's suggestion that Gavin might try to murder her was intolerable to her. It was one thing to disparage Gavin herself, and another to hear Tony disparage him. She turned on Tony furiously. "First of all, he *didn't* strangle me . . . he only *shook* me. Second of all, it's bonkers to think he killed my father. You *yourself* told me that was far-fetched!"

Tony regarded her with consternation. "You dragged me here all the way from London to tell me that Gavin murdered your father, and now you're telling me I'm crazy for believing you. If you're so sure he's innocent, then order an autopsy."

"Why would I do that, when I *know* he's innocent?" she shouted. "You're just jealous of him. You've always been jealous of him, because he's more of a man than you!"

He gaped at her; her denial was worse than he had thought. "Goodbye, Judith," he said, and he turned and left the room.

She didn't bother to show him out.

31.

The Torture Chamber

Judith was dozing on the drawing room sofa when Gavin entered. She heard a soft voice say, "Wake up, sleeping beauty." She looked up groggily, and her eyes widened with fright as she saw his face hovering inches above her.

"You've been sleeping for hours. Care for a cocktail?"

Her head was splitting, and she needed something to take off the edge. "Gin and tonic," she said.

Day had turned into night. The room was streaked with shadows, and the chandelier threw scattered rays of light onto the room, giving the red velvet wallpaper an even more lurid aspect than usual.

Gavin, dapper in his blue velvet smoking jacket, strode to the bar and fixed her drink. He handed it to her, his heavy garnet ring sparkling on his finger. She took a few sips, and her head started to clear. He perched himself at the edge of the sofa, an inscrutable smile on his face.

"Why the suitcases? Were you planning to leave me?"

"No. I . . . I was going to spend the night with Anne."

"Without telling me?"

"She canceled, so I didn't bother."

"I spoke to Anne. I called to offer my condolences about your father. She was surprised you hadn't rung her about it."

A cold fear crept over her. "I *did* ring her, right after you did, and she invited me to stay the night. But then she called back and said she'd take a raincheck."

"I can check your story, you know."

"Go ahead and check." Her fear began to spread as she gulped down the remainder of her drink.

He held her chin in his hand and chucked it. Normally she experienced this gesture as affectionate, but now she found it oddly violating.

"One more?" he asked, and she nodded. As he went to the bar and whipped out a fresh glass, he said, "Didn't you wonder why I was at the police station for so long?"

She declined to answer. He continued, "I was waiting for the coroner's report."

"What did he say?" she asked dully, knowing what the answer would be.

"He ruled it a heart attack." His tone was suitably reverent, but she thought she detected a gleam of triumph in his eye.

There was a heavy silence as Gavin prepared her drink, broken only by the sound of the ice cubes as he plonked them into the glass with the silver tongs.

The funeral came and went, and Anne and Judith dressed alike, in black crepe Dior dresses with full pleated skirts, black patent-leather Mary Janes, black silk gloves, and little hats with black net veils. It was a grand affair, for Sir Wilfred had been an important man, and Anne and John had done an impressive job of arranging it. She saw all of Sir Wilfred's ghoulish friends there and listened to their endless eulogies droning on and on. Anne was devastated about their father's death, but Judith felt little. She had no pangs of regret the way she'd had with her mother, no tragic feelings of "too late," no self-incriminations. Her relationship with him hadn't been bad; it had simply been indifferent.

She had long put all thoughts of foul play concerning his death out of her mind, but when she saw Gavin exaggeratedly crying when he passed the open coffin, she felt a surge of contempt for him, and she said to herself, *Fake, fake, fake, it's all a performance.* She was surprised at herself for thinking this. It was as if there was another person inside her, a little demon that thought bad things about Gavin and disparaged him in a scary *Exorcist* voice in her head. She tried not to listen to the demon, but it clamored in her mind until she felt nearly possessed by it. And no amount of sprinkling holy water on herself, or drinking Christ's blood, or eating his body, could drive it from her.

But aside from the demon in her head, and her frequent nightmares, and her excessive drinking, and her insomnia, she was happy and productive. She had begun to take long walks again, and to ride Valancourt, and to groom herself better, and to eat properly, and to drink slightly less often. She even began to love Gavin passionately again, and she felt like the luckiest woman in the world to have him for her husband. She finished *Bluebeard's Castle* and ended it with good conquering evil. It was a gruesome and satisfying ending, and she knew her readers would be pleased with it.

One night, she had a nightmare. She was in her nightgown, walking with a candle through the labyrinthine corridors of Bluebeard's Castle, until finally she came to a door beneath which pools of blood seeped. She opened it with a little golden key, and within she observed a large basin full of bloody water, and a bloody chopping block with an axe stuck into it. On the block was Lady Mordaunt's severed head, and in the basin were the body parts and heads of several women who had been murdered and chopped to pieces. She removed the parts from the basin one by one and placed them on the floor, adding to them Lady Mordaunt's head from the chopping block. Then she sat on the floor and proceeded to gather the parts together, placing them back in order: head, neck, torso, arms, and legs, and she sewed them up with a needle and thread, just as she had done once with some dolls she had assembled for a craft fair. When all the parts were joined together, the women opened their eyes and looked at her. Then they started to pull her towards the chopping block, and she screamed.

Judith awoke, feeling a chill of dread. She glanced at her husband lying beside her, quietly sleeping, as fragments of her dream floated in and out of her consciousness.

This story of dismembered women in a vat was familiar to her—it was from a fairy tale. But what did it mean for her to dream this ghastly tale? That she was next on the chopping block? Or was it about her longing to stitch female victims of male violence together and bring them back to life, like a mad feminist Doctor Frankenstein?

As she lay there in the dark and listened to her husband's gentle breathing, she thought, *I'm* not a victim of male violence. I'm not like those women who are such doormats that they'll endure anything from a partner. I only agreed to take him back after he accepted all of my terms . . . so I *can't* be a victim. But Tony compared me to those women they bring in on stretchers. Why would he do that? Because he's jealous. He's trying to split us apart.

But even as she denounced Tony in her mind, she knew he was right — she was in danger. She was desperately unhappy, and her grief was seeping from every crevice in her mind, like a pool of blood seeping from under a corpse. And then the wind began to sigh and moan, and she heard the distant sobbing of a woman, and lugubrious chains dragging across the floor. She clapped her hands over her ears to drown out the sounds. She wouldn't listen — nor would she listen to Tony. All of these people and ghosts judging her, wagging their fingers at her, trying to force her to leave the man she loved. But they wouldn't get their way. They could haunt and scold her all they wanted, but she would never leave him.

She fell asleep again, and she had another nightmare. This time, she dreamed she was lying nude on a canopied bed in a sumptuous medieval bedchamber, her limbs tied to the bedposts. She thought she would die of shame as Gavin, himself clad in eighteenth-century dandy attire, stood grinning at her naked body, his eyes ferocious. "What are you going to do?" she asked, her heart pounding with terror. But he merely chuckled and said, "*You* know."

"Please, release me from my bonds," she pleaded. "That is my right, as your wife."

He laughed diabolically. "As my wife, you have no rights."

He gloated and rubbed his hands together in villainous anticipation. Then he removed his clothing, and he used her body in various ways. Over and over again she cried out for him to stop, but he refused to heed her cries. Instead, he took the greatest delight in abusing her flesh with his hands, his mouth, and various implements, some of which she recognized from his torture chamber. She experienced excruciating pain, and blood flowed from her wounds, and she thought she would faint from the torture. She wept abject tears at this brutal violation of her person, but her distress only compounded his pleasure. And then, with one last abomination of her flesh, he brought himself to the peak of ecstasy. When he had finished, he untied her and laid his head on her chest, cradling her in his arms, as if what had passed between them had been sweet and tender, a tryst between equal lovers. In this attitude, he fell asleep. As she listened to his gentle breathing she wept silently, aflame with pain and tormented with shame and grief that her husband could be so vicious and inhuman.

She awoke to find herself weeping, and wet with her tears. Soon the sound of her quiet sobbing broke through her husband's sleep, and he awoke and switched on the lamp. "What's the matter, Princess?" he asked, with drowsy concern.

"It was just a nightmare. Go back to sleep."

"All right." And he switched off the lamp and went back to sleep.

Soon she heard his gentle breathing once more. And as she lay there in the dark next to the man she loved, she was seized with panic. She was not consciously aware of any hidden aversions to her husband's sexual kinks, nor did she experience him as a sadist. But the emotional terror of the dream felt familiar, and it reminded her of the way she'd felt when he had approached her with stockings in his fists, his eyes full of cruelty, that first night in Cornwall. She wondered if she had been repressing a latent terror of him, or if this was a new terror, brought about by his recent escalation of sexual violence in the bedroom. He had been pushing her boundaries of late, and her response had been to suppress any discomfort, and inure herself to any pain; after all, the last thing a man wanted was a prudish, sex-negative wife.

Her mind wandered to specific incidents, which suddenly, although they had seemed harmless at the time, now seemed traumatic and obscene. Everything they had done in the bedroom had been consensual, but that's because she had never said no. She had decided early on to submit to her husband's every whim, and to follow him wherever he might lead; but she didn't know how much of that decision was due to her pleasure in submission, and how much to her fear of him. And if she *did* say no, would he stop? She was afraid to find out.

She wondered what her true sexuality was. It had never even occurred to her to introduce kink into her lovemaking with Tony. And their two trysts — the night of the ball, and the morning after — had been wildly pleasurable. Gavin had remarked on her sexual responsiveness when he had taken her virginity, and it was true. Her body was incredibly alive to a man's touch, and the way Tony had used his hands and his lips had driven her mad, without the need for special implements or role-play.

Her pleasures with Gavin were more intensely orgasmic, but with him the pleasure was intermixed with humiliation, pain, and shame. He liked to pretend that she was a prostitute and he was a punter, and in this aspect he would hurl the most harrowing verbal abuse at her. Nearly every game he invented involved depreciating her in some way, and sometimes the play became fused with her identity, so that she became convinced that she was a worthless piece of trash, to be used and discarded at will. She would tell herself, "It's my *choice* to be objectified and debased. It's fun and empowering!" But the truth was more complicated.

She indeed reveled in his amorous attentions, even when they were demeaning and belittling, grateful for any focused attention after a childhood of utter neglect. At the same time, she was ashamed that she should take pleasure in his abominable treatment of her, and that she should regularly achieve orgasm to the most shocking abuse. She knew it wasn't *actual* abuse, as it was proper within the guidelines they had established, but the line for her was often blurred. And she *did* take pleasure in it — even now, her senses became inflamed as she remembered his amorous excesses — not because she enjoyed abuse, but because everything they did together was inseparable from her love for him. She could have endured anything as long as he loved her, and it was in this spirit that she had allowed him to lead her to the darkest and most dangerous places. *That's* my sexuality, she thought: sex with someone I'm in love with, who also loves me. Everything else is a question of style.

But sometimes she observed on his face expressions of cruelty that made her blood run cold. It was as if he meant all of the demeaning things he said to her during sex, and was secretly gloating at having slipped them in under the guise of fantasy role-play.

As these expressions of malicious triumph flashed through her mind, she began to wonder if he was indeed possessed by the spirit of the evil Lord Mordaunt, whom she imagined had taken innocent girls into his bed, only to ruthlessly murder them once they ceased to arouse his lust. At this fancy, she drifted into a deep and dreamless slumber.

32.

The Haunted Castle

When she awoke, Gavin had already gone down to breakfast. She lingered in bed, peeking through the filmy curtains of her princess bed and thinking about her nightmares, whose torments the light of day had banished to the shadows. She now felt no fear of her husband, and she was disturbed to think that her unconscious mind was so prudish in contrast with her conscious mind, which was game for anything he might suggest.

She donned a silk dressing gown and sashayed over to her vanity table, gazing into the mirror and brushing out her hair, her nerves shattered. I can't go on like this, she thought. I'm the beautiful, glamorous wife of a highly desirable man, and I have everything I've ever wanted. And yet I'm a nervous wreck, I never sleep, and my nightmares are destroying me. Why am I so *fearful* all the time?

For the past two years, she had exhausted every possibility as to why she might be afraid of her husband, nearly always avoiding the obvious one — that she was afraid of him because he was a genuinely terrifying person—and now she tried to discover a new solution to the problem. It came to her suddenly, in a flash. It's this *castle*, she thought. It's *haunted*. It's turned my husband into a sadistic villain, and myself into a woman in peril!

That the castle might be haunted was something she had always pushed away from her as an impossibility. Although she had read, and indeed written, many stories about evil houses, she had never taken them seriously. But now the evil-house angle seemed as plausible as any other, and she became fixated on the castle as the reason for everything that was wrong between them. We've never been truly happy since we've lived here, she thought. It's where he shook me on Halloween night, and where my cat died in a trap, and where my father died of a heart attack, and where I've had dozens of nightmares, and where my husband and I have either slept in separate rooms or engaged in sex that felt like being in a torture chamber. It's where I've been terrified of his brooding glances, and where he impregnated our maid, and where I committed adultery with my lover, and where I had sex with a ghost, and where I contemplated suicide.

The more she thought about it, the more she was convinced that the house itself had caused all of these things to happen, especially in terms of its evil influence over Gavin's character. It had started working on him instantly, when they had first driven up to the castle and he had given her that cruel, menacing glance. Living at the castle had enhanced his grandiosity, making him feel like a fine lord, and intensifying both his pleasure in hunting and killing, and his lust for money. He had become obsessed with the castle, and his preoccupation with it had consumed him so demonically that there was no room left for their innocent love. Houses have auras, she thought, and the aura here is *evil*. The castle, the money . . . it's *all* evil. I don't want any part of it!

She determined to sell the castle at once. Reflecting that if she kept her father's money it would only compound Gavin's greed, she decided to donate most of it to the Church, keeping just enough to support them comfortably in a townhouse in London. They would still be well-off, but they would both need to work. The spell would be broken, and the castle would have no further hold over them. They would turn back the clock to the way they had been in Paris: young, carefree, and in love.

As soon as she made this decision she felt wonderfully rejuvenated, and she went to find Gavin. He was breakfasting on the drawing room sofa, resplendent in his striped pajamas and silk dressing gown, his feet on the coffee table, buttering a piece of toast. As Judith joined him, Jane hurried in with the coffee pot. "And what would Madam like for breakfast?"

"Oh . . . a Miss Crumpet with butter and strawberry jam."

"A *what*, Madam?"

"A crumpet! And some berries with sweet cream."

"Yes, Madam." Jane freshened Gavin's coffee, poured Judith a cup, and hurried out of the room to fetch her mistress's breakfast.

Gavin sipped his coffee with gusto. Then he devoured a piece of bacon with his fingers, licking the grease off them, and turned to Judith. "Happy, Princess?"

She smiled beatifically. "Yes, darling."

"It's wonderful to have so much money to play with. Let's take a second honeymoon. We'll go back to Paris. Or the Riviera."

"We'll see. I know we're rich now, but I don't want to spend the money frivolously."

He sat up, surprised. "What do you mean? Taking a holiday is hardly frivolous. We haven't had one in ages."

"I know. But we have to economize now. I'm donating most of my money to the Catholic Church. And we're selling the castle and moving to London."

Gavin snorted with laughter. "Good joke!"

"It's not a joke," she said, smiling. "This castle is haunted. And the money is haunted, too."

"So you believe in all that rubbish, do you?"

"Not literally. But the castle has changed us. The atmosphere here isn't healthy. We'll be much happier if we start all over again, just the two of us in a little house, all cozy the way we were at Hampstead Heath."

"That's a terrible idea. Are you daft?"

"Well, I'm not going to *argue* about it. We agreed that the household decisions would be left to me, and this is what I've decided. In time, you'll see that it's best. I'll connect you with some new business partners in London, and we'll keep enough money to start you off with a bang."

Gavin sat there glowering, and she mussed his hair and laughed. Her attitude was so gay and amusing that she felt she could have charmed the pants off anyone, with no more than a studied nonchalance and an effervescent laugh.

"Are you sure you want to do this?" he asked, looking miserable. "Why not at least keep the money?"

"No. The money will only tempt you to buy another castle, and we'll be back where we started."

"There's no need to rush things. You may think better of it later."

"No, this is best. I've made up my mind, and I'm not going to change it." She sipped her coffee with satisfaction, finally feeling like a proper wife. She had taken her husband in hand and decided what was best for him, and she was amazed at how easy it had been. For nearly two years now she had been terrified to say anything that might cause his temper to explode, and now she realized that her fears were entirely of her own creation. As long as she was charming and assertive, she could have anything she wanted.

But his rage hadn't gone; it had only gone into hiding. And just as she was congratulating herself for her new husband-taming skills, he was staring at the back of her head with an expression of pure hatred.

The weeks passed, and they went up to London and picked out a lovely townhouse in Chelsea. It was elegant and expensive, but Gavin didn't care for it. He's still pouting about the castle, she thought; well, he'll get over it. It will be so much more fun living in London that he'll soon forget all about living in a castle.

One day, Judith was folding laundry in the bedroom. Lovelace was rolling all over it, and she had to drag it out from under him, at which he meowed and clawed her. She didn't mind; she loved him unconditionally, and he could do no wrong. But she had just finished pressing Gavin's shirts, and now they were rumpled. So she smoothed them as best she could, folded them neatly, and brought them over to his dresser.

As she was putting them in, she felt something lumpy at the bottom of the drawer. And to her surprise she found, tucked within one of his shirts, a clear plastic bag containing several strange, hairy roots. She stared at them, mystified. They didn't look like ginger or horseradish; rather, they looked like something you might find on a Wiccan altar. But she didn't care what they were. If he wanted to hide strange roots in his drawer, it was none of her business.

She determined to put the shirt back exactly as she had found it, because she remembered his wrath when she had gone into his desk drawer. But just as she was about to wrap it up again she recognized the roots, and she cried out in horror. "Aconite root!" she gasped.

She folded the shirt carefully, tucking the bag of roots inside and shoving it back into the bottom of the drawer. Then, in a panic, she called her sister. "Anne, can I come over?"

"Of course. What's the matter?"

"I'll tell you when I get there."

She texted Gavin, telling him she was popping up to London to see Anne, and she took off in a hurry.

Three hours later, she was sitting on Anne and John's magenta brocaded sofa, drinking a whisky sour. They lived in a lavish townhouse in Kensington, dripping with antiques. Anne was knitting a scarf, and John was playing a Schumann piece on the black Steinway grand, over and over again. The tune was familiar; she knew it was the theme of a noir film, but she couldn't remember which one. Was it *Possessed*, the one where Joan Crawford is mentally insane and obsessed with Van Heflin? Whatever it was, John played it rather well. As the romantic music tinkled through the air, Judith recounted to her sister the events of the past few weeks.

"Anyway, Gavin wasn't pleased with my plan of selling the castle, but he seemed to have accepted it. Then, this afternoon, I found some aconite root at the back of his drawer. I recognized it, because I use it in one of my books as a poison. We used to have it growing in the garden, remember? I pointed it out to you once."

"Yes, I remember. Is it used for anything else, like gardening?"

"It's used in very small doses for things like migraine."

"Does Gavin get migraines?"

"Yes, he does. But he's no chemist. A mistake in the dose could be fatal."

"Then why does he have it?"

"Do you know what I think? I think he's making a poisoned tincture to murder his wife with!"

Anne and John exchanged meaningful glances. Judith was unaware of the drain it had been on Anne's time and energy, and on her relationship with John, when she had lived with Judith for weeks on end at the castle. Anne had only done it because she had thought she was saving her sister from her evil husband. But at the very first opportunity Judith had run back into his arms, and it had all been for nothing. And now she was devaluing him again, and even accusing him of planning her murder. Judith had lost all credibility with the couple when she had returned to Gavin, and now they took his side over hers. How could anyone keep up with her erratic mood swings? How did poor *Gavin* put up with them?

Anne sighed. "So now you're accusing him of attempted murder? That's ridiculous."

"It's *not* ridiculous. I think he really is plotting my death!"

"But what's the motive?"

"He was upset when I told him I was going to sell the castle. I also told him I'm giving away most of my money . . . and he *wants* that money!"

"Judith, you're being hysterical. If he was going to kill you for your money, he'd have done so long ago."

"Yes Judith, you're being hysterical," chimed in John from the piano. "Gavin is a fine man. Everyone I know likes and respects him. You're making him out to be a perfect Dracula."

"How would *you* know? Maybe he *is* a Dracula. And he might even be a *Bluebeard*!"

Anne put down her knitting. "A Bluebeard? As in, the fairy tale?"

"Yes. A Bluebeard — a woman-killer. He may have even murdered his ex-wife!"

Anne laughed derisively. "If he's a murderer, then why haven't you gone to the police?"

"Because I have no proof — only my suspicions. You say I'm hysterical, but if I am, it's because he scares me. Men aren't like us. They have *secrets* . . . and *moods*." At this, Anne glanced involuntarily at John. "I never know if he's just having a bad day," continued Judith, "or if he's planning to *kill* me!"

322

Anne rolled her eyes. "You read too many novels."

Judith felt anger and indignation rising up in her with a fury. "Why is everyone so blasé about the danger I'm in? You think I'm being dramatic or causing a scene. Is that it?"

Anne looked mildly vexed. "Judith, I never said—"

"You don't care if I live or die!" Judith's voice had risen to a shriek. "None of you do. You'd be *glad* if I were dead!"

John stopped playing, and they both stared at Judith. There was a ringing silence, and half a minute went by. Finally Anne said, "That's not true. Of course we care. If you think he's going to murder you, then you have to leave him."

Judith realized that her sister was right. This was the first time Anne had given her any real advice, and it meant more to her than she could express. Tears formed in her eyes. "Thanks, Anne. I won't forget this."

Judith felt warmed by her sister's loving words. She was reminded of one of her favorite novels, *The Woman in White*. In it, the beautiful heiress Laura is in grave danger from her evil husband, Sir Percival, but her sister Marian saves her. Without Marian's love, Laura would have been murdered or locked away in a mental asylum forever, friendless and forgotten. Nothing like that will happen to me, thought Judith, because I have Anne.

33.

The Crypt

Judith returned home and had a late supper; Gavin had already dined. He wanted to make love, but she begged off, saying she had a headache. His words and gestures seemed especially fake and theatrical to her now, and she was watchful of his every expression. She saw nothing out of the ordinary — he was pleasant and attentive as usual, a real Stepford husband — and she marveled once more at his capacity for dissimulation. He was planning to murder her any day now, and yet no anxiety, nervousness, or anger marred his handsome face; he was truly a monster.

The following morning, a Tuesday, she waited until Gavin left for London, and then she went into the library and sat at her Louis XV secretaire to compose a letter. She opened a box of stationery and wrote in her elegant hand:

Dear Tony,
    I'm leaving Gavin. If I should die suddenly, I want you to alert the police that Gavin killed me. Whatever

the apparent cause of death, make sure they perform a toxicology report, and that they test for aconite. I am not suicidal, nor am I planning on standing on any precipices or taking any baths where I might carelessly slip and fall, so anything that appears to be an accident should be treated as a murder. I am leaving him, but he may follow me and try to kill me. I know you have always cared for me, and that you would wish to see my murder avenged. Forever yours, Judith.

She folded the letter and put it in an envelope. Across the top, she scrawled in capital letters, "TO BE OPENED IN THE EVENT OF MY DEATH." She stamped it with her wax seal and enclosed it in a larger envelope, which she addressed to Tony. She knew that posting such a letter was like something out of an old thriller, but she didn't know what else to do. If she rang Tony one more time to rescue her from Gavin he would tell her to go to the devil, and she didn't want to appear hysterical or melodramatic. She was determined to take care of the situation herself, rather than relying on a man to protect her.

She had booked a room in London for Friday night, using a false name on the register, and from there she would charter a private plane to Capri. Now that Gavin was out of the picture, she saw no reason to give her money away; in fact, she found it extremely convenient to be rich, now that she was going into exile. If he found her in Capri, she would flee to Morocco, or Turkey, or Mexico. She would keep fleeing him until they were divorced, and he posed no further threat to her. The thought of being rid of him was incredibly empowering, and she breathed freely for the first time in months.

In high spirits, she rang the bell. Presently, Jane entered. "You rang, Madam?"

"Jane," said Judith, affixing a stamp to the letter. "Can you post this when you go out today?"

"Yes, Ma'am." Jane took the letter and put it in her pocket.

Later that morning, Jane dropped the letter into a postbox in the village.

Judith bided her time until Friday. She knew Gavin would be home late that night, as he was dining with a financier in London—or so he claimed. He left just after tea, and she stood on the doorstep and watched ruefully as he drove away.

She packed two suitcases, choosing her clothes carefully. Everything she touched filled her with an ineffable sadness: not only her lingerie and nightgowns, but also her dresses, her riding clothes, her suits, and her jewelry, each article triggering a fond memory of making love with him, walking with him, riding with him, cuddling with him, traipsing about with him in Paris. When she had finished, she started to touch and smell Gavin's clothes. Holding up one of his jackets to her nostrils and sniffing its musky fragrance, she went into a kind of trance. Life with him was pleasure and pain. Tony was right; she was an addict. But she had finally hit rock bottom.

After she finished packing, she lay on her bed and kissed and stroked Lovelace, inhaling the scent of his fragrant fur to intoxication. Then she kissed him one last time on his wet nose, bundled him into the carrier with his favorite toys and treats, and brought him downstairs. The doorbell rang, and she carried him outside and handed him to the driver, who was to leave him at Anne's house until she could safely return and retrieve him.

Tears streamed down her cheeks as she watched Lovelace disappear down the drive. She stood on the doorstep, feeling empty and forlorn, and then she went into the kitchen and fetched some marrow bones, apples, and sugar cubes. She walked across the garden to the kennel and said goodbye to the dogs, giving them the bones and patting them on their sweet heads. Then she visited the stables and said goodbye to Valancourt and Montoni, handfeeding them the apples and sugar cubes, kissing their horsey noses, and stroking their silky manes.

After that she returned to her bedroom, slipped on a Valentino gown, and downed two shots of Scotch for good luck. She left a letter for Jane, instructing her and the rest of the staff to remain in service and take care of the castle, the grounds, the horses, and the dogs until she returned, and she texted Gavin that she was on her way to Paris for a last-minute lecture arranged by her speaker's bureau. Then she gathered her traveling cloak, her suitcases, and her handbag, and she descended the stairs.

She hurried through the heavy oak doors, tripped down the steps to her car, and set down her suitcases with a sigh. And as she took one last lingering look at the castle, she felt a terrible sense of loss. Leaving Manderfield was leaving *him*, and she still loved him, in spite of everything. But now she was forced to flee, because he was going to kill her. *My husband is going to kill me.* She repeated this to herself over and over again, and the tears streamed down her cheeks in a steady flow. She thought about the various methods he might use to try to kill her, and then she went over their relationship in detail from the first day she had met him to the present.

When she had finished, she was chilled to the bone. The chapel bell rang the midnight hour, and she was amazed to realize how long she had been standing there. She was lucky he hadn't returned in the middle of her reverie and shot her down with his revolver, or blown up her car . . . Her *car*! She had never considered her car as a murder weapon, but now she feared she might be blown to pieces the moment she turned the key in the ignition.

She stood there, paralyzed with indecision. Should she call a taxi to take her to Anne's? In this part of the country, and at this hour, it could take ages to arrive. Maybe it was better to stay put and take her chances until morning.

Then, as she stood shivering in the night air, she wondered if she was making a mistake by running away. Why can't I just march my suitcases back into the house, and have a bath, and put on my Paris lingerie, and get into to bed, and wait for Gavin, and make love with him, and have everything go back to normal? she thought. I can tell him I no longer want to sell the castle or give away my money, and he'll kiss me, and we'll laugh, and that'll be that.

She began to move towards the house, but then she stopped in her tracks as more fears began to overtake her. What if he fell in love with another woman? What if he planned to kill her regardless of what she did with her money? Would she ever truly be safe with him?

Her vigilance renewed, she reached into her handbag to call a car to take her away from Manderfield forever. But as her hands groped in her purse, they touched her rosary, and she was seized with an urgent desire to visit the chapel once more and pray. So she gathered her cloak about her to shield her from the biting wind, and she made her way towards the ancient building.

She strode across the tall grass, through the rose garden, and into the churchyard, pausing before a headstone on which was carved, in gilt-edged lettering, *ROMEO. REST IN PEACE, MY FELINE LOVE*. She cried, letting her tears fall on the little grave. And then she continued to the chapel, shivering as she creaked open the door and entered the lofty room.

She faded up the lights and lit the altar tapers one by one. Then, suddenly, she heard the sound of a woman weeping.

She stopped and listened. The woman's plaintive sobs rang through the air, along with her labored breath, her terrible wailing, and the sound of chains dragging unevenly across the floor. Listening more closely, she determined that the sounds were coming from the crypt.

Sick with fright, but determined to finally solve the mystery of the weeping ghost, she grabbed a candelabra and moved to the back of the sanctuary. She swept aside a velvet curtain, revealing an ancient wooden door, which she unlocked with a key secreted in a panel in the wall. Then she entered the stairwell, and the door closed behind her with a heavy clang.

Suddenly, the sobbing and chain-dragging stopped. She paused and listened, but all was still. Full of trepidation, she made her way down the cold, dank stairs to the sepulcher.

The lights in the lower chamber were out of order, and aside from the light cast by her tapers, the crypt was sunk in utter blackness. She crept slowly across the vaulted room, which was filled with the foul odor of mold and decay, for a small but persistent leak had caused damp to permeate the chamber. She could hear the steady drip of water as it leaked through a crack in the wall, the surface of which was overspread with black mold, poisoning the air with its deadly spores. As it fell, the water seeped into cracks in the floor, through which grew horrible pale plants that thrived without sunlight.

Avoiding festoons of elaborate spiderwebs, she paused before a niche in which stood a replica of Saint Catherine's mummified head, just as it was displayed in the Basilica of San Domenico. Below it was a small altar and a wooden box containing ancient relics. Within the box she found a small dagger, a tarnished silver goblet, a decomposing Bible, a wooden cross, and a small parchment book listing the names of the dead lying in the graveyard and the crypt. She picked up the goblet and examined the attached tag, written in a faded calligraphic scrawl. It read, "Here lie the goblet from which Lady Mordaunt drank the poisoned wine that ended her life, and the dagger she plunged into her breast when she knew she had been murdered." She replaced the goblet and shuddered, closing the box.

She passed several stacks of coffins along the wall, some of them rotting away. A skull clattered to the floor and she screamed, watching as it rolled away into a loathsome corner. Then, moving through a number of medieval arches held up by stone pillars, she reached the center of the room, where she beheld the crowning glory of the crypt: the cadaver monuments of Lord and Lady Mordaunt.

She paused before Lord Mordaunt's tomb and held up her candelabra, gazing upon his magnificently sculpted form. At first glance he looked merely proud, but when she peered more closely she detected a vicious cruelty in the line of the mouth, and a hardness in the expression of the eyes. She imagined him as he must have been in life: handsome and brooding, clad in magnificent armor, wielding his sword in battle, and raising a whip-hand in anger against the intractable women and servants of his household.

Then she moved away from the tyrant, and her flickering candles illuminated the tomb of Lady Mordaunt. She gazed in wonder at the effigy of the noble lady, her translucent face peaceful and serene, the folds of her garments lifelike and natural, her hands folded across her chest and pressed together in prayer.

Judith placed her guttered candles on the tomb, which was draped with rotting crimson velvet trimmed with silk fringe, and she lowered her head. And then she heard herself murmur, "Lady Mordaunt, I'm sorry your husband poisoned you. I was planning to flee, because I thought my husband was going to poison me too. But my husband would never hurt me; my husband loves me."

She was startled to hear herself utter these words, for she had not intended to make any sort of declaration. But she kept her head bowed and declaimed fervently, "O Lord, look upon this soul suffering in purgatory. Cleanse her of her sins and fulfill her desires. May she soon be united with thee."

Suddenly the chain-dragging started up again, along with the sound of lugubrious sobs. She raised her head, and to her shock and amazement, she observed that the marble effigy of Lady Mordaunt had come to life. She appeared to be a flesh-and-blood woman, and she was breathing softly in a coffin lined with purple velvet, her enormous dark blue eyes glistening, her long black tresses tumbling loose about her shoulders, her bony white hands folded across her chest. She was beautiful and ghastly pale, and she was bedecked in an ivory lace wedding gown which was stained with blood.

As Judith watched, Lady Mordaunt rose to a sitting position. She felt an unspeakable terror at the sight of this ghost, this wraith, this demon, this wight, this Ligeia, this nightmare, this specter, this shade, or whatever it was — staring at her with her brilliant eyes blazing. Then the wraith clutched Judith's wrist like a vise with her waxen fingers and she hissed, "You little fool — your husband doesn't love you. You must flee from this place. Flee! Flee! Flee!"

Judith screamed at the pain of the specter's fingernails digging mercilessly into her wrist, at her incandescent burning eyes, and at her words, uttered in such a vicious tone. Her scream extinguished her candles, and she was plunged into a Stygian blackness. Then she was struck by a sickening wave of vertigo, and she fell to the floor in a faint.

When she came to, she was lying nearly lifeless on the cold stone floor, with a searing pain at the back of her head. She was strangely disoriented, and she realized that she must have had a concussion. She had never felt so sick, sad, and shaken, and so near death. And as she lay there in the dark, delirious and moaning, macabre images flashed before her eyes: Her mother sobbing in the halls. Her mother going over a cliff to her death. Gavin's silhouette against the sky. Running out of a church in an ivory lace wedding gown. Bloody rabbits on a dressing table. Gavin strangling her. Romeo with his neck in a noose. Aconite roots in a bag. Newspaper clippings of dead brides. And then she uttered a cry of horror as she recalled her sister's words: *According to the legend, the brides see the ghost of Lady Mordaunt just before they die.*

She languished in the blackness, letting despair wash over her. This is it, she thought. I've seen the ghost, and now I'm going to die. She folded her hands across her chest in imitation of Lady Mordaunt's effigy, and she prepared for her final sleep.

But as she lay there in a torpor, waiting for death, she became disgusted with herself for her passive acceptance of her fate. She was slipping into old habits: feeling sorry for herself, being melodramatic, romanticizing her own suffering and death, the way she used to as a child. But she had outgrown those childish conceits—she no longer wanted to be a dead maiden, the aesthetically pleasing subject of a beautiful poem. She liked herself now; she was a good writer; her life was worth something. Hot tears coursed down her cheeks, and she thought, I don't want to die! I will not remain in this godforsaken place and wait for my husband to murder me. I've got to get out of here!

She tried to rise, but her limbs refused to support her, and she collapsed. She feared she would die alone in the crypt, swallowed up in the darkness. It would be a fitting end for her: she had come into the world alone and unloved, and that's how she would die. I've sealed myself in my own tomb, she thought, and she cried her eyes out in despair.

At length it struck her that her weakness was due to a combination of shock, concussion, and lack of nourishment;

she had consumed nothing all day except lemon drizzle cake and coffee in the morning, and Scotch in the evening. If she survived, she must not emulate her idol Saint Catherine, and starve herself to death!

But now her task was to summon the strength to rise. So she tried to relax, and her slow, gentle breathing eventually calmed her nerves. Soon her heart stopped racing, and her limbs regained some of their strength. She rolled onto her stomach and supported herself on her hands and knees, and from there she grasped onto the side of Lady Mordaunt's tomb, her knees buckling under her, until she was on her feet. Then, inching her way forward, her arms outstretched like Frankenstein's monster, she reached the wall and felt along its cold, damp surface until she found the stairwell. She continued to grope her way up the stairs until she reached the top, and then she pushed open the door and found herself back in the sanctuary of the chapel.

Amazed at her return to the world of the living, she dusted herself off and adjusted her eyes to the light. Her teeth were chattering, so she turned on the radiator and stood next to the grate, and the heat brought her frozen limbs back to life. Then she made her way to the altar, which was bright with the blaze of dozens of candles.

She washed her hands in rose water, and she took a wafer from a little box and placed it on the paten. Then she poured wine into the chalice, and she ate Christ's body, and she drank his blood. And she intoned, "Let not the partaking of thy Body, O Lord Jesus Christ, which I presume to receive, turn to my judgment and condemnation; but through thy mercy may it be unto me a healing remedy both of soul and body. Amen." But she could barely speak the words, because she was sobbing so violently. She was leaving her husband because he was going to kill her, but she didn't want to live in a world in which he wanted her dead. Whether she fled or remained, her life was over.

In her abjection, she gazed up at the statue of the Virgin Mary. But as she viewed it through the prism of her tears, she staggered back, perceiving an extraordinary atmosphere of light surrounding the Virgin, glancing off her like thousands of tiny stars. And as Judith's eyes became dazzled by the light, her body became flooded with love. All of her doubts and fears suddenly seemed like deplorable weaknesses, in contrast with the pure, unwavering light of love.

She was experiencing something which few achieve in their lifetime: for Christians, beatific vision, direct communion with God, seeing the light; in transcendental meditation, unity consciousness, a sense of being one with everything in the universe. She felt herself as a drop of water in the ocean, blending into a sea of infinite love. Where once there had been inner and outer, self and non-self, real and unreal, there was now only One. The love in her heart was so enormous that it filled her entire being, and her energy was so light and joyous that she felt she could have healed multitudes with her touch.

Tears of joy trickled down her cheeks as she felt this sublime love coursing through her body. She fell to her knees and cried, "Mother Mary, I lost my faith in love. But now I love everything in the universe — the planets, and the stars, and the wind, and the blades of grass, and even myself — and now my husband and I will live happily ever after. Because love conquers all. Isn't that right?"

The Virgin Mary stood there shining magnificently, and Judith basked in her glorious light. And then the statue said, "Yes, Judith. Love conquers all."

Judith's heart burst with happiness. Mary had been there for her when her mother had died, bestowing on her that celestial embrace, and now she had come through for her in the greatest crisis of her life. She gazed at the Virgin with tears of gratitude shining in her eyes, and then she crossed herself and said, "Sancta Maria, Mater Dei, gratias tibi ago. Amen."

Judith turned her eyes heavenwards, humbled by the miracle that had just occurred, and thanking Mary over and over again in her heart. Then she blew out the candles and exited the chapel, picking up her suitcases on the way back to the castle.

She unlocked the front door with her key, and she strode into the hall and up the stairs. As soon as she entered her bedroom, she hid the suitcases at the back of her closet and heaved a deep sigh. Phew, she thought. That was a close call.

34.

Constance

Judith shoved the last vestiges of a trifle loaded with strawberries and whipped cream into her mouth, licked her fingers, and set the dish down on her vanity table. Then she entered her bathroom, with its blue Italian marble and gold-streaked mirrors, and turned on the gold bath taps in the shape of swans taking flight, sprinkling into the steamy water Epsom salts, essential oils, and bubble bath. She slipped out of her filthy, cobwebbed things and stepped into the water, washing away her cares and sighing with happiness.

She couldn't believe how perfect her life was; she didn't know any other woman who was as happy and as lucky as she. Her marriage up until now had been fraught with anxiety, because she had been ambivalent about her husband. But now she would love him unconditionally, and she would live without worry or fear. As soon as he came in, she would tell him she was keeping the money and the castle, and they would go away somewhere extravagant on a second honeymoon — perhaps to the Riviera, or maybe even to Capri. She already had a reservation there, after all.

She was eternally grateful to Mary for restoring her faith in love. Now that she believed in love again, nothing could stop her. She knew she was beautiful, but beautiful girls are a dime a dozen; and she knew she pleased her husband in bed, but neither was that sufficient to hold him. The only edge she had over the competition was that she loved him more than any other woman could. Love was her secret weapon, the only real power she had. Loving compliance had always been her magic wand, convincing her mother to allow her to remain in the house, and deflecting her abuse and violence. And now she would use the same magic wand on her husband. Through intense and targeted love, she would eventually win his heart, so that he would never dream of straying or hurting her in any way. She didn't care how long it would take for him to truly love her, but he *would* love her. She would lead the lion by his leash, and he would become her pussycat. Once again, she tasted victory. She had won, and no one would ever reject or abandon her again.

She stepped out of the bath and put on her bathrobe. Then she went into her bedroom and slipped into a pretty satin nightgown with a marabou-trimmed robe and matching slippers, and she adorned her fingers with her garnet, ruby, sapphire, and diamond rings. Finally, she sat at her vanity table and started to brush out her hair.

Soon she heard Gavin's car pull up in the driveway, and a few moments later she heard the front door open and slam shut behind him. She quickly applied lipstick and ran a mascara wand through her lashes. She waited, but he didn't come up. Then she remembered how late it was, and she realized he was probably fetching her nightly cognac. How thoughtful he is, she mused. How could I ever have considered leaving him? I must have been insane. He loves me as much as ever! And she smiled, thankful that his delay would give her time to finish her face.

Judith was right about the cognac. When Gavin saw her car in the driveway, he realized she had changed her mind about going away. So he entered the house, donned his blue smoking jacket, and poured out a glass of Rémy Martin from a small bottle he retrieved from a secret panel in the bar. He then placed the glass on the silver tray and started up the stairs; but he paused on the landing, thinking. Despite Judith's tortured fantasies about what went on in his mind, he was a simple man who rarely let anything disturb him. But now something was troubling him — a persistent memory he couldn't shake.

His mind drifted back to a certain day two years earlier, just before Halloween. He had gone up to London to see a friend, but he had wanted to surprise her. So he had swooped into a flower shop and bought her a large bunch of yellow roses — her favorite color — and then he had followed her from the Marylebone Farmer's Market, whence she had just emerged with a bag of shopping, and down Weymouth Street, a lovely old avenue peppered with historic eighteenth-century buildings. She was an exceptionally handsome woman: tall and slim, with long blonde hair, large blue eyes, full lips, high cheekbones, a tiny waist, and perfect legs — the model type. And she dressed well: she had impeccable taste, and she spent a small fortune on designer clothing. Just then, she was wearing a long-sleeved yellow Gucci minidress with a ruffled neckline and white knee-length boots. She was his quintessential physical type — in fact, he had married her — but that chapter of his life was long over.

As he followed her down the street, he recalled the day they had first met. He had stalked her for two months before finally approaching her, during which time he had learned, among other things, that her father was extremely rich and well connected, and that she worked at a prestigious fashion house as an illustrator. She didn't need to work, but she had a talent for design; in any case, she far preferred it to her previous vocation as a lingerie model, where she had attracted an upsetting amount of male attention.

Sexual harassment was still a problem for her; indeed, due to her striking good looks, her life was lonely and guarded. He was amazed to observe how many stalkers and creeps accosted her daily. And he soon discovered, by listening in on her conversations with a girlfriend at the pub, that this unwanted attention had begun when she was fourteen, and had not relented since. She was an intelligent woman with a wonderful sense of humor, but men rarely noticed this, so attuned were they to her physical charms. She had always had terrible luck with men, as all of her boyfriends had turned out to be interested only in her body. She'd had it with rock stars, artists, actors, and party boys; she just wanted to meet someone normal and nice.

He had seen an easy entry into her life: all he had to do was to treat her like a human being, and she would fall at his feet. He was somewhat amazed that other men didn't think of this, but he supposed that most men were either too intimidated to approach her, too self-centered to consider her needs, or too afraid of commitment to risk a serious love affair. Having no fears of any kind, he intrepidly took the plunge.

During this period, he created a new identity for himself — a shy, unassuming investment banker with horn-rimmed glasses — and he compiled a list of impressive friends and relatives, both real and fake. Some of these, he managed to befriend. By the time he approached her at a cocktail party, she had already heard great things about both his character and his background. His father was an English baron, and his mother was a French viscountess, and he was due to inherit a sizable fortune.

When they first bumped into each other at the buffet table he was nervous and bumbling, pretending to be more impressed by her intelligence than her beauty. She liked him right away, and they texted back and forth for a few days, until finally she insisted that they meet in person. They met for tea at Claridge's, and it was the most romantic date she'd ever had.

They went on more dates, and she took him to the best menswear shops and made him switch to contact lenses, and it was like that wow moment in movies, where the girl takes off her glasses and lets her hair down. When they finally made love a few weeks later, she was mad for him. Soon afterwards, he proposed to her with an antique garnet engagement ring that had belonged to his mother, and she said yes, yes, yes.

She purchased a house for them in London, and for a while they were perfectly happy. But one day he told her he had lost all his money in a risky stock, and she became saddled with the mortgage and all of the bills. He promised he was coming into his inheritance soon, and she believed him.

Then, about a year later, things began to fall apart. He became controlling and jealous, sometimes raging so violently that she felt genuinely terrified. The chaos was too much for her, and finally she asked him for a divorce. To her surprise, he agreed without putting up a fight; the only stipulation he made was that she return his mother's ring.

After the divorce they put their house on the market, and he handled the sale while she was away on holiday. But just beforehand he transferred the property to himself, hiring a woman to impersonate her and forge her signature. She had paid for the house in cash, and now all of that money was gone.

When she discovered the crime she was furious, and she made up her mind to go to the police. But he showed up at her apartment in tears, explaining that his father's business had fallen into ruin, and that he had borrowed the money to avoid a scandal and bankruptcy. He promised to pay it all back with interest, reminding her that his trust fund on his mother's side would soon be due. She forgave him instantly, and he knew it was because she was still in love with him. That night they prepared a meal together, and drank two bottles of Château Lafite Rothschild, and made love by the fire.

She waited months for him to pay her back, and in the meantime he remarried. This cut her to the core, for she had been hoping for a reconciliation. She traced him to a dilapidated castle in Somerset and confronted him there.

He promised to get her the money, and she agreed to give him more time. But he had been stringing her along for five months now, and he was afraid that if he didn't pay her back soon she would go to the police.

He hadn't intended to swindle her; it was just that the money had been at his fingertips, and he had desperately needed it. *Gelegenheit macht Diebe*, as they say. He hadn't had the advantages she'd had, so it was only right that he should even the score a little. The only social currency he'd ever had were his good looks, and to those he'd added a studied charm and an upper-class accent. He was determined to use women to get what he wanted, and he had no shame in doing so. They were lucky to have him, he thought, these bored, lonely women with their fat bank accounts, for he had learned to act the perfect lover and to mirror a woman's every fantasy, something normal men are too honest, or too stupid, or too lazy to try. He had used Constance to make the deposit on the castle, and he had used Judith to pay the mortgage. One day, the castle would be his.

He continued to follow Constance down Weymouth Street, and on to Fitzroy Square. He watched as she entered her building, a fancy Georgian townhouse. Then he buzzed from below, peering into the marble entrance hall with its white Grecian statues.

Soon he heard her voice blaring through the speaker. "Who is it?"

"It's me, Sammy."

"All right. Come up to the first floor."

The street door buzzed. He pushed it open and climbed the stairs.

He rapped lightly. He heard her heels clattering across the floor, and then she opened the door and stood staring at him. He thrust the bouquet into her arms and pushed past her, finding himself in a lovely vaulted room, exquisitely furnished and painted in period-accurate pastels. He looked around, impressed.

"Hello, Constance. Nice place."

She stared at him with icy hostility. "What do you want?"

"I want to square things with you."

"Well, you certainly took your time."

"I couldn't come any sooner."

She selected a vase for the roses, but then she thought better of it and tossed them unceremoniously on the table. She turned and glared at him. "You're lucky I didn't blow the whistle and let your new wife know what's going on."

"I appreciate that, Constance. I really do."

"I didn't prosecute after you stole my money, because you promised to pay me back. But I've waited and waited, and I haven't seen a penny. I've been very nice, laying low for you. You don't deserve it."

"I know I don't. You're the best. How much do you want?"

She frowned. "You got a big chunk of cash for selling the house, and I was the one who paid for it. I should really get all of it, but I don't want to drag this into court. So I'll take half."

"I can't give you half right now. I don't have it."

"What did you do with all of that cash?"

"I bought a castle."

"You *what*?"

"I bought a castle. The deposit."

"You mean you used *my money* to buy that dump of a castle? How dare you! You know, I can seize the castle tomorrow if I want. It doesn't belong to you."

"There's no need to get stroppy. I'll pay you back every penny. But you'll have to wait."

"I've been waiting long enough. Get your mother the viscountess to give it to you."

"She hates me — she'd never lift a finger to help me."

"Then squeeze it out of your new wife. She's loaded."

"She can't get that much at a time."

"How much can you give me right now?"

"Ten thousand quid."

"Ten thousand quid! Have you lost your mind? I'm telling your wife."

"Don't tell my wife."

"You bloody fraud! I should have reported you to the police ages ago. I think I'll give them a ring right now."

She reached for her handbag and grabbed her phone, but he seized her wrist so hard that she cried out in pain and dropped it. She stared at him in anger, struggling to free herself, but he pulled her roughly to him, giving her a long, lingering kiss. She yielded to it as if she'd been craving it. "I've finally got you out of my system," she murmured over his shoulder. "Don't start that again."

"I still want you, Constance. I think I'll always want you."

She laughed bitterly. "Tell it to your wife."

"You wouldn't tell her about us, would you, Princess? It would ruin everything."

"You can't tell me what to do. I'm not your wife anymore."

He kissed her neck, and she shuddered; whether from

pleasure or horror, it was hard to tell. "Of course you're my wife," he whispered, his lips still grazing the soft hairs on her neck. "You'll always be my wife."

She stiffened and pushed him away, as if the feeling of his mouth on her felt violating. "What do you mean, I'll always be your wife? We're divorced . . . or hadn't you heard?"

He stepped back in confusion, her sudden assertiveness shocking him.

She uttered a contemptuous laugh. "Now I remember why I had to get away from you. You're all about power and control, and frankly, it's frightening. But I'm not afraid of you anymore, because I *know* you. Men like you are the enemies of women."

He clenched his teeth. "No woman speaks that way to me. You need to watch your tone."

"What are you, the tone police? Well, you don't scare *me*. I'll need that money soon, or I'm telling your wife. I'm going to lie down now. Lock the door on your way out." And she turned and walked away from him.

Suddenly he was filled with a blind rage. "Don't you dare walk away from me!" he screamed. Then he seized a silver candlestick and smashed her on the back of the head with it, and she collapsed to the floor in a heap. He stared down at her lifeless body in horror. He hadn't meant to kill her; but then again, she shouldn't have laughed at him.

He bent down and lifted her wrist. He thought he detected a faint pulse, but he couldn't be sure. In any case, it was too late; if she wasn't dead, he would have to kill her. Moving with mechanical precision, he took off his jacket, rolled her body onto a towel, and dragged her into the bathroom.

He put the plug in the clawfoot bath, turned on the taps, and undressed her, removing first her boots, then her dress, then her bra and knickers. Then he turned off the taps and lifted her under the arms, getting behind her and wedging the towel under her bloody head. He dragged her upper body into the tub and then lifted her legs in, while Judith's words from the cocktail party echoed through his mind: *Well, think about it. If you found someone dead in the bath, how could you prove it was murder and not an accident?*

He held her head under water for an inordinate length of time, and then he dragged it up by the hair and propped it at the edge of the tub. She lay there with her eyes open, blood trickling out of her eyes and her mouth. She was definitely dead.

He returned to the drawing room and replaced the candlestick on the mantlepiece, wiping it carefully, and he cleaned the blood off the floor with the towel, wetting it and adding some dish soap to make sure all traces of blood were gone. Then he folded the bloody towel and placed it inside his coat, deposited her groceries in the refrigerator, and stuck the roses into a vase. Returning to the drawing room, he opened the front door, wiped the knob of prints, and closed the door behind him.

Gavin came back to himself, standing on the stairs. Recalling this scene brought tears to his eyes. He had been fond of Constance. And he hadn't intended to kill her; if she hadn't laughed at him, she would still be alive. Thinking about the way Constance had died made him feel sad. Did he really want another murder on his conscience? He almost turned back and threw out the cognac, but he stopped himself as he thought seriously about his situation.

Judith was fine in her way, but she had become rather stubborn of late. She thought she was a queen now, but really she was just a bitch, and he mourned the loss of the old, compliant Judith. He didn't mind having sex with her, as long as she let him do whatever he wanted. And she was pleasant enough as a rule, as long as he didn't have to listen to her inane chatter—he was more interested in what was between her legs than what was between her ears, as he often joked to her—but honestly, she wasn't very bright. He chuckled as he remembered how he had gaslighted her by pretending to be a ghost, making love to her and reigniting her passion for him before swooping in for the kill. All he'd had to do was pull a few strings to get Anne hired for the *Vogue* shoot that was to take her away from the castle, leaving his victim alone and vulnerable. Everything had gone exactly as planned.

Or nearly everything; he had not planned for her find out about his affair with Nancy. Once she knew, he had hoped to use it to erode her boundaries about monogamy, pegging her as someone who had been so abused and neglected that he could destroy any and all boundaries she might erect. But she had offered a surprising amount of resistance, so he had been forced to change course. Neither had he planned to insult her looks and sexual performance the night she had confronted him about Nancy, but she had been so dull and irritating that he had been unable to control himself.

That had been a mistake, and she had kicked him out for it, but it had been easy to get her back. Once they had separated, he had deliberately ceased all communications with her, so that she would have time to miss and crave him. He hadn't been overly concerned about Tony, for he had known that once he could reclaim his sexual dominance over her, all thoughts of Tony would be erased. She was trauma-bonded to him forever through his act of spilling her virgin blood, and by her need to believe that the man who had so brutally violated her was not a rapist, but her own romantic creation.

In fact, she had been the perfect victim, with her romantic fantasies, her history of abuse, her mental instability, her Catholic guilt, and her desire to please, and he had greatly enjoyed raping her, tricking her, and keeping her in line, more than any other woman he had preyed on. But he'd nearly had to strangle her to death to keep her from prying into the Constance situation, and he'd had to kill that damned cat, because it was a wretched creature, always hissing at him. His dominance in the bedroom, besides being the only way he could take his pleasure, had been necessary to keep her fearful and submissive at all times, and he had discovered early on how remarkably effective his sexual violence was in breaking her to his will. But she had grown accustomed to his sadism, even as he had escalated it of late, so he would have to resort to stronger measures to continue to subdue and terrify her. And frankly, he didn't have the energy.

She had been easy to manipulate, and fun to terrify, but the whole thing had taken a lot of work, and he was tired. He had already invested too much time in her, and he needed to move on with his life. If he hadn't already murdered her father and Constance he might have thought better of it, but he wasn't about to let their sacrifices be in vain. Besides, it was a great stroke of luck that she had decided not to flee to Capri, and that he didn't have to chase her to the ends of the earth to achieve his purpose. So he took a deep breath and continued stoically up the stairs, balancing the tray of cognac in one hand as steadily as an experienced maître d'hôtel.

35

The Monster of Manderfield

He entered the bedroom and came behind her with the tray as she put the finishing touches on her makeup.

"Here's your cognac, Princess," he said, setting down the tray and knocking her handbag off the table. As he bent to pick it up, he removed her phone and slipped it unseen into his pocket.

She misted some perfume over her décolletage and gazed at him, love blazing in her eyes. Then she walked over to the bed, removing her robe to reveal her pretty nightgown and lying back against the quilted satin headboard. She felt like a pin-up girl, and she knew she looked it. She pouted. "What took you so long? I heard you come in ages ago."

"I was getting a snack. What happened? I thought you were going to Paris."

"I decided it was too last minute, and I canceled."

"That's my girl."

He handed her the cognac, and she warmed the snifter in her hands. "Mmm. This is what I've been waiting for. This, and you."

Unseen by her, his eyes gleamed as he watched her drink.

"It's very bitter," she complained. "Have Sarah order a new bottle. This one's no good."

She lay back on the bed, outstretching her arms and looking at him languishingly. "Come here. Come to mama."

He stooped down and kissed her. Then he tried to straighten up, but her bejeweled red-lacquered fingers clung to his neck.

"Don't go," she pleaded.

He detached himself from her grasp and stood up. "I must. I have some work to do. I'll come to bed a little later."

"I love you, Gav. Do you know how much? I love you so much that I've decided to keep the castle, and the money too. I don't care if it's all you love me for, as long as you love me."

He turned pale, and a strange, pained expression crossed his face.

"What's the matter?"

"Nothing. Goodbye, Princess."

She laughed. "Goodbye? You mean goodnight."

He forced a smile. "Yes. Goodnight."

He crossed to the door and paused, giving her a sad backward glance. Then he left the room, and she heard the key turn in the lock. The shadow of his feet lingered under the door, and his footsteps receded down the hall.

She stared at the door, frowning. Why had he locked her in? And why had he looked at her like that? Then her eyes fell on the glass. Suddenly she remembered the bitter taste of the cognac, and she gasped in horror.

Her vision was starting to blur. She staggered to her feet, knocking the glass and the lamp off the table and going down after them. When she rose again the room was swirling, and she vomited and collapsed once more. She careened over to the door, striking against it and sliding to the floor. She grasped the knob desperately, but it wouldn't turn.

"Gavin!" she screamed. "Gavin, open the door!"

She wept and pounded, but her efforts were in vain. Heaving and gasping, she rolled onto her belly and dragged herself over to her handbag. She dumped its contents onto the carpet, searching for something. "He stole my phone!" she wailed. She thought of ringing for Jane, but the bell was no longer there.

Her head spinning, her stomach churning, her lungs heaving, she dragged herself to the window. "Help, help!" she screamed. Then she remembered that all of the staff were off that night.

She staggered back into the room, planning to try the door again. But her legs gave way and she fell to the floor, delirious, vomiting blood, her head splitting with migraine. Soon, she began to lose consciousness. And then she dozed off, and she had a dream.

A screeching noise filled her ears, along with the sound of a beating heart. She heard voices indistinctly speaking. And then she saw, through a warped haze, Tony pacing back and forth in Anne and John's house, holding a letter.

"It says to open it in the event of her death. But do you think she'd be angry if I opened it now?"

"She might be," said Anne. "She was acting very strangely the last time she was here."

"Strangely? What do you mean?"

"She said she thought Gavin was trying to kill her."

"Did she say why she thought that?"

John walked over from the piano. "She found some poison, didn't she?"

"That's right," said Anne. "It was some sort of root. Agonite, or something."

Tony started in alarm. "Do you mean *aconite*?"

"Yes — that's what it was."

"But aconite is a deadly poison!"

Now he was tearing open her letter. "Oh my God!"

Judith's eyes flew wide open. But although she was awake now, everything still looked strange and hazy, and the heartbeat sounds continued.

The next thing she knew, she heard the front door slam, footsteps pounding up the stairs, and the key turning in the lock. Her bedroom door was flung open, and Tony rushed in. He grabbed a glass of water and knelt next to her, cradling her head in his arms and taking a handful of black pills from his pocket.

"Drink these down."

Judith opened her mouth and Tony shoved the pills in, pouring water after them. She choked on the water, heaving.

He smiled gently. "Darling, you'll be all right now. I've given you charcoal to absorb the poison, and I'm taking you to the hospital. I love you — I'll never leave you."

As she gazed up at Tony, all of their time together flooded back to her. She remembered waltzing with him at the ball, and as a tender and affectionate lover afterwards. She remembered his chivalry, and his patience, and his kindness, and his sense of humor. Most of all, she remembered how persistently he had loved her, from the very beginning.

"Tony, I'm sorry. Now I see that you're the only person who has ever loved me."

"I told you I'd always be here for you."

She thought he was the most beautiful man she had ever seen. "I love you, Tony."

"Try not to speak."

"Tony, I'm dying."

As she said this, Tony's loving, attentive face went blurry, and then it disappeared along with the rest of him. She stared around in a panic, but he was nowhere to be seen. He had vanished into thin air, and she was utterly alone. Then she realized, with an excruciating pang of grief, that Tony had never been there at all, and that the whole thing had been a dream. She cried bitterly, and her heart broke. And then it stopped beating, and she died.

When she opened her eyes again, she saw Constance standing before her, beautiful and radiant in a diaphanous crystalline gown. She smiled at Judith and said, "Now you are dead. Do you know our husband's name? It is Bluebeard."

Constance took her hand and led her through a tunnel towards a light that was blindingly pure, bright, and sublime. She felt joyous and free, and there was no more pain. As she went into the light, Romeo bounded up and jumped into her arms, licking her face with his rough tongue. She wept with joy and pressed him close to her, kissing his wet nose. And then she saw the Virgin Mary, and Saint Catherine, and all of the other saints and martyrs of history, along with Lady Mordaunt in her sparkling gold dress. Behind Lady Mordaunt floated the souls of countless other women who had been murdered by men throughout the centuries: rich women and poor women, courtesans, slaves, and queens, including the village girls murdered by Lord Mordaunt, and the wives of King Henry VIII. These souls were beautiful and sad, and full of their stories that had been lost to history, and she felt bonded to them in eternal sisterhood. And then Noël Coward and Marlene Dietrich waltzed up and greeted her with warm affection, she in a Travis Banton confection, and he in a silk dressing gown. Other classic movie stars, writers, and directors joined them, and they all exchanged witticisms and were kind and respectful to her, and she was happier than she had ever been in her short life.

Judith's body lay on the floor of her bedroom, the empty glass by her hand. Her eyes stared heavenwards, and a trickle of blood escaped from the corner of her mouth. She was alone in her bedroom, and she was dead.

In the middle of the night, Gavin came in and found the body. Just after he had locked Judith in, he had gone into his dressing room and typed a text from her phone addressed to Anne that said, "Having chest pains. Going to hospital." He hadn't sent it; it was merely a plant for the police, and he didn't want to alert anyone before Jane had the chance to discover the body.

He had heard Judith's screams faintly from across the castle, and they had been horrible to hear, but everything had been over quickly. Afterwards he unlocked the door and went in, and he found her lying there, her nightgown splattered with vomit and blood. The sight of her dead body gave him a tremendous sense of relief; so much work, and it had all paid off beautifully. Then he washed out the glass, cleaned up her body, scrubbed the bloodstains and vomit off the carpet with towels and a bar of soap, changed her into a fresh nightgown, and placed her phone beside her on the floor. After that, he put on his pajamas, robe, and slippers, gathered the incriminating evidence, and left the room. He burned the bloody clothes and towels in the incinerator, returned to his dressing room, and slept like a log.

Jane discovered the body early the next morning, and she screamed so loudly that she awoke the entire houschold. Gavin tumbled out of bed, sleepy and frowsy. He feigned extreme shock and grief at the news. "Why would she just die all of a sudden like that?" he wailed. "Do you think it's because of her excessive drinking?" No suspicions rested on him; the coroner ruled the death a cardiac arrest, and there was to be no autopsy or investigation.

Even Anne accepted the official diagnosis, ignorant of the fact that aconite can stop the heart, and attributing her sister's sudden collapse to her agitated mental state. It was lucky that Judith never knew this; if Anne, who was constantly on the internet, could have taken two minutes to search for "aconite poisoning," she would have discovered that aconite can cause ventricular arrhythmias, which in turn can lead to cardiac arrest. Her failure to do so lay in her conviction that Judith was a drama queen, who had merely been causing a scene when she had gone to her and sought her help. That's what Judith had meant when she had accused Anne of not caring whether she lived or died, and her heart would have broken twice over if she had discovered that she had more or less been right.

But then Tony, who had been too busy to look at his mail, read Judith's letter and alerted the police, and Gavin was arrested at the castle. Per Judith's instructions, a toxicology test was performed which showed aconite in her system. Tony requested autopsies of Sir Wilfred and Constance, and they showed strychnine in the blood of the former, and wax and bits of silver in the head wound of the latter. Gavin was convicted of first-degree murder for Judith and Sir Wilfred, and second-degree murder for Constance, and sentenced to life imprisonment. In the meantime, calls began to flood in when his picture was published in the paper, and earlier cases were dug up. Soon, two more trials were under way of women who had died suspiciously after intimate relations with Gavin Garnet, aka Samuel Jones, aka Thomas Grey, and his estranged parents in Swindon were heartbroken to learn of their son's horrific crimes.

As for the sobbing that had caused Judith innumerable sleepless nights, it had been heard by so many other people over the centuries that it cannot be dismissed as a mere product of her fancy; but we will never know whether the ghost was real, or whether all who had heard it had been similarly affected by the power of suggestion. It's more difficult to account for Judith's vision of Lady Mordaunt on the night of her death, but, again, there are two possibilities: either she had succumbed to the castle's deadly curse, or it was the fevered product of a fragmented psyche already prone to visions, and under great duress.

And as for Judith's conviction that she had invented Gavin in her mind as a dream lover, that had been nothing more than an illusion. He had simply read her novels, and styled himself as a hero from one of them. In reality, he had none of the qualities she desired in a lover; he was a simple and brutal man who loved only money, sex, hunting, and winning, and who understood nothing of the finer things in life. He was the opposite of the sublime, the antithesis of everything she had ever dreamed of. And yet none of the blame for loving him could be placed at her feet.

As her own research had shown, *anyone* can fall for a sociopath, even the best and cleverest among us. No woman could have resisted his onslaught. And his initial attack had been so effective that it had withstood even the two occasions on which he had lost his temper and revealed his true colors. In the end, it had not been stupidity, weakness, or madness that had undone her, but the fact that she'd had the misfortune to cross paths with him in the first place. If she had possessed any weaknesses that may have contributed to her downfall — naïveté, low self-esteem, depression, an obsessive-compulsive drive, mental instability, and an addictive personality — these were more than balanced by her strengths: idealism, intelligence, curiosity, adaptability, spiritual strength, an active imagination, a compassionate nature, and a boundless capacity for love.

Some readers might be inclined to blame Judith for returning to Gavin, but he would have killed her regardless of her movements. He was already prepared to hunt her down in Capri, and he would have pursued her to the ends of the earth to claim his prize. He felt as entitled to her money and property as if it had been a buried treasure he'd dug up on a desert island. Since he had done the work of seducing her, the reward was his to claim, and a little thing like her flight would not have stopped him. For a man with his sense of entitlement, murder is an expedient to rid himself of obstacles, either to his ambition or to his vanity. Thus, far from instilling remorse, each new crime he masterminded further entrenched his feelings of grandiosity.

And as for those readers who believe that Judith brought the tragedy on herself by coddling the monster, what type of behavior would have stopped him? Surely not Constance's cheeky assertiveness, which caused her to be killed even more abruptly and violently than Judith. As much as we like to believe in fairy tales, where only stupid or bad people meet tragic ends, women are not murdered because they bring it on themselves through their actions or their inactions; women are murdered because they find themselves in the vicinity of a murderer.

Judith was buried in the churchyard at Manderfield, as there had been no place reserved for her in the family vault. Her white marble tombstone was engraved with gilt letters, and it was the only inscription, besides the one on Romeo's grave, that could be clearly read, the others having long ago been worn away with time. The funeral was a small and simple affair with few people in attendance, and it rained all day. Tony stood over the open coffin at length, and then he broke down and cried, throwing himself on the body and letting his tears fall on her lifeless form. He never knew what Judith's final thoughts had been, and that she had discovered too late that he was her one true love, but it was just as well; such a thing would have haunted him forever.

Judith had loved Gavin more than she had loved herself, and she had paid dearly for that love. But she had the last laugh, as she'd had the presence of mind to write that letter to Tony, and thus to ensure that not only would her murder be avenged, but that the Monster of Manderfield would claim no further victims.

36.

Abigail's Revenge

Abigail sat at the sumptuously appointed table in the great hall as the sun rose, still wearing her crimson damask gown, for she hadn't been to bed all night. She persisted in trying to scrub the blood off the key with rags, solvents, and abrasives. And although her fingers were raw from the effort, she was so terrified of her husband's wrath that she refused to give up. But it was a magic key, so each time she succeeded in removing the stain, back it would come.

Finally submitting herself to failure, she heaved a sigh, ensconced the blood-stained key in her bosom, and strode to the hearth, tossing fresh logs onto the smoldering faggots. As she watched the flames blaze up, she was amazed to realize that it was only yesterday that she had discovered Beaumont's hideous room full of dead wives. She had often tried to imagine what secret could be so grim as to merit murdering one's wife for discovering it, but the answer was contained in the question. Question: What in this chamber is so frightful that I must die if I see it? Answer: Your own death, for asking the question.

She could scarcely believe she was married to a man who would so readily kill her for unlocking a door, but her excuse was that she had fallen in love with him. Love had blinded her to his essential nature and bewitched her to follow his every command. But now she understood that he was a special kind of sadist: a man who murders women *because he can*. His lust for power was so great that he was compelled to kill any woman who displayed the least bit of assertiveness; thus, his riddle of the secret chamber, which was designed to keep his wives in a state of suspended terror.

As Beaumont's wife, Abigail had been forced to submit to his every whim, no matter how perverse, and she reflected that this was the lot of all married women. She knew that many men were good and kind to their wives and would never think of using them in harmful ways; but she also knew that whether one's husband was good or bad was a matter of sheer luck. If a man wanted to keep a series of wives just in order to torture and murder them, as long as he was rich and powerful, no one would dare utter a word against him.

Gilles de Rais, for instance, who had violated and murdered hundreds of peasant children, never would have been arrested and executed had he not insulted a male member of his own class, although his crimes were prolific and well known—and so it was with any man rich enough to keep a fortified castle. The fact that Beaumont had dispatched six wives already, with no harm either to his person or his reputation, told her everything she needed to know about the worthlessness of women in the eyes of men.

She had once loved him passionately, and she had tried for months to draw out the finer points of his character, but now she laughed with bitter irony at the memory of those fruitless efforts. He had been indefatigable in his attempts to depreciate and subdue her, and in response she had tried to cast a feminine spell over him, imagining that if he loved her, she would be safe from his violence. But now she despised the monster with a burning rage, and the fact that she had formerly shared his bed filled her with revulsion. She had loved him, and she had writhed with pleasure beneath him as she had felt his naked body against hers. Yet soon he would murder her and add her body to the trophies in his gruesome private collection.

Suddenly, she was jolted from these unwholesome thoughts by the clatter of hooves on the drawbridge. At length, she observed Beaumont through the window alighting from the golden coach, and she heard his key turn in the lock. She gasped with fright as he stood in the doorway, tall and handsome, sweeping into the room with his cape swirling, the feather in his hat cocked, his face hard, chiseled, and handsome. She tried to conceal her fear, but her big, dark, terrified eyes gave her away. And although she was trembling violently, she said in the gayest tone she could muster, "Welcome home, my Lord."

"Good evening, Abigail," he replied, his voice deep and sonorous. "I have returned earlier than I expected from my journey. Pray, return my keys."

He extended his hand, and she hesitantly handed him the massive ring. After he had examined each key, he frowned. "Where is the little golden key that I forbade you to use?"

Abigail retrieved it from her bosom, quaking as he turned it over in his hands.

"Why is there blood on the key?"

"I do not know, my Lord."

"You do not know! Well, I know! You went into the closet, did you not? Very well, Madam; you shall go back, and take your place among the ladies you saw there!"

He brandished his poignard, about to plunge it into her breast, but Abigail took up the tallow candle and flung it in his face. It burned his flesh, and he cried out in pain. While he was thus distracted, she seized the dagger and thrust it into his breast with all her might.

He screamed, and his face registered shocked surprise, but she stabbed and stabbed in a blind fury until he toppled heavily to the floor. She laughed to see him thus powerless, and she licked his blood triumphantly off her bejeweled hands as she watched him bleed to death. After he was dead, she stabbed him several times more, and she stomped on his chest where the wounds were and smeared his blood all over the floor.

Then she dragged him by the hair down the steep stone steps and into the forbidden chamber, which she unlocked with the bloody key, and she hoisted his body up onto a hook. There it hung, added to the bodies of his six dead wives, his arrogant, handsome eyes now dimmed forever. "You will never have power over me again!" she cried.

. Abigail had never in her life expressed any violence, except that which had been directed inwards in endless self-incriminations, so this manifestation of her vengeful bloodlust initially plunged her into shock. But soon she came to feel great satisfaction in his murder, and her feelings of horror yielded to feelings of pride and accomplishment.

Indeed, her pleasure at having killed him was so great that she was afraid she might now have recurrent fantasies about stabbing random men to death and nailing them to the wall. She might be forgiven for thinking such a thing, as her present state was one of heightened fear and vigilance. But she had nothing further to fear from him, and none but herself to thank for ridding the world of the monster.

She climbed the stairs to the great hall, and then up to the ramparts. She walked along the parapet and surveyed the extensive grounds and the manicured gardens, realizing with pleasure that all of this was now her property. The queen would be forced to acknowledge, once she was made aware of the baron's other dead wives, that Abigail had killed her husband in self-defense, and the guards, who were posted at intervals around the castle, would be obliged to obey her every law and command. Tomorrow she would drive the golden coach to her darling Frederick's house — sweet, noble Frederick, whom she had spurned for a worthless tyrant — and she would confess her undying love for him, and they would live out their remaining days happily at the castle.

That night she supped on partridges, roasted apples and chestnuts, cakes, and wine, and the next morning she informed the guards that their lord was dead, and she instructed the coachman to get the draught horses ready. But before she left, she was compelled once more to visit the forbidden chamber, where she triumphed at the sight of the dead monster, hanging by his hair on a hook.

And as she took one last parting glance at his handsome face, now gruesome in death, she recalled the terrifying moment in which he had put his hands on her neck in a murderous rage, and had later tried to convince her that he had only been shaking her. She now gazed at his lifeless face, and she said with the utmost contempt, "No one strangles *me* and comes out alive." Then she quit the bloody chamber, and she closed and locked the door, and she ran out of the castle to start her new life with Frederick, forever ending that sordid but fantastical chapter of her life.

THE END

ACKNOWLEDGMENTS

First of all I would like to thank Robert Greene, who ordered me to write this book, and whose calm energy, brilliant suggestions, and sense of humor kept me going throughout the writing process. (He insists this story is based on him, which isn't true.) I would also like to thank Cian McCourt and Mark Martin from Verso Books, who have been absolutely wonderful in every way. And I would like to thank Jared Sanford, who has been wildly supportive and enthusiastic about every draft, and my Twitter friends, who offered invaluable feedback, and the fairy tales that sustained me throughout my childhood. Finally, I would like to thank my cats, because without cats nothing is really possible.